"According to Tex's will, you are officially Tess's legal guardian."

"No," Megan whispered, stunned not only by the concept, but by the weight of the responsibility. She tried to imagine taking a kid back to New York with her, fitting her into a life already stretched to the limits. Her imagination, always vivid, failed miserably. "There has to be another way. Mrs. Gomez...."

"Not quite," Jake said. "You can't just dump Tess with Mrs. Gomez and take off."

"Why the hell can't I?" she all but shouted as panic flooded through her.

"Because Tex has spelled it all out in his will."

His intimate familiarity with the details of Tex's wishes stirred suspicion. "How do you know so much about Tex's will?" Megan asked, her gaze narrowed.

"Because I'm the one who drew it up. Believe me, it's airtight."

Megan wondered just how many shocks her heart could take. "You're a lawyer?"

"A damned good one, if I do say so myself. You renege on the terms that Tex has spelled out and the ranch is up for grabs." Jake's expression turned triumphant. "In other words, it'll be all but mine, Megan, and there won't be a damned thing you can do to stop it."

Watch for the newest blockbuster from
SHERRYL WOODS

ANGEL MINE

Coming in September 2000
Only from MIRA Books

SHERRYL WOODS

AFTER TEX

MIRA®

If you purchased this book without a cover you should be aware
that this book is stolen property. It was reported as "unsold and
destroyed" to the publisher, and neither the author nor the
publisher has received any payment for this "stripped book."

ISBN 1-55166-542-5

AFTER TEX

Copyright © 1999 by Sherryl Woods.

All rights reserved. Except for use in any review, the reproduction or
utilization of this work in whole or in part in any form by any electronic,
mechanical or other means, now known or hereafter invented, including
xerography, photocopying and recording, or in any information storage or
retrieval system, is forbidden without the written permission of the publisher,
MIRA Books, 225 Duncan Mill Road, Don Mills, Ontario, Canada M3B 3K9.

All characters in this book have no existence outside the imagination of the
author and have no relation whatsoever to anyone bearing the same name
or names. They are not even distantly inspired by any individual known or
unknown to the author, and all incidents are pure invention.

MIRA and the Star Colophon are trademarks used under license and registered
in Australia, New Zealand, Philippines, United States Patent and Trademark
Office and in other countries.

Visit us at www.mirabooks.com

Printed in U.S.A.

For my father
As strong-willed as Tex and every bit as great an
influence on my life. I'll miss your wit,
your generosity, your tomatoes
and our Beanie quests.
October 23, 1917—August 28, 1998

1

Megan O'Rourke swept through the elegant marble and glass lobby of the prestigious Manhattan skyscraper, acknowledging a half-dozen greetings that followed in her wake.

"Hey, Megan."

"Good morning, Miss O'Rourke."

"Miss O'Rourke."

"Hi ya, sweetheart."

This last from the newspaper vendor, who also handed over a copy of the latest issue of her competitor's glossy life-style magazine.

"Nothing you haven't covered and done better," he assured her with a wink.

"Thanks, Billy. I hope the day never comes when you tell me she's beat me on something."

"Won't happen," he said with confidence. "That staff of yours doesn't miss a trick."

Megan knew that because her staff was every bit as eager and ambitious as she was, every bit as tenacious and determined to take *Megan's World* to the top, right along with the weekly TV show that had launched just weeks ago. The people she'd hired were young and savvy, quick to spot trends, sometimes just as quick to start them, she acknowledged as she got onto the elevator.

Not until the doors had whooshed closed did she pinch herself, a daily ritual that had started with her meteoric rise in publishing. She still couldn't believe she was right on the brink of becoming a phenomenon as successful and renowned as Martha Stewart, dabbling in a whole slew of media pies, from magazines to books to television, her finger on the pulse of American culture.

Pretty impressive for a small-town girl from Wyoming who'd grown up on a ranch with a grandfather who was about as sophisticated as flannel—shirts, not designer sheets. Tex O'Rourke wasn't into trends or styles or much of anything except land and cattle and making money. If Megan ever saw another cow again it would be way too soon.

Still, as Tex liked to remind her, she owed a lot to those cows she hated so much. They'd enabled her to go off to New York at twenty-one with money in her pocket. She'd been able to rent an apartment where she didn't have to fear for her life every time she walked out the door.

After she'd served a suitable apprenticeship on three other magazines, starting in the lowliest of capacities, those blasted cows had allowed her to buy a faltering bimonthly publication, rename it and, in two short years, turn it into must-have reading from New York to Los Angeles. Even the people who set the trends read it, just in case she'd gotten the jump on them. Her readership demographics were an advertiser's dream. These were the people who spent money—a lot of it—to stay one step ahead of the Joneses.

But if Tex's money had given her a boot up, she knew it was her own drive and dedication and vision that had accomplished the impossible. *Megan's World* was on financially stable ground now all on its own. Her first book—a hefty tome on entertaining—had been a bestseller. The second—on turning flea market bargains into treasured heirlooms—was flying off shelves at an even faster pace.

Six months ago she had started a local cable TV show in Manhattan, used that to assemble sample tapes, and just weeks ago had taken the program into national syndication. She was the media world's latest hot property. Her demanding schedule was packed with talk show appearances and newspaper interviews. Ironically, that ability to crowd every hour with work was another lesson learned from the inexhaustible Tex, even if he didn't approve of the way in which she'd put it to use.

Life was good. Life was very, very good. Alone in the elevator, she pinched herself again just to make sure it was real and not one of those summertime daydreams she used to have on the rare occasions when Tex had allowed her to laze around down by the creek during breaks from school.

When the elevator opened on the thirty-second floor, Megan stepped off into chaos. The rapid expansion of her media interests had jammed the offices, but no one had the time to steal away to look at new space. Her Realtor was at her wit's end.

"Jasmine called again," her executive assistant said, as if to reiterate that fact as he trailed her into her office. "The penthouse floor over on Madison is going today unless you get your tail over there to put in a higher bid."

"Can I fit it in?"

"No."

"Can you?"

"No, not unless you clone me."

Megan stared, intrigued by the idea. "Can I do that?"

"They did it on *Guiding Light,* but as a practical matter, I'd say no," Todd Winston said.

Todd—with his all-American face and biceps to die for—had been an aspiring actor until Megan had gotten her hooks into him when he'd taken a temp job between acting roles. She'd turned him into an executive assistant, the ultimate Yuppie with his neatly trimmed brown hair, oxford cloth, button-down shirts and trendy glasses that couldn't hide mysterious eyes the gray-green color of sage. She had a hunch he'd taken the job as an acting assignment and chosen his wardrobe—and the glasses—accordingly. She knew for a fact he could see better than she could, and her vision was twenty-twenty.

He still taped at least three daytime dramas at home every weekday and fast-forwarded through them in some sort of bizarre soap ritual every weekend. He claimed the women in his life loved it, and if it satisfied some deep-seated need in him and kept him working for her, Megan wasn't about to complain. Nor was she going to voice any disapproval of his tendency to discuss the story lines as if talking about old and dear friends. She had offered sympathy on more than one occasion only to discover that the

death in question had been scripted and filmed in a
studio on the west side of Manhattan.

"What do I tell Jasmine?" Todd asked.

"To start looking for alternative space. Then find
a hole in my schedule and pencil her in sometime
before the millennium."

"I'll write it in pen," he countered. "Otherwise,
you'll just erase it and write in something else. I will
not listen to another one of that woman's perfectly
justifiable tirades. You hired her to find new space so
we wouldn't all be crawling over top of each other.
The least you can do is look at what she finds."

Megan grinned at his testiness. "I thought you enjoyed crawling all over the staff, especially Micah."

Micah Richards was a bright, ambitious producer
who was responsible for whipping Megan's TV production into shape in record time. With her close-
cropped black hair, angular features and long legs, she
was stunningly beautiful in an unconventional way.
Mere mention of her was enough to bring color to
Todd's cheeks.

"Micah's the kind of woman who'll slap me with
a harrassment suit if I sneeze in her general direction," he protested. "I do not crawl anywhere near
her."

"But you want to, don't you?"

Todd gave her a jaundiced look. "My private
yearnings are none of your concern."

"Sure they are. It makes up for having absolutely
none of my own."

"I thought you had a date last night."

"It was a business meeting," she countered emphatically. "No yearning involved."

"How many so-called business meetings does that make with Peter? Your finances must be very complicated if you need to see your accountant that often."

That was the trouble with an efficient assistant. He knew her habits all too well. "Do I pay you to keep tabs on my social life?"

"You pay me to keep tabs on everything."

True enough, she acknowledged, but only to herself. "Okay, then, tell me what's on the agenda for today."

Todd ticked off a daunting schedule that was already running late, thanks to his penchant for scheduling nine o'clock meetings when he knew perfectly well Megan refused to be civil to anyone before ten. Too many years of ranch living and rising at dawn had made her rebellious. Fortunately, most of those nine o'clock meetings were with staffers who knew her habits. They worked steadily until she called for them, she crammed an hour's worth of talk into fifteen minutes and Todd got to enjoy his little game. It was a small price to pay for his otherwise incredible efficiency.

Her first meeting was with her food editor, who wanted to do a feature on edible flowers. She littered Megan's desk with bright nasturtiums and encouraged her to sample them to prove her point. Megan eyed the perky little flowers with distaste and agreed to take the woman's word for it.

That was followed by a quick session with a free-lance photographer hoping to do an architectural photo shoot on the new waterfront home of a man who'd made megabucks in the computer industry.

Megan had to tell him they'd been there and done that—months ago, in fact.

She had lunch with her editor to talk about the next book, followed by nonstop meetings to cover every facet of the magazine, as well as the topics for the next four tapings of the TV show.

"Are you satisfied with these?" Megan asked Micah, who was pacing around the room with an edginess that was typical of the woman's nervous energy.

"All but that last one," she said. "To be honest, I'm not sure anyone gives a fig about figs."

"Isn't it our job to show them the possibilities?"

Micah nodded. "Okay, I'll buy that, but consider this. The people watching this show have to go to their neighborhood market later to get the ingredients. Just how many varieties of figs do you think the stores in Middle America will carry?"

"In other words, we'll excite them, then frustrate them," Megan said thoughtfully.

"Exactly. It's all well and good to suggest new, trendy foods, but if we do, we'd better be sure there's a mail-order link or something for the hard-to-find ingredients. See what I mean?"

Megan nodded. "Mail order, huh? Maybe a catalog?" She beamed. "I love it. Put somebody on developing it. Let's not just offer exotic gourmet foods, but a sampling of everything we talk about on the show. Anything else?"

"Nope. I'll take care of this and get back to you."

"Thanks, Micah." Megan regarded her hopefully. "I don't suppose we could get the first catalog out in time for Christmas."

"Not without having the entire staff crash and

burn. Maybe next Christmas, if we want to do it right.''

"Okay, I'll settle for summer," Megan compromised.

"Done," Micah said, then grinned. "I would have gone for spring."

It was a game they often played, tempering their natural tendencies toward eagerness and excitement with reality checks.

"See you tomorrow," Micah said. "I'll find something to sub for the figs."

After her meeting with the producer, Megan retreated to a test kitchen to sample the recipes slated for nine months from now, in the July issue's feature on backyard entertaining. She prided herself on the fact that *Megan's World* had never once mentioned the word *hamburger* in connection with such an informal social event.

She thought of her grandfather and smiled. Tex referred to her suggested alternatives as "sissy food" and refused to allow his housekeeper to put any of it on his table. Megan knew, because on her last whirlwind visit home she'd asked Mrs. Gomez if she'd ever tried any of the recipes.

"Only at my own home, *niña*. Your grandpapa wants only meat and potatoes, nothing so fancy as what you write about."

"Does he even look at the magazine?" Megan had inquired, unable to hide the wistful note in her voice. For all of her claims to independence, she still craved Tex's approval, which he gave out with stingy rarity.

"Of course he looks. He even got cable last month so the picture of you on TV would be clearer. He is very proud of you.'' The older woman had shrugged. ''That does not mean he understands the choices you have made or the food you write about, *sí?*''

''Yes,'' Megan had agreed with a sigh.

Megan was a mystery to her grandfather, just as Tex was an enigma to her. He had taken her in when she was barely nine and abandoned by a mother who no longer wanted any part of raising a difficult child. That was the last time Megan had seen Sarah O'Rourke. She had never seen her father, at least not that she could recall, and no one mentioned him. She didn't even know his name. Given Tex's tight-lipped reaction to her hesitant inquiries, there was some question whether her mother did, either.

Tex had been mother and father to her from that moment on. He'd done the best he could, but he was not an especially warm man. He believed in plain truths and harsh realities with no sugarcoating. He'd given her a roof over her head, food and clothes, but he thought toys and dolls were foolishness, television a waste of time and books on anything other than ranching only marginally better.

Megan had never doubted, though, that he loved her. And when the time had come to let her go, he'd railed about it, but he'd given her the wherewithal to make her dreams come true and the knowledge that home would be waiting for her if she failed.

That Megan had succeeded beyond her wildest expectations and his was still baffling to him. Not a conversation passed without him asking when she was going to ''give up that damn fool nonsense'' and come back where she belonged. She'd put off another visit for just that reason, because the pressure to come home—both overt and subtle—would be relentless. Seeing the hurt and disappointment in his eyes when she refused took some of the joy out of her accomplishments. Better, she'd concluded, to stay away.

Tex thought she should be satisfied that she'd proved what she could do in a competitive world. He simply couldn't understand that every single TV show, every single issue of the magazine was a new and exciting challenge. His attitude was proof that his early support had been an indulgence, not a genuine exhibition of faith in her abilities. He still dreamed of turning her into a rancher.

That lack of understanding and his refusal to set foot in New York grated on her and made every conversation with her grandfather a minefield. Their last one had ended with an explosion that had shaken her. She'd been avoiding his calls for the past week, letting Todd and her answering machine deal with Tex because she simply couldn't, not without adding to the mountain of guilt already weighing her down.

She was tapping her pencil against her desk, still lost in thought, when Christie Gates burst into her office carrying an *I Love Lucy* lunchbox and a *Howdy Doody* puppet. Christie was Todd's assistant and an aspiring writer who spent every lunch hour searching for some story angle she could sell to Megan. Most of the ideas had been outlandish and way off the mark, but this one had potential. Megan could feel it.

"Are these not the greatest?" Christie said enthusiastically, setting the two pieces of memorabilia on Megan's desk with surprising reverence for someone who hadn't even been born when either classic show was originally on the air.

Megan examined them closely. "Definitely originals," she concluded.

"Would I bring back anything else?" Christie demanded indignantly. "I know a reproduction when I see one."

"What do you propose we do with them?"

"I was thinking of a feature on using decorative accents like this to rediscover the child within. Talk about a whimsical touch. I mean, how could you not smile every time you walk into a room with Howdy Doody or Lucy staring you in the face? I've even heard that people are collecting those really old sand pails to remind them of when they were kids at the beach."

She paused and watched Megan closely. "So, what do you think?" she finally prodded.

Megan considered the idea thoughtfully, deliberately taking her time, then grinned at Christie's bouncing impatience. "I think it's terrific. Congratulations! You have your first story assignment."

"Oh, wow! You mean it?"

"I mean it. At a fee above and beyond your salary, of course. Have Todd draw up the contract and make sure accounting reimburses you for whatever you have to buy for the photo shoot."

"Like a real freelance deal?" Christie asked.

"Yes, ma'am."

Christie rushed around the desk, embraced her, then backed away self-consciously. "Sorry, Miss O'Rourke."

Megan grinned. "No apology necessary. And I think from now on you should call me Megan."

The girl's eyes brightened. "Really? Oh, wow."

Megan might have been amused by the unabashed excitement if it weren't for the fact that not very long ago she had reacted in exactly the same way to every triumph—minor and major. Still did, if the truth be known, but she tried to confine it to the privacy of her office.

"One last thing," Megan added, "you might ask around, see if any decorators know of a home doing anything like this. Todd can give you a list of people to call."

Christie bounded toward the door to share her news, but Megan stopped her. "Hey, Christie, when the story's done and all the photos have been shot, I'd like you to bring Howdy Doody back to me, okay?"

"You want the puppet?"

"Sure. I need to remember being a kid, the same as everybody else," she said. The pitiful truth was, though, she couldn't really remember ever being a kid at all.

Slowly the outer offices fell silent. Megan worked on her column for the next issue of the magazine, not coming up for air until darkness had fallen outside and the sky was lit with the twinkling lights of endless rows of skyscrapers. It was her favorite time of day in New York, when the streets were emptying of traffic, the impatient blare of horns was dying and the view from her office turned into a picture postcard. Daytime might offer a glimpse of Central Park in all its orange-and-red autumnal glory, but this was the view that had been on the one postcard she'd ever gotten after her mother abandoned her.

Some days Megan wondered if New York's pull

had been professional or personal. Had she subconsciously come here hoping to spot Sarah O'Rourke on a street corner? It was a question she rarely asked herself and had never adequately answered, just as she never examined too closely how a woman whose own background was so dysfunctional was qualified to promote life-style choices for others.

To her surprise, given the hour, one of the phone lines lit up and she heard Todd answering. She was even more surprised when he stepped through the door rather than buzzing her. The sympathetic expression on his face set her pulse to pounding.

"What is it?"

"It's Mrs. Gomez."

No doubt the housekeeper had been persuaded to play intermediary for her grandfather. "I can't talk to Tex tonight. Please just tell her that for me."

Todd stayed right where he was. "You need to take the call, Megan."

If she hadn't already had this gut-deep feeling of dread building inside, his somber tone would have set it off. With reluctance, she reached for the phone.

"Mrs. Gomez," she said.

"Ah, *niña*," the woman murmured, her voice suspiciously scratchy, as if she'd recently been crying. "I am so sorry to be calling like this. It is your grandfather."

The pounding pulse slowed to a dull thud. "Is Tex okay? Has something happened to him?"

"There is no easy way to say this. He is gone, *niña*. Your grandfather passed away a few moments ago."

The words echoed, nonsensical, impossible.

"No," Megan protested in a whisper.

"I am so sorry, *niña.*"

"No," Megan said again as tears welled up and spilled down her cheeks. "Not Tex." He was big and blustery and strong. Indomitable. Immortal.

"I am so very sorry," Mrs. Gomez repeated. "It was very fast. There was no time to call you. His heart, the doctor said. There had been signs, but your grandfather ignored them. Like always, he thought he knew best."

"I'll be there on the first flight," Megan told her, dimly aware that another phone line had lit up, indicating that the ever-efficient Todd was already making the arrangements. He would clear her schedule, see that things ran smoothly in her absence. More than ever, she thought what a godsend he was.

"I'll let you know when I'll arrive," she promised. "And I'll arrange for a rental car."

"No need to do that. There are cars here you can use. I will tell Señor Jake. He will pick you up."

Megan was not so distraught that the name of a man she'd thought long gone from Whispering Wind, Wyoming, slipped past her. "Jake?"

"*Sí.* Señor Landers. You remember."

Oh, yes, she remembered. All too well. Sexy. Arrogant. Big-time trouble. Also a man her grandfather had once despised. Tex had worked very hard to see that Jake was out of both their lives.

"Why is Jake Landers there?"

"I am sure he will explain it all to you."

"You tell me," Megan insisted.

"I do not know your grandfather's business," Mrs. Gomez said. "Just hurry home, *niña.*"

It was too late to worry about hurrying, Megan

thought bleakly. It was too late for so many things she had vowed to do to let her grandfather know that she loved him, that she would be forever grateful for all he had done for her.

"I'm coming home, Tex," she murmured.

But, of course, it was too late for that to matter, too.

2

"Is she coming?" Jake asked Tex O'Rourke's housekeeper after she had talked to Megan.

"Well, of course she is," Mrs. Gomez replied with a touch of indignation. "Did you think she would stay away at a time like this?"

The truth was Jake didn't know what to think about Meggie after all these years. Once he'd had a world-class crush on her, but she'd been as out of reach to him then as if they'd lived on different planets. In a very real sense, they might as well have.

As Tex O'Rourke's granddaughter, Megan had been part of Whispering Wind's elite social circle, such as it was. Jake had been the son of the town whore and a troublemaker in his own right. No one was more stunned than Jake himself that he had wound up a lawyer. Then again, few people knew both sides of the law as well as he did.

Jake still wasn't entirely certain what perversity had drawn him back to Whispering Wind a few months ago. Some would say he was returning to the scene of his crimes. Others would probably assess his motives even less charitably. The bottom line, though, was that he was back, and predictably enough, the whole town was still talking about it.

Ironically, Tex O'Rourke had been one of the few who hadn't cast judgment, but then the old man knew better than most that not all of the tales about Jake's misdeeds had been accurate. When Tex had turned up in Jake's office late one afternoon asking for legal help, Jake wasn't sure which of them had been the most uncomfortable.

The last time they'd met, Jake had been charged with trying to rustle cattle from Tex's ranch. Even though he'd eventually been cleared of the charges, it had left a bitter taste in his mouth. As for Tex, he'd bought his way out of that misjudgment by sending Jake off to college, then funding his way through law school.

When his mother died before his graduation, Jake had had every intention of never setting foot in Whispering Wind again. He'd joined a prestigious law firm in Chicago, married and settled down, chasing after money the way he'd once chased after stray cattle.

Then he'd discovered his wife in bed with one of his law partners who was on an even faster track. In the midst of their very messy divorce, he'd won an acquittal for a guy who was a perpetual loser, only to discover the kid was guilty as sin. It hadn't taken all that much encouragement from his stuffy, uptight, publicity-shy partners to get him to quit. Jake had taken his considerable savings and investments, his bruised and battered ego, and retreated to Whispering Wind. Maybe, he reasoned, if he finally dealt with his past, he'd be able to figure out his future.

Opening a law practice here had been a halfhearted gesture, a way to keep his old neighbors from referring to him as that lazy, no-account Landers boy once again. He'd figured not a soul in town would turn to him for legal advice, but he had enough money tucked away and enough income-producing investments not to care. In fact, whole days often passed before he stopped by to check his answering machine for messages from potential clients. He should have known the most powerful man in town—his reluctant benefactor—would be the first to show up and actually catch him sitting behind his desk.

"Surprised to see you back here," Tex had said, sinking heavily into a chair opposite Jake.

"Displeased, too, I'll bet."

"No, the truth is, I'm glad for the chance to make it up to you for what happened back then. You'd done some foolish things. It was easy enough to believe you'd taken the cattle. I latched on to the notion when I shouldn't have."

It was more of an apology than Jake had expected. He shrugged, as if it made no difference at this late date. "You paid my way through school, old man. We're even."

"Not just yet," Tex insisted. "I want to hire you. That'll bring the rest of the folks in town flocking to you."

Jake had shuddered at the prospect. He hadn't actually wanted to be successful all over again. It certainly hadn't suited him well the last time. "Thanks all the same, but I came home to take it slow and easy. I don't need you building up business for me."

"Yeah, I heard about that kid. Must have shaken you pretty bad." Tex had regarded him knowingly. "Almost as bad as finding out your wife was cheating on you with a man you'd thought of as a friend."

"I see you've kept up," Jake said dryly, not the least bit surprised at the old man's ability to ferret out secrets. Tex had always known what Jake and Megan were up to, that was for sure, and he'd done his best to see that things between them never went too far.

"You cost me enough," Tex said, explaining away his interest. "I figured it was my duty to see how my investment was paying off."

Anger, long denied, surfaced. "No, what cost you was misjudging me. I was never a thief, old man, and you should have known it. I respected you, looked up to you like a father. I gave you an honest day's work for every penny you ever paid me, and then some."

Tex nodded in agreement. "True enough. And that's exactly what I expect of you now."

"What kind of legal work do you want me to do?" Jake asked reluctantly.

"I want you to write up my will, make it airtight, so no legal shark can pull it apart after I'm gone."

Jake studied him and noticed something he should have spotted earlier. Tex O'Rourke's color was bad, his complexion ashen. His words came with a hitch in his breath. For a man not yet seventy, a man who'd always been in robust health, the changes were dramatic.

Jake was surprisingly shaken by the thought of his old nemesis dying. He'd realized in that instant that, even after all this time, he wanted to prove himself to this cantankerous old man. Until the day Tex had charged him with cattle rustling, he'd been the closest thing to a father figure Jake had ever known. The realization that there might not be much time left shook him.

"Is it your heart?" he asked, trying not to let his dismay show. Tex would hate pity more than most men, hate it coming from him even more.

"So the doc says. It's my opinion I'm too contrary to die, but you never know where God stands on something like that, so I'm not taking any chances." He leveled a look straight into Jake's eyes. "Will you do it?"

Filled with reluctance, Jake reached for a yellow legal pad and a pen. "Tell me what you have in mind."

An hour later he was reeling. "Megan's going to be fit to be tied," he said.

Tex shrugged. "She'll adapt. It won't be the first time life's tossed her a curve."

"Being dumped on your doorstep as a kid was one thing. She had no choice. Now she does. She has a successful career in New York. Why should she come back here?"

Tex slammed his fist on the desk, proving he still had power enough to make his point. "Because, by God, she's my flesh and blood. She'll do what's right, because that's the way I raised her."

"She doesn't know anything at all about this?" Jake asked. "You've told her nothing?"

"Not a word. She hasn't been home in months now and this isn't something I wanted to get into on the phone. If the doc's right, she'll find out soon enough."

"And I'm the one who gets to break the news."

Tex grinned at Jake's discomfort. "You'll enjoy it, son. Don't even try to deny it. You've been itching for a way to get under Meggie's skin since the first time you laid eyes on her. Now's your chance to do it. Better yet, you'll have my blessing. That ought to satisfy you.''

It was evident that afternoon that the old coot had thoroughly enjoyed the bombshell he'd dropped and the fix he was putting Jake in. Now it was time for Jake to follow through.

But how the devil was he supposed to tell Meggie that her beloved grandfather had had a short-lived liaison with what could only be described as an unsuitable woman? Moreover, Jake was expected to explain that Tex had fathered a child who was now eight years old and had only recently come to live with him, abandoned on his doorstep just as carelessly and indifferently as Megan had once been.

Even worse than all that, though, he was going to have to break the news that Megan O'Rourke—hotshot media executive—was now this child's legal guardian and that she was expected to raise the girl on the very ranch she had fled a decade earlier, or she would lose her inheritance.

Even in death, Tex O'Rourke was destined to turn several lives upside down—Jake's among them. Tex was probably laughing all the way to hell.

Megan had done everything but beg. Nothing she'd said, though, had dissuaded Mrs. Gomez from sending Jake Landers to pick her up at the airport.

"He will be there, *niña*. Look for him. You will recognize him, *sí?*"

Recognize Jake? Oh, yes. She would be able to pick that low-down, conniving son of a gun out of a crowd of thousands. Her personal radar had been attuned to him practically from the second she'd hit puberty. It had taken several long and painful years for her to discover that her radar was not capable of exercising good judgment. When he'd stolen Tex's cattle, she'd finally realized her mistake. Jake had been securely locked behind bars when she'd left for college. His name had never once been mentioned in all the years since.

So what on earth was he doing at the ranch now? she wondered. And why was he running errands for Mrs. Gomez? Had her grandfather hired him once he'd been released on parole, maybe given him an undeserved second chance? Tex wasn't sentimental, so she doubted it. Jake had probably pulled some scam to get back in her grandfather's good graces.

When the plane landed in Laramie, Megan was the first one off. It didn't take more than a quick glance around the waiting area to spot Jake. He was propped against a railing, dressed in black from head to toe, the stereotypical western bad guy from his Stetson to his boots. Even his reflective sunglasses spelled trouble. At least they prevented her from getting a good look at his eyes. He'd always been able to make her weak kneed with a glance from those piercing blue eyes.

"I'm glad to see you're on time," Megan said briskly, handing him her baggage claim slips. "Four bags, all matching, Gucci."

He grinned. "Of course, they would be."

His amused tone, the wash of his deep baritone, raised goose bumps. The sarcasm irritated. "What is that supposed to mean?" she snapped, already breaking her vow to remain cool and impersonal for however long she had to put up with his company.

"Just an observation, Meggie. Don't get your drawers in a knot."

"My drawers are none of your concern."

He waved the luggage claim slips under her nose. "Apparently they are, unless you're wearing the only ones you brought." He tilted his head consideringly. "Or don't you bother with them these days?"

"Your mind's in the gutter as always, I see," she said, casting an imperious look his way and sweeping past him. She all but raced for the baggage claim area. Ten seconds, maybe less—that was how long it had taken the man to not only rile her, but remind her that she'd once wanted him with a passion so powerful it had threatened to wreck her life.

There had been a time when she would have chosen Jake Landers over anything. She would have ditched her dreams, settled for an uncertain future, if only this man were a part of it. Nothing anyone said could persuade her that Jake was all wrong for her. Then the cattle had gone missing, Jake had gone to jail and, brokenhearted and disillusioned, Megan had left Wyoming.

There hadn't been a single day since that she had looked back with regret. He'd betrayed her as well as her grandfather. It was something she wasn't likely to forgive or forget.

She supposed a case could be made that she owed him. His crime had revealed her first significant error in judgment, forced her to reevaluate her priorities. She now had the career she'd been destined for, thanks to Jake's betrayal. She socialized with men who were rich and powerful and, most important, honest. Thanks to lessons learned, she was slow and cautious before trusting anyone. People took advantage of her at their own peril, because she had a reputation for being ruthless with those who tried.

Megan stood by while Jake gathered her luggage, then followed him to the parking lot. Though it was only mid-October, the air had the sharp bite of winter in it. She shivered as it cut through her lightweight wool jacket.

"I hope you brought something heavier than that to wear," Jake said, opening the door for her. "They're predicting snow for later tonight or tomorrow."

"Don't worry about it. I'll be fine. I've been dressing myself for years now."

"When was the last time you were in Wyoming when cold weather hit?"

"Not that long ago," she responded evasively, aware that there was a guilty flush in her cheeks.

"Does Christmas four years ago ring any bells?"

The accuracy rankled. "What have you been doing, grilling Mrs. Gomez?"

"Didn't have to. She likes to talk," he said as he started the engine. He glanced her way. "You're one of her favorite subjects."

"I'll have to speak to her about that. I'm not sure I like being a topic of discussion for her and one of the hands."

Jake's posture behind the wheel of the fancy sports utility vehicle had been surprisingly relaxed, but his shoulders tensed at her remark. He turned toward her and, for the first time, removed the glasses and seared her with eyes that sparked blue fire.

"Maybe we should get something straight right now, Meggie. I'm here as a favor to Mrs. Gomez and, in a way, to your grandfather. I don't work at your grandfather's ranch. In fact, if things turn out the way I hope they will, before too much longer I'll own it."

If he'd roped her and dragged her feetfirst through the mud, she wouldn't have been any more stunned. "Never," she said fiercely. The idea of turning the ranch over to a man who'd stolen from her grandfather was thoroughly repugnant.

Her vehement response, however, only seemed to amuse him. "You planning on sticking around to run it?"

The question threw her. She actually hadn't considered what was to become of the ranch. From the moment she'd heard about Tex's death, all she'd thought about was the huge, gaping hole in her life. Even at a distance, Tex O'Rourke had been very much with her. Never again would she hear the gruffly spoken, "I love you, girl," with which he'd ended every conversation, no matter how contentious. The hated ranch hadn't once entered her mind.

Of course, it would be hers now. She was Tex's only living relative, unless Sarah were around somewhere. He would expect Megan to run his cattle empire, no doubt about it. It wouldn't matter to him that she knew precious little about ranching, that she hated it or that her life was exactly the way she wanted it—in New York. *Duty,* a word that had been bandied about enough over the years, was what mattered to Tex.

Megan's grief gave way to despair. She couldn't do it. She could not stay here, and that was that. She didn't have to think about it, didn't need to examine the moral dilemma she faced from every angle. She would stay in Whispering Wind long enough to take care of Tex's affairs and then she would go back to New York.

"Well, Meggie, what is it? You going to stay or go?"

"I'll be going," she said at once. "But it'll be a cold day in hell before I sell the ranch to you. I'll let the place fall to ruin before I let you have it."

She didn't even stop to consider his arrogance in assuming he could afford it. If the man had accumulated millions, it still wouldn't be enough to buy Tex's ranch, not with the price tag she would put on it to keep it out of his reach.

"We'll see," Jake said. "There's time enough to decide."

His quiet confidence that she would eventually change her mind rattled her. The old Jake would have raged at her insulting dismissal, forced her to dig in her heels. This Jake with his mild response was leaving her wiggling room, a way to extricate herself from a hasty decision without losing face. Why? she wondered. What was he up to now? Had her grandfather made an agreement with him that she knew nothing about?

She felt his gaze on her and forced herself to face him. "What?"

"I haven't said it before now, Meggie, but I am sorry about Tex. I know you loved him. More than that, I know he loved you. You'll need to hang on to that in the days to come.''

There was genuine sympathy in his voice. That alone would have startled her, but she was pretty sure she heard something else, as well. A warning, perhaps, that there were shocks to come? Or was it no more than his awareness that making burial arrangements, the funeral itself, dealing with death's aftermath would be grueling? That had to be it, she assured herself. What else could he have meant?

Unwanted and unexpected tears stinging her eyes at Jake's sympathy, Megan turned away and stared out the window as he put the car into gear and headed for home. The drive took over an hour, with barely a word spoken. He seemed content enough to leave her to her thoughts. More than once she wished he'd say something, *anything,* just so she could pick a fight with him. Silence left her too much time to grieve, too much time to think about walking into the ranch house for the first time without Tex there to greet her.

By the time they turned into the ranch's long, winding drive, the sun had vanished behind a bank of heavy, gray clouds. Snow, thick and wet, splashed against the windshield. The air, when she finally stepped out of the car's warmth, was raw.

Leaving the luggage to Jake, she ran toward the front door, only to skid to a halt on the porch when the door was opened by a child of eight or nine, her eyes puffy and red from crying, her hair a tangle of thick auburn curls.

"Who're you?" she demanded, glaring up at Megan.

"I'm Megan O'Rourke," Megan responded automatically, then realized that she was the one who ought to be asking questions. "Who are you?"

"I'm Tess. I live here," she declared with a hint of defiance.

Megan stared at her, as shocked as if the girl had uttered an especially vile obscenity. "That can't be," she murmured, just as Jake bounded onto the porch and tucked a supporting hand under her elbow to guide her inside.

The child regarded him with only slightly less hostility. "We're about to have dinner. You gonna stay again?"

Jake ignored the lack of warmth in the invitation and grinned. "Chicken and dumplings?"

She nodded. "Mrs. Gomez said they were her favorites," she said, gesturing toward Megan. She gave Megan another defiant look. "I hate chicken and dumplings."

That said, she stomped off in the direction of the kitchen. Megan watched her go, then sank down on the nearest chair. "Who is that child and what is she doing here?" she demanded, already dreading the answer. There wasn't a doubt in her mind that whatever his response was, she was going to hate it. That red hair all but shouted that the girl was an O'Rourke.

"Her name is Tess," Jake began.

"She told me that much."

"Tess O'Rourke."

The confirmation sent a shudder washing over her. Her gaze shot to his. "Please, don't tell me..." She couldn't even say it.

"She's your grandfather's daughter," he said. "Which technically makes her your aunt, but I think you can be forgiven if you decide not to call her Auntie Tess.''

Megan had hoped for a distant cousin, maybe. Even a sister. But an *aunt?* It was ludicrous. "I don't believe this," she murmured. "I don't believe it."

"Believe it."

"But how?"

"The usual way, I imagine. All I know for sure is that Tex just found out about her himself a few months back. She was abandoned on his doorstep. He didn't think he should mention it on the phone."

"Yeah, I can see why he might not want to," Megan said wryly.

Jake was studying her sympathetically. "You okay?"

"Just peachy."

"Good, because it gets more interesting."

Megan shook her head. "I don't think I can handle anything more interesting."

"You'll adapt. Isn't that what you do best?"

He said it in a way that sounded more accusatory than complimentary. She didn't have time to analyze why before he continued.

"According to your grandfather's will, you are officially Tess's legal guardian."

"No," she whispered, stunned not only by the concept, but by the weight of the responsibility. She hadn't planned on having kids, at least not without going through the usual preparations—marriage, pregnancy, nine months to get used to the idea. She hadn't even had nine seconds.

She tried to imagine taking a kid back to New York with her, fitting her into a life already stretched to its limits. Her imagination, always vivid, failed miserably.

"There has to be another way. Mrs. Gomez…"

"She'll help out, certainly," Jake said. "She's told me she intends to stay on here as long as you need her."

"Well, that's it, then," Megan said gratefully, relieved to have the issue settled so expeditiously.

"Not quite," Jake said. "You can't just dump Tess with Mrs. Gomez and take off."

"Why the hell can't I?" she all but shouted as panic flooded through her.

"Because Tex has spelled everything out in his will. I'll give you a copy later."

His intimate familiarity with the details of Tex's wishes stirred suspicion. "How do you know so much about Tex's will?" she asked, gaze narrowed.

"Because I'm the one who drew it up. Believe me, it's airtight."

Megan wondered just how many more shocks her heart could take before she wound up in a grave right next to Tex. "You're a lawyer?"

"A damned good one, if I do say so myself. You renege on the terms Tex has spelled out and the ranch is up for grabs." His expression turned triumphant. "In other words, it'll be all but mine, Meggie, and there won't be a damned thing you can do to stop it."

3

Jake wasn't sure what had gotten into him in the car. Why had he declared his intention to get his hands on Tex's ranch? He'd been toying with the idea in the back of his mind, but he hadn't decided on it. Far from it. He was still painting the inside of the modest little house he'd bought in town, discovering that he liked fixing leaky faucets and patching cracks in the walls. What did he need with a ranch?

Sure, owning such a spread would represent respectability. Even the doubters in Whispering Wind would have to take him seriously if he became the area's biggest rancher. Mrs. Perkins at the general store might stop trailing him around as if he were about to steal a loaf of bread. The explanation made sense, but he had a hunch his motives were a whole lot more complicated than that.

Like making Meggie crazy, for one thing. Maybe just to taunt her into sticking around for the sake of that little girl who was in desperate need of someone to love. Though Tess hadn't exactly warmed to him, he had to admit he had a soft spot for her.

The child had come from a background not all that different from his own. Whether she knew it yet or not, Tess had lucked out when her mother had dumped her on Tex's doorstep. For all of his gruff demeanor, Tex was a man a person could count on. Losing him so unexpectedly and so soon had been a bad break. Getting Meggie for a mother, well, it remained to be seen how that would turn out.

While Megan went upstairs to clean up for dinner—and probably to gather her very rattled composure—Jake wandered into the kitchen, where he'd felt at home the very first time he'd walked through the door years and years ago. Mrs. Gomez had always fit his image of the perfect mother, such a far cry from his own that he thought she'd been conjured up straight out of a fairy tale. She was blustery and affectionate by turns, and she always had some treat in the oven.

"Sit, sit," Mrs. Gomez encouraged now, waving him toward the table.

The aroma of sugar and chocolate competed with that of the chicken stewing on the stove. Unable to resist, Jake snatched a still-warm cookie from the baking sheet, then sat as she'd asked.

"How come he gets to have a cookie before supper and I don't?" Tess demanded.

"Because he's a grown-up and I can't boss him around," the housekeeper said.

"You can't boss me around, either," Tess said. "I'm not your kid."

"No, *niña*, but you are my responsibility, and I will see that you do right, because that is what your father would have wanted."

"Some father," Tess muttered. "He didn't even know I existed till I showed up here. I guess he and my mom weren't real close."

Jake caught Mrs. Gomez's helpless look and stepped in. "He was here for you when it counted, wasn't he? He took you in, made a home for you. The last few months haven't been so bad, have they?"

Her bright green eyes shimmered with tears, reminding him of another little girl, another time. Tess's lower lip trembled, but that O'Rourke chin jutted defiantly.

"Fat lot of good that does me now," she declared. "He's dead and I ain't staying here with her." She nodded toward the door to indicate the absent Megan, no doubt.

"I will be here, too," Mrs. Gomez promised. "We will all get along just fine."

"And I'll be around," Jake added.

"Over my dead body," Megan retorted, striding into the room and heading straight for Mrs. Gomez, who opened her arms wide to embrace her.

"Ah, *niña,* it is good to have you home, but not so good that it is under these circumstances," the housekeeper said. She tucked a finger under Megan's chin and looked her in the eye. "You are holding up okay? Shall I fix you some tea? I have all of your favorites—raspberry, orange spice, whatever you like."

Jake detected a hint of puffiness under Megan's eyes and guessed she'd indulged in a good cry upstairs, where it could be done without witnesses. That had always been her way, ingrained in her by Tex, no doubt. Tex had been critical of emotional displays. Jake had seen Meggie swallow back tears no matter how much pain she might have been in, physical or emotional.

"I'm fine," Megan insisted. Like Jake, she reached for a cookie and bit into it, oblivious to Tess's expression of disgust.

"Geez-oh-flip, does everybody get to break rules around this place but me?" Tess demanded, scraping her chair away from the table. She shoved open the back door and disappeared into the gathering darkness.

"She does not have her coat," Mrs. Gomez said worriedly, moving toward the hook by the door where the red, down-filled jacket hung. "It is too cold for her to be outside."

"I'll go," Jake said, his hand on her shoulder. "You stay here with Megan."

Glad of an excuse to escape the restlessness that seeing Meggie stirred in him, he grabbed Tess's coat from the hook and flipped on an outdoor light as he went out. He spotted the child racing toward the barn, ducking into shadows. He suspected the new litter of kittens he'd heard about was at least part of the reason for her destination.

Sure enough, he found her kneeling beside a box that had been lined with an old flannel shirt, one of Tex's favorites, if Jake wasn't mistaken. He wondered if it had been confiscated for this particular duty before or after his death. Jake grinned at the sight of orange-and-white balls of fluff tumbling around inside the box, scrambling to get to their mama's milk.

"They're getting big," he observed, hunkering down beside Tess. "Do you have a favorite?"

"Not really," she said, but her gaze was fixed on the runt of the litter, who couldn't seem to squeeze in to feed.

Jake reached down, picked the littlest kitten up and made room for it. "Looks like this one needs some extra attention," he said, thinking it was a lot like Tess herself. Megan, too, though she would have hated the comparison.

"I suppose."

"Maybe you should consider adopting it and taking it inside. It's big enough now, especially if you bottle-fed it for a couple of weeks."

"I can't," she said, though her expression was wistful.

"How come?"

"Tex said."

"Did he say why?"

"He said he wasn't having some damned cat bringing in fleas and tearing up the furniture."

Jake held back a grin. He had a hunch she'd nailed the old man's exact words. "You know what I think?"

"What?"

"That if Tex could see how lonely you've been feeling the last day or so, he'd change his mind."

Her face brightened. "Do you think so?"

"I know so," Jake insisted, because there wasn't a chance in hell the old man could contradict him. Tess needed something weaker and needier to tend to right now. He doubted Mrs. Gomez would have any objections. He knew for a fact there were cats crawling all over her own house. She took in every stray that ever came to the door, him included. On more than one occasion, she'd been the one he'd run to when he couldn't bear one more night in the same house with his mother and her "gentlemen callers."

He glanced up from the kittens and caught Tess studying him intently.

"Can I ask you something?" she asked.

"Of course."

"Is *she* going to keep me?"

"You mean Megan?"

Tess nodded, her expression bleak. "I don't think she likes me much."

"You just took her by surprise, that's all. No one had told her about you."

"Well, having her come busting in here like she owns the place ain't no picnic for me, either."

"She does own the place," Jake pointed out gently.

"Then how come she doesn't live here?"

"Because she's got a job in New York."

"That TV show," Tess said, feigning disinterest despite the spark of fascination that lit her eyes. "Tex used to watch it sometimes. He didn't think I knew that, but I did. Sometimes I'd hide out in his office behind that big old chair of his. Right after dinner, he'd come in there, put in the tape and watch, muttering to himself."

"Ever hear what he said?"

"That it was damned fool nonsense," she quoted, probably precisely. "You know what I think, though?"

"What?"

"That he was real proud of her. He never looked at me the way he looked at that show of hers." Her lower lip trembled. "I don't think he gave a damn about me at all."

Ignoring the substance of the remark for the moment, he chided, "You know, kiddo, you really do need to clean up your language. Ladies don't swear half as much as you do.''

"Maybe I don't want to be no lady."

Jake grinned at the defiance. "What do you want to be?"

Her expression brightened. "A rancher, just like Tex," she said decisively. "Then I could boss people around and make lots of money and ride horses." She met Jake's gaze. "He was teaching me to ride. Did you know that? That's when it happened. He fell right down on the ground. I screamed and screamed for somebody to come, but it took forever. I didn't know what to do. I've seen that CPR stuff on TV, but I didn't know how to do it. Not the right way, anyway. I tried and tried, but nothing helped."

Sobs shook her shoulders. "I didn't mean for him to die," she whispered brokenly, launching herself at Jake. Her skinny little arms wound so tightly around his neck that he could scarcely breathe. "Sometimes I said I hated him and sometimes I said I wished he were dead, but I never meant it. Never."

"Oh, baby, I know that," Jake soothed, feeling totally out of his depth. "Tex was sick. It wasn't your fault."

"But if I hadn't come, maybe he wouldn't have gotten sick."

"No. That's not the way it works. He'd been sick for a while. He told me that himself. His heart just gave up. It could have happened anytime. I promise you, you had nothing to do with it."

Slowly Tess's sobs subsided. She sniffed, accepted Jake's handkerchief and blew her nose. She blinked away the last of the tears and regarded him evenly. "I got an idea."

"What's that?"

"I'm thinking I should come and live with you."

Jake realized he had walked right smack into that one. He'd made it a point to spend time with Tess the past couple of weeks, anticipating what might happen, knowing the kid would need a friend until she adjusted to all the upheaval.

Not that seeing Tess had been any sacrifice. She was bright and funny, and she did have a mouth on her. She didn't like him, didn't trust him and had no qualms about telling him just that. Jake had overlooked it all and stayed the course. The fact that she was willing to turn to him now proved he'd done the right thing. With persistence, he'd slipped past her defenses. It was critical to tred carefully.

He took her hands in his and kept his gaze on her face. "Honey, you know that's not possible. I explained it to you before. Tex named Megan your legal guardian in case anything happened to him."

"But she doesn't want me," Tess said, wrenching herself free. Hands on hips, she faced him. "You know she doesn't. I'll mess up her life."

"It's going to take a little time for her to get used to the idea, just the way it took time for you to get used to being here with Tex. Everybody's real upset about Tex right now. I told you before, I'll be around. You can come to me with any problem, but you can't live with me."

"Then I'll go find my mom."

Jake had anticipated that sooner or later that thought would occur to her. Rather than squashing the notion outright, he asked quietly, "Any idea where she is?"

"No, but I can find her. I'll just ask a lot of questions till somebody tells me. She's probably back in Laramie. That's where we lived before she brought me here."

Jake knew better. He'd searched Laramie for some trace of Tess's mother himself. "Honey, she's probably moved on."

"I can find her. I know it."

"Tell me something," Jake said. "Do you study geography in school?"

"Sure."

"Then you know it's a big country. Your mom could be anywhere."

She stared at him, then. A look of utter defeat crossed her face. "It could take forever, then, couldn't it?"

"I'm afraid so."

"It's not fair," she whispered. "Nothing's fair."

"No," he said gently. "There's nothing fair about losing your dad almost before you really got a chance to know him. There's nothing fair about your mama running out on you. But it is going to work out, Tess. I swear to you. Megan's got a good heart. You'll get along well enough."

"You can't make her care about me," she said, with the weary resignation of someone who'd learned too early that love was never a guarantee, not even from a parent.

"I can't make her, no, but she will, honey. I know she will." If he had to hog-tie her and explain a few facts of life, Megan O'Rourke would do right by this child. Just as Tex had predicted, Jake would enjoy every single minute of seeing to it.

If it had been up to Megan, Tex's funeral would have been private. It was Jake who handed her a letter with Tex's wishes spelled out. He wanted something lavish, even though he hadn't set foot inside of a church in years.

"The service isn't for me. I'll already be wherever I'm heading," he'd written. "It's for you, Megan. I want you to be surrounded by the steady, solid folks around here. Maybe it'll help you to remember what it's like to have friends who can share your grief, who'll be there for you and expect nothing in return. Seems to me like you've accumulated enough of the other kind in New York."

She sighed at his words. Leave it to Tex to take a dig at her life-style while laying out his own funeral arrangements. She forced herself to read on.

"After all the hoopla's over, bury me quietly on that rise overlooking the creek," he'd instructed. "I've already made arrangements for my tombstone. It's nothing fancy, so don't you go adding any flowery sentiments to it. Plain and simple will do me just fine."

When she'd finished reading, she folded the letter precisely and tucked it back into the plain white envelope with her name scrawled across the front in Tex's careless script.

"I suppose you know what it says," she said to Jake, irritated that he'd been taken into her grandfather's confidence when she had not.

"The gist of it," he agreed. "Obviously, the details are up to you, but he made his feelings known."

"And, of course, I'll do as he asked," she said wearily.

Jake studied her intently. "About everything?"

"You're talking about Tess, aren't you?"

"Of course."

"Jake, I can't think about that now. I really can't. I'm feeling..." Her voice trailed off and she held up her hands in a rare gesture of helplessness.

"Lost? Overwhelmed? Angry?" he supplied.

She caught herself wanting to smile at the litany, which was eerily accurate, reminiscent of a time when Jake had read her mind with ease. "Pretty much," she admitted.

"Some of this you'll have to handle yourself, but in terms of the funeral, if you're agreeable to what Tex wanted, you can sit back and leave the rest to me," Jake offered. "I'll make the arrangements for the service and the burial."

She balked at letting him take on that task. Duty came to mind again. "It's my responsibility."

He shook his head and grinned. "Ah, Meggie, you never did know when to let go, did you? I'm surprised you haven't gone up in flames with all that's on your plate in New York. Do you trust anyone to handle even the tiniest detail?"

She thought of Todd and his incredible efficiency. "Of course," she snapped.

Jake's steady gaze was skeptical. "Really?"

Okay, she admitted to herself, the truth was that not much got past without her final approval. Her staff sometimes chafed at the lack of faith, but she reminded them repeatedly that it was her name on the magazine, her image on the television screen, her reputation on the line. Admitting any of that to Jake, though, was not an option.

"It's a funeral, not a presidential inauguration. I can handle it," she informed him. "I'll be sure and call your office when the time is set."

He grinned and settled back in the easy chair opposite her—Tex's chair, the leather one that was oversize to fit a big man. Jake looked as at home in it as Tex ever had. The relief she felt at Jake's being there unnerved her. The house was too empty without Tex. She accepted the fact that it would have felt that way even if it had been crowded with people. She told herself that a cattle thief was a poor substitute for the honorable man her grandfather had been, but she was a little too grateful for the company just the same. That made it all the more important to see that he left.

"Didn't you hear what I said?" she asked testily.

"You trying to get rid of me, Meggie?"

"I was hoping to, yes," she said bluntly. "I'm tired, Jake. It's been a long, grueling day."

"I'm sure it has been," he agreed. "But there are matters we have to discuss."

"Tonight?"

"I think so."

"Such as?"

"Tess."

Her head pounded just thinking about Tess. "I told you I am not talking about Tess."

"You can't ignore the subject, Megan. She's not going to vanish overnight."

Megan closed her eyes as if to deny the truth of

what he was saying. Unfortunately, Tess was very
real and apparently very much her responsibility. Megan didn't have to see the terms of Tex's will in black
and white to prove it. She doubted that Jake, for all
of his flaws, would have the audacity to lie about
something so important.

"I can't deal with this now."

"You have to," he insisted.

"Aren't you the one who just finished saying that
Tess wasn't going anywhere? I'll deal with that situation tomorrow."

"Or the next day or the one after that," he suggested sarcastically. "She's a kid. You can't just
back-burner her until it's convenient. She needs some
reassurance that things are going to work out, that
you'll take care of her now. She's already convinced
you don't want her. Can you imagine how insecure
that makes her feel?"

The memory of another terrified, insecure little girl
came back to haunt her. Megan tried to push it aside,
bury it where it belonged, in the past. "Where did
this show of concern come from?" she asked Jake.
"I don't remember you being the fatherly type."

"I'm talking common decency here. Tess is scared.
Can you blame her? Of all people, you ought to know
what it feels like to be dumped on someone's doorstep."

Megan shuddered despite herself. The memories
flooded back once more. It had been more than two
decades ago and she still remembered how terrify-
ingly alone she had felt in a strange house, knowing
that her mother had gone away, more than likely for
good.

What was it about the women in Tex's life—his own daughter, Tess's mama, even Megan herself—that they all fled? Had they been overwhelmed by the sheer force of his personality? Had they needed to escape to find themselves?

"I'll check on Tess when I go upstairs," she said, resigned to the fact that he wouldn't leave her in peace without such a promise.

"It'll take more than a kiss on the cheek and tucking the blankets around her to fix things," Jake pointed out, still not satisfied.

"Dammit, I know that," Megan said, frustrated by his persistence. "I'll do what I can. You've known about this for how long now? Weeks, maybe. Months. I've had less than a day. You'll have to excuse me if I'm inept at the maternal bit. As you just reminded me, I never had an example to go by."

He looked vaguely guilty. "Sorry. I didn't mean to reopen old wounds."

"Of course you did. And you were right," she admitted with a sigh. "I should be more understanding, since I went through the exact same thing." She thought of Tess's attitude. The child had deliberately done everything in her power to goad Megan all through dinner. "She's not making it easy, you know."

Jake clearly wasn't persuaded. "Did you?"

She thought back. She'd pretty much challenged Tex every chance she got until the ground rules were laid out and had taken hold. "I suppose not."

"You're the grown-up now, Meggie. Do what you wish had been done for you way back then." That said, he finally seemed satisfied that he'd done what he could. He stood up and headed for the door. "You need anything, call."

"I'll manage."

He shook his head. "Whatever." At the door, he paused. "We'll go over the rest of Jake's will after the funeral, okay? That'll be soon enough."

Megan doubted there were any more bombshells to be dropped. Just in case, though, she muttered, "I can't wait."

As soon as Jake was gone, she slipped over to Tex's chair just as she had so many times in the past the instant her grandfather had left the room. The leather was still warm from Jake's heat. She could almost pretend that Tex himself had just been sitting there, but it was Jake's scent that surrounded her tonight. Despite her reluctance to accept anything at all from him, she curled up in the spot where he'd been and took comfort from the lingering traces of his presence.

She thought of the pushy, irritating man who'd just left, the angry little girl upstairs and the sneaky old coot who was gone forever.

"Oh, Tex," she whispered, battling fresh tears. "What have you done to me?"

4

The slightly plump woman standing on the front porch with an armload of casserole dishes had a wary expression in her eyes, as if she were uncertain of her welcome. Her arrival had taken Megan by surprise. In New York she wasn't used to people dropping by, and even if they did, there was a whole layer of security built in before they ever reached her. Surprise didn't take away the pleasure, however. It had been way too long since she'd seen her onetime best friend.

"Megan, it's me, Peggy," the woman announced in an insecure rush before Megan could acknowledge her. "I probably should have called first, but we don't stand on ceremony much around here. It's probably not like that in New York. What with all you do, you probably have a zillion secretaries to keep people from bothering you." She thrust the food toward Megan. "I'll just leave this and run along."

If she'd slowed down for even a second, Megan would have welcomed her with a hug, but Peggy had always chattered on without pausing for breath. Being ill at ease only made her worse. Megan snagged her friend's arm as she turned away.

"You get in here, Peggy. You're not going anywhere," Megan insisted.

Peggy's expression brightened. "Are you sure? I just wanted you to know I was thinking about you. I don't want to be a bother."

"How could you possibly be a bother? Now get in here. Let me take this into the other room and I'll be right with you."

She waited until Peggy had come inside before carrying the still-warm casseroles toward the dining room table, which was already heaped with offerings from other neighbors. When she returned to the foyer, Peggy was still regarding her uncertainly.

"I wasn't sure you'd even remember me," she confessed.

"And why wouldn't I?" Megan said, startled by the statement. "We grew up together. I slept over at your house whenever Tex would let me. You know more of my secrets than anyone else on earth. How could you possibly think I wouldn't remember you?"

Peggy shrugged. "It's been a long time." She said it without judgment or rancor, just a statement of fact that spoke volumes about the way Megan had cut not only Whispering Wind, but everyone in it out of her life. There'd been no cards, no letters, not even a quick, occasional phone call to Peggy.

"I'm sorry," Megan said sincerely. "I never meant for so much time to go by. Can you stay for a bit? We can make up for lost time."

Even as she said the words, she realized just how much she had missed having a real confidante, someone who knew her inside out and never judged. She had hundreds of acquaintances now, but few good friends and absolutely no one who shared a lifelong history with her. Seeing Peggy and remembering middle-of-the-night confidences, shared dreams and irrepressible giggles made her feel the absence in a way she never had before.

"Are you sure?" Peggy asked. "I know you must have a million and one things to do. We're all real sorry about Tex. If there's anything you need, you just have to ask. Wilma at the funeral home said you'd been in to arrange for the services. Everyone'll be there, of course. Tex touched a lot of lives around here. I never realized how many till I was grown and on my own. Kids never do, I guess." She paused and grinned. "I guess you can tell I still go on and on. Just hush me up whenever you're tired of hearing my voice. Johnny says I could talk a man to death. He believes that's how I get my way so often."

Megan searched her memory. The image of a freckle-faced blond boy with an untamable cowlick and a shy smile came to mind. "You married Johnny Barkley?"

"Who else?" Peggy said. "I mooned over him long enough. I guess I just wore him down. We have three children, two boys and a girl, which explains how I've managed to put on twenty pounds I don't need and turned most of my hair gray, though you can't tell it because of the blond rinse I've been using. I'll be darned if I'm going to look old before my time the way my mama did. Of course, she looks terrific now that she's down in Arizona. She had herself a facelift last year. I swear she looks almost as young as me."

"Well, you certainly look wonderful," Megan said with total sincerity. Despite the extra weight, Peggy looked healthy and happy—contented in a way that

Megan found herself envying without knowing why. Her green eyes sparkled with merriment, just as they had when she and Megan were children.

"Go on into the living room and have a seat," Megan urged. "I'll have Mrs. Gomez fix us some tea. Or would you rather have coffee?"

"I'll have a soda if she has one. Any kind will do."

"A Dr Pepper," Megan said, suddenly remembering. They had gone through cases of the stuff. "I'll bet there are some in the fridge."

In the kitchen, she found the housekeeper trying to stuff the already overloaded refrigerator with yet another casserole that had just been delivered to the back door by a neighbor who hadn't wanted to bother Megan.

"It's a good thing the funeral's tomorrow or all this food would go bad," she said. "Not much of a loss, if you ask me. There's not an enchilada in the lot of them."

"Maybe folks figure your spicy cooking is what put Tex in his grave and they're not taking any chances," Megan teased, then regretted it when she saw the sheen of tears in the housekeeper's eyes. Megan wrapped her arms around her. "Don't you dare cry. If you do, you'll have me weeping."

"Crying might do you some good. Better to let your emotions out than keep them all bottled up the way Tex made you do," the housekeeper said with undisguised disapproval. "You remember when that boy—Bobby Temple, *sí?* He shoved you down in the mud in your brand-new winter coat. You were crying and carrying on. Tex gave you one of those looks of his and said, 'Girl, an O'Rourke always holds his chin up high and we never, ever cry over things that are over and done.'"

Mrs. Gomez had captured Tex's words exactly. Megan had heard them often enough. She gave the housekeeper another hug. "Oh, I'll do my share of crying before this is over," she assured her. "Right now, though, Peggy's here and we were wondering if there's any Dr Pepper around."

Mrs. Gomez's expression brightened. "I believe there's some in the pantry. I'll fill some tall glasses with lots of ice the way you used to like it, and I'll bring it right along."

"I'll get it. You have enough to do." Megan found an entire case of the soft drink in the pantry. Emerging with a couple of cans, she regarded the housekeeper with a wry look. "I take it you were expecting Peggy to drop by."

"Of course, *niña*. She is your best friend. Where else would she be at a time like this?"

Some friend I've been, Megan thought as she took the drinks into the living room. Peggy was married and had three children Megan had known nothing about until today. She'd never even asked after her friend when she'd talked to Tex, and he wasn't one to volunteer information.

In the living room she found Peggy perched on the edge of the sofa as if she still might take off at any second. Once she would have been curled up in a corner of that same overstuffed sofa with her shoes kicked off and a fat pillow hugged to her middle.

Megan handed a glass to her friend and sat at the

opposite end. "Okay, then. Married. Three kids. What else have you been up to?"

Peggy gave her an amused look. "I can tell you don't have kids, if you have to ask a question like that. Three of them, all under the age of ten, pretty much eliminates anything except sleeping six hours a night if I'm lucky."

Megan thought of Tess and the disruptions she faced to her own life, and shuddered. "I imagine I'll be finding out for myself soon enough," she said, testing the idea aloud for the first time.

Though she'd been praying for some other solution, Jake's words and a long night of restless tossing and turning had left her fully aware that she couldn't simply abandon the girl, no matter how much either of them would have preferred it. She wouldn't be able to live with herself if she simply walked away.

Peggy gave her an understanding look. "Then you know about Tess? I'd wondered."

"Oh, yes, I know. I found out when I got here."

"Sweet heaven! Not before?" Peggy asked, clearly shocked. "It's been the talk of the town for months now. I thought surely Tex would have told you."

"No one thought to tell me," Megan said with undisguised bitterness. "Of course, Mrs. Gomez wouldn't think it was her place. And apparently Tex didn't think he should mention it in passing during one of his phone calls. Better to let the bomb drop when he's not around to see the fallout. According to his lawyer, I'm expected to rise to the occasion."

"It'll be an adjustment, I'm sure, but it won't be that bad. She's a good kid," Peggy said. "She's spent some time at our house. She and my girl are friends, at least most days. Tess doesn't make it easy. Then, who can blame her? It can't have been easy having a mama walk out and getting left with a man she'd never even met before. That mama of hers ought to roast in hell for what she did.''

"Apparently that place in hell is going to be crowded with Tex's women," Megan observed. "The habit goes all the way back to my mother—beyond if you consider the fact that Grandmother died when my mother was barely five."

Peggy's cheeks turned bright pink. "Oh my gosh, I'm sorry. I wasn't _thinking_. It's just that it was so long ago, what happened to you. You've done so well, I suppose I never think about the scars it might have left inside."

"No scars," Megan insisted staunchly. "You're right. My life is as close to perfect as anything I could ever have imagined."

"Perfect, huh? That's certainly the impression you give on TV and in your magazine. Makes the rest of us downright envious. How's Tess going to fit into that?"

Megan sighed. "I wish to heaven I knew."

"Well, if anyone can make it work, it's you," Peggy said with absolute confidence. "After all, aren't you the woman who tells the whole world how to turn lemons into lemonade? I swear to goodness, I think you could take the rattiest old thing lying around and turn it into some fancy decorative accent. I watched that show of yours one day and dragged an old cradle out of the basement and turned it into a planter. Johnny thought at first I was hinting about having another baby, but then I stuck a couple of

ferns in there and he admitted it looked right nice.
Said the watering's likely to rot the wood before the
next generation comes along, but so what? I doubt
they'll appreciate anything that doesn't come from
some discount store, anyway. Plastic's practical. Even
my mama says that, though it makes me shudder
when she does. Last time I went down to Arizona to
see her, I swear to goodness I was shocked. Her idea
of decorating is picking up whatever's on sale at Wal-
Mart. You should have seen the mishmash. It would
have brought tears to your eyes.''

Megan chuckled. ''Oh, Peggy, I have missed you.
No one cuts through to the heart of things the way
you do. Don't ever change.''

''I don't suppose I could if I wanted to. This is
who I am and, thank goodness, Johnny loves me for
it.'' She paused and studied Megan carefully.
''You've changed, though.''

''How?'' Megan asked, expecting her to say something about the expensive highlights in the sophisticated, yet casually short hairstyle that had replaced
the ponytails of her youth. Or maybe something about
the elegant clothes that were a far cry from the worn-
out blue jeans and frayed cotton shirts she had once
favored.

''You're warier,'' Peggy said thoughtfully. ''Jake's
responsible for that, I suppose. It must have come as
a shock to find him here. I know everyone in town
was certainly stunned when he came back. Then he
and your grandfather got to be thick as thieves at the
end, no pun intended, and no one knew what to make
of it. To give the devil his due, Jake's still the hand-
somest thing walking around Whispering Wind.

"Not that I'd trade my Johnny," she added hurriedly. "No, indeed. Johnny's a man you can rely on. No surprises. Jake Landers is the kind of man who can break a woman's heart, but who would know that better than you?"

"That was a long time ago. Jake Landers means nothing to me now," Megan said firmly. "Nothing."

Peggy looked startled by her vehemence, then a slow grin spread across her face. "Oh, my, so that's the way it is, is it?"

"I don't know what you're talking about," Megan insisted, despite the heat she could feel climbing into her cheeks.

Peggy went on as if she hadn't spoken. "Of course, he's a respected lawyer now. I suppose it could work. And Tex isn't around to stand in your way—"

"Enough!" Megan interrupted. "I am not the least bit interested in Jake. That was over and done with a very long time ago. He stole Tex's cattle, for heaven's sake. How could I give two figs about a man who would betray my grandfather that way after Tex had brought him out here and given him work?"

Peggy regarded her oddly.

"What?" Megan asked.

"He didn't do it," Peggy said. "Surely you knew that."

She sounded so confident, so sure of her facts that Megan was taken aback. "Jake didn't steal the cattle? Are you sure?"

"Well, of course I am. I can't believe you didn't know that." Peggy shook her head. "No, I take that back. It makes perfect sense. Tex certainly wouldn't tell you. Not only was he a man who never cared for admitting a mistake, but he wouldn't have wanted you running straight back to Jake. I always wondered if he didn't have something to do with those charges being trumped up in the first place, but then I couldn't imagine a man as upstanding as Tex O'Rourke doing such a low-down thing.''

"Peggy, what are you talking about?" Megan demanded, cutting into the rambling monologue.

"There were no stolen cattle," Peggy said succinctly.

"Of course there were. Why else—"

"No, it was all some huge mistake. Or so they claimed once the dust settled. That's why your grandfather paid for Jake to go to college and law school, to make up for misjudging him."

"Tex paid for Jake's education?" Megan repeated, stunned.

"Every penny."

"And the cattle were never stolen." She couldn't seem to grasp the implications of that.

"Nope. They'd just wandered off to some other pasture, according to the story that came out eventually. They were grazing a few miles up the mountain, happy as could be."

"He never said a word," Megan whispered. "Not one word."

"Who, Tex?"

"No. Jake. All these years he's let me go on thinking the worst of him."

"What did you expect? The man had his pride. You were supposed to know him better than anybody on earth and you thought he was a thief. Never even had a doubt about it, as far as I can recall. Is it any wonder he never said a word, after the way you let him down?''

The accusation stung, in part because of the truth of it, in part because it was coming from a woman who'd never been a particularly big fan of Jake's back then. Now Peggy sounded like a blasted cheerleader. Obviously the tide had turned in Whispering Wind.

"I wonder if he'll ever be able to forgive me," Megan said, surprised and dismayed to find that it suddenly mattered. All those years of thinking of Jake as the bad guy were nothing more than wasted time and wasted regrets. It was just one more thing to hold against Tex. At this rate, by the time the funeral came along in the morning, Megan was going to be glad to see the sneaky old coot buried.

There was a light dusting of snow on the ground when Tex was finally laid to rest on the hill overlooking his spread of land. A mountain of flowers covered the grave, from the splashy, elaborate arrangements he would have loved to the simple bouquet of daisies that Jake had helped Tess pick out at the florist in town.

All during the service Tess had kept her hand tucked in his while huge, silent tears rolled down her cheeks. He had a feeling it was the only display of genuine emotion in the entire crowd of mourners. Most people were here because it was expected. Some had come out of curiosity, because they wanted to see the hotshot from New York who'd once lived just down the road.

As for Meggie, she certainly didn't appear all that broken up. Dry-eyed and coolly competent, she looked as if she were worried about nothing more than catering details, when he knew for a fact her heart had to be breaking. Still, five minutes after the service ended, she was back at the house, issuing orders to the temporary kitchen staff and putting the final touches on an elaborate buffet for the mourners. She did it all with a brisk efficiency that proved entertaining a crowd this size was second nature to her.

As he watched her place steaming platter after steaming platter on the table, Jake couldn't help wondering what had happened to all the food the neighbors had dropped off in Pyrex dishes covered with foil. Probably not up to her fancy standards.

She stood by the table and frowned at some flaw Jake couldn't detect. He wandered over to stand beside her.

"Something wrong?"

Megan barely glanced at him. "There's something missing, but I can't pinpoint what it is," she said with evident frustration.

"Nobody's going to notice if you've left off a salt-shaker or a serving spoon. They're coming by to show their support and their sympathy, not to see if Megan O'Rourke can throw a great party," he reassured her, even though he'd been thinking exactly that about the mourners' motives earlier.

When she would have protested, he tucked a finger under her chin and forced her gaze to his. "Meggie, it's not a test."

For a moment tears swam in her eyes. She looked lost and surprisingly vulnerable. "I have to get it right," she whispered. "For Tex."

"Then you should have thrown a barbecue and

been done with it. That was Tex's style, Meggie. Not all this fancy silver.''

He'd meant it to be reassuring, but he knew instantly she took it the wrong way. Fire flashed in her eyes.

''Are you saying I've gotten this wrong, too? Well, who the hell are you to tell me what my grandfather would or wouldn't like?'' she exploded. ''He was *my* grandfather, dammit. Just because you somehow managed to cozy up to him these last few months doesn't mean you knew him better than me, Jake Landers. It doesn't.''

With that she burst into tears and fled to the kitchen. Jake hadn't intended to goad her into an outburst, but he couldn't help being glad he'd broken through that tough act she'd been putting on for everyone's benefit. He was about to follow her when the housekeeper put a hand on his arm.

''Let her go,'' Mrs. Gomez said.

''I should have been more sensitive, I suppose,'' he said, but without much real regret.

''No. She needed a good cry, but she won't like you seeing it. You being the cause gives her an excuse she can handle right now. Thinking of Tex being dead and buried is still too much for her.''

''Is she going to be all right?'' he asked, still staring worriedly after her.

''Oh, I imagine she'll be just fine in time. Megan's a strong, resilient woman. She's had to be all her life. Her world's a little topsy-turvy right now, but she'll set it straight soon enough.''

It sounded kinder when Mrs. Gomez said it than it

had when he'd sarcastically accused Megan of being adaptable. "Will she be okay with Tess?"

"As I said, she is resilient. She is also good-hearted. She will do what is right for the child."

Still staring after Meggie, Jake sighed. "There have been a lot of times these last few months when I've regretted letting Tex talk me into drawing up that will of his. This is one of them."

"If you hadn't done it, someone else would have. Better that it was someone who knows Meggie, someone who cares about her and can see her through this."

His gaze shot to hers. "I never said..."

She patted his cheek. "You didn't have to. It is in your eyes. It always has been." She gestured toward the table. "Now pile a plate up with some of this food and eat. You will need your strength for what's to come, *sí?*"

Jake had a feeling he could eat every last scrap on the buffet and still not be strong enough to deal with Meggie when she found out about Tex's final devious scheme to get her back to Wyoming for good.

5

Tears streaming down her cheeks and, no doubt, destroying her carefully applied makeup, Megan retreated to the back steps, where she was pretty sure no one would find her. The fight with Jake had been absurd. She knew that. But it had set off a whole slew of insecurities and stirred up anger and resentment that she'd kept pretty well tucked away inside for the past couple of days.

The anger had been misdirected, of course. It was Tex she was furious with, not Jake. She was mad at him for being sneaky and conniving and, most of all, for being dead.

Now she'd never have the chance to tell him that she loved him, that she owed him or that she was sorry they'd fought. It was too late to take back what she'd said—not that she would have—about belonging in New York, not Wyoming, no matter how much it hurt him to hear it.

The cold air was drying the tears on her cheeks and setting up goose bumps when she heard a soft, shuffling sound and noticed Tess creeping up beside her. The girl's face was streaked with dried tears and dirt, and her hair was a tangle of mussed curls and straw. Obviously she'd paid another visit to the barn. As pitiful as she appeared, she still shot a defiant look at Megan.

"Why are you crying?" Tess demanded, as if Megan had no right to shed tears over Tex.

"Same reason as you, I imagine."

"You didn't care about Tex," Tess accused.

"Yes, I did," Megan corrected mildly.

"Sure didn't show it. I been here six months and this is the first I've seen of you."

"Because I work in New York."

"So? You make a lot of money, least that's what Tex said. You could have come home, if you'd wanted to."

Megan sighed. "Yes, I suppose I could have."

Tess seemed startled by the quick admission. "How come you didn't, then?"

"It's complicated," Megan said, for lack of a better explanation.

"Complicated how?" Tess asked, refusing to be put off.

Was this what life was going to be like from now on? Was she going to be asked tough questions by a kid, rather than a reporter? Megan struggled to find a plausible answer that would satisfy an eight-year-old. "Tex and I didn't always see eye to eye about the choices I made."

"Like what?"

"Like me living in New York."

"You liked it better than here?"

"Yes."

"I don't get it," Tess said. "This place is the best. There's stuff to do and it's real pretty. Why would you rather be in some big, ugly city, all crowded in?"

The characterization of New York had Tex's stamp all over it. Megan had heard it often enough over the years. She supposed now was as good a time as any to contradict it, to get Tess excited about the prospect of moving east.

"Because my work is there," she explained. "And because it's filled with people from all over the world. It's amazing, like no place else I've ever been. It's bright and glitzy and energetic. There's something going on every minute. There are museums and plays and wonderful restaurants. You'll see."

Tess regarded her suspiciously. "What do you mean, I'll see?"

"When you come there to live with me."

Tess backed up, her expression as horrified as if Megan had suggested taking her on a spaceship to an alien world. "I'm not coming there. No way. You can't make me, either."

Megan reached out a hand, but Tess moved farther away.

"This is where I live. It's where I belong," the girl all but shouted. "Tex said. He promised!"

Tess turned then and ran, leaving Megan shaken. She hadn't expected such a violent reaction. Why hadn't Tex prepared Tess? Foolish question. Because he hadn't believed he was going to die. Then again, there was the will, naming her as Tess's guardian. That proved he had known. He'd just chosen not to stir things up. He'd left that to Jake.

As if just thinking about him had conjured him up, Jake appeared at the doorway behind her, his expression filled with concern.

"You okay?" he asked.

"Just peachy," she said without looking up.

"I'm sorry for upsetting you earlier."

Megan started to lie, to protest that he wasn't even capable of upsetting her, but she didn't have the energy for the debate that would have inevitably followed. Instead, she just shrugged, as if it were of no consequence.

"People are beginning to leave," he said. "They'd like to say goodbye, if you're up to it."

Because it was expected, she stood and brushed herself off, patted her cheeks to smooth out her makeup, and offered Jake a bright smile.

"Of course I'm up to it. The O'Rourkes don't indulge in self-pity."

"No one would think any less of you today if you did," Jake noted.

"I would," she muttered, and swept past him. In her business world, appearances mattered. In Wyoming, they mattered, too, though for very different reasons. Here it was important not to seem standoffish, to be the good neighbor that Tex had been, to show what O'Rourkes were made of.

Megan kept that smile plastered on her face for the next hour as she accepted condolences from dozens of people she'd never met before and dozens more she hadn't seen in years.

When the last of them had left, she sank into a chair and breathed a sigh of relief. But she realized she'd done it a bit too soon when Jake settled into a chair opposite her. He'd shed the jacket of his black suit and loosened his tie, which gave him a rumpled, sexy look that would have been hard to resist if she hadn't been so utterly exhausted.

"I thought you'd gone," she said.

"Sorry to disappoint you," he said wryly. "But we have business to take care of, unless you'd rather come into town tomorrow."

She was sorely tempted to take him up on the delay, but that would be cowardly. "No," she said finally. "Let's just get it over with. I can see you won't be happy until you've spilled whatever deep, dark secrets have been nagging at you ever since I got here."

He pulled a sheaf of papers from a briefcase. "Want me to do a formal reading of the will or would you rather scan it yourself?"

She held out her hand for the papers. The document in a blue folder was the will, she concluded after a glance. An envelope held a letter from Tex. Her fingers trembled as she took out the pages and stared at his familiar scrawl.

"Darling girl," it began, as his letters always had, even when he'd been mad at her. Tears stung her eyes. She wouldn't break down now, not in front of Jake. Swallowing hard, she lifted her gaze to his. "I'm not so sure I can do this right now, after all."

He took the papers. "Let me." Putting the letter aside, he started with the will, reading through a lot of legal jargon that held no surprises. There were bequests for Mrs. Gomez and other employees, a trust fund for Tess, and the legal guardianship arrangement putting Megan in charge of Tess's future.

"Is that it?" she asked when Jake paused.

"Not quite. On this last part, though, I think the letter spells out his wishes better than all the legalese that's in the will. Maybe you'll understand his reasoning better. If it's too painful, I can read it aloud for you."

His words, his tone alerted her that what was to come wasn't going to thrill her. Perhaps she could do a better job of concealing her reaction if she read the letter to herself, after all.

"I'll read it," she said, taking the letter from Jake's outstretched hand.

It began with a plea for her understanding about Tess, an apology of sorts by Tex's standards.

I know I'm leaving you with a burden that, by rights, isn't yours to shoulder, but I'm counting on you, girl. Be a mother to that child. Lord knows, she hasn't had much of one up till now.

Megan glanced at Jake. "Do you know anything about Tess's mother?"

"Her name—Contessa Florence Olson."

"Contessa?"

"A name, not a title, I assure you," he said wryly. "She goes by Flo. From what Tex told me she was waiting tables at a restaurant in Laramie when he met her about nine, maybe ten years back. They saw each other from time to time over a year or so. A matter of convenience, I believe he called it."

So, Megan thought, it had begun about the time she'd gone away to college. Tex had been lonelier than she'd realized and had turned to a stranger for companionship. Funny, Megan had never thought of Tex as being lonely. He'd seemed like the most self-contained man she'd ever known.

"He had no idea she was pregnant?" Megan asked.

Jake shook his head. "Not until Flo appeared one day about six months ago, said she was tired of the hassle, that it was his turn to take responsibility for the kid. Off she went without a backward glance. She hasn't been heard from since. I've checked and there's no sign of her in Laramie. No one there has heard from her."

"Poor Tess," Megan murmured, knowing precisely how she must have felt the night she'd been left behind. Pity wasn't what Tess needed, though. She needed a home, and Megan wasn't the least bit convinced she could provide one. Tex, however, hadn't given her much of a choice. She returned her attention to the letter.

When I'm gone, give the child some time right here on the ranch to adjust. Don't go dragging her off to New York. Thanks to the way her mama dumped her here and ran off, Tess's world has been turned upside down too much as it is. You should remember what that was like, Megan. It'll be a bond between you. Seems to me you'll be good for each other. You both need family whether you realize it or not. It's been sorely lacking in both your lives. I regret that more than I can say, but I did the best I could by both of you.

So far, Tex's request wasn't much of a shocker. It made sense to stick around for a couple of weeks to give Tess a little time to get her feet back on the ground again. With Todd and Micah to handle things in New York, Megan could juggle her responsibilities and make that work.

Then she recalled Tess's earlier reaction to the idea of going to New York, and she realized with dismay that her grandfather hadn't intended this to be a temporary adjustment at all. He wanted Megan back here permanently. Jake had pretty much laid that out for her, too, when he'd said if she didn't follow her grandfather's wishes, the ranch would be up for grabs, and that he was first in line to claim it.

A terrible sinking sensation settled in the pit of her stomach as she read on.

Whatever it is you have to do to keep all those balls you're juggling in the air can just as easily be done from here. That's what faxes and computers were made for, leastways that's what you're always telling me. Put technology to good use. Make this one of those challenges you're always talking about. You can make it work, Megan, if you want to badly enough.

Could she? Tex certainly had more faith in her than she had in herself, at least in this one area. Megan glanced back at the page and saw that there was more.

If you choose to go, if other arrangements need to be made for Tess, well, Jake knows what to do. You've made your own way. You don't need anything I could leave you. I have to take care of the child, Meggie. I have to see to what's best for her.

He'd phrased the letter in the form of a request, but it was evident from this final paragraph that it was a whole lot more than that. Megan was to stay on the ranch with Tess indefinitely, become the rancher he'd always wanted her to be—or lose everything. Her choice, or so he wanted it to seem.

"He expects me to stay here?" she demanded, staring at Jake for confirmation of her own interpretation of the letter.

"Yes."

"Or?"

"The ranch will be sold—to me—and the money will be put in trust for Tess."

"He can't mean it," she whispered, even though she knew that he had.

"He did."

"But I can't go on living here. I can't just walk away from my career, everything that means anything to me."

Jake shrugged. "You have a choice. Stay, or go and lose the ranch. Tess can stay on here with me."

"That's no choice. I don't give a damn about the ranch. I never have."

"Then walk away. You certainly don't need his money or his land, right?"

"No," Megan agreed. She didn't need land or money, but she had always craved Tex's approval, and she knew that even from the grave he'd withhold it if she didn't at least try to do as he asked.

Besides, she thought, who else was there? Not Jake, no matter how calmly he had declared his willingness to step in. She wouldn't have him doing what was by rights her duty. She—Lord help them both—

was all Tess had, just as Tex had once been all Megan had had. She would manage just as Tex had. O'Rourkes always did what was expected of them. It had been her grandfather's mantra.

"So, what's it going to be, Meggie? Will you stay or go?"

"You'd just love it if I left, wouldn't you? You'd stay here, do the noble thing, be a hero."

"I'm not sure I'd be declared a hero, but your leaving would ease the way toward me getting this ranch." He shot her a lazy grin. "But I can wait. Having you around again might be even more fascinating."

That night was the longest of Megan's life. She felt as alone and every bit as afraid as she had when her mother had abandoned her on Tex's doorstep years before. The only thing that kept her from sinking into despair was knowing that, as bad as she felt, Tess probably felt worse—more frightened and even more alone.

Not that the child would show it. Tess had avoided her for most of the evening, and when Megan had offered to go upstairs with her and tuck her in, the girl had jeered, "I ain't no baby," and stalked off with shoulders squared proudly.

In the moments that followed, Megan had longed for someone she could confide in, but the only person who came to mind was Jake, and she refused to give him the satisfaction of seeing her vulnerable and uncertain.

By the time it occurred to her that Peggy would

have listened and probably offered sensible, down-to-earth advice, it was too late to call.

"Get a grip," Megan muttered to herself when the illuminated dial on her bedside clock ticked on toward four o'clock.

She reminded herself that she ran an entire media conglomerate, that she had all sorts of resources at her disposal, that she was known worldwide for her creative solutions to all sorts of social dilemmas. Surely she could come up with something that fit the fix she was in.

By five she was up, dressed and in the kitchen searching for the coffee grinder. When she found nothing but a store brand of already ground, ordinary Colombian beans, she sighed heavily, put them into the automatic coffeemaker and waited to see what sort of pitiful brew emerged. She grimaced at the taste, but it was hot and loaded with caffeine, so it would do.

At five-thirty she reached for the phone and called her office. Todd picked up on the first ring.

"How's it going back there?" she asked, suddenly unsure just how much she was ready to tell him about the upcoming upheaval in all their lives. No matter what her final decision, some things would inevitably change.

"We're managing," he assured her. "What about you?"

"Same here."

"When will you be back?"

"Well, that's the thing," she began slowly.

"Megan, is there some sort of a problem?" he asked sympathetically. "I know losing Tex can't be easy, despite the way you two argued all the time. We can cope around here for a couple of weeks if you need more time.''

She drew in a deep breath. "It may be a little longer than that.''

Todd fell silent. "How long?'' he asked eventually.

"I'm not saying it's going to happen. It's certainly not what I want—"

"Spit it out, Megan. What's the worst-case scenario?''

"Worst case? Unless I can find some other way to handle certain things, and believe me I am trying, I could be here permanently.''

"Permanently?'' he echoed, as if the word were unfamiliar. "As in forever?''

"That's the definition I'm most familiar with.''

"What the hell is going on out there?'' Todd demanded. "Have you been taken captive or something?''

"The days of the Wild West are pretty much over,'' Megan assured him, grinning despite herself.

"Then what?''

"It's gotten complicated,'' she said, settling for the same word she'd used with Tess.

Todd was no more satisfied with the response than Tess had been. "Complicated how? The estate and stuff?''

"You could say that.''

"Megan, why don't you just spit it out?'' he repeated with a rare touch of impatience. "I need to know what we're up against here. Are you closing things down? Selling out?''

"Absolutely not!'' It was more certainty than she'd

displayed with Jake, but she realized she'd made her decision about that overnight.

"Then explain."

"Tex's legacy wasn't exactly what I expected."

"More money? Less? The ranch? What?"

"An eight-year-old daughter."

That silenced her unflappable assistant.

"Todd?"

"I'm here. I'm just grappling with this. He left you a daughter?"

"That pretty much sums it up, except for the part where I have to stay here to raise her."

"You've got to be kidding me."

"I wish to hell I were."

"You with a kid," he said with evident amazement. "It boggles the mind."

"Doesn't it just?" she agreed. "But that's where I am. I'm still trying to figure out how to make all this work, so don't go blabbing the news around and set off a panic, okay? My goal is to get back to New York, but that could take time and some legal tap dancing, okay?"

"My lips are sealed," he assured her. "Uh, Megan, just what are some of the options you're considering? Commuting, maybe?"

"It's on the list," she agreed, though even she had to concede that as a practical matter it was seriously lacking. She wasn't sure Todd was ready to hear another option she'd been toying with all night long. Envisioning Todd and the others—savvy, sophisticated New Yorkers one and all—trying to adapt to life in Wyoming had given her one of the only good laughs she'd had overnight. Last resort, she'd finally conceded. That was definitely her last resort.

"Commuting could work," Todd said, as if eager to convince her. "There are faxes and e-mail. And just imagine all those frequent-flyer miles. Plus you'd be halfway to the West Coast, so trips to L.A. would be a breeze, too. Just say the word and I'll start writing up a plan."

"Not just yet. I still have some thinking to do. In the meantime, I'll pick up a fax machine and a computer for Tex's office here. I'll call as soon as I can get everything set up. Now tell me what's happening there. Everything on schedule?"

"Running like clockwork," he assured her. "I shifted the taping schedule on the show till next week. If you can't make that, we'll adjust, despite Micah's dire predictions that it'll be a disaster. There are enough shows pretaped to hold us for a while. The lead story for the magazine's been laid out. I can fax you the pages as soon as you say the word."

"Terrific. I don't know what I'd do without you. I'll talk to you later. Tell Micah I'll check in with her before the end of the day, too."

"Right." He hesitated. "By the way, Megan, don't think I haven't noticed that it's practically the middle of the night there. Now that I know your brain does actually function in the morning," he taunted, "I might start scheduling those a.m. meetings for eight."

"Don't even think about it," she warned, but she was chuckling as she hung up.

"Everything okay at your office, *niña?*" Mrs. Gomez asked from behind her.

Megan turned. "I didn't hear you come in. I hope

I didn't wake you with all my commotion in here. I really appreciate you staying over till things settle down.''

"This is not a problem. I can stay as long as you like. My sister will take care of things at my house. As for waking me, we're early risers here. You know that. Tess will be down any minute wanting breakfast.''

"And then what?" Megan asked, at a loss about what sort of routine the child had.

The housekeeper regarded her quizzically. "I don't understand what you are asking.''

"Does she go to school?''

"Well, of course she does, though I thought it best that she not go this week because of Tex. She will return on Monday and things will settle back to normal.''

Megan wanted to scream that things would never be entirely normal again. She wanted to ask what could possibly be normal about Tex's empty office or his empty place at the table. She wanted to ask what was normal about becoming an overnight mother to a child she hadn't even known existed a few days ago.

"You will see, *niña*," Mrs. Gomez consoled, as if she had read Megan's mind.

Before Megan could argue, Tess wandered into the kitchen, gave Megan a distrustful look and sat down at the far end of the big oak table.

"I thought you'd be gone by now," she said.

"Did you really?"

"I know what a busy life you have in New York,"

she mocked. "You told me so yourself. Go, if you want. We don't need you here."

"Tess," Mrs. Gomez scolded, placing a hand on the girl's shoulder. "Be polite."

Tess retreated into scowling silence. Megan didn't have the strength or the ingenuity just then to try to coax her out of it. Besides, Tess's distrust was justified. Megan hadn't done much to prove she intended to stick it out in Wyoming. How could she when she didn't know herself what decision she would finally reach? Maybe her actions today would help give them both some breathing room, though.

"If you'll excuse me," Megan said, pushing her chair back, "I have to go into town for a few things today. I'm going into Tex's office to make a list."

"A trip into town will do you good," Mrs. Gomez agreed a little too enthusiastically. Then she added slyly, "Why not take Tess along?"

"No way," Tess blurted, just as Megan was about to protest as well.

Mrs. Gomez went on as if their reactions had been more positive. "Tess can show you where things are. There are new stores since the last time you were here."

"I suppose that makes sense," Megan conceded grudgingly. "Tess, would you like to come along?"

"Not really," the girl grumbled, but at a sharp glance from the housekeeper, she shrugged. "Might as well. I ain't got nothing else to do."

"Working on your grammar might be one alternative," Megan muttered, but she forced a smile. "Terrific. We'll leave in an hour."

But in an hour, there was no sign of Tess. If it had

been up to Megan, she would have left without her, but Mrs. Gomez seemed to be determined to send the two of them off on some sort of bonding experience.

"She will be in the barn," she told Megan. "There are kittens there. They seem to give her some comfort."

Thinking of Tess turning to a litter of helpless kittens for consolation shamed Megan sufficiently that she walked to the barn in search of the girl. Sure enough, she was hunkered down with kittens scrambling all around her.

"They're cute," Megan said, drawn to them despite herself.

"I'm not giving them away," Tess stated defiantly.

"Did I ask you to?"

"No, but you will."

Megan imagined that was what Tex had insisted on. He'd always allowed a single cat to wander the barn in search of mice, but no more, and never one in the house as a pet. She had longed for one of her own, a warm ball of fluff who would curl up in her lap and sleep on her bed, but she had dared to ask only once. Tex's curt refusal had kept her silent about wanting a pet from then on.

"You could bring them up to the house, if you like," Megan suggested casually. "When they're a little bigger and the mother won't mind."

Tess stared at her with wide eyes. "I could?"

The longing in her voice brought a lump to Megan's throat. She nodded. "I don't see why not."

"Jake thought it might be okay, too, but I figured you'd never go for it."

"I will on one condition," Megan said.

Tess frowned. "I knew it! I knew there'd be a catch."

"No catch, just a condition. I want one of the kittens for my own."

Tess simply stared, clearly too shocked for words.

"Is it a deal?" Megan asked.

"Yeah!" Tess said excitedly, then caught herself. "I mean, I suppose that would be okay."

Megan held back a grin. It wasn't much, she concluded as they walked to the car, but it was a start. If only the next ten years or so would go as easily, maybe they would survive them.

6

Jake was at loose ends. With his biggest—okay, his only—client dead and buried, his workload was back to zip. That was exactly the way he wanted it, or so he'd thought. Rather than relaxing, maybe going off on a long horseback ride through the countryside, however, he was restless. He knew exactly where to lay the blame for that: Megan.

He'd pushed aside a lot of old resentments the past few days. He wanted to go on hating her for thinking the worst of him all those years ago. He wanted to steal Tex's ranch right out from under her just to get even. But for some reason, he couldn't work up much enthusiasm for the all-out war he'd once envisioned. It was probably because of that sad, lost look in her eyes. He'd always been a real sucker for vulnerability, especially in a woman normally as tough as Meggie.

The smart thing would be to steer clear of her. Even if she made a halfhearted attempt to comply with Tex's wishes, it wouldn't be long before she found some way around the terms of the will and hauled Tess back to New York with her. There wasn't a doubt in his mind that was what she desperately wanted to do. He'd seen the wheels clicking away the instant she'd realized what Tex's will meant.

Somehow Megan had turned into a city girl. Maybe she'd always been one, though how that had happened living in the middle of nowhere with Tex was beyond him.

As for Jake, his foray into the urban thing had been pure rebellion. He'd had something to prove to himself and to Tex and to all the judgmental people of Whispering Wind.

He'd been damned good at it for a time, but in the end he'd accepted the fact that he was happier right here in Whispering Wind. The pace was slow, the demands and expectations were few. And he had enough money now to enjoy the spectacular scenery at his leisure without anyone being able to label him that "no-account Landers kid."

He glanced around his office, took stock of the fancy artwork on the walls, the bronze of a bucking bronco on his credenza, the thick carpeting and well-cushioned leather sofa and chairs, the wall of bookcases filled with leather-bound legal volumes, the state-of-the-art computer setup.

Unlike his home, which could best be described as a fixer-upper, he'd taken pleasure in designing his office to impress. Of course, he hadn't bothered to hire a secretary or to solicit new clients. As restless as he felt this morning, he regretted that. Maybe if he'd had a few cases to sink his teeth into, Meggie's image wouldn't be popping into his head with such annoying regularity.

He heard a commotion on the street, then a howl of protest. He was on his feet and dashing for the door before it registered that that howl was distressingly familiar.

He found Tess outside, her expression indignant, the fist of the red-faced sheriff, Bryce Davis, clamped tightly over her shoulder. Lyle Perkins was standing in the doorway of his mama's general store with a smug expression on his face.

Jake had been exactly where Tess was a few times himself, though Lyle had been a boy back then, but no less of a bully. Apparently he hadn't outgrown the tendency. Jake's hackles rose as he strode toward the group. He couldn't wait to tangle with Lyle and Emma Perkins now that he was on equal footing with them in the community.

The instant Tess caught sight of Jake, she broke free and ran straight for him, then turned and shot a defiant look at the sheriff that would have withered a less confident man. She didn't look at Lyle at all. Fortunately, Jake supposed, Bryce Davis wasn't lacking in ego. Jake had tangled with the sheriff a time or two himself. It would take more than a fiery eight-year-old to intimidate Davis.

"Okay, what's the problem here?" Jake asked, directing the question at the beefy sheriff, while ignoring Lyle.

"I need a lawyer," Tess announced before Bryce could open his mouth. She slapped a quarter in Jake's hand. "Here's your retainer. It ain't much, but it's all I've got. I want to sue him for false arrest, police brutality and whatever else you can come up with." She jerked a thumb toward Lyle. "Sue him while you're at it."

Jake hid a grin at her riled-up declaration. "You've been watching too much TV, kiddo. I don't think you're under arrest yet."

Tess trembled with indignation. "Oh, yeah, try telling that to him. He was about to slap handcuffs on me and take me to the slammer."

Jake figured there was another side to the story that he'd better hear before he leaped too trustingly to Tess's defense. "Bryce?"

The sheriff didn't mince words. "Aunt Emma caught her shoplifting. Lyle called me to get over here. He tried to hold her till I arrived, but she made a break for it. I nabbed her out here."

Jake turned to Tess. "Is that so?"

Tess's gaze met his and never flinched. "I didn't take anything from the old bat's store. All she's got is a bunch of junk, anyway." Once again she cast a disparaging look toward Lyle. "*He* probably put her up to it. He's mean as a snake and everybody in town knows it."

"Why, you little punk," Lyle began, taking a step in Tess's direction. He backed off at a sharp look from his cousin.

Since Jake had had his own run-ins with the paranoid shopkeeper and her spoiled son, he would have been inclined to believe Tess, even if she hadn't just hired him to be on her side. Lyle had always been eager to make trouble for anyone weaker than he was. In those days, Jake's only weakness had been his lack of anyone to stand by him. He'd settled more than one argument with Lyle with his fists. Fortunately, he had grown out of the habit.

"What'd she steal?" Jake asked the sheriff.

Bryce rocked back on his heels and looked vaguely uneasy. "That part's a little hazy, what with the commotion of catching up to Tess before she got away."

"Then I suggest we all go inside and get our facts straight," Jake said, starting for the general store, where Mrs. Perkins waited in the doorway just behind her son, hands on ample hips.

"I might have known you'd take the girl's side," she said, scowling at Jake with a sour expression before turning an equally sour look on Bryce Davis. "I expected more of you, Sheriff, especially since you're family."

"Nobody's taking sides, Aunt Emma," Bryce said soothingly. "We just need to figure out what happened here. What did you see?"

"She was right over there," Mrs. Perkins said, gesturing toward a case filled with school supplies. "I looked up and saw her hand go in her pocket. When it came out again, it was empty. She stole some of them pens, or maybe the stickers the kids like so much."

"Did you see her with either pens or stickers in her hand?" Jake asked.

Bryce scowled at him. "I'll ask the questions, son."

Jake shrugged. "Be my guest, but I reserve the right to ask a few of my own if you don't get at the truth in a hurry."

"Well, Aunt Emma, did you see the girl with those items, or anything else, for that matter?"

"No, but I know what kind of mischief her kind gets into."

The hairs on the back of Jake's neck stood up at the characterization, but he forced himself to deal with one thing at a time. Most important was clearing up whether or not Tess had shoplifted so much as a paper clip from the old bat.

"Tess, honey, did you ever pick up any of the things Mrs. Perkins mentioned?"

"Do I look like I play with stickers?" she shot back, giving the storekeeper a belligerent glare. "As for pens, Tex practically bought them by the case because he was always chomping off the end, once the doc told him he had to stop smoking cigars. I sure as heck don't need hers."

Jake hid a grin. "That's not the issue," he admonished. "Did you put anything into your pockets?"

"No. If you want to, you can check." She shot a triumphant look at the shopkeeper, but when the sheriff stepped forward, she scowled. "Not you. Jake."

"That okay with you, Bryce?"

"I suppose," he said with obvious reluctance.

Jake emptied Tess's pockets, turning them inside out for the sheriff's benefit. He came up with a candy bar wrapper, a couple of pennies, some lint and a wilting daisy, which he suspected came from Tex's funeral bouquet.

"Satisfied?" Tess demanded, eyeing them all belligerently.

"My apologies," Bryce said, then looked toward Jake. "I had no choice. You know that, don't you?"

"Can I sue him now?" Tess asked. "Her, too?"

"We'll talk about it," Jake said. When Tess appeared ready to balk, he added, "Over ice cream."

She followed him docilely enough after that. When they were back on the sidewalk outside, he paused. "How'd you get into town, anyway? And why would you go into that store when you know how Mrs. Perkins is? She thinks every kid in town is out to rob her blind.''

''I came in with Megan. As for the other…'' Tess shrugged. ''I guess I just like to see her get herself all worked up watching me every second. That Lyle, though, he gives me the creeps.''

''Then I suggest you steer clear of the place. Now, where's Megan?''

''Beats me. I pointed her in the direction of the new office-supply place, then took off. She didn't seem real disappointed to see me go.''

''Did you arrange to meet her someplace?''

Tess shrugged. ''I figured we'd both turn up at the car sooner or later.''

Jake sighed. Clearly Tess intended to make him work for his answers. She was volunteering nothing. ''Where'd she park?'' he asked next.

''A couple of blocks that way,'' Tess conceded, jerking a thumb over her shoulder.

''Let's go see if she's there.''

''I thought we were going for ice cream.''

''We will, after we find Megan and let her know you're okay.''

''Like she'd care,'' Tess muttered.

Obviously things weren't going smoothly with the bonding. ''Don't you think maybe you should give her a break?'' he asked.

''Why? She doesn't give a rat's behind about me.''

''Maybe because she hasn't had a chance to get to know you, any more than you've taken the time to get to know her.''

''What's the use? She'll leave.''

To his very deep regret, Jake's heart thudded at that. "Has she said that?"

"No, but she will. Everybody does."

Jake gave up trying to argue the point. All the evidence in her young life was on her side. It would take time to prove that Meggie was different, that she had staying power. For Tess's sake, he prayed to God he was right about that. She was already jaded enough without another disappointment.

"Any idea what she was getting at the office-supply place?" he asked.

Tess shot him a disgusted look. "Duh! Office supplies would be my guess."

"You know, kid, one of these days somebody's going to take exception to that smart mouth of yours."

"Oh, yeah? Who?"

"Lyle Perkins for one. You did your darnedest to rile him back there."

She grinned. "I know," she said proudly. "Who else?"

"Me."

"And then what?" she asked, clearly unintimidated. "You gonna lock me in my room?"

"No. I'll wash your mouth out with soap, the way my mama used to do with me."

Tess's eyes widened. "She did that? Oh, gross."

"Gross pretty much sums it up, but it was effective. I cleaned up my language. Think about it."

Jake fell silent, as did Tess, though whether she was actually pondering his warning was anybody's guess. She trailed along a step or two behind him, scuffing the toes of her sneakers on the sidewalk.

He spotted Megan up ahead, looking predictably more impatient than worried.

"There you are," she said, when she noticed Tess behind him. "Where on earth have you been? I've been waiting here for a half hour at least."

Tess shot an imploring look his way. Jake relented and left the encounter with the sheriff and Mrs. Perkins unmentioned. "Visiting with me," he said. "We were going for ice cream and came to ask you to join us."

"I was hoping to get back to the ranch so I could get all this equipment set up. I have work to do."

Jake peered into the back of the sport utility vehicle. There were a half-dozen cartons, along with bags that appeared filled with reams of paper and other supplies. He took heart from the sheer amount and extravagance of the purchases.

"Was this stuff cheaper here than it would be in New York?" he inquired lazily.

"Of course, but that wasn't the point."

"What was?"

"I need a few things if I'm going to be able to get anything done while I'm here."

He took a better look at the cartons. "A fax machine, a copier, a computer, a printer, a scanner. Yep, that ought to get you through the afternoon, all right."

"I'm delighted you approve. Now, if you don't mind, we'll be on our way."

"I mind," Tess protested. "Jake promised me ice cream, after what happened."

Only when the words were out of her mouth did she realize her mistake. She slapped a hand over her mouth and backed away a step.

"After *what* happened?" Megan asked. When Tess remained stubbornly silent, she turned to Jake. "Well?"

"Sorry. Attorney-client privilege."

"She hired you to represent her? Why, for heaven's sake?"

"Now, Meggie, you know I can't answer that."

"Somebody had better answer me," Megan declared, foot tapping and arms folded across her chest.

Amused by the display of temper, Jake glanced toward Tess. "I don't think she's crazy about being left out of the loop. How about we all go for ice cream and explain once she's mellowed out on hot fudge?"

"You're going to tell her no matter what, aren't you?" Tess demanded. "Geez-oh-flip, nobody around here's any good at all at keeping secrets. What about professional ethics?"

"I can only tell her if you say it's okay," Jake agreed. "It's up to you."

"But that's the only way I'm getting ice cream, right?"

He nodded.

"Okay, fine. Blab your heart out." She turned and marched off.

Jake turned to follow. Megan regarded him impatiently, but eventually fell into step beside him.

"I'm not going to like this, am I?" she asked with weary resignation.

"On a scale of one to ten, compared to some of the other things you've heard in the past few days, this can't be more than a two."

"I'm so relieved."

"Don't worry, Meggie, I've handled it. There's nothing for you to worry about."

"Why does that make me even more nervous?"

"Because you have control issues?" he suggested.

"Oh, go to hell," she retorted, and snapped her mouth shut. She didn't say another word to him until after the awestruck waitress had begged for an autograph, chattered endlessly about Megan's TV show and then—finally—taken their orders. Sundaes with double hot fudge prevailed.

"Well?" Megan asked, turning her attention back to them. "You might as well get it over with. What happened earlier?"

After a glance at Tess, Jake gave her a quick overview of the encounter with Mrs. Perkins, Lyle and the sheriff.

"Why, that pompous old witch," Megan declared, with every bit as much indignation as Tess had displayed earlier. "I'll have a thing or two to say to her when we're finished here. As for Lyle, I never liked him and it seems as if time hasn't improved his judgment or his temper."

Tess regarded her with wide-eyed amazement. "You're going to take on Mrs. Perkins?"

"Well, of course I will," Megan said emphatically. "Nobody messes with an O'Rourke."

Jake settled back onto the bench beside her. "Go, girl," he murmured, delighted by her reaction, by the quick rush to Tess's defense.

There'd been a time when she'd been equally protective of him, when she'd stood defiantly beside him in the face of all sorts of accusations, a good many of them trumped up by the envious Lyle.

But when the most serious charge of all had been made, when he'd been accused of rustling Tex's cattle, she'd failed him. He'd guessed that years of silent doubts had added up at last. Even with him understanding that, the pain of her turning on him had been worse than sitting in a jail cell in which he didn't belong.

She turned and met his gaze. "So, how did you happen to be so handy just when Tess needed an attorney?"

"My office is next door to the general store."

Megan grinned. "Was that an in-your-face decision aimed at Mrs. Perkins?"

He shrugged. "Could have been," he conceded, though no one beside Meggie had guessed it.

"Wasn't that the old barbershop?"

Jake nodded. "When Pete died, the space sat empty for a year. When I got back to town, it seemed to make sense to set up my practice right on Main Street."

"Were you able to get the smell of that awful shaving cologne out of the place?" she asked, nose wrinkling in disgust. "You used to be able to smell it half a block away."

"I think it's gone. Want to check it out?" The invitation was casual enough, but his tone turned it into a challenge. He could see her struggling with herself—stubborn resistance versus innate curiosity.

"Sure. Why not?" she said eventually.

Her response proved that the old Meggie hadn't gotten entirely lost in all the glitter and glamour of her new life. He took hope at that.

"You coming, Tess?" he asked as he stood.

"Geez, I'm surprised you remembered I was still here. The two of you have been making goo-goo eyes at each other ever since we sat down."

Jake laughed. "What do you know about goo-goo eyes?"

"I used to watch a lot of old movies after Tex went to bed," she said. "You learn things."

"None of them good, from what I've heard coming out of your mouth," he admonished. "Maybe you ought to switch to reruns of *The Brady Bunch*."

"Oh, yuck," Tess said. "Were those people for real?"

"Real, no. But they were trying to make a family work," Jake responded. "It might give you some ideas." He glanced at Megan. "You, too."

Megan frowned at him. "If I conclude we need family counseling, I don't think you or the Bradys are the people I'll turn to."

"It was just a thought." He headed for the register to pay their bill, then went outside to join Tess and Megan on the sidewalk. "This way, ladies."

"Not just yet," Megan said, her gaze focused on the general store. "I think I'll drop in and pay a visit to Mrs. Perkins."

"You're really going to tell her off?" Tess asked, clearly still skeptical.

"Let's just say she won't be messing with you again anytime soon," Megan declared. Shoulders squared as if she were going off to battle, she marched straight into the store.

"Well, come on," Tess said, grabbing Jake's hand and tugging. "I've got to see this."

They entered the store with its crowded shelves and

wide-plank wooden floor just in time to hear Mrs. Perkins greet Megan with enthusiasm.

"It's been too many years, young lady. We thought you'd forgotten all about us," the woman said. "I'm real sorry it had to be under these circumstances that you finally came back. Your granddaddy was a good man. I always thought he'd have been better off if he'd had a woman out there at that ranch to look after him and a son to take over for him in his later years, but after your grandmama died he didn't seem inclined to marry again."

Obviously she'd had herself and Lyle in mind for the positions, Jake concluded. Tex had been wise enough to avoid all the snares she'd laid for him.

Mrs. Perkins glanced over and caught sight of Jake and Tess. Her lips turned down. "Of course, I suppose he was otherwise occupied, if you know what I mean."

Megan smiled innocently. "No, I'm afraid I don't. What do you mean?"

"You know," she said, jerking a shoulder toward Tess. "Her mother. Everyone in town knows all about *that*."

"Which would explain why you chose to accuse Tess of shoplifting, I suppose," Megan said. "Because you disapprove of my grandfather's relationship with her mother. Or were you jealous, Mrs. Perkins?"

The older woman looked shocked. "Why, Megan, how can you ask such a thing?"

"Well, after your husband died, you did bring an awful lot of meals out to the house, even though you knew we had Mrs. Gomez there to cook for us," Megan pointed out. "*Everyone* knew what *that* meant."

Mrs. Perkins cheeks were stained with pink. "Young lady, do you have any idea who you're talking to?"

"Yes, ma'am, I believe I do," Megan said politely. "And in the future, I hope you'll remember with whom you're messing when you make unfounded accusations against a member of *my* family." She smiled, locking eyes with Lyle, too, as he wandered over to join them. "I'm sure you'll both want to apologize to Tess for the mistake you made this morning. Tess, come on over here. Mrs. Perkins has something she'd like to say." She fixed her gaze on the woman. "Don't you, Mrs. Perkins?"

"Why, yes, I suppose I do," she said, clearly flustered. "I was mistaken this morning, and for that I am truly sorry. Lyle's sorry, too, aren't you, son?"

Lyle scowled, but at a sharp look from his mother, he nodded. "Whatever."

"Gee, thanks," Tess said, clearly unmoved.

"It was lovely to see you again, Mrs. Perkins," Megan said without much sincerity. "You, too, Lyle. Tess, shall we go?"

As the two of them walked toward Jake, he heard Mrs. Perkins mutter, "Well, I never..."

"Mama, she's just turned into a rich bitch. Forget about her," Lyle said. "She always was a stuck-up thing. Folks around here will bring her down a peg or two. You'll see."

Jake chuckled at the exchange. "I don't think she'll be selling *Megan's World* on her magazine rack anytime soon," he observed as they left the store.

"I'm sure our circulation director will bear up under the loss," Megan said, then grinned. "That felt good."

"You were awesome," Tess declared. "She looked like she'd been hit by a truck."

"Don't go getting any ideas," Megan said sternly. "You don't get to run around putting people in their place. That's my job."

"Hey, whatever floats your boat," Tess agreed. "I ain't interested in picking fights with people who are twice my size. She started this one."

"And now it's finished," Jake reminded her sternly. He eyed Megan as well. "Right?"

She beamed. "Whatever you say, Counselor."

Suddenly, he couldn't help wondering if Whispering Wind was prepared for a native daughter to come blasting through and upset more than a hundred years of status quo. For that matter, was he ready to have the nice, dull life he'd carved out for himself turned inside out?

Glancing at Megan, who was looking mighty pleased with herself, he concluded it was too late now to turn back.

7

Megan had enjoyed putting Mrs. Perkins in her place just a little too much. Only part of that scene had been for Tess's benefit, and she doubted there was anyone in the room who hadn't known that. Megan had said what she'd longed to declare years ago on Jake's behalf. Then she'd been too cautious, too young to be rude to an adult, no matter how deserving they were of a sincere put-down.

Back then she'd also been intimidated by Lyle. He'd been tall for his age and heavyset. Because his mama thought the sun rose and set with him, he'd believed he could get away with anything, and he usually had. He'd been the worst sort of bully, picking out his targets with impunity. Megan hadn't wanted to be one of them and not only because she hadn't wanted Jake to be drawn into a fight with him in her defense. She hadn't liked the glint in Lyle's eyes when he watched her. She'd found it unnerving, without fully understanding why until she was older. By then, she had known enough to avoid him.

Mrs. Perkins and Lyle hadn't been the only people in town who'd looked down on Jake and made his life hell. A lot of fine, churchgoing people had made judgments and found him lacking just because of what his mother had done for a living. None had stopped to think that Lettie Landers might have reformed if anyone in town had ever given her a break, hired her to do some other kind of a job to put food on their table after Jake's daddy walked out on them.

Megan had always thought it remarkable that Jake had turned out as well as he had, living in that tumbledown shack that was all his mama could afford after spending most of her money on booze. Megan distinctly remembered how Jake had spent his first paycheck from Tex all those years ago. He'd bought wood and nails and gallons of paint and made all the repairs the house had needed, repairs that should have been made by Josh Wilson, their sleazy landlord.

But the change had been only cosmetic. Inside the house, his mother had still been in an alcoholic stupor. Seeing Jake's disappointment at that, Megan knew he'd been hoping his work would set his mother on a fresh path.

Now, standing on the sidewalk in front of what had once been Pete's barbershop, she was stunned by the difference he'd made to the old frame structure. The barbershop pole remained as a whimsical touch, but the wood glistened with bright white paint. The trim was a businesslike black. The wide window—once dingy from customers smoking—gleamed in the late morning sun, and discreet gold lettering in one corner announced that the building held the offices of Jake Landers, Attorney-at-Law.

"I'm impressed," she told him. "Pete wouldn't recognize the place."

"Wait till you see inside," Tess enthused. "He's got these big, ol' western paintings on the wall, just like they came from a John Wayne movie or something.''

"Lead the way," Megan told them, curious to see what Jake's taste was like.

As Tess had suggested, there was a western theme to the decor, but it had been done tastefully. She recognized immediately that the oils were by the finest western artists and that the bronze on his credenza was an original Remington. Obviously Jake had done very well for himself over the last decade or so.

"Is your secretary out to lunch?" she asked, glancing around the empty outer office.

"I haven't gotten around to hiring one yet. Didn't seem much point since I'm hardly ever here."

"Why not?"

"I haven't been actively pursuing clients. Other than your grandfather's estate, my caseload is zero."

Her gaze narrowed. "Your choice?"

"Yes, darlin'. I'm taking it easy by choice," he assured her. "Don't go getting your dander up on my behalf now. The town's not snubbing me the way it once did. Tex hiring me saw to that."

"Good."

"Would you go out there and whup a few of them, if I asked you to?" he inquired, his expression amused.

"Oh, something tells me you're perfectly capable of fighting your own battles these days."

"Too bad. I was kind of looking forward to seeing you in action again."

His intense gaze settled on her in a way that suggested the kind of action he had in mind wasn't some battle of wits with the local townsfolk. Megan turned away rather than deal with the feelings his look stirred inside her. She reached haphazardly for the first thing she saw, the bronze.

"This is beautiful."

"You admired it once before," Jake said, moving to stand close beside her.

"I did? When?"

"We were on our class trip to Denver. We walked past a gallery. It was in the window. You couldn't take your eyes off it. I told you I'd get it for you one of these days. I doubt you believed me, but I remembered."

"But how?" she murmured. "It had to have been years before you could afford it."

"I bought it six months ago," he confirmed.

"From the same gallery? Surely it wasn't still there after all this time. Museums and collectors snap up Remingtons as soon as they come on the market."

"No. It was in a private collection. I persuaded the owner to part with it."

She forced her gaze to his. "Why?" she asked, as tension shimmered between them.

"I wanted to own it."

"Why, Jake?" she persisted, not entirely sure why she wanted him to say the words.

"Because you liked it," he said finally. "And because the promise I'd made meant something to me."

Megan swallowed hard. The cool bronze seemed to heat beneath her touch. She was pretty sure her skin was turning just as hot. Finally she forced herself to turn away, to place the bronze on the credenza.

"I need to get back to the ranch," she said, her

breath hitching in the most annoying way. She glanced around. "Where's Tess?"

"She went outside a few minutes ago. I suspect she wanted to give us some privacy."

"Do you actually think she's that sensitive? More likely, she was just bored watching us make goo-goo eyes."

He stepped in closer. "Is that what we've been doing, Meggie? Making goo-goo eyes?"

She swallowed hard and shook her head. "Not me."

"Me, either," he claimed.

But his head lowered just the same, and when his mouth met hers, her lips parted on a sigh. No one in the universe could kiss quite like Jake, soft and slow and gentle with a hint of urgency and heat. Megan's breath caught in her throat. Her senses swam. She reached out and grabbed on to the first thing she found—Jake—to steady herself.

It wasn't supposed to be like this, not after all this time. There wasn't supposed to be a curl of heat, a shimmer of desire. But the fire was there, and the yearning, and the amazing, shocking sense of being exactly where she belonged. In the end, that was what terrified her and had her shoving hard against Jake's chest to put some much-needed distance between them.

"No," she said, intending a shout, but managing little more than a whisper.

Jake's grin was lazily insolent. "Some things never change, do they, Meggie?"

"Everything's changed," she insisted, fighting the oddest sensation of panic.

He shrugged. "If you say so."

Feigning composure was second nature to her. She forced a cool little smile. "Thank you for the ice cream and for coming to Tess's defense," she said primly.

His grin returned. "Anytime."

Megan dragged her attention away from his face— from that sneaky, clever mouth—and turned to the door. She'd almost managed a clean getaway when he spoke.

"Have dinner with me, Meggie."

"I don't think so," she said, without even taking a second to think it over. Of course, he put his own interpretation on her response.

"Scared?" he suggested.

"Of course not."

"Look me in the eye and say that."

The man did have an ego, that was certain. She faced him squarely. "You don't scare me, Jake Landers." She managed it without so much as a blink, without any telltale tremor in her voice. Covering her nerves on camera served her well.

"Then why not have dinner with me?" he persisted. "A couple of old friends catching up. What's the big deal?"

It shouldn't have been a big deal, Megan agreed to herself. If it had been Peggy asking, for instance, it would have been just fine. But it was Jake and that meant it was very, very dangerous. He had more than dinner on his mind. He'd made that clear minutes ago.

"I'm sorry. I doubt I'll have the time."

"You're not planning on sticking around, then?"

Too late, she realized the trap he'd set. She could

hardly claim that she'd be jetting off to New York without him reiterating the terms of Tex's will.

"Just because I'm here doesn't mean I won't have work to do. It'll be even more complicated because I am here."

"Tex seemed to think you were pretty good at juggling a million details. What's one more? It's dinner, Megan. Think of it as business."

"Business?" With Jake it couldn't possibly be that simple, that uncomplicated.

"There will be details of Tex's estate we can discuss over dessert," he explained.

"Such as?"

"Oh, I'm sure I can come up with something by tomorrow evening. Say, around six."

"Okay, fine." She relented at last, because it was clear that anything less than acceptance was going to be viewed as cowardice. "Come to the ranch. I'll have Mrs. Gomez fix one of the Mexican feasts you love so much."

"Your turf, then?" he said. "We really do need to talk about those control issues of yours."

Her temper rose, but she managed to keep it from showing. "Make it seven, though. I'll be on the phone with my office until then."

"Your turf, your timetable," he murmured with a shake of his head.

"Oh, for heaven's sake, will you be there or not?"

"I'll be there, Meggie. I wouldn't miss it for the world."

"So, what's the deal between you and Jake?" Tess inquired, as she and Megan headed back to the ranch.

Megan feigned innocence. "There's nothing at all between Jake and me."

"Then how come the two of you were playing kissy-face in his office?"

Horrified, Megan stared at her sternly. "Spying is not an attractive trait, young lady."

"Who was spying?" Tess retorted. "Anybody walking down the street could have seen. It's not like there were shades on the windows, you know."

Megan barely contained a groan. "Please tell me that you were our only audience."

"Me and Tommy Morgan, but he won't blab. He's only six. He didn't even know who you were."

"Where was Tommy Morgan's mother?" Megan asked.

"At the beauty shop down the block. She works there. Tommy thinks it stinks in there, so she lets him play outside. Everybody looks out for him, so he doesn't get hit by a car or something."

"It sounds as if you know Tommy's habits pretty well."

Tess shrugged. "Yeah, well, Tex brought me into town a lot when he was meeting with Jake. I hung out on the street just like today. Tommy kinda got used to me being around."

"You didn't mind?"

"Nah. He's okay, for a kid. It's kinda like having a little brother."

Megan recalled how often she, too, had longed for brothers and sisters. It was tough enough being an only child, but that had been compounded by the isolation of Tex's ranch and his strict rules, pretty much eliminating most after-school activities that might have widened her circle of friends. Peggy had been the one person who hadn't seemed to mind spending her visits to the ranch helping out with Megan's chores.

"You know, Tess, if you were in New York, there would be people around all the time," she suggested casually. "You could have lots of friends."

"I told you, I ain't going to New York," Tess shouted, the tenuous, temporary truce between them shattered. "If you need to go back, go. I ain't stopping you, but I'm staying right here on the ranch."

Megan was at a loss. "Do you love it that much?"

Tess seemed taken aback by the question. "It's where I live, that's all." She regarded Megan defiantly. "Tex said I could stay there, no matter what."

"I know that."

"Good. That's settled then," Tess said with satisfaction.

But from Megan's point of view, nothing was settled at all.

After Megan and Tess had gone, Jake sat in his big leather chair, propped his booted feet on his desk and considered the kiss he and Meggie had shared. It had certainly livened up his day, even more than battling wits with Mrs. Perkins, Lyle and the sheriff.

Why was it that no other woman could turn him on the way Meggie did? She was irritating and prickly and jumpy as a june bug. He wondered what her fans would think if they could see how rattled she'd been by a little ol' kiss. They looked to Megan for cool competence in the face of any social crisis. They probably figured she walked away from a tumble in bed with every hair in place.

She hadn't been cool when his lips had brushed across hers, though. Her skin had heated as if she'd been standing squarely in the noon sun on a blistering hot summer day. Her expression had turned dreamy and flustered at the same time. He'd been fully aware of just how angry that had made her, but she'd still managed to come off sounding haughty and imperial. He'd concluded right then that he was going to spend however long she remained in Whispering Wind doing his darnedest to shake her composure at every opportunity. It was the first hobby he'd considered that he could pursue with enthusiasm.

He was thoroughly enjoying contemplating the future when his phone rang, startling him. "Yes?"

"Is this Jake Landers?" a woman demanded, her voice thick and vaguely slurred.

"Yes. Who's this?"

"Are you the one handling Tex O'Rourke's estate?"

Jake's feet hit the floor and he sat up straight at the question and its tone. "Who wants to know?"

"You haven't said yet if you're the one who's in charge of the estate."

"Yes. I'm handling it. Now tell me who you are or I'm hanging up."

"How much does the kid get?"

Ah, Jake thought with disgust, so this was Tess's mama. No further introduction was necessary. The nature of her questions, the slurred voice told him everything he needed to know about Contessa Florence Olson.

"I'm not at liberty to discuss the terms of the will except with those directly involved."

"I'm that child's mother," she admitted finally, "so I guess that makes it my business. Tex took real good care of her, didn't he?"

"As I said, that's between me and Tex's heirs. Once the will is filed for probate, you can pick up a copy at the courthouse."

"Oh, you can bet the ranch I'll be doing just that," she declared.

Because he had a hunch that he was going to need to know the answer before all was said and done, he asked, "Where are you calling from?"

"I don't see that that's any of your business," she said, clearly mocking him. "That's between me and my girl."

"Stay away from Tess," he said coldly. "You have no rights where she's concerned."

"Who're you to tell me to stay away from her? She's my baby, isn't she?"

"No. That's where you're wrong. You gave up any claim to her the day you left her with Tex. I have the papers you signed saying just that."

"Tex is dead. All bets are off. She needs her mama."

"Tess doesn't need the likes of you," he countered emphatically.

"Who's taking care of her now?"

"Tess is being well taken care of. You have no need to worry on that score."

"I think I'd like to see that for myself, rather than taking your word for it."

"Stay away," Jake said again. "If you go near

Tess, I'll have you slapped with a restraining order so fast it'll make your head spin.''

"She's my baby.'' She said it with a whine that set his teeth on edge.

"You should have thought of that before you ran out on her,'' he said coldly, and hung up.

Jake stood up, grabbed his jacket and headed for the ranch. Megan needed to know about this.

So did Tess, he supposed, though he wasn't looking forward to being the one to tell her. He had no idea how he would handle it if Tess got the idea in her head, as she had a few days ago, to go off with her mama. Legally he could prevent it. She was in Megan's care now, but Megan would have to be the one to fight to keep her. Would she do it? Or would she see this as the perfect out, a chance to get her own life back?

He made it to the ranch in record time, then went in through the kitchen. Barcly pausing to give Mrs. Gomez a quick kiss on the cheek, he asked, "Where's Megan?''

"In Tex's office playing with all those gadgets she bought this morning.'' She regarded him with a knowing look. "There is a problem, isn't there?''

"Just something I need to talk over with Megan.''

As he started to leave, she stopped him with a hand on his arm. "The woman called you, didn't she? That's why you look so troubled?''

He hesitated, searching her face. "Tess's mom?''

The housekeeper nodded, her concern evident.

"You know, then, that she's asking questions? How?''

"*Sí.* She called here earlier. I refused to let her talk

to the girl. I gave her your number. It's no surprise she's calling out of the blue. She's heard of Tex's death and thinks there will be money, yes?''

"That would be my guess," Jake agreed.

"She has no claim to the child, does she?"

"That depends."

"On?"

"Whether Megan will fight her."

"She will."

"You sound so certain," Jake said, wishing he were half as sure.

"I am. She is Tex's granddaughter, isn't she? O'Rourkes stick together."

Jake squeezed her hand. "For Tess's sake, I pray to God you're right."

8

It had taken Megan most of the afternoon to get all of her new equipment up and running. The minute she had everything set to go, the fax began humming with paperwork from her office. She'd been deluged ever since.

For the past hour she'd been on the phone with Todd, dictating memos, rearranging her schedule and getting a strong lecture on staying in better contact with her staff.

"I'm telling you, Micah's bouncing off walls. You promised you'd call her this morning. She thinks you're deliberately keeping her out of the loop," Todd said. "Then there's Caitlyn. She's champing at the bit to get that wedding cake art finalized, and you're not in your office, so she can't bust in and get your okay."

"I'll call them," Megan promised.

"Now," Todd stressed. "Micah first, so she doesn't latch on to the idea that she's even less important than your magazine art director."

"Okay, fine. Transfer my call to her."

"Thank you," Todd said fervently.

"Anytime. I know I've left you with enough on

your plate without having the staff coming down on your head, too.''

The conversation with her producer was every bit as tense as Todd had predicted. After a few minutes, Megan decided to deal with her bluntly.

"Micah, do we have a problem here?"

"Haven't I just been reeling off a hundred of them?" she snapped in response.

"I'm not talking about the show. I'm talking about you and me."

Silence greeted that. Megan sighed. "Apparently we do. Look, I know this isn't easy. I'm not overjoyed about throwing the schedule into chaos, but these are extraordinary circumstances. My grandfather just died. I've been hit with a whole lot of things I didn't expect." It was a massive understatement, but she was unwilling to discuss Tess right now. "I know I'm putting a lot of the burden on you, but I'm doing the best I can."

Micah drew in a deep breath. "I'm sorry," she said with what sounded like genuine regret. "I got so caught up in my own stress, I didn't even stop to think about what you must be going through. It won't happen again."

"Hey, we all get stressed out from time to time. Just try to keep things in perspective, okay?"

"Deal."

"I'll talk to you soon, then. If problems crop up, call me or fax me here."

"Any idea when you'll be back?"

"Not yet. I'll keep you posted, or Todd will."

"I'd rather hear it from you," Micah said irritably. Megan sensed that she'd accidentally hit on the real crux of the problem. "Is that what this is really about? Don't you and Todd get along?"

"It's just that I'm the producer of your show. He's a secretary, for God's sake. Why should I hear what's going on from him instead of you?"

So that was it. Her ego was bruised. "Micah, I tell Todd what's going on because it's one call and he can handle things from there. He's not a secretary. He's my executive assistant. For all intents and purposes, he's as close to a second in command as I have. I'll try to be more sensitive to your feelings, but I can't swear it won't happen again. Todd and I have had a strong working relationship for several years now. You and I are just finding our way."

"And I'm telling you that I need to know you trust me, that you see my role as important."

"Well, of course it is," Megan said impatiently. "And I do trust you. If I haven't demonstrated that, I'm sorry. I'll work on it. I've got to go. I have other calls to make."

Megan hung up before she gave in to the temptation to tell the woman to grow up and concentrate on doing her job. Micah was the best producer around. She intuitively sensed which ideas would translate into strong segments for the show. Right now, though, Megan didn't have a whole lot of patience for the ego stroking she apparently required.

In her next call, she soothed the ruffled feathers of the art director, whose layout for the lead story wasn't nearly as effective as it could have been. Megan doubted the news would go over well. She took a deep breath and told her anyway.

"The picture of that wedding cake has to be bigger," she explained to Caitlyn Holmes. "Readers have to be able to see every detail of the decorations. It's a masterpiece. I want them to know that, so when they follow the directions and duplicate it at home, they'll know what they've accomplished. I want every prospective bride in the country to want just that cake at her reception."

"Then they'd better go to a professional, because if they try it at home, it'll be a disaster," Caitlyn retorted. "How many people do you know who can actually find edible gold in their neighborhood grocery store, much less manage to get it on a cake so it looks like anything other than little gold nuggets?"

"That's what the directions are for," Megan explained patiently. "Anybody can follow directions."

"Have you made that cake?"

"No, but—"

"Dare you to try," Caitlyn said. "Call me back when it's done and I will personally fly out to Wyoming—at my own expense, no less—and arrange a photo shoot of the one you've baked and decorated. In fact, I'll talk to Micah and you can do it live for the TV show."

On another occasion, Megan might have been inclined to accept the challenge, but a prickling at the back of her neck told her that Jake was in the vicinity. She turned toward the door and found him watching her, a storm brewing in his eyes.

"I've got to go," she told the art director. "Fax me the new pages when you have them."

"But—"

"Just do it, Caitlyn. We can debate the clarity of

the recipe directions some other time.'' She hung up slowly and faced Jake.

''You're early by about twenty-six hours,'' she said.

''We've got trouble.''

Megan was struck by his somber tone. It matched the grim expression. ''Come in, then.''

He came into the room and shut the door behind him.

She gestured toward a chair. ''Have a seat.''

He ignored the suggestion and began to pace.

His mood was beginning to make her nervous. ''Jake?'' she prompted.

''I had a call earlier from Tess's mother.''

The tone was casual and not especially revealing. Still, it was evident that he was deeply troubled by the call.

''Why did she call you?''

''Mrs. Gomez told her to.''

Megan was surprised by that. The housekeeper had said nothing to her. ''Was she checking on Tess?''

''In a manner of speaking,'' he said, his expression wry. ''She wanted to know how much Tess had inherited.''

''I see,'' she said, realizing she should have expected it. ''What did you tell her?''

''That it was none of her business.''

''Good.''

He shot her a worried look. ''She's going to come here and stir things up, Meggie.''

''We can handle her.'' Her gaze narrowed. ''Can't we? She doesn't have a claim on anything, does she?''

"Only on Tess, not the money."

She realized then what was really worrying him. "You're afraid I'll let her have Tess, aren't you?" If she hadn't understood only too well that she'd given him reason for concern, she might have been insulted.

He regarded her intently. "Will you?"

"No," she said at once, not sure which of them was more surprised by the vehemence of her response.

"It would be a way out for you," he said. "Tess would be back with her mother and you could return to New York with a clear conscience."

She was hurt that he would think so little of her. Then again, maybe it was no less than she deserved after doing much the same thing to him. "You don't know me very well, do you?"

"I thought I did," he said. "Once upon a time."

"I don't take the easy way out, Jake. I never did."

"You're wrong. You did back then," he accused. "You heard the story going around, you took it at face value and you ran."

She sighed. She had known it would come up sooner or later. Better to get it over with. "I'm sorry. I made a mistake. Tex seemed so certain that you were behind the rustling. I thought you had betrayed him and me."

"You left without even talking to me, without even asking my side of it. That was what hurt the most."

"Tex said—"

Jake leaned across the desk, eyes blazing. "Didn't it ever occur to you that Tex might lie to keep us apart?"

"Not at the time, no," she retorted heatedly. "Tex

had never lied to me, not once. That was one of the first things he promised me when I came here—that he would never lie.''

"He never told you I'd been cleared of the charges, either, did he?''

"No,'' she admitted.

"A lie of omission. That's two big ones that we know of, then. I can only imagine how many more there were.''

She could see how deeply Jake had been hurt, could imagine him waiting for her to come to his defense, only to learn that she had left town without even saying goodbye. "I'm sorry. I know it doesn't mean much now, but I truly am sorry. I should have had more faith in you.''

"Not just in me, Meggie. In us. I could never have betrayed you.'' He backed away, shoved his hands in his pockets and shrugged. "But like you said, it was a long time ago.''

"But you haven't forgotten, Jake.''

"No, obviously I haven't. But that's hardly the issue now,'' he said, straightening up, his expression coolly businesslike again. "This is about Tess.''

"I'm not running out on her, Jake. I'd like to go back to New York. I'd like my life to be exactly the way it was before Tex died, but that's not possible. I may not have all the answers yet, but I do know one thing. Tex wanted Tess with me and somehow, some way, I intend to make that work.''

He gave her a curt nod of satisfaction. "Good. Then I think we should go to court now and ask for a restraining order. That could prevent a whole lot of heartache down the road.''

"Will Tess's mother pay any attention to a restraining order?"

"She'll have to, or land in jail. That's not what she wants."

"What about Tess? How will she feel when she finds out?" Megan thought back nearly two decades. "I would have been furious if Tex had kept me from seeing my mother." Given everything that she'd just discovered about Tex's role in separating her from Jake, she had to wonder if maybe he hadn't kept her and Sarah O'Rourke apart. It was something Megan would probably never know.

"Tess is an eight-year-old kid," Jake retorted. "It's not up to her."

Megan smiled. "Try telling that to her. She's eight going on twenty. Besides, she has to be prepared. She has to know that her mother could turn up here, and what the stakes are."

"Are you going to be the one to tell her that her mother might want her back, now that she stands to inherit some money?"

The prospect held little appeal. "Hey, you talked to the woman, not me," she said.

"We'll tell her together," Jake decided, his expression grim.

As it turned out, Tess took the news in stoic silence. When they finished explaining about the phone call and its implications, she nodded.

"I'll be in my room," she said dully, then turned to go.

"Tess?" Megan called after her, but the girl refused to turn around.

"I think you'd better go talk to her," Jake said.

Megan had never felt so helpless in her life. "What do I say?"

"I don't think the words are important. Being there is what counts."

Megan climbed the stairs with reluctance. Outside Tess's room, she hesitated, drew in a deep breath, then knocked. "Tess, may I come in?"

"Suit yourself. I'm just a kid. You'll do what you want, anyway."

Megan couldn't help smiling at the snippy retort. Tess might be down, but she definitely wasn't out. Megan opened the door and walked into the room, surprised to find it neat as a pin. There were none of the kind of posters she'd had as a girl, no hodgepodge of toys scattered on the floor. It looked as if the occupant had just arrived, a guest in a new home.

A child prepared to be uprooted at any moment. Megan scanned the room for some sign of a packed bag.

"Did you just come in to stare or what?" Tess asked.

"Actually, I came to see if you were okay."

"Why wouldn't I be?" Tess held her, chin defiantly high.

A few days ago the bluff might have worked. Megan would have wanted it to be easy. She could see past Tess's tough facade now, too. More and more of her own past—carefully shut away for years—was coming back to remind her of what Tess must be feeling.

"All that stuff that Jake and I laid on you just now was pretty heavy," she said casually. "It would be understandable if your feelings were hurt, or you were worried, or even scared.''

Tess's eyes blazed. "I ain't scared of nothing.''

"I'm not scared of anything,'' Megan corrected.

"Who asked you?''

Megan ducked her head as a smile came and went. "Never mind. How do you feel about seeing your mom?''

There was the faintest hint of worry in Tess's eyes. "Do I have to?''

"No. That's the point. You don't have to, but I thought a part of you might want to." When Sarah had disappeared, Megan would have done anything to see her again. Was she projecting her own feelings onto Tess? More than likely.

"She dumped me. Why would I want to see her?''

"My mom dumped me, too," Megan said quietly. "I never stopped wishing she'd come back, though.''

Tess's mouth gaped. "Your mom left you?''

"Pretty much the same as you," she explained, a lump forming in her throat even after all these years. "She brought me by to visit with Tex, then disappeared during the night. I've never seen her again. I only heard from her once, a long time ago. I don't even know if she's dead or alive.''

Tess crept a little closer and scanned her face. "And you still care about her, after what she did?''

Megan nodded. "I know it doesn't make much sense. I should probably hate her, right? And in my head, I do. But right in here—'' she tapped her chest "—I still love her.''

A huge tear spilled over and streaked down Tess's cheek. "Me, too.''

Megan opened her arms. "Come here, baby."

For once Tess didn't have a smart retort, a protest about the term of endearment. She raced into Megan's embrace and clung to her tightly. Sobs shook her shoulders and dampened Megan's blouse. They remained that way, rocking together on the edge of the bed, until a soft tap on the door had Tess jerking away.

"You guys okay in there?" Jake called out.

"Fine," Megan said. "We'll be down in a few minutes."

"I talked Mrs. Gomez into making pizza. Mind if I hang around?"

"Could we stop you?" Tess demanded. Her voice, hoarse from crying, had lost some of its belligerence.

"Probably not," Jake agreed.

Megan could hear the amusement in his tone—and the relief.

"See you downstairs. And hurry up. I'm starved."

Tess regarded Megan shyly. "Jake's not so bad."

"No," she agreed. "He's not so bad."

"But he's always starving."

Megan grinned. "He was that way as a kid, too. He would eat anything that wasn't hidden. Tex used to swear our grocery bill went up a hundred bucks a week when Jake was working here."

"Know what?" Tess said.

"What?"

"Tex said that about me, too," she confided, then grinned impishly. "But I don't think he really minded."

Megan reached out tentatively and brushed a damp

lock of hair from Tess's cheek. "No, I imagine he didn't mind at all."

Exhausted by the emotional turmoil, Megan crawled into bed at ten and sank into a sound sleep. Todd woke her from it practically in the middle of the night. Oblivious to her groggy state, he launched straight into a barrage of questions that had her head reeling.

"Hey, wait!" she protested, finally cutting in. "Give me a chance to wake up."

"It's after nine," he responded.

"Not here."

"Oh," he murmured, obviously chastened. "Sorry. You've been checking in so early most days that I forgot."

"Yes, well, post a big sign about the time difference on your desk. Now slow down and start over. What has you in such a tizzy?"

"The syndicator's been calling. Dean Whicker's nervous because you're not in production and there are only a few backup tapes left."

"I'll call Dean."

"And say what?"

"That they shouldn't worry."

"Why shouldn't they?" Todd demanded. "I'm worried."

Megan ignored that. "What else?"

"The real estate agent says she's not going to look at office space anymore until you give her a firm appointment."

"Fine. What else?"

"Caitlyn's still ape-shit over redoing that layout."

"She'll get over it. Anything else?"

"For nine in the morning, that's enough, don't you think? Megan, when are you coming back?"

"I can't answer that."

"Those tapes will buy you till the end of next week. No longer."

She sighed heavily. "I know. I swear I'll give this some thought today and try to finalize some plans. I'll call the syndication company, the real estate agent and Caitlyn right after I've had my first cup of coffee, okay?"

"Thank you."

"Hold down the fort, Todd. This won't last forever."

"It already feels like longer."

"Just imagine what it feels like on my end," she said quietly, and hung up before he could respond. Predictably, the phone rang again at once. Todd with an apology, no doubt. She ignored it. But when the ringing stopped, then began again, she sighed and reached for the phone. "It's okay, Todd. I know you're sorry."

"Who the hell is Todd?" Jake demanded.

"Ah, and a pleasant good morning to you, too."

"Sorry. Who's Todd?"

"My executive assistant, who is currently charged with juggling all the balls that I ought to be handling. He's having a tough day."

"Taking it out on the boss?"

"Something like that. You're up early."

"I've been thinking about your problem."

"Which problem is that?"

"Staying here and keeping your career alive."

"And?"

"I may have a solution. Can you be ready to go in an hour?"

"Go where?"

"Can't you trust me, just this once?"

"Give me an hour and a half and I'll try."

"You've got it. See you, darlin'."

Megan rolled over and let the sound of Jake's voice linger in her head. There'd been a time when just a whisper would have made her pulse hum. It was beginning to have that effect again and that was worrisome. Jake was a complication she didn't need. Todd had just ticked off a whole long list of things that ought to be preoccupying her. Instead, she was propped up against her pillows daydreaming about a man who'd been out of her life—out of her heart—for years.

"Dangerous, Megan," she murmured. "Definitely dangerous."

That warning didn't stop her from taking extra care with her clothes and makeup before she rushed through her calls back east. Dean Whicker at Whicker Television professed understanding of her dilemma, but she could hear the concern in his voice. Jasmine was also sympathetic, but stuck to her refusal to look for another piece of property for their offices without Megan's firm commitment to check it out in person. Caitlyn expressed chagrin that Todd had passed along her continued complaints about the layouts.

"You know me, I was just grumbling. I know who the boss is. You're a pushy, know-it-all broad, but I do respect your instincts for this sort of thing. Otherwise, I'd have bailed a long time ago."

"Thank you, I think," Megan said, sure there was a compliment in there somewhere. She resorted to some flattery of her own. "I wouldn't demand so much from you if I didn't know you could do it."

"Yeah, yeah, whatever. I'll have the new pages faxed to you by the end of the day."

"Thank you, Caitlyn."

"You're going to love them."

"I'm sure I will."

Caitlyn laughed. "You always do when you get your way."

Three crises and it wasn't even nine o'clock in Wyoming. What was happening to her? Megan wondered. She was never up to speed at this hour. It was a point of honor with her, her own little rebellion against years of predawn rising. Less than a week on the ranch and she was drifting back into old habits even without Tex nagging at her.

She sighed and closed her eyes, trying to relax away the headache that was on the verge of becoming full-scale pounding. She was startled when strong hands settled on her shoulders and began massaging. Jake's hands, she thought, allowing herself to sink into the sensation.

"When did you get here?" she murmured.

"A couple of minutes ago. You look wiped out. Tough morning?"

"Nothing unusual," she assured him. "It just started earlier."

His fingers worked on a knot in her shoulder until she sighed with pleasure. She had to try very hard to keep her imagination from taking a wicked turn about the magic those hands of his could perform.

"Anytime you get tired of law, you could hire out as a masseuse," she murmured with lazy contentment. "People in New York would pay a fortune for your services."

"Sorry. I only take on very special clients." He gave her shoulders one last squeeze. "Okay, that's it. Let's get a move on. The day's a'wasting. I want to check into that restraining order while we're out."

She groaned. "Good God, why am I surrounded by people who are perky in the morning and can't wait to get started with the day?"

"Just lucky, I guess. Come on. We'll do breakfast first. Another jolt of coffee and some blueberry pancakes will improve your mood."

Megan's spirits brightened at the suggestion. "The Starlight Diner's still here?"

"Of course. It's an institution. I think the whole town would collapse if Henrietta decided to retire. That's where everybody goes for mental and physical sustenance."

"Gossip, you mean."

Jake grinned. "Gossip and those blueberry pancakes. I'm relieved to see you haven't gone too high-falutin' to love them. I was afraid you'd prefer kiwi and homemade granola, both of which are in short supply in Whispering Wind."

"There are some basics that I would never presume to mess with," she said, sweeping past him to tell Mrs. Gomez she was leaving.

"Where are you going?" Tess demanded, looking up from her own breakfast. After the prior night's turmoil, she had obviously gotten a late start.

"Into town," Megan told her.

"Can I come?"

Megan almost grabbed at the chance to have a chaperone, then chided herself for cowardice. Besides, Tess didn't need to know all the details about the restraining order. "No. Not this time. Jake and I have some business to take care of."

"Monkey business, I'll bet," Tess retorted.

"Niña," Mrs. Gomez chided. "That is enough. We have plenty to do here today. You are going to help me with the canning before all the green beans from the garden spoil."

"Oh, yippee!" Tess grumbled sarcastically. Suddenly her expression turned wary. "You aren't thinking my mom's going to be in town today, are you? Is that why you don't want me around?"

"No," Megan reassured her at once. "Absolutely not. It's just because we're going to take care of some business. That's it. You'll have more fun here with Mrs. Gomez."

"Have you ever actually canned anything?" Tess asked.

"As a matter of fact, I have," Megan replied, amused to see Tess gape. "Every year, right up until the day Mrs. Gomez pleaded with me to stay out of her kitchen."

"Why'd she ask you to stay out?" Tess demanded, clearly brimming with curiosity.

The housekeeper grinned. "There was a little accident. It was nothing."

"That wasn't what you said when the jars started exploding," Megan reminded her.

Tess giggled. "You blew up the vegetables?"

"I just made a bit of a miscalculation," Megan insisted. "It could have happened to anyone."

"Oh, man, if your readers knew about that, your magazine would probably fold, right?"

"Don't go getting any bright ideas, kiddo. I told all in a column I wrote once."

Tess sighed, looking disappointed. "I guess blackmail's out, then."

"Definitely."

"Too bad. I've had my eye on a pair of really neat boots for a long time. Tex said I couldn't have 'em till I learned to ride." Her expression clouded over. "I guess I'll never get 'em now."

Megan stared at her. "Why would you say that?"

"Who's gonna teach me?"

"I will," Megan promised recklessly, not pausing to consider just how long it had been since she'd been on a horse. "And you will have those boots, Tess. Count on it."

The western supply store would be her first stop…right after she finished the blueberry pancakes her mouth had been watering over since Jake had mentioned them.

9

The Starlight Diner, with its neon sign in the window, bright red vinyl seats and tabletop jukeboxes filled with oldies, was a Whispering Wind tradition. It was one of those rare places where the home-style food was every bit as savory as the gossip. Most folks in town passed through it on a weekly, if not a daily basis. Teenagers for two generations had done their courting there over burgers, cherry sodas and milk shakes. Ranchers dropped in when they came into town for feed. Housewives met for lunch when they drove in to shop for groceries. There was hardly an hour of the day when it wasn't busy.

This morning heads swiveled and a hush fell over the place when Jake and Megan walked in the door. Jake realized too late that he should have anticipated the reaction, given the awed response of the waitress at the ice cream parlor the day before. Megan gave everyone an awkward little wave, then slid into the only available booth, one right in front, in plain view of the gawkers.

Owner Henrietta Hastings, tall and lanky with gray hair as short as a boy's, bustled out from behind the counter, scowling. "What's the matter with you people? Didn't your mamas teach you any manners?"

she demanded of the crowd in general, hands on narrow, jeans-clad hips. "It's not polite to stare."

Chastized, the customers dutifully returned to their food and their conversation, but surreptitious glances slid in Megan's direction every few seconds.

Order pad in one hand, coffeepot in the other, Henrietta blocked their view. She filled Jake and Megan's cups to the brim, then beamed at Megan. "Child, it surely is good to have you back again. Are you here to stay?"

Eager as always to discover her intentions, Jake watched Megan's reaction. She looked as if the woman was trying to pin her down to a long-term contract that wasn't written in her favor. Megan squirmed, her gaze shifting from Jake to Henrietta and back again.

"It's hard to say," she responded finally. "There's a lot to consider."

"Well, of course there is," Henrietta soothed. "I never meant to push. It would be good to have you back, though. No question about it. Too many of our young people take off and never set foot in Whispering Wind again. If that keeps up, the town will just die of old age one of these years."

"It can't be that bad," Megan said. "This place is as busy as ever. Isn't that Barbara Sue you've got working behind the counter? You never had another waitress in here before."

A cloud seemed to pass over Henrietta's face, but it came and went before Jake could pinpoint the cause.

"She helps out when she can," Henrietta said vaguely. "Still doesn't change the fact that the town's all but dying. Look at the gray hair, what there is of it on some heads," she pointed out, nodding toward the balding Realtor, Josh Wilson. "Aside from you and Jake, do you see a soul in here under forty? Not a one."

She paused, apparently to allow them to survey the customers, before adding, "Of course, some of the young ones do go on out to that fast-food place that opened up on the highway. What kind of breakfast can you get in a place like that, I ask you? Nothing healthy, that's for sure. Now what can I get you? Do you need to see the menu? Haven't changed a thing in twenty years, but could be you've forgotten."

"Not a chance," Megan told her. "Blueberry pancakes."

"Two or three?"

"Three," Megan said with gusto. "I've been dreaming about those pancakes all morning."

Jake grinned. "Double that, Henrietta. Then I'll finish whatever Megan can't."

"If you want more than three, you'd better order your own, pal, because I intend to eat every bite," Megan countered. "I hardly had anything for dinner last night. Somebody I know grabbed up most of the pizza."

"Must have been Tess. That girl sure can eat."

"Tess, my eye," Megan retorted.

Henrietta listened to the exchange with a grin tugging at the corners of her mouth. "You two still battle over every little thing, don't you? All that fire ought to lead somewhere, if you ask me." She sashayed off without waiting for a response.

"Interesting observation, don't you think?" Jake said when she'd gone.

Megan regarded him with feigned innocence. "What observation was that?"

He chuckled. "Okay, we'll let it go for now."

When the pancakes came a few minutes later, he watched with amusement as Megan attacked them as if she hadn't eaten in months. He suspected she hadn't consumed anything like this in that time or longer. She looked as if she lived on skimpy little salads, cartons of yogurt and grapefruit. If she was going to withstand the Wyoming winter, she needed a little meat on her bones.

She lifted her gaze from her plate and caught him staring. "What?"

"I was just thinking maybe I ought to give you my pancakes, instead of the other way around."

"Why?"

"You're too skinny."

"I am not," she retorted indignantly. "I've weighed exactly the same thing for years now."

He recognized her ploy. "Going back how far?"

"Since I was fourteen."

He vividly recalled the gawky teenager, all arms and legs and still growing. "How much taller are you now?"

"An inch or so," she grumbled, clearly aware that she'd fallen neatly into his trap.

"More like three or four."

"I had no idea you were paying such close attention."

"Darlin', I've always paid attention to you. At fourteen you barely reached my chin." He deliberately lowered his gaze from her eyes to her lips. "At sixteen, your mouth was conveniently level with mine." He met her eyes again. "You can still look me in the eye, and believe me, I've grown, which puts you at five-ten, easy."

"Five-nine-and-a-half," Megan countered, as if that half inch made him a liar.

"Do you really want to quibble over that?"

"I don't want to discuss this at all," she declared huffily.

"Because you know I'm right. You obviously hang out with too many fashion models, who'd blow away in a stiff wind." He picked up a pitcher and reached across. "Here, add a little cream to your coffee."

She regarded him balefully. "I don't think a teaspoon of cream is going to have a big impact on my weight, one way or the other."

He reached for the syrup. Megan scowled. "Don't you dare. I won't have these pancakes ruined with syrup."

"More butter, then," he suggested hopefully.

She brushed away his hand. "If you do this every time we share a meal, it's going to get to be very annoying."

"I'll try to restrain myself—that is, if you'll promise to share lots of meals with me."

"Don't press your luck, Jake. At the rate you're spoiling this one for me, there's not a big inducement to repeat the experience."

He held up his hands in a gesture of surrender. "You win. Not another word. Enjoy. Eat up." He grinned. "Whoops. Sorry."

"You are not sorry."

"Sorry for what?" Peggy Barkley inquired, standing beside the booth and regarding them both with undisguised curiosity.

Megan's expression brightened. "Peggy, slide right in here beside me," she said, scooting over. "Jake and I were just having a discussion about food."

"Sounded to me like he was apologizing. I thought maybe you were talking about..." She glanced at Jake. "Well, you know."

"The infamous missing cattle," Jake suggested, surprised at the lack of bitterness in his voice. After getting into it with Megan the night before, maybe he was finally letting go of the anger. "We've pretty much exhausted that topic."

"Along with this other one," Megan added. "No more talk about food, okay?" She turned to her friend. "What brings you in here? Henrietta made it sound as if no one our age ever darkens her door."

"Actually, that's true enough. I can put on five pounds just looking at those pancakes," Peggy said, waving off Henrietta's offer of coffee, as well. "I was in town to pick up some supplies from the feed store for Johnny. I spotted you sitting here as I was walking past and thought I'd sneak in long enough to say hi and invite you over to dinner tomorrow night—that is, if you don't mind having three kids underfoot. You can bring Tess, too." She glanced toward Jake. "You're welcome to come along, too. It won't be fancy, because the kids won't eat it if they don't recognize it, but it will be filling."

"I'd love to come," Megan said.

The ready response surprised Jake. Even though the two had been close once, he'd expected Megan to keep some distance between herself and old friends to make the break easier if she decided to go back to New York eventually. But Megan seemed genuinely pleased by Peggy's invitation. As for Peggy, she looked...what? Relieved, maybe. As if she'd feared a rejection.

"What can I bring?" Megan asked.

"Just yourself," Peggy insisted. "If you show up with some dish you've whipped up that puts my food to shame, I'll never forgive you."

"Can I bring a bottle of wine or some beer?" Jake asked.

Peggy chuckled. "I doubt they make a wine that'll go with whatever I whip up. Bring some beer if it suits you, though Johnny always has a six-pack on ice." She stood up. "I'd better run. I've got a million things to do and no time to do them."

She leaned down and brushed a kiss across Megan's cheek. "See you, sweetie. I'll be looking forward to seeing you both tomorrow night."

Jake watched her go, then shook his head. "I get breathless just listening to her."

"She hasn't changed one iota in all these years," Megan said. "She's so happy."

"She does seem that way, doesn't she?" Jake said, his tone neutral.

Megan stared hard at him. "You sound as if you think she might not be. Do you know something I don't?"

Rumor and innuendo, Jake thought, deciding to keep both to himself. "Of course not. I've hardly seen Peggy since I've been back."

"And Johnny?"

"I've run into him once or twice. Don't make a

big deal out of it,'' he admonished. "I wasn't implying anything.''

"If you say so,'' she said, but she was clearly skeptical.

"Are you ready to go see the judge about the restraining order?''

The question served its purpose. Her spine straightened and fire sparked in her eyes. "Absolutely.''

It took little persuasion to get Judge Lawton Kinsey to agree to the restraining order. He was one of Tex's oldest friends, and he knew all about Tess, right down to the agreement Tex had made with her mother.

"You take this on over to the sheriff. If that woman shows her face anywhere around Whispering Wind, Bryce will sit her down and have a little chat with her telling her what's what.''

"Thank you, your honor,'' Megan said.

"That's Lawton to you, Meggie. We go back too far to stand on ceremony while we're in my chambers. Tex was mighty proud of you, you know. Never had a talk with him that he didn't tell me everything you were up to and all you'd accomplished.''

"Thank you. It means a lot to hear that,'' she said, a suspicious sheen of tears in her eyes. "He never...well, Tex wasn't much with words.''

Hearing the pain in her voice, Jake cursed the old rancher for not having said as much to her on occasion. It would have meant the world to Meggie to have had his approval. Jake reached over and grasped her hand, gave it a squeeze.

"Let's go, darlin'. We still have things to do.''

They dropped off a copy of the restraining order with Bryce, then went by the western supply store, where Megan asked Nate Hollings if he had any idea which boots Tess had her eye on.

"I believe it was these right over here," he said, leading the way to a pair in soft, fine leather. "She's come in here a half-dozen times and just stood and stared at 'em. She said Tex had promised 'em to her when she learned to ride."

"We'll take them now," Megan told him. "I'll have to guess at the size, but she can bring them back if they don't fit, right?"

"Absolutely. We'll get 'em custom fitted, if need be. When you spend this much on a boot, it ought to be right. It's meant to last."

"She'll outgrow them in a year," Jake warned.

"It doesn't matter," Megan said. "She needs these boots."

"And you need to give them to her," Jake murmured under his breath as Megan went off to pay for them.

"Where are we going now?" Megan demanded when Jake turned in the opposite direction of the ranch as they drove out of town. She was still clutching the package with Tess's boots. For some reason she couldn't entirely explain, she didn't want to let go of them. "I want to take these home to Tess."

"All in good time. Have you forgotten what I said when I called you this morning?"

She tried, but came up blank. "What?"

"I promised you a solution to your problems."

"Oh, that," she said. She'd assumed that was little more than a ploy to get her away from the ranch for the day, and had dismissed it. "I didn't think you were serious," she admitted.

"Where you're concerned, Meggie, I am always serious."

She scowled at his teasing. "Jake, it would take half the advice columnists in the country, along with a few financial experts and military logistical strategists, to solve my problems these days."

"Give me first crack at it and see if you still feel that way."

She sat back. "Sure. Why not?"

It took only a few minutes to reach the western outskirts of Whispering Wind. A few years before the town had made a halfhearted bid to bring in high-tech businesses and light industry. Tex had written her about it. The result was this unimpressive complex of mostly vacant offices and warehouses. It had been an ill-conceived idea. No one in town had had the marketing skills to go after the right sort of tenants. Josh Wilson was the only Realtor in town, and he pretty much waited for folks to come to him. Now weeds had grown up and overtaken the pitiful attempt at landscaping. Harsh winters had left the paint peeling and the sidewalks cracked.

She stared from it to Jake. "This is what you wanted me to see?"

"Like it?"

"What's to like? The buildings are ugly and nobody's tended the lawn or gardens since they were planted, probably. Everything looks decrepit and neglected."

"But it's functional," Jake corrected. "Perfect for a media empire."

He gestured toward the row of offices. "Headquarters." Then to the warehouses. "Studios. Bring in some fancy furniture, some equipment, and bingo, you're in business."

Megan stared at the property, incredulous. "You have to be kidding. Here? You want me to bring my entire operation to the middle of nowhere?"

"Unless you plan to abandon the ranch...and Tess."

"Never."

"Then what choice do you have?"

Backed into a corner, she said rashly, "I'll commute. I've been toying with that for the past couple of days. It could work. I have a very efficient staff in New York. They can handle the day-to-day stuff. I'll fly in, tape my shows, catch up on whatever needs my personal attention and fly back."

The brash statement flew straight in the teeth of very recent evidence that her staff would probably rebel within a month. Maybe less.

"How many connections did you have to make to get here for Tex's funeral?" Jake inquired reasonably.

"One. In Denver. It wasn't that complicated, Jake."

"It's still a huge waste of time, isn't it? With all you have to do, isn't time a very precious commodity, not meant to be wasted?"

"I'll buy a damned jet if I have to."

He shrugged. "If that's really how you want to spend your money and your time, don't let me stop you. To me, this looks more practical."

"You're talking about relocating dozens of people."

"Dozens?"

"Okay, a couple of dozen. They're New Yorkers, for God's sake. They'd go nuts out here."

"Better for you to wear yourself out commuting," he said with an annoying edge of sarcasm.

"I'm one person. I can handle it."

"If you say so."

"I can," she shouted.

"Tell me one thing," he said quietly, reasonably. "If the head of your company, the star of your show, the editor of your magazine—that's you in all three cases—collapses, what'll those dozens of people do for jobs then?"

"I won't collapse," she said, but the words came out with far less certainty than she would have liked.

"No matter what those press releases of yours might say, you're not Superwoman. She was a figment of someone's imagination. You're flesh and blood, merely human." He touched a finger to her cheek as if to remind her of that. "Soft and fragile."

"Tough as nails," she corrected, but with a catch in her voice that was all too human, all too feminine.

"If you say so," he murmured, right before his lips touched hers.

The kiss was quick and tender, clearly meant to do no more than prove his point. The swirl of sensations it set off was devastating.

"I'm doing it my way, Jake," she said, making her own point.

He watched her with hooded, doubting eyes. "Suit yourself. But I think I'll take out an option on this place, just in case."

"You're wasting your money."

"I'll worry about my bank balance, Meggie. You worry about keeping all those damn balls in the air."

10

Jake told himself he shouldn't have been disappointed by Megan's reaction to the industrial complex, but he was. If she'd liked it despite its sorry state of disrepair, if she'd taken his idea and run with it, he would have felt more confident that she was going to stay in Whispering Wind and do right by Tess. As it was, he was more certain than ever that she was keeping all of her options open, that she already had one foot out the door despite Tex's very clear wishes.

Even so, he dropped by the real estate office after leaving the ranch and negotiated a deal for the property. If Meggie didn't want it, someone else would. It was just a matter of putting a spin on the town's more attractive features and getting that spin into the right hands. With the number of actors living at least part-time in Wyoming, convincing one of them to open a production facility close to home should be a breeze.

"You're turning into a regular land baron around here," Josh Wilson declared after Jake had signed the papers. "You hoping to own the whole dang place one of these days?"

"Could be," Jake said, thinking of the satisfaction

he'd feel in virtually controlling a town that had once shunned him. It might be an interesting goal to contemplate when he had some time on his hands.

"Who was that actress who bought a town down South awhile back?" Josh asked, his expression thoughtful. "You know, that real pretty one. Kim something."

"Kim Basinger," Jake told him. "And she didn't buy the town. She found some investors, sold them on the town's potential and lent her name to the deal."

"Whatever," Josh said, clearly not especially interested in the facts. He rarely had been. "Anyway, that's the one." He shoved a second set of papers in front of Jake. "Sign here and here. We'll schedule the closing whenever you're set with the money."

"Schedule it," Jake said.

Josh blinked. "You know, son, even in a small town like this, it takes time to get loan approvals, that sort of thing."

"Not a problem," Jake assured him. "Just set the closing, Josh. I'll be here with the money."

Obviously enthused by the prospect of a quick, hefty commission from the sale of the town's abandoned property, Josh grabbed Jake's hand and shook it. "A pleasure doing business with you, son. A pleasure."

Jake gave him a wry look. The older man must have a far shorter memory than he did. Not twenty years ago, Josh Wilson had been among the first to label Jake as a troublemaker. He and his wife had led the crusade to have Jake and his mother driven out of town. Only Tex's intervention, his hiring Jake and advancing him the money to pay the rent on their ramshackle house—which happened to be owned by Josh—had kept the Wilsons from making good on their threat to see mother and son banished from Whispering Wind.

Jake could remember seeing his mother coming home from yet another confrontation with their landlord, her shoulders slumped, her head bowed, her cheeks red from the humiliation he had subjected her to. Impotent fury that he'd had no outlet for had raged through Jake time after time. He had vowed with a child's fervor that one day Josh Wilson would pay. Nothing that had happened in the intervening years had dulled his determination.

If there had been another Realtor in town with whom he could have done business, Jake would have. Instead, he concentrated on lowballing every piece of property he bought, coming as close to stealing it as he legitimately could. He was collecting property like squares on a Monopoly board, accumulating them one by one so that one day there would be nothing left for Josh to buy or sell. Only when the Realtor was all but penniless would Jake be satisfied. He looked forward to the day when Wilson would need something from him and he could send him packing, just as the Realtor had done to Jake's mother time and again.

The walls were closing in on Megan. Funny, she thought, staring out the window. Here she was, surrounded by wide-open spaces, in a house that sprawled over several thousand square feet, and she felt more claustrophobic than she did in her comparatively cramped New York apartment with skyscrapers blocking every view.

A lot of that feeling had to do with Jake's sneaky attempt to back her into a corner that morning. It wasn't so much that she'd hated the industrial park on sight. It was what it represented. She'd seen it as a trap. If she'd leased that property, even on a temporary basis, it would have been as much as an admission that she was back in Whispering Wind to stay. She wasn't ready to admit any such thing.

"I brought you a cup of tea," Mrs. Gomez said, bustling in and giving Megan a welcome break from her dark thoughts.

The housekeeper placed a tray on the corner of the wide oak desk that only a few days earlier had been Tex's. Ranching books and magazines had been piled high, along with a haphazard array of bills and a box of the fancy cigars Tex had favored. Megan had dealt with the bills an hour ago and had moved the books and magazines to the shelves behind her. Now the desk was littered with her own papers, crowded with a computer and a fax machine and a three-line phone that the phone company had installed while she was out.

"Two cups," Megan noted, glancing at the tray Mrs. Gomez had brought. "And a very big slice of your sour cream cake. That must mean you want to talk."

The housekeeper nodded. "If you've got the time."

"For you, always." She caught Mrs. Gomez's worried expression. "What's on your mind? Is there a problem?"

"More than one, I'd say. I haven't wanted to burden you before now. You've had enough to deal with."

"Just tell me," Megan urged.

"There's the ranch, for starters. The men want to know if you intend to keep it operating or if you plan to sell out. Winter's coming on. There are decisions to be made. Up till now, Jake's been handling some of it, along with Tom Hagen, but you're in charge now. You owe it to the men to give them fair warning if you intend to sell out. They'll need to find other jobs, and winter's not the best time for doing that."

Megan stared at her, grappling with the concept of being a rancher whether she wanted to or not. "I don't know anything about ranching."

"Nonsense," Mrs. Gomez said sternly. "Of course you do. Your granddaddy saw to that. He had you working with him from the day you arrived here. You've been on cattle drives. You've done your share of branding."

"But I hated it."

"That doesn't mean you didn't absorb at least some of what he tried to teach you," Mrs. Gomez contradicted. "Tex always believed you had what it took."

"Tex was wrong."

Mrs. Gomez regarded her sympathetically. "Megan, I'm not saying whether you should keep the place running or not, just that if you do, then you'd best get to it. This ranch was your granddaddy's pride and joy. It would be a shame to see it suffer from neglect. The men Tex hired work hard. They're loyal. You won't find a better foreman anywhere than Tom.

But it's not the same as having an owner who keeps a close eye on things.''

The walls seemed to creep another foot inward, crowding her. "I see," she said tightly. "Anything else?"

"There's my own position to consider. If you're going back to New York, do you want me here? I've got a place with my sister in New Mexico whenever I want it. My other sister would move there in a heartbeat, if I'd agree to go, too. I'm at the age when the prospect of slowing down some holds some appeal. Tex's legacy would be enough to keep me going."

Alarmed, Megan stared at her. "No. Please, I need you here."

The woman who'd been as close to a mother as anyone Megan could recall smiled softly at her response. "Is that just panic talking or do you really intend to keep this place going and me here with it?"

Megan put her hands over her face. It was all she could do to keep from screaming in frustration and confusion. "I wish I knew what was right," she whispered. "I only know what Tex wanted."

"Tex was wise in many ways, *niña,* but he didn't know everything. You must look into your heart and see what is right for you."

"And for Tess," Megan said. "Don't forget about her."

"I could not if I tried. But she will be happy only if you are. If you stay out of a sense of obligation or duty and are miserable, you will only hold it against her. She is a very bright child. She will feel that, even if you do your very best to hide it."

"But when I so much as mention going to New

York, Tess reacts violently. She loves it here. She feels secure. How can I take that away from her?''

''She did not feel that way when she first arrived,'' the housekeeper reminded her. ''She was frightened and angry, just as she is now. Think back to how you felt the first few weeks you were here. You were lashing out at everyone, me included. Time helped you, as it has Tess. If she feels secure here, it is because Tex did what he could to make her feel that way. Could you not do the same for her in New York, if that is where your heart is?''

''Are you telling me to go?''

Mrs. Gomez smiled sadly. ''No, *niña,* I am telling you that your options are still open. Do not make a decision for the wrong reasons.'' She stood and patted Megan's hand. ''For the moment, we will leave things as they are. I will tell the men they are to go on as they would have if Tex were here. Shall I tell Tom he has the authority to make whatever decisions he thinks are for the best?''

''Yes, and thank you. I won't take too much longer, I promise.''

''Tell me one thing.''

''Anything.''

''Where does Señor Jake fit into all of this? Are you struggling with that decision as well?''

''He doesn't,'' Megan insisted.

''But he is coming for dinner tonight, *sí?*''

Megan had forgotten. ''Yes,'' she admitted with a sigh.

''He is a good man.''

''You always believed that, didn't you?''

''Always.''

"Even when my father accused him of stealing the cattle?"

"Even then."

Megan felt that sense of having failed Jake more deeply than ever. "I wish I had."

"I was old enough to reach my own conclusions," Mrs. Gomez told her. "You were still very much under your grandfather's influence."

"Do you think he lied about it deliberately?"

"I would not like to think so."

"But you believe it's a possibility," Megan persisted.

"A possibility, *sí*. Your grandfather loved you very much. Just as now, he thought he knew best. It was a way to be sure you would go off to college as planned. Little did he know that it would wind up with you staying so far away. Perhaps if he had been able to see the future, he would have been less likely to interfere in such a way."

"He made it possible for me to go to New York."

"I think it might have been his way of punishing himself for being so foolish where a young boy was concerned."

"Not a boy," Megan said fiercely. "Jake was a man even then."

"*Sí*," the housekeeper agreed. "Perhaps that is what your grandfather feared the most." She reached for Megan's hand and held it in her own. "Let it go. It is in the past and cannot be changed. The present and the future are what matter now."

But the present and the future were filled with such uncertainty, Megan thought as she tried to concentrate on her work for the rest of the afternoon. Either because she was distracted or because she was overdue for a run of bad luck, nothing went well.

She fielded a dozen calls from Todd, each one more frantic than the last, until she finally agreed to fly to New York on Sunday so she could be in the office first thing on Monday. She called Peggy right away to postpone their dinner party until her return. "I'm sorry to do this to you. Next weekend will be great, if it works for you."

"I'll be looking forward to it," Peggy said. "Don't worry about me. You have a real safe trip, okay?"

Only after she'd hung up did Megan realize there had been genuine disappointment in her friend's voice. Obviously Peggy had been counting on their get-together more than she had realized. It was just one more thing for her to feel guilty about.

To make matters worse, Jake spent the entire evening pestering her with a hundred little decisions that needed to be made about Tex's estate. What annoyed her even more was that he never once looked her directly in the eye. He seemed to have distanced himself from her because she hadn't immediately fallen in with his plans for that industrial park.

Then, to top it off, right after dinner Tess disappeared. When Mrs. Gomez announced that the girl was nowhere to be found, Megan didn't believe it.

"She has to be around somewhere," she responded with exasperation. "Did you look in the barn? She's been spending a lot of time with the kittens."

"I looked there, in her room, in the attic, even in Tex's room."

At Megan's quizzical look, the housekeeper shrugged. "She seems to be more at ease when she sits in his chair by the window. I saw no reason to forbid her from doing it.''

"No, of course not,'' Megan said. She glanced at Jake. "Any ideas?''

"Is it possible she overheard you talking about flying to New York on Sunday?''

"It's possible. In fact, if she was anywhere near Tex's office at the time, it's likely. Todd and I were arguing about it.''

"The words or just the yelling could have frightened her,'' Mrs. Gomez suggested. "Perhaps she assumed you would insist on her going, too.''

"I actually thought about it. I thought she might enjoy a few days in New York. I told Todd to make a reservation for her, just in case. Afterward, I thought about the kind of schedule I'm going to have to keep and decided it was a bad idea.''

"But, of course, she wouldn't have known that,'' Jake pointed out. "She would have jumped to the obvious conclusion that you were taking her with you against her wishes.''

"You're assuming this is because of something I did,'' Megan retorted, not wanting to accept the blame he was all too eagerly heaping on her. "What about her mother? Is it possible that she's shown up, contacted Tess in some way? Tess could be hiding from her.''

Mrs. Gomez sketched a cross across her chest. "I hope you are wrong. The poor child has enough to deal with without that.''

Jake stood up and strode toward the door. "We may all be overreacting. We're accomplishing nothing here. I'll search outside and talk to the men. You two go through the house again from top to bottom."

"Mrs. Gomez can do that," Megan insisted. "I'm coming with you."

Jake regarded her with surprise. "Whatever. Let's get going. There's a storm blowing in tonight. We have to find her before it hits full force. If the temperatures drop much more we'll have snow instead of rain."

Megan grabbed Tex's old sheepskin coat off the peg by the back door. It was miles too big for her, but it was warm. The icy wind that smacked her in the face when she stepped outside proved it had been a wise decision. Jake had been wrong. It was already snowing.

"Where should we start?" Megan asked.

"I want to go back to the barn. I can't believe she'd go far from those kittens."

"Mrs. Gomez said she'd looked there."

"Maybe not in the hayloft or in every stall."

But a thorough search revealed not a trace of Tess. Even though she desperately wanted to believe that Tess was merely hiding from them, Megan was beginning to get a sick feeling in the pit of her stomach. Years ago, on a night not so very different from this one, she had run away. She had set out to find her mother, to prove to herself that Sarah O'Rourke still loved her.

She had plodded out to the highway, then turned toward town, intent on getting to the bus station. Snow had begun falling before she even reached the road—big, wet flakes that had soaked through her coat and piled up all too quickly on the slick highway.

Her hands and feet had been so cold she'd barely been able to feel them. Tears streaming down her cheeks had all but frozen. She hadn't gone far before she had wanted desperately to go home, to crawl back into her warm bed, but stubborn pride had kept her going.

Tex had found her an hour later. He had blustered and carried on about how foolish she'd been, but she realized now how badly his hands had been shaking when he'd gathered her close, how frightened he had been. She knew that same kind of fear when she glanced toward the stall where Tex's horse should have been.

"Jake," she called out, panic threading through her voice.

He was at her side at once. "What?"

"Midnight is gone."

"Tex's horse?" Jake's gaze flicked to the empty stall. "She wouldn't have…"

"She wanted to learn to ride. I gave her those boots today. Maybe she got it into her head that she had to earn them."

"Or maybe she just decided to run away," he said grimly. "I'll saddle up the horses. You round up as many men as you can find and let Mrs. Gomez know we're going to search. She can start calling some of the neighboring ranches."

Megan raced from the barn. She alerted the foreman first. Tom promised to have the men ready to ride out immediately.

"We'll find her, miss," he said with quiet confidence. "Don't you worry. The men all like that little gal. She was like Tex's shadow. He pretended not to notice that she was never far away, but we could tell it pleased him. She's learned a thing or two since she's been here. She'll be fine. She's a real feisty one.''

"That she is," Megan agreed, then ran on to the house.

"I will make the calls," Mrs. Gomez promised.

Megan swallowed hard, struggling with guilt and fear. "If something happens to her—"

"Nothing will," the housekeeper declared. "You will find her and bring her home."

Hearing the reassurances repeated so often should have helped, but Megan kept seeing Tess's face the day of the funeral. She'd looked so lost and alone, so terribly frightened. Even when she'd been snapping and snarling, the vulnerability had been plain in her eyes.

"Think back," Megan ordered herself as she mounted the horse Jake had saddled for her. Would Tess have struck out for town the way she had?

"Let's try the highway," she suggested, turning in that direction.

Jake didn't question her decision. He rode silently alongside her. When she turned toward town, he said, "You did this once, didn't you?"

Megan nodded. "But I wasn't on horseback and I didn't get far."

There was no sign of hoofprints in the deepening snow. After little more than a mile, Megan concluded she had been wrong.

"Where else would I have gone?" she asked aloud, struggling to put herself into Tess's place. Surely the same hiding places that would have lured her years ago would prove irresistible to Tess, as well.

She'd always been drawn to the creek. But on a night like tonight, with the wind howling and snow piling up rapidly, surely Tess wouldn't have wanted to be out in the open.

But there was a place, Megan realized finally, that would be safe and dry.

"I think I know," she said suddenly to Jake.

His gaze clashed with hers and it was as if her thoughts were silently communicated. "The cave," he said at once.

"Our place," Megan whispered.

It wasn't really a cave at all, just a niche nature had carved out in the side of a rocky cliff. There had been barely enough room for two people sitting side by side, but that was more than enough for one small, frightened girl.

Jake led the way, his horse stepping carefully over the rocky, treacherous terrain. The sky was thick with clouds that shadowed the moon and left the night dark as pitch. Megan's horse stumbled on the slick ground, rocking her wildly in the saddle before he steadied.

Her gasp of dismay drew Jake's attention. "You okay?"

"Fine," she said, teeth clenched against the jarring her body was taking. Once, riding had been second nature to her, but in recent years there had been few opportunities. Obviously she could use a little practice. Who'd ever heard of a rancher who couldn't ride worth a damn?

"It's just beyond this next rise," Jake called back.

Megan peered through the inky darkness and saw

little more than the shape of Jake ahead of her. "How can you tell?"

"There are some things a man never forgets," he called back, laughter threading through his voice. "Like the time that big ol' snake slithered in front of us and you threw yourself straight into my arms."

"I don't remember that," she retorted.

What she remembered was Jake kissing her for the first time in that cave, his lips soft and tender and tentative against hers. Her shy response, the first womanly stirrings of her body. It was not a memory she intended to share just now.

"I recall the kiss, too, Meggie," Jake said quietly. "All the sweet wonder of it."

"What kiss?"

"You can pretend if you like, but you're remembering it, too. You're blushing."

"How the hell can you know that?" she grumbled. "It's dark as sin out here."

"Because you always blush when I catch you in a fib. That's why you're such a lousy liar."

"Maybe I've gotten better with age."

"Shall I turn my flashlight on you and check it out?"

Knowing her face was burning, Megan tried to distract him. "Is that the opening up there on the left?"

After the briefest hesitation, he turned in the saddle. "You're right. That's it."

His horse nickered. From somewhere nearby came a response.

"That has to be Midnight," Megan said. "Tess! Tess, are you out here?"

Jake dismounted and moved toward the opening in the cliff. "Tess, sweetie, where are you?"

"Here." The tearful reply came not from the cave, but from the same direction as the horse's soft neighing.

"I think she's over there, Jake." Heart pounding and almost dizzy with relief, Megan slid to the ground, skidded on the snow, then ran toward the sound of muffled sobs.

Tess was on the ground, with Midnight standing protectively nearby. Megan hunkered down beside her. Only then did she realize that she was trembling, just as Tex had been all those years ago.

"Oh, baby," she whispered, gathering Tess close. The sense of déjà vu, the swirl of powerful emotions, stunned her. Was this what it meant to be a mother?

Tess was soaked through and shivering.

"Are you okay?" Megan asked, trying to warm her. She pulled back and examined Tess's tear-streaked face. There were no cuts or bruises.

"It's my ankle," Tess whispered. "There was so much snow, I slipped and fell when I got off Midnight. It's twisted. I tried to get up again, but I couldn't. I couldn't get the boot off either, 'cause my foot's all swollen."

"We'll cut the boot off," Jake said, kneeling down and examining the injured leg.

"No," Tess protested with a cry. "The boot's brand-new."

"I'll get you another pair," Megan told her.

"But these are the ones Tex promised me. I can't ruin 'em," she insisted, clearly on the verge of a fresh round of tears.

Jake stared at Megan. "Any ideas? The boot has to come off."

"Could you maybe work it loose at the seams, so it can be repaired?"

"I'll give it a try." He glanced at Tess. "That okay with you?"

She sniffed, but her expression was hopeful. "You really think it can be fixed after?"

"I'll see to it," Megan promised.

Tess sighed. "Then go on and cut," she instructed Jake. "But if you mess up, I'm gonna hurt you."

Jake grinned. "Now there's an incentive," he said as he carefully sliced along the inner seam.

As the boot loosened, Megan gingerly pulled Tess's foot free. She winced at the swelling and the already visible black-and-blue bruising.

"You think it's broken?" she asked Jake.

He probed the tender ankle, then shook his head. "We probably should have it x-rayed to be certain, but I think it's just a bad sprain. Let's get her back to the ranch, get some ice on it and see how it looks then. We can take her in to Doc Lee's office after that."

"I ain't going to no doctor," Tess protested. "No shots."

"An X ray doesn't hurt," Megan reassured her. "No shots are required."

"Yeah, but what if it's broke? He ain't gonna set it without jabbing me with a needle and you know it."

"Let's cross that bridge when we come to it," Jake said. "Let's get you up in the saddle with me."

"What about Midnight?" Tess demanded. "We can't just leave him here. He took care of me."

"Midnight will come along on his own now that he knows you're going home," Jake assured her.

They rode back toward the ranch at a careful pace. When they were within sight of the house, Tess asked, "Am I in trouble?"

"Oh, yeah," Megan replied. "Big time."

"But I'm hurt and I'm just a kid."

"It's because you're a kid that you're in trouble," Jake said. "You had no business taking off like that and scaring everybody half to death. Do you know how many people have been tied up all evening looking for you?"

"A lot?" she asked.

"Every man on the ranch."

"Oh, boy," she murmured.

"That about sums it up," Megan said. "But we'll discuss all of that in the morning. In the meantime, let's get that ankle of yours checked out. Then I intend to lock you in your room for a month."

"You won't know if I'm locked in or not," Tess retorted. "You'll be in New York."

So, Megan thought, she did know about the trip, and more than likely, that was what had set her off. "Sweetie, I could be in Timbuktu and I would still know every little detail about what is going on where you're concerned. Remember that next time you get some crazy idea in your head."

"I figured..." Tess began, sounding surprisingly meek.

"I think I know what you figured," Megan replied more gently. "But you figured wrong. I wasn't going to take you to New York against your will. And I wasn't going to go away like your mother did and never come back. Whether I'm here or in some other state entirely, I'm in your life to stay. Got that?''

A slow smile spread across Tess's face. "Yeah," she whispered. "I think I do.''

11

Tess was still laid up in bed when Megan had to leave Sunday for New York. The girl looked so forlorn when she went in to say goodbye that guilt washed over Megan, even though she knew Tess would be in good hands. Mrs. Gomez and Jake were both hovering over her. To Megan's surprise, though, Tess grabbed her hand and clung to it.

"You'll be back on Friday, right?" she asked for the hundredth time. Megan's reassurances never seemed to satisfy her for very long.

"It will probably be late, but yes, I will be here."

"And I can call you anytime I want?"

"Anytime. Mrs. Gomez has the number."

"What's your assistant's name again?"

"Todd."

"And he'll let me talk to you?"

"No matter what I'm doing."

Tess finally seemed satisfied with that. "I probably won't call at all, you know," she said, her bluster back.

"I know," Megan said, hiding a smile.

"You might as well go. There's a show coming on now I want to watch."

Surprised by another of those oddly maternal

twinges, Megan almost bent down to drop a kiss on Tess's cheek, but obviously Tess anticipated it. She scowled. "Don't even think about it."

Megan straightened and settled for smoothing the comforter on Tess's bed. "I'll be seeing you."

"Yeah, whatever," Tess said, her gaze already focused on the TV.

Outside the room, Megan sighed. "So much for greeting card moments."

"She does not wish to seem as if she needs you," Mrs. Gomez explained.

"I know. And it's not as if I'm any good at this."

"You are doing fine, *niña*. Nobody is ever perfect at being a parent."

"Forget perfection," Megan retorted. "I'll be content if she just survives my parenting skills."

"She will survive," Mrs. Gomez assured her. "In fact, she will thrive. You will see."

Jake offered the same opinion as he drove Megan to Laramie to catch her flight. "You're doing just fine with Tess. Now, go to New York, put everything here out of your mind for a few days and concentrate on your job. I'll hold the fort."

To her surprise, on the long trip to New York with its flight connection in Denver, Megan was able to follow Jake's advice. She finally managed to push Tess, the ranch and even Jake out of her mind. She concentrated on the latest batch of faxes from Todd. It was late when she got to her apartment, later still when she finally pushed away the last of the papers and fell into a troubled sleep.

She'd set the alarm for six, determined to use every single second she was in New York to full advantage.

Grumbling when it went off, she stumbled out of bed and into the shower. An hour later she was on her way to the office. When she walked through the door, Todd's gaping expression made all the effort worthwhile.

"Okay," she said briskly, moving into her office. "What's up first?"

Though he looked as exhausted as she felt, he efficiently ticked off a list of meetings that would have daunted anyone else. Megan merely nodded.

"Let's get to it."

"Sorry. We can't."

She stared at him. "Why not?"

"Because you are never ready for real meetings before ten. Since you were traveling yesterday, I figured you'd be late. I didn't even schedule the first one until then. Right this second you and I are the only ones in the office."

She heaved a sigh of relief. "Thank God," she murmured, folding her arms on top of her desk and resting her head on them. "Wake me at 9:59."

"Oh, no," Todd protested, nudging her arm until she lifted her head. "I can have someone in here in thirty minutes. I'm not wasting the precious few days you intend to stick around. For tomorrow and Wednesday Micah has scheduled back-to-back tapings. Five each day. That'll give us two weeks of shows, which should relieve the anxiety level for the syndicator. If you can stand the pace, I suppose we could work on this schedule every month. Can you get here every other week? Or do you intend to be back here full-time?"

"I wish I knew," Megan said. "And I don't intend

to discuss it without coffee. Lots and lots of coffee, brewed from those vanilla hazelnut beans you grind yourself.''

Todd brought the coffee, then sat down across from her, his expression worried. ''This can't go on, you know. Not indefinitely. Look at you. You're beat and this is the first time you've tried the cross-country thing. Just imagine how exhausting it will be if you try to pull it off twice a month. Top that with Micah's stress level when you're not around to rein her in and we've got trouble on the horizon.''

''I'll get used to it,'' Megan insisted. ''So will Micah.''

''What about the rest of us? What if we can't get used to it?''

She studied him intently. ''What are you telling me?''

''I'm just saying that it's not easy keeping things afloat when the boss is half a continent away. People are used to you signing off on every little thing. When you're not here, everyone starts to second-guess themselves. Either you're going to have to be a day-in, day-out presence here like always, or you're going to have to start giving people more autonomy. There are already serious cracks in the smooth-running machinery around here.''

''It's only been a little over a week. We're still working out the kinks. Except for Micah and Caitlyn, I thought it was going pretty smoothly with the faxes and e-mail.''

''Because that's what everyone wanted you to think. After all, this was a tough situation. Nobody expected you to bounce right back here after Tex's funeral. Now they suspect it could last indefinitely, and it's grating on their nerves, not being able to pop in and out of your office for a quick response. If they figure out it could turn permanent, they'll freak.''

"I can't uproot Tess," Megan said in a plea for understanding. "Not yet. You should see her, Todd. She's angry and hurting. She's already run away once and scared the living daylights out of us. She's just waiting for me to walk out and abandon her like her mother did.''

If she'd expected his sympathy, Megan would have been disappointed. He was straightforward as always. "You do what you have to do," he said, "but I just thought you ought to know how stressed people around here are beginning to feel.''

She looked him in the eye. "You, too?''

His gaze shifted away, then came back to clash with hers. He removed his glasses so she'd get the full effect.

"Me most of all," he said quietly, but emphatically. "I'm on the front line for all the flack when you're not here, but I don't have answers and I can't get them fast enough to suit anyone. It's not a position I like being in.''

Megan grinned ruefully. "I know. You're an approval junkie, just like me. To top it off, you're organized and efficient, the two skills I prize most in you. The circumstances aren't allowing you to be either one, right?''

"Exactly.''

"I'll figure out a solution, Todd. I promise you. I won't leave you hanging out there for much longer.''

"I'm sorry if I'm making things more difficult for you, but I thought you ought to know."

"You were exactly right," she assured him. "I needed to know."

And now that she did, Megan discovered that the terrible panic that had begun nagging her in Whispering Wind had followed her right back to New York. In the city where she'd once felt on top of the world, she was suddenly filled with uncertainty, and she didn't like it. Not one bit.

Even though he professed a lack of interest in actually having clients, Jake found himself spending afternoons in his office more often than not while Megan was away. Now that he was beginning to finish up the last of the little projects he'd planned for his home, he'd discovered he wasn't half as crazy about having time on his hands as he'd thought he would be. He was itching to get control of Tex's ranch, to have active, sometimes back-breaking work to do. He could have bought another, smaller ranch, but Tex's place was the only one that interested him. There were probably a dozen perverse reasons why that was so. Retaliation for Tex's misjudgment, for his outright lies to Meggie topped the list.

In the meantime, going into his office at least gave his day some sort of structure, even if all he did once he got there was to prop his feet on his desk and stare out the window. With Megan in New York, he was more restless than ever and irritable because of it. He'd been to visit Tess earlier and she'd kicked him out because of his dark mood.

"You're no fun now that *she's* not here," she had

complained. "You might as well go and moon over her somewhere else. I have better things to do."

The accuracy of the eight-year-old's assessment had been irksome. He'd left with a promise to return with ice cream later in the day.

"Cherry vanilla," she'd demanded. "With hot fudge sauce, okay?"

"It'll melt by the time I get here."

"Not if you have 'em put the hot fudge in a separate carton, then put it on when you arrive." Her gaze had narrowed. "Did you really have some kind of big-shot career in Chicago?"

"Yes. Why?"

"'Cause you don't seem to get the easiest stuff."

"I'll work on it," he'd assured her wryly.

Thinking back on the conversation, he smiled. Tess was a treasure, all right. He wondered if Megan had realized that yet. She'd been worried about Tess the other night, no doubt about it. She'd even seemed uneasy about going off and leaving her while the girl was recuperating. Had that been anything more than a sense of duty? he wondered. For Tess's sake he hoped so. He hoped that Tess was sneaking into Megan's heart just as she had into his.

Funny how his thoughts had tracked right back to Meggie again. He really needed to do something about that.

"Coffee," he muttered, lowering his feet to the floor. "Maybe a decent cup of coffee will help."

He strode across the street to the diner, which was still busy with the lunchtime crowd. He found a spot at the end of the counter closest to the register.

"What can I get for you, Jake?" Henrietta asked

as she passed out hamburgers to the customers on his left. She had a pencil tucked behind her ear and worry lines in her forehead.

"Just coffee." He studied her intently. "You okay?"

She nodded curtly. "We'll talk later." She grabbed a cup with one hand, the pot with the other, and poured. "I hear Megan's gone off to New York again."

"For the week."

"She'll be back then?"

"That's the plan."

"Well, good. I know of at least one person who must be thrilled with that."

Jake glanced up. "Who?"

"You, of course. You always did have eyes for that girl."

"That was a long time ago, Henrietta."

"Some things never change." She glanced toward a booth. "Gotta go. You holler if you decide you want something to eat."

Jake stared glumly into his coffee and tried to figure out why Megan had such a hold on him. The coffee cooled and he still had no answers. Glancing around, he realized that the diner had emptied out except for a party of four strangers in a back booth. Tourists from the looks of them, with their stiff, unfaded jeans and fancy, spotless Stetsons.

Henrietta slid onto the stool next to him, eased her feet out of her shoes and sighed. "I'm getting too dadgum old to be on my feet all day long."

"I thought you'd hired Barbara Sue Perkins to help out."

"I did," she said with a weary expression. "Unfortunately, she's already taken off more days than she's been on. Today's another one of them."

"Fire her and hire someone more reliable."

"Can't," Henrietta said succinctly. "Barbara Sue needs the work."

"But if she's not showing up…"

"It's not that she doesn't want to or that she's irresponsible. She's embarrassed." Henrietta glanced around, then lowered her voice. "That's one of the things I wanted to talk to you about. She's got bruises again. That fool she married hit her when he found out she'd gotten work. He's scared she's about to walk out on him, which truth be told, she ought to do."

Jake absorbed the information with a mounting sense of anger. "Lyle Perkins beats her?"

"Only when she needs it, to hear him tell it."

"Why the hell does she stay?"

"Low self-esteem would be my guess, but then I get that from watching all them TV talk shows."

"She ought to get out while she still can. Do they have kids?"

"A boy and a girl. It can't be easy for them seeing their mama messed up like that. Makes me want to go out there and wring Lyle's scrawny old neck myself."

"Do you think it would help if I talked to her?" Jake asked. "Or to Lyle?"

"I wouldn't go near Lyle, if I were you. It'd just make him meaner. The two of you never did get along. That's why I stay away, much as I'd like to give him what-for. But talking to Barbara Sue might be good. You could tell her what her options are.''

''Will she listen?''

The diner owner sighed. ''I doubt it, but we have to try, Jake.''

He knew the fruitlessness of talking to abuse victims before they were ready to hear their options. ''Send her to see me,'' he said anyway. ''I'll do what I can.''

Henrietta studied him intently. ''Does this mean you're actually going to start taking on a few clients?''

''I hung my shingle out there months ago,'' Jake reminded her.

''You also made it pretty clear that it was a half-hearted gesture. Till Tex came along, I thought you didn't much care if you practiced law again or not. To tell the truth, it seemed to me like you were just drifting, trying to sort out some things.''

''I think that's exactly what I've been doing,'' he admitted, acknowledging to himself that he'd been driven all these months by some sort of vague need for revenge, rather than any sort of positive purpose.

''And now?''

''Why are you asking?''

''Because folks around here need a good lawyer every now and again. They get tired of going all the way down to Laramie to get legal advice. I'd send 'em your way if I thought you wanted the work.''

''Who else besides Barbara Sue?'' he asked, realizing that she had only been a trial balloon Henrietta had used to test the waters.

''That Morgan girl over at the beauty shop needs

some advice. Josh Wilson is her landlord and he's giving her fits. Won't fix things and charges an arm and a leg for that pitiful house he rents to her and her boy.''

The story was one that was all too familiar to Jake. He'd lived it. ''Tell her to come see me,'' Jake said tightly. Taking Josh Wilson to court would be a pleasure. He'd do it for nothing but the satisfaction. ''Anyone else?''

Henrietta grinned. ''I suppose that's enough for today. I wouldn't want you to get overworked after such a long layoff.''

''You're too good to me.''

''Well, I just think it's a shame to waste all that education of yours, especially when there are folks nearby who could benefit from it.''

''I suppose you know someone who needs a job as a secretary, too.''

She grinned. ''I'll think on it. I imagine I could come up with a name or two.''

''I'm sure you can.'' He dropped a dollar bill on the counter for the coffee. ''Remind me to put a coffeepot in my office so I can steer clear of here.''

''The coffee might be as good, but you'd miss the company,'' Henrietta retorted.

Yes, he conceded, he would at that.

12

The tension in the air was palpable. Megan had taped four of the five shows scheduled for production on Tuesday, but it was clear to everyone that her energy was flagging. It was also evident that everyone's patience had been stretched to the limits.

"Maybe we should give it up for the day," Todd said, regarding her worriedly.

"Don't be ridiculous," Micah objected, scowling at him. "It's a half-hour show, not *Gone With the Wind*. She can do it."

Megan cut in before a full-blown argument between the two could erupt. "It's okay, Todd. I'd rather get it over with than try to cram it into tomorrow's schedule or bring the crew back on Thursday."

Micah shot a look of triumph in Todd's direction, then went off to find Kenny Hawkins, the director.

"That woman—" Todd began.

"Is doing her job," Megan filled in. Micah's edgy nervousness had been obvious to the whole production crew all day. Megan had spent too much time smoothing ruffled feathers.

"Settle down," she instructed Todd gently. "Is all the gift wrap here? I want to show viewers how to make their packages every bit as personal and unique as the gifts they're giving."

"Over there," Todd said, pointing toward the display being wheeled onto the set. "Everything you asked for."

His cell phone rang. "Yes?" His expression turned grim. "Now's not a good time." He paused, then sighed heavily. "Okay, yes, she's right here."

Turning to Megan, he mouthed, "Tess."

Megan took the phone and tried to inject a pleased note into her voice. "Hey, Tess, how are you?"

"He didn't want to let me talk to you," Tess accused.

"It's just that we're right in the middle of taping some shows."

"You said—"

"I know, Tess. I'm here now. What's up? Everything okay back there?"

"When are you coming back?"

Megan had told her at least a hundred times before she'd left and a dozen more since. "On Friday night," she said once more, clinging to her patience by a thread. "It'll probably be late, though."

"Can I wait up?"

"No. You need your sleep. I'll see you first thing Saturday morning. We'll do something special."

"What?"

Megan couldn't think of anything to save her soul. "Whatever you want."

"Can we go to a movie?"

The last thing Megan wanted to do after flying home and making the drive from Laramie was to turn around and drive right back there. "If that's what you want," she said anyway.

"Good. I'll tell Jake. He said you wouldn't go for it, 'cause you'd be too tired."

If only he'd told her that he'd tried to get her off the hook, she thought wearily. "Look, sweetie, I've got to run. The crew's ready to go."

"Yeah, okay. I didn't have anything else to say, anyway."

"Stay off that ankle," Megan admonished. "I'll talk to you tonight."

"Whatever."

Megan handed Todd's phone back to him, then drew in a deep breath. Her gaze skimmed across the set to confirm that everything for the gift-wrapping segment was in place—tissue paper, pretty little decorative boxes in various shapes and sizes, elegant ribbons.

"Looks good to go to me," she called over to the director. "Are you guys ready?"

Kenny, the most unflappable man she'd ever met, nodded. He'd spent most of the day staying out of Micah's path. "Let's do it."

Megan started toward the set, only to have Todd snag her wrist.

"You might need this," he said lightly, reattaching the portable mike to her collar. "Hey, Ken, have them do a sound check to make sure this is positioned okay."

"Will do." He signaled to Megan. "We're rolling. In five, four, three, two…" He pointed to her.

"Good morning, everyone. Today we're going to

talk about special occasions and how to make the gifts you give memorable.''

"Cut,'' Ken called over the intro. "Sorry, Megan.''

"What is it?''

"Weren't you supposed to change between episodes? That's the same outfit you had on for the last show.''

"Damn,'' she muttered, stripping off the mike and racing for her dressing room to slip into yet another outfit, this time chocolate brown linen slacks and a cream silk blouse with some simple, chunky gold jewelry. It had all been chosen and laid out ahead of time. She'd just flat-out forgotten to change.

"My fault,'' Todd said, meeting her at the door. "I stopped you on the way to the dressing room, Micah interrupted us and then Tess called.''

"Forget about it. I'm distracted, too.'' She ran a brush through her hair, then reached out a hand. "Have you got the mike?''

"Right here.''

She was back on the set in less than five minutes. Ken's gaze skimmed over her before he nodded in satisfaction. "Perfect. Let's do it, people.''

It took two horrible hours to get the half-hour show done to everyone's satisfaction. Micah seemed determined to reshoot everything until it was perfect. It was as if she considered this her one shot at a daytime Emmy. Megan finally called a halt.

"Micah, it's not going to get any better than this. If anything, it'll just get worse because none of us can see straight.''

The producer shrugged. "Whatever. It's your show.'' With that she turned and left the studio.

Megan stared after her, then shook her head.

It was going on midnight by the time she was able to leave. On her way out she promised Kenny she'd be there by 10:00 a.m. to do it all again—five more shows back-to-back. The pace was far more grueling than she'd ever imagined. She was used to doing two shows a day for three days one week and two days the following week to pick up the total of ten needed for a two-week run. With everyone rested and prepared, things ran smoothly ninety percent of the time. Even the other ten percent didn't rise to the level of stress or mistakes that today's tapings had induced.

Worse, as exhausted as she was, she knew she had to do it all over again the next day.

By the end of Wednesday, Megan had absolutely no idea whether she'd even been coherent. In fact, she'd had to redo a fruit tart twice because she'd forgotten to put the fruit into the prebaked crust the first time and had dumped it onto a glass pie plate lined with raw dough. She was too much of a perfectionist to simply laugh it off and move on.

By the time she'd ended the segment, she'd made a mental vow to do nothing more complicated than open canned soup ever again. Of course, that would take the edge off her reputation for whipping up the extraordinary with little effort.

Once again, Micah had left in an apparent huff, though Megan hadn't actually seen her do so. Megan was too tired to worry about it. She was still in her dressing room with her feet propped up when Todd walked in without bothering to knock. She barely glanced up.

"I thought you'd gone home hours ago," she mur-

mured as he moved behind her and began massaging
her shoulders. It was another of the skills she admired
in him. The man had incredibly clever hands. "God,
that's wonderful." Almost as good as Jake's touch,
but without the edge of sensuality.

"We live to serve," he muttered. He'd long since
stripped away his tie and rolled up his sleeves, ruining
the sartorial perfection in which he normally prided
himself.

"Why are you still here? Didn't I tell you to go?"

"You did, but I wasn't about to leave you here
without protection."

"Protection from what?"

"Those exhausted people out there. As tired as
they are, they'd have let just about anything on the
air to get the taping over with. I nominated myself to
do quality control, since Micah cut out before the last
taping."

Megan glanced up. "Before the last show? Are you
sure? I thought she was in the booth."

"Nope. I watched her walk out the door. She didn't
say a word to anybody. Something's up with her, but
I can't get a handle on it."

"Stress?" Megan suggested.

"Nope. It's more than that. She's been in a snit
ever since you took off for Wyoming."

"She's felt out of the loop," Megan reminded him.
"We talked about it."

"Well, you're here now and she could be very
much in the loop, if she'd just stick around and do
her job."

"Well, I'm not going to get into it with her yet.
We're all under too much pressure. Let's keep an eye

on the situation. If things don't improve, I'll handle it.''

"I can talk to her," Todd offered.

"Thanks, but she already resents the fact that so many of her marching orders come via you. I'll speak to her directly," Megan said, then yawned. "What's on the agenda for tomorrow?"

"Nothing till noon. I cancelled all your morning appointments. You have lunch with Peter at one, a meeting with Caitlin about the magazine's next cover design at three, a TV interview at five. It's a light day."

"Why am I having lunch with Peter?"

"You tell me. He called. I scheduled it. I assumed it was social."

Megan sighed. Peter probably thought the same thing. He'd been trying for years to take on a more important—more personal—role in her life. She had to give him points for persistence. If he weren't such a fine, totally trustworthy accountant, it would have been a whole lot easier to make it clear that she wasn't interested.

Todd regarded her quizzically. "Should I cancel lunch?"

"No. I have to eat and there's worse company to have than Peter's."

"Now those are the words a man waits a lifetime to hear," he retorted lightly. "Why don't you cut him loose and put him out of his misery?"

"Who'd deal with my finances?"

"I can show you **pages** of classifieds in the phone book. Manhattan's a big place. The world's financial markets are all represented here. I'll just bet there's another qualified accountant in the city.''

Megan hated change, even when she knew it was time. She also feared putting her finances into the hands of someone she didn't know with absolute certainty was honest. Tex had always handled every last detail of his own bookkeeping and preached to her to do the same. She hadn't gone that far, but once she'd found Peter, she'd uttered a sigh of relief and considered herself in good hands.

Peter's pursuit of a relationship with her had muddied the waters. Maybe she could extricate herself from that without losing their business relationship, but it was doubtful. She would always wonder if he harbored some secret grudge over the rejection, if he'd take out his revenge on her books. Nope, better to make a clean break of it.

''I'll think about it,'' she said at last. ''Get some names for me.''

''They'll be on your desk in the morning. Now go home and get some sleep. You have bags under your eyes.''

''Thank you for sharing that with me.''

He grinned. ''My pleasure.''

''It doesn't matter, you know. There's no taping tomorrow.''

''Just that TV interview,'' he reminded her. ''And your date.''

''Maybe the bags will scare Peter off.''

''Doubtful. If the man weren't totally smitten and oblivious, he'd have figured out by now that you're only interested in his calculator.''

When she would have retorted, he held up a hand and backed off. "I'm outta here. See you tomorrow."

"Good night, Todd."

Left alone, Megan gathered up her papers and jammed them into her briefcase. She shoveled an assortment of jars and tubes into her makeup bag and left the studio. Outside, a limo was waiting to whisk her to her apartment. The ride was less than ten minutes long, but the service was an extravagance she could afford. On rainy nights, when taxis vanished from Manhattan streets, it more than paid for itself.

"Good night, Ms. O'Rourke," the driver said as he held the door for her in front of her building. "You have a pleasant evening."

"You, too, Bill. I'll see you on Friday."

"Right. What time is your flight?"

"Six-thirty."

"Shall I pick you up here or at your office?"

"The office, I think. If that changes, I'll call."

Upstairs, she found a dozen messages on her answering machine. Her first instinct was to ignore them. Then she thought of Tess and punched the play button.

Most were from friends, calling to offer sympathy over Tex, inviting her to dinner, suggesting lunch. Buried among them, though, was one from Jake.

"I talked to that protective assistant of yours today. He didn't seem inclined to give me your itinerary for Friday. If you'll tell him I have security clearance or call me back yourself, I'll pick you up at the airport. I hear Tess conned you into promising a movie for Saturday. Guess you're already turning into one of those guilt-ridden moms who overcompensates for her absences.''

Moms? Megan stopped the machine and considered the word. She'd barely grown used to the idea of being Tess's legal guardian, but a mom? Her? She supposed that's what her new role amounted to, but hearing Jake express it was a shock just the same. The very thought made her tremble.

How could she be anyone's mother, when she'd never had an example? She tried to remember what it had been like when she'd lived with Sarah O'Rourke, but the memories—even the good ones—had faded. She could remember the scent of chocolate chip cookies baking in the oven, but that memory had been reinforced by Mrs. Gomez over time. Now it wasn't clear whether the smell brought back memories of her mother or the housekeeper who'd become her surrogate mom.

Of course, a case could be made that Megan knew precisely what not to do as a mother. She knew not to run off and abandon an impressionable kid. It wasn't exactly an inspirational guideline, but it would do for a start. Beyond that, she and Tess would just have to muddle through.

With that in mind, Megan reached for the phone and dialed Todd's number. True to form, he responded at once, sounding as alert as he did at midmorning.

"Can you clear my schedule for tomorrow and Friday?"

"What? Why?"

"I'm going home," she said, making it clear that

it wasn't open for discussion. "Do whatever it takes to make that happen."

"You're the boss," he said, but there was an unmistakable edge of disapproval in his tone.

"Yes," she said decisively. "Yes, I am. I'll call you from the plane tomorrow."

"I'll be looking forward to it," he said in a way that suggested he might have more to say on the subject when he knew she was trapped in a plane several thousand feet in the air.

"You're a wonder, Todd."

"An *expensive* wonder," he suggested.

Megan laughed. "I'll take that into account when we talk tomorrow."

"We're talking bonuses, a promotion and who knows what else," he warned.

"Not a problem," she assured him.

When she'd hung up, she began to consider just what it would take to persuade the ultimate New York whiz kid that he'd always wanted to be a cowboy.

"She's coming home *early*?" Tess repeated Jake's words, her expression torn between amazement and confusion. "How come? Am I in trouble or something?"

"As far as I know, she just decided to cut her schedule in New York short and come back a day early," he told Tess. "She called from the plane an hour ago."

"From the plane? Doesn't that, like, cost an arm and a leg?"

"I doubt she worried about that," Jake said dryly. "Now, the question is, do you want to ride to Laramie with me to pick her up? We could maybe catch that movie you're so gung ho to see while we're there.''

Tess's eyes widened. "Really? You mean it?" Then her expression fell. "Won't Megan be mad if I'm there? She'll figure if I'm fixed up enough to come to Laramie, then I should be in school. Besides, you said she was gonna be tired when she got back.''

"This was her idea," Jake assured Tess.

The girl seemed unwilling to accept the offer as the thoughtful gesture it was. "Probably just 'cause it saves her from having to go back on Saturday," she said.

"Maybe she wanted to do something nice for you, since you've been cooped up in the house for a few days," Jake suggested. "Now, do you want to go or not?"

Her expression brightened at last. "Don't get all worked up. I'll be ready in five minutes," she said, bouncing out of bed and hobbling unsteadily toward the bathroom.

"Slow down," he warned. "Don't go spraining the other ankle.''

"You were the one in such a hurry," she reminded him.

He chuckled at the defiant tone, always ready, always just below the surface. But even so, it couldn't undercut the excitement threading through her voice. To his astonishment, he thought he'd heard the same tone in Megan's voice.

"Brush your teeth," he called after Tess.

"I know better than to go out with doggie breath," she shouted right back. "How about you? Did you use that minty stuff so you can give Megan a big ol' kiss when she gets off the plane?''

"Don't you worry about what I plan to do when Megan gets off the plane. Keep bugging me and you'll wait in the car.''

She poked her head out of the bathroom. "No way. I ain't never been inside an airport before. I want to see the planes.''

Jake stopped in his tracks. "You've never seen a plane?''

"In the sky. Not up close.''

He regarded her intently. "Is that why you were so dead set against going to New York? Because you didn't want to fly?''

She stared back at him belligerently. "Are you saying I'm scared?''

"It wouldn't be such a terrible thing to admit. Lots of people who've never flown are uneasy about it. So are some who do it all the time.''

"Like you?''

"Actually, I like to fly," he said, then grinned. "I just like being on the ground and in control more.'' Before she could guess his intentions, he scooped her up and carried her down the stairs.

"I can walk, blast it.''

"I know you can, but we'll get going a lot faster this way.''

Once they were settled in the car and headed to Laramie, he glanced over at Tess. "You didn't give me a straight answer before. Did you refuse Megan's offer to take you to New York because you didn't want to fly?''

"Maybe that was part of it,'' she admitted, staring

out the window rather than at him. "But mostly I just didn't want to leave here."

Jake released a breath he didn't realize he'd been holding. If Tess's only reservation about going to New York had been a fear of flying, it would be all too easily overcome. Megan would whip her away from Whispering Wind in a heartbeat. He knew it was selfish, knew it was wrong, but he was glad it was more than that.

"You really love Tex's ranch, don't you?"

"It's okay," she said with feigned indifference, then finally turned to face him. Unshed tears made her eyes seem huge. "It was better when Tex was there."

"Oh, baby, I'm sure it was."

"Megan could turn out to be okay, I guess, as long as she doesn't make me do all that prissy stuff she does on her show."

"She'll be great," he said, making a promise he had no way of keeping.

"You'd say that if she locked me in a closet every night."

"I would not," he denied.

"You think she's perfect."

"I think she's special," he corrected. "There's a difference."

"Yeah, well, you couldn't prove it by me."

"You'll see."

"You know what Tex used to say?" she asked, regarding him slyly.

"What?"

"That once the sale is made, a man should know enough to shut up."

Jake held back a laugh. "And you think that applies here?"

"Oh, yeah. You are downright pitiful."

"I'll try to contain my enthusiasm in the future."

She gave a little nod. "Playing hard-to-get works. I've seen it in the movies."

"I'll keep that in mind," he said with a shake of his head. He really was pitiful. He was actually hanging on the advice of an eight-year-old. But the truth was, maybe hard-to-get wouldn't be such a bad idea.

13

There was something on Megan's mind. Jake watched her during the movie and would have bet his life's savings that she had no idea what the story was about or even who was starring in it. She'd been the same way on the drive from the airport into town. Her gaze had been focused on the scenery as if she'd never seen Laramie before. And all during dinner before the movie, she'd made only a cursory attempt at conversation, responding to Tess with distracted murmurs of agreement.

Had something gone wrong in New York? he wondered, watching her. Was she now convinced that she couldn't commute and that Tess would simply have to make the move east? Or was Megan considering abandoning Tess, after all? He didn't buy that last possibility. He was pretty sure she'd made a legal—if not an emotional—commitment to keeping Tess. So what the devil was on her mind?

Jake realized when they were finally in the car heading back toward Whispering Wind that he'd been no more aware of the movie than Megan had. Tess's excited attempts to discuss what they'd seen drew blank stares from both him and Megan.

"Geez-oh-flip, did you guys sleep through the

whole thing?'' she grumbled. "I might as well have gone by myself."

"Sorry, sweetie," Megan said, reaching into the back seat to give her hand a squeeze. "I guess I was distracted. If you enjoyed it, that's all that matters."

"It was totally awesome," Tess declared, and proceeded to explain the action plot in mind-numbing detail.

"Sounds spectacular," Jake said, trying to muster up some enthusiasm.

"Like you give a rat's behind," Tess retorted. "You weren't paying any attention, either, not then or just now."

"Of course I was. I heard everything you said," Jake protested.

"Okay. Who played that teeny-tiny part on the elevator when the bad guys tried to sneak into that skyscraper and blow it up?" Tess challenged.

Megan regarded him with amusement. "Yes, Jake, who was that?"

"Lauren Bacall," he guessed wildly.

"It was a guy," Tess said with disgust. "Geez-oh-flip, what is wrong with you?"

"I must have nodded off in that part."

"I just told you not ten minutes ago," Tess reminded him.

"Oh. Tell me again."

"Forget it. I'm going to sleep. Obviously you two are way ahead of me on naps."

After they'd driven another few miles, Jake glanced into the rearview mirror. Tess had stretched out across the back seat. He glanced over at Megan.

"Everything okay?"

"Fine," she said, without meeting his gaze.

"How was your trip?"

"Okay."

"You're back a day early. How come?"

"I taped the shows and took care of the most critical things. After I looked over my schedule, I decided I could handle the rest from out here."

Despite her responses, Jake wasn't buying the idea that everything had gone smoothly. Something had happened. "The tapings went okay?" he asked, convinced her mood must have something to do with those.

She shrugged. "It's hard to tell at the pace we were shooting them. Todd's going to overnight the finished tapes so I can take a look. We crammed a lot of work into a little bit of time. I just pray it doesn't look rushed."

He realized he had no idea just what her work schedule must be like. "How many did you do?"

"Ten."

He stared incredulously. "Ten shows in three days?"

"In two days, actually. I spent Monday in the office, catching up on everything there."

"Sweet heaven! No wonder you were practically comatose in the movie. I'm surprised you didn't fall sound asleep."

She gave him a weary smile. "I slept on the plane."

"Megan, how long do you think you can keep this up?"

"As long as I have to, I suppose. I'll get used to it."

He noticed she didn't sound nearly as confident as she had the last time the subject had come up. He thought of the property he'd bought a few days earlier and wondered if now was the time to bring it up again.

"Wouldn't it be easier to do the tapings here?" he probed.

"Easier, but not terribly practical," she said. "We'd have to find facilities, bring the crew out here, find housing. I can't just uproot all those people. Whispering Wind isn't exactly loaded with four-star hotels, and Laramie's too far away to be practical."

"Couldn't you hire people here, or maybe out of Chicago?"

"Absolutely not," she said at once. "I took a lot of time putting together a great team to do the show. I can't just say, 'Sorry, guys. It's all over. I'm going to do the show in Wyoming and you're out of work.'"

"Then give them the option of coming here," he suggested. "Let it be their decision."

She scowled at him. "Why are you pushing this so hard?"

"Because it's plain to me that it's not working this way," he said.

"It's been one trip, Jake. Naturally there are adjustments to be made. I'll make them," she said defensively, then sighed. "I am thinking of bringing Todd out here for a while."

"Your assistant, right?" he said, thinking of the brisk, protective man he'd spoken to the day before.

She nodded. "It'll be a hard sell, though. Todd isn't exactly into wide-open spaces. I can't imagine what he'll have to say when he discovers that Whispering Wind doesn't have a sushi bar."

"To our credit, if you ask me," Jake said.

"What's sushi?" Tess asked sleepily from the back seat.

"Raw fish," Jake said.

"Oh, yuck."

"My sentiments exactly," he agreed.

"Don't knock it till you've tried it," Megan admonished Tess, then turned to Jake. "And you stop trying to influence her. Let her try it and reach her own conclusions."

"She's the one who said it sounded yucky," Jake protested, grinning at Tess in the rearview mirror. "Didn't you?"

"Uh-huh," she murmured, clearly half-asleep again.

"Okay, so Todd will miss his sushi. Anything else?"

"Oh, yes. Add in the lack of an upscale men's store and he'll probably be traumatized. Todd does like his designer clothes."

"I'll explain to him about mail order, in case he's never heard of the concept," Jake promised.

"I'll ask you again, what's your stake in this? And don't tell me you're worried about the strain it's putting on me. That's hogwash."

He shrugged off the accusation. "Okay, I'll admit it. I don't give a damn what you do. I'm not the least bit worried about you. I'm just in it for the fun of hassling you."

Megan's scowl deepened. "I'm not buying that, either."

"Then you tell me what I'm up to, since you're such an expert on my motivations."

"You want me to use that industrial park for some reason," she said, her expression thoughtful as she studied him. "It can't be because you care about the economy of Whispering Wind, so it must mean there's some way you'll benefit from it."

Her gaze narrowed. "You bought it, didn't you? You bought that property and you're looking to make a killing on it."

He was impressed. She'd always had great powers of deductive reasoning. "Well, you're half-right, anyway. I did buy it, but not for the reason you think. I'll loan it to you rent free on a temporary basis, if that's what it takes to prove that my intentions are honorable. You turn it into a first-rate production facility and we'll call it even, if you decide to pull out later."

Megan seemed thrown by the offer. "Why would you do that?" She followed the direction of his gaze, obviously saw his quick glance into the rearview mirror. "Ah, I think I get it. For Tess, of course."

He nodded, then called Tess's name quietly. Only when she didn't respond, indicating that she'd finally fallen soundly asleep, did he say any more. "Tess wants to stay right here, in Tex's home. If I can see to it that that happens, I'll do it."

"You amaze me."

"Why?"

"I never figured you for a softie."

He glanced at her. "Don't be fooled, darlin'. I can play tough when the circumstances call for it. Do anything to hurt that child and you'll see."

"What is this bond between the two of you?"

"Maybe I just like her. She's a good kid."

"Try again."

"You know me so well. Why do you think it is?"

Megan hesitated only briefly. "You identify with her, don't you?" she said slowly. "You remember when times were tough for you, when you didn't have a mom you could count on."

"And?" he taunted.

She regarded him with less certainty. "There's more?"

"Of course."

"Tell me."

"I can also remember a time when the only person in the world I had to count on was you," he said quietly. "I don't want Tess to be let down the way I was."

Megan looked as stunned as if he'd slapped her. For a moment, he almost regretted bringing her betrayal up one more time, but the sad truth was it was at the core of everything that had happened between them. He might be over the bitterness and anger, but clearly on some level, as painful as it was for him to acknowledge and for her to hear, he still didn't trust her to do the right thing. Maybe he never would. Trust was a fragile bond. It didn't take much to sever it forever.

Unfortunately, that didn't seem to have stopped him from wanting her.

After her conversation with Jake, Megan would have preferred going to a public hanging over going with him and Tess to the postponed dinner at Peggy's on Saturday night. However, she refused to cancel on her friend again. She knew Peggy had gone to a lot of trouble. The last time they'd talked, she'd worriedly gone over the menu to make sure that she was having dishes Megan liked.

"With all that fancy stuff you fix on TV, I wasn't sure if you'd eat plain old barbecue anymore," she'd explained.

"It's been ages since I've had really good barbecue," Megan insisted. "I'd love it."

Peggy's sigh of relief was audible. "Good. Then that's what we'll have. I'll see you guys at six. Johnny likes to eat early, because his day starts at the crack of dawn. You probably prefer stylishly late, but—"

Megan had cut her off. "Six is just fine. I know what ranch schedules are like."

No, Megan thought, she couldn't back out on Peggy now. It would be a slap in the face. Besides, Tess was looking forward to it. She'd been on the phone off and on all day with Peggy's daughter, deciding what CDs to bring along. Maybe Jake would have the good grace to call and cancel, but it was almost time to leave and Megan hadn't heard from him yet. Obviously he intended to stick it out, too, probably just to irritate her.

Megan's wardrobe no longer ran to denims and cotton. She had to search long and hard to find an outfit that was casual enough for the occasion. She didn't want anyone to think she was putting on airs, flashing around in fancy clothes and jewelry just to prove what a big success she'd become.

She finally settled for the same chocolate-brown linen slacks she'd worn for one of the tapings and a tweedy hand-knit sweater in shades of orange, brown and rust. Though the sweater was from a designer collection, anyone who was adept with knitting needles could have recreated it. She knew, because she'd demonstrated the pattern on her show a month back. If she could master it with her clumsy fingers, anyone could.

When Jake arrived at five-thirty, he surveyed her with such thoroughly masculine approval that it brought heat flooding to her cheeks. She was pretty sure they had to be one shade brighter than the rust yarn in her sweater. How could he make it so clear one minute that he hadn't forgiven her and then look at her as if he wanted to devour her the next? Of course, no one had ever said the brain and the libido were directly linked.

"Is Tess ready?" he asked.

Megan merely nodded, worried that any words she spoke would come out sounding vaguely breathless. She refused to give him that satisfaction after the painful note on which they'd parted.

"Shall I go get her?" Jake asked, regarding her with knowing amusement.

"No, I will," she said, and fled.

At the top of the stairs, as she paused to catch her breath, literally and figuratively, Tess emerged from her room.

"Did I hear Jake?"

"He's downstairs."

Tess regarded her solemnly. "You okay? You look kinda funny."

"I'm fine."

"You guys didn't fight again, did you?"

"Why on earth would Jake and I fight?"

"Beats me, but you seem to be pretty good at it. You were talking and laughing when I went to sleep in the car the other night. When I woke up, there was practically frost on the windshield."

Because it seemed pointless to continue the denial, Megan shrugged. "Old habits, I suppose."

"I thought you used to be friends."

"Sometimes even friends have disagreements."

"Is that what happened with you and Jake? You had a fight on the way home? Was it about me?"

Megan regarded her curiously. "Why are you so interested in this?"

Tess shrugged. "No reason."

"I'm not buying that."

"I just thought it might be okay if you and Jake…" She shrugged. "You know."

Megan had a terrible sinking feeling that she did know. "No, sweetie, nothing's going to happen between Jake and me."

"Why not?"

"It's just not, okay? Now let's get going before we're late."

Tess gave up with obvious reluctance and trailed downstairs after Megan. Jake gave them a troubled look.

"Everything okay?"

"Let's go," Tess said, bolting past him and out the door.

Jake turned to Megan. "What just happened here?"

"Tess had some crazy idea in her head. When I told her she was wrong, she was disappointed."

A knowing expression stole across Jake's face. "About you and me?"

"Why would you say that?"

"Believe me, I know all about being a neglected kid and looking for a happy ending."

"Well, I told her she was wrong, that nothing was going to happen between you and me except regular disagreements."

Jake grinned. "Did you, now?" He reached over and deliberately trailed a finger along her cheek. "Are you so sure about that?"

Megan slapped his hand away, because his touch *had* set off all sorts of old yearnings. "I'm sure," she insisted.

"Good."

The response startled her. "Good? What do you mean, good?"

"It's just going to be that much more fun proving you wrong."

"Jake, this isn't a game. You've made it plain how you feel about me because of what happened years ago. I don't blame you, but let's not muddy the waters with sex."

"Sweetheart, life is a game. If you don't take chances, you're not really living. You ought to know that better than anyone. Who would have thought a small-town girl from Wyoming could slip into New York, take a failing magazine and turn it into a publishing wonder? Who would have thought that a woman who used to burn oatmeal would become the gourmet guru of society?"

"Did it ever occur to you that I burned oatmeal

because I hated it, not because I didn't know how to cook?"

"I think you're deliberately missing my point."

"Which is?"

"That none of us know what's around the next corner. You can swear up and down that there's nothing between us. You can even fool yourself into thinking that there never was and never will be a connection—" his gaze locked with hers "—but I can prove you wrong."

Megan swallowed hard under that intense gaze. "How?"

"A kiss," he said softly. "Just one kiss."

"See, you're back to sex again."

"Are you going to accept the dare or not? I say you're chicken."

Desperate to prove him wrong, she said, "Okay, go ahead. One kiss. I dare you."

He stepped closer, crowding her, making her aware of every masculine inch of him, of the heat radiating from him. One hand circled her neck. His gaze—hot enough to forge steel—settled on her lips.

And, then...*nothing*. He didn't touch her mouth with his, didn't slide those clever fingers into her hair or skim his knuckles along her jaw. He simply waited, and all the while Megan could feel her resistance slipping away, could feel the slow, inevitable buildup of yearning, the coiling of tension in her belly. Another few seconds and she would be kissing him with the kind of desperate hunger that would more than prove his point.

The corners of his mouth tilted up in a knowing little smile, as if he'd read her mind, guessed her deepest secrets. He took a step away, released her. When she almost staggered backward, his grin widened.

"See, darlin'," he said with a touch of purely male arrogance. "It doesn't even take a kiss, merely the anticipation. Now imagine what would happen if my mouth actually covered yours, if my tongue slid inside."

Megan's knees went weak just listening to him. She found her reaction—the whole game, for that matter—to be infuriating. She hated this power he had over her, hated the weakness in herself that gave it to him.

But that didn't stop her from wanting him, and the knowledge of that scared the living daylights out of her.

14

Peggy had obviously read every last chapter of Megan's books, as well as every issue of her magazine. Even though she'd invited them for a barbecue, her table was set formally with a clever fall flower and leaf arrangement in the center. More flowers, displayed in every room, brought the outdoors in. Not a speck of dust would have dared to land on the highly polished furniture. Megan had a feeling that all three of her children had been locked upstairs all day to keep order in the downstairs rooms. It had never looked like this when she and Peggy had been kids.

"The house looks wonderful," Megan said, feeling nostalgic just stepping inside the familiar rooms.

"It's still the same old place," Peggy said, downplaying her efforts. "Johnny and I have painted a little here and there and refinished the floors, that's all."

Still wearing his work clothes, his blond hair mashed down from his hat, Johnny came in just in time to hear the last.

"She's had me working like a fool around here for the past week," he grumbled, though he gave his wife an affectionate peck on the cheek. "If you're coming over again, Megan, give me some warning so I can get out of town."

Peggy scowled at him. "It's not as if the house didn't need some work. We'd been talking about it forever."

Even though the dissension between the two was lighthearted enough, it made Megan uncomfortable. Before she could think of anything to say, Jake stepped in.

"These floors must have been a bear to do," he said to Johnny. "Mind telling me what you did to restore them? I'd like to do some work on the floors over at my place."

"Yeah, I heard you'd bought the old Harper house," Johnny said. "I thought a hot-shot lawyer would want someplace bigger."

Jake didn't take offense. "It suits me," he said simply. "I've enjoyed working with my hands."

Megan was fascinated by the exchange. For the first time she realized she had no idea at all where Jake had been living since coming back to town. She'd seen the office, knew he wanted Tex's ranch, but obviously he had to be staying someplace other than that tumbledown shack his mother used to rent from Josh Wilson. Megan remembered the Harper house. It had been next door to his mother's house, a safe haven for Jake when things had gotten too difficult at home. She wasn't all that surprised that he had bought it, but she couldn't help wondering what he had done with it.

For the moment, though, she was simply grateful that he'd distracted Johnny. The two of them went off to look at floor polish and sanders. No doubt they would wind up with more guy talk about hardware and tools. Peggy sighed, obviously also relieved that they were gone.

"I'm sorry. I thought Johnny would get back sooner and have time to clean up. I'd have told him to do it now, but he'd have bitten my head off. Some days I can't say anything right."

"Don't be silly," Megan protested. "Just promise me that the next time you invite me over you won't go to so much trouble. It's the company that's important, not the decor."

"It's not like you're just anybody," Peggy countered. "Look at what you do for a living. You must live in this perfect place with the latest of everything. Besides, it's been so long since you've been here and you're such a celebrity now, I just wanted things to look nice at least, even if we couldn't go out and buy the latest furniture."

"Well, everything looks wonderful. More important, it takes me back to when we were kids. Now what can I do to help with dinner?"

"Nothing," Peggy said sharply, then winced. "Sorry. Everything's under control. Would you like a drink? I think I'll have a glass of wine."

"Wine would be lovely," Megan agreed, following Peggy into the cheerful kitchen with its bright yellow curtains and sparkling white appliances and countertops. The refrigerator looked suspiciously new and state-of-the-art, too. In fact, it was the exact one Megan had on the set of her TV show.

Her expression still tense, Peggy reached for a wineglass and filled it with an expensive chardonnay before handing it to Megan. She grabbed her own half-filled glass from the counter and added more wine.

"To you being back in Whispering Wind," Peggy said, touching her glass to Megan's. "Welcome home."

"To old friends," Megan added, watching worriedly as Peggy drank half her wine in one long swallow. Only after that did the lines in her forehead ease. Uncertain whether she had any right to ask anything so personal, Megan couldn't seem to stop herself from touching Peggy's arm. "Is everything okay?"

Peggy regarded her with eyes that were far too bright. "Of course. What could possibly be wrong? I'm married to the man of my dreams, I have three wonderful kids and my best friend's back home at last."

Megan let the subject drop, because it was obvious that was what Peggy wanted, but she couldn't help watching her and Johnny intently for the rest of the evening. Thanks mostly to Jake's skillful handling of Johnny, dinner went smoothly enough. The swirling undercurrents of tension never got a chance to take over. The kids were polite and well-mannered. Even Tess seemed subdued. Jake filled all of the awkward silences, praising Peggy's cooking, questioning Johnny about the ranch. Still, by the time the meal was over, Megan was so tense her shoulders ached. She couldn't wait to make her escape.

Jake must have known going in that something was wrong in the Barkely household, but he hadn't prepared her. She couldn't ask him about it in the car with Tess listening, but the very second Tess had gone off to bed, she turned on him.

"Okay, what do you know that I don't?"

"About?"

"Peggy and Johnny. There would have been full-scale warfare over there tonight if you hadn't interceded."

"Maybe they were just having a bad night. It happens," he said, shrugging it off.

Megan wasn't buying it. "Peggy was trying too hard and drinking too much. Johnny was sniping at her, even when he tried to make it sound as if he was only teasing. I think he deliberately came in late, just so he wouldn't have time to clean up for dinner, because he knew it would make her crazy. Is their marriage in trouble? Peggy made it sound as if they were ecstatically happy the first time she came to see me."

"Megan, this is none of my business—or yours, for that matter."

"She's my best friend."

"She *was* your best friend. A lot has gone on since you've been away."

Irritated by the dig, Megan wasn't about to let the subject go. It was true she and Peggy hadn't stayed in touch, but she still cared about her and hated to see her hurting. Maybe she could help.

"Okay," she said quietly. "You're right. There are a lot of things I don't know about. Fill me in."

"What makes you think I know anything about Peggy and Johnny's marriage? Maybe I'm just a nice guy who spotted a bit of tension and tried to help out."

Megan ignored the disingenuous response. "Is it her drinking? Is she an alcoholic?"

"She had a few glasses of wine at a dinner party,"

Jake said dismissively. "I've known people who could drink the whole bottle on a special occasion. It didn't make them a drunk. Believe me, I know all about alcoholics, Megan. I lived with one. You don't have a clue."

"Why are you getting mad at me?"

"Because you're poking and prodding me for information that I don't have and wouldn't share if I did. If you want to know what's going on over there, then the people to talk to are Peggy and Johnny."

She didn't understand his anger. "Jake, I just want to help."

"Obviously Peggy went out of her way tonight to make a good impression on you. She wants you to think her life is perfect. Let it go at that. Maybe the best way to help her is to leave it alone unless she comes to you for advice."

"Then she does need advice," Megan said.

Jake shook his head. "In all the years I've known you, there's only been one surefire way to shut you up," he said, just before settling his mouth firmly over hers.

The earlier promise of that withheld kiss exploded through her, stealing breath and thought. His lips were wickedly clever in silencing her and stirring her senses at the same time. His tongue—well, whole volumes could have been written about *that* sensual assault. Her skin burned under his touch. Her knees went weak. And every last thought of meddling melted away as his hands slid upward over her hips, caressed her breasts, then came to rest on her shoulders.

When the kiss ended, Megan was too dazed to recall what they'd been talking about. She barely remembered her own name.

"Well, hell," she murmured.

Jake grinned.

"I guess you were right."

"About?"

"The connection."

"Connection?" he repeated, his expression innocent.

"Between you and me."

"Ah, that connection."

"It's just chemistry," she said, trying to put the least damaging spin on what had shaken her.

"I don't know about you, but I've always found science fascinating," Jake said. "Chemistry, electricity, anatomy, all that sort of thing."

"Go take a course," Megan grumbled.

"Why do that when you're a lesson all by yourself?"

"This was an experiment, Jake. Nothing more."

"A successful one, if you ask me."

"Then it doesn't need repeating."

He gave her a lazy once-over. "Oh, darlin', anything that volatile bears repeating. Something tells me we're going to have to do that one over and over to make absolutely sure it always has the same result."

Jake was sitting behind his desk with his feet propped up a few days later, contemplating the feel of Megan's lips under his, when he realized he wasn't alone. Six-year-old Tommy Morgan was standing in the doorway, hands jammed in his pockets as if he'd been told not to touch anything.

"Hey, Tommy."

"Hi," he said shyly, inching into the room.

"Everything okay?"

The towheaded boy with the huge brown eyes nodded. "Guess so."

"What brings you by?"

"My mama wants to know if you gots time to see her."

Jake pretty much had nothing but time. "Sure. When does she want to come?"

"Soon as you say so."

"Then you go tell her that now's as good a time as any."

Tommy's solemn expression brightened. "Okay. Bye."

"Bye," Jake said, grinning as the boy took off, his chubby little legs pumping furiously.

A few minutes later Janie Morgan, who had the same huge, sad eyes as her son, came into his office, still wearing a big plastic apron that had been discolored by hundreds of hair dying jobs. She barely looked old enough to be out of school, much less to have a son Tommy's age. She reminded Jake of his mother.

"Tommy said this was a good time. Is it okay?"

Jake gestured toward a chair. "It works for me. What can I do for you?"

She perched on the edge of the chair and twisted her hands nervously in her lap. "I was talking to Henrietta the other day. She said maybe you could help me out with Josh Wilson."

"He's your landlord, right?"

"He owns the property, if that's what you mean.

As for keeping it up the way a landlord should, forget it. He's never done a lick of work around that place. He says repairs will cost more than it's worth.''

Old anger burned in Jake's belly. He hadn't just heard this story before, he'd lived it. He reached in a desk drawer and took out a legal pad. ''What's the address?'' he asked grimly.

''You'll help me, then?''

''Oh, yes,'' he said. Maybe it would make up for the impotent rage he'd felt years ago.

''I can't pay much.''

''Don't worry about it,'' he told her. ''Think of this as repayment of an old debt.''

Janie looked confused. ''I'm not sure I understand.''

''Let's just say I have an old score to settle with Mr. Wilson and let it go at that. Now tell me everything that needs doing around the place, how many times you've made the requests, what his responses have been. Do you have any of it in writing?''

Janie laughed. ''You could sum up his responses in one word—*no*. As for putting it in writing, I tried that, but he ignored my letters. All I've gotten is that same verbal response when I've cornered him in the general store or the diner. Most of the time, he pretty much avoids me.''

''Why haven't you moved?''

''Where would we go? There's not a lot of property around Whispering Wind that I can afford. I have my own business, but, face it, you can only do so many perms and dye jobs in any given month. The ladies of Whispering Wind aren't the kind who'll come in regular once a week for a shampoo and set. That would be an extravagance. Between food and clothes for Tommy, who's growing like a weed, there's not a lot left over to save for a house, especially when I wind up getting the roof on that rental patched once a month with my own money.''

''Do you have receipts for that?''

''Every one. I threatened to take the money out of the rent, but Mr. Wilson said he'd toss us both out on our behinds if I did that. Said such things were specifically forbidden under the terms of the lease.''

Jake nodded as he made notes, then looked up and gave her a reassuring smile. ''Okay, Janie, I'll take care of it. Don't pay the man another dime unless I tell you to. I'll stop by this evening and take a look at what needs to be done.''

''Do you think you can get it fixed up?''

''One way or another, you won't have to live like this much longer,'' Jake promised. Not if he had to buy a decent place himself for her and Tommy to move into. In fact, doing just that and setting things in motion to have Josh Wilson's property condemned was going to make his day.

At ten-fifteen Thursday morning Megan got a call from Tess's school. Tess was in the nurse's office throwing up. It was clear that something was expected of Megan, but what? This was the first time she'd been in this position.

''Should I come and get her?'' she asked the nurse.

''That would be best. She doesn't seem to be running a fever, but clearly there's some sort of upset. Maybe a day in bed would do her good. I know she missed some school with her sprained ankle, but if she has the flu, it would be better for her and the other kids if she weren't here.''

Megan had been planning to have a conference call in fifteen minutes with Todd and the syndicator about the taping schedule. For a half second she considered sending Mrs. Gomez into town after Tess, but then abandoned the idea. She could remember one occasion when she'd been sick with the flu and the school had called the house. Tex hadn't come, though she had dearly wanted him to. It had been Mrs. Gomez who'd made the trip, and while she was probably better able to cope with Megan's illness than Tex would have been, his refusal to come had hurt her. Already insecure about her importance to him, she had felt even less certain that she could count on him.

Running into the kitchen, Megan explained to the housekeeper what had come up. ''I'll take my cell phone along and try to reach Todd. If I don't get him and he calls here, please explain what's happened and ask him to reschedule the call with Dean Whicker for later this afternoon.''

''Of course. Would it be better if I went for Tess?''

''No. I think I'd better go.'' She regarded Mrs. Gomez with puzzlement. ''It's funny, though. Tess seemed fine at breakfast.''

''Perhaps it is nothing more than stress. These have been difficult days for her. Even children feel the effects of grief more than we realize.''

Megan nodded. ''You're probably right.''

On the way into town she finally managed to get Todd on her cell phone.

''I thought I was supposed to make that conference

call,'' he said, when he heard her voice. ''You're early.''

''We need to postpone it.''

''What?''

''Tess is sick. I'm on my way into town to pick her up at school. See if you can get everyone together a couple of hours from now.''

''Fine, if you say so.''

''Todd, I know things aren't running as smoothly as usual. Give me a break here. This isn't easy for me, either.''

He sighed heavily. ''I know and I don't mean to make you feel guilty.''

''Of course you do,'' she replied. ''Not that you can make me feel any worse than I already do. I have one solution in mind, though. We'll talk about it later, after the conference call.''

''Okay, whatever. I'll let you know what time works for everybody. I can't wait to break the news to Micah. She's already ticked that you had me set up the call instead of her.''

''She'll live. Meantime, you can reach me on my cell phone for the next hour or so. I'll be at the house after that.''

When she walked into the school office a few minutes later, she was directed to the nurse's office. She found Tess sitting on the side of a cot, looking more bored than ill. Her color looked fine, too. She seemed surprised to see Megan.

''You came?''

''Did you think I'd just leave you here?''

''I figured Mrs. Gomez would come.''

Megan sat down next to her and picked up her

hand. It was cool enough, as was her forehead when she touched that. "No fever."

Tess shrugged and avoided her gaze. "I guess it was one of those stomach things. Probably something I ate for breakfast."

"You're feeling better now?"

"I guess."

"Well, the policy is to send you home, so let's go."

"I could stay, I guess."

"Afraid not," the nurse said. "I can't let you back into class until we're sure you're okay. If you don't feel any worse overnight and you don't have a temp, come back in the morning."

"Have you got your books?" Megan asked.

Tess shook her head. "I had to leave class in a hurry."

The nurse gave Megan a smile. "I'll run down and get them for her and see if there's any homework she should be doing."

Tess regarded Megan worriedly. "Are you mad?"

"Why would I be mad? You can't help being sick." A sudden suspicion crossed her mind. "Can you?"

Tess's cheeks flushed.

Something in her expression set off alarms. "Can you, Tess?"

"Maybe I did make myself throw up," she admitted in a tiny voice.

Megan stared at her. "But why, Tess? Why on earth would you do that?"

"To see if you'd come," she admitted.

Megan pulled Tess into her arms. "Oh, baby, of

course I'd come. I may not be much good at this mom stuff yet, but I will always be here when you need me.''

Tess sniffed. ''Promise?''

''I promise.''

''I guess you're gonna ground me for a month now, huh?''

''No, but I am going to take you for ice cream and make you eat it without hot fudge sauce.''

Tess's eyes widened. ''Really?''

Megan grinned. ''Really.''

''Can Jake come, too?''

Megan hesitated, then shrugged, feigning indifference. ''Sure. Why not?'' She tucked a finger under Tess's chin and forced her to meet her gaze. ''Just don't make this a habit, okay? It worked once. It won't work another time.''

Tess's grin spread. ''Got it.''

As soon as the nurse returned with Tess's books, they drove into downtown Whispering Wind. At Jake's office, Megan sent Tess inside to invite him to join them for ice cream. As she sat propped against the bumper of her car, her cell phone rang.

''Megan, I've got that meeting rescheduled for two o'clock your time. Will that work for you?'' Todd asked.

''That's perfect. I'll be home by then.''

''How's Tess?''

''She's had an amazing recovery,'' she said dryly. ''I'm sure she'll feel even better after we've had ice cream.''

''I don't get it.''

"It was a test. She wanted to see if I'd come when she needed me."

"And you're rewarding her with ice cream?"

"No hot fudge sauce. That's punishment enough."

"My mom would have tanned my hide," Todd said.

"I like my plan better."

"You actually have a plan?" Todd inquired skeptically.

"No. To be perfectly honest, I'm winging it, but I prefer to think there's a method to it."

"She'll turn into a spoiled brat," Todd warned.

"Who made you father-of-the-year?"

"Unless you have another candidate in mind, I'm as close to you as any husband on your social horizon. I figure that makes me a sort of absentee dad." He sounded more than a little disgruntled by the prospect.

Megan grinned. "Actually, that's what I intended to talk to you about this afternoon."

"Marrying you?" he asked in a horrified tone.

"No," she said with a laugh. "Not being quite so much an absentee."

"Oh, no," he said as her meaning sank in. "I'm not coming to Wyoming, Megan. You can get that notion right out of your head."

"We have cable TV," she assured him. "All the modern conveniences."

"You also have blizzards and wild animals and who knows what else."

"We'll talk about it later," she said soothingly. "You spend the next couple of hours getting used to the idea."

"You can't convince me to come," he repeated.
"No way."

"We'll discuss it after the conference call."

"I'll hang up," he said.

"No, you won't."

"I will."

"Todd, it is not in your nature to hang up on your boss."

"I'll make an exception. Forget it, Megan. You can't pay me enough money to get me to Wyoming on a permanent basis. I've never been near a horse, much less a cow. I want my beef straight from the meat section at the corner grocery."

"You haven't lived till you've had it barbecued over an open pit."

"A gas grill on a deck in the Hamptons suits me just fine. There's not an ocean within hundreds of miles of where you are. I checked the map."

"Just wait. You'll love it."

"Megan, listen to me, please. I—will—not—love—it."

"Sure you will. Have I ever lied to you?"

"Let me count the times," he muttered. "I am not discussing this. Not now. Not later. Goodbye."

Megan turned off her cell phone, a grin on her face. She thought it had gone pretty well, all things considered. He hadn't quit. She figured it would take three days, tops, to convince him it was his duty to come to Wyoming to bail her out of a jam.

Getting him to stay was going to be a little trickier.

15

"So Megan came to school to get me and then she figured out that I wasn't really sick, but she wasn't mad," Tess told Jake as she perched on the corner of his desk, legs swinging. "Ain't that neat?"

"Listening to you talk, it seems to me she ought to have left you in school long enough for another grammar lesson," he observed.

"Huh?"

"Never mind. The bottom line is that Megan brought you into town for ice cream, even though you'd faked being sick. Have I got that right?"

"Yep. She said you could come with us. Wanna?"

Jake might disagree with the reason for this so-called special occasion, but he wasn't about to pass up an opportunity to see Megan. "Where is she now?"

"Outside waiting, I guess." Tess offered him a disgusted look. "Probably on the phone. She spends more time on the phone than any teenage kid I know."

Jake barely restrained the urge to chuckle. "And how many teenage kids do you know?"

Tess scowled. "Maybe not that many in real life, but I see 'em on TV," she informed him airily.

"That's all they do. Yak, yak, yak, mostly about boys and stuff. What a waste! I'm never gonna date and I'm sure as heck never gonna get married. It's nothing but heartache."

"You'll change your mind," Jake assured her, wondering if he should insist that Megan restrict Tess's television viewing to Saturday morning cartoons. "Come on. Let's go find Megan and get that ice cream."

Tess regarded him wistfully. "Do you think you could get her to forget about that dumb ol' hot fudge rule? I'd really, really like a sundae. Besides, what kind of punishment is that, anyway?"

"If I were you, I'd count your blessings and leave well enough alone, kiddo. If it were up to me, you'd be locked in your room waiting for Mrs. Gomez to deliver bread and water."

Tess looked shocked. "You would do that to a kid?"

"Oh, yeah."

"I don't believe it."

"Just pull a fast one on me and you'll see."

Tess gave him an impish grin. "I pull fast ones on you all the time and you never even guess."

He stared at her, gaze narrowed. "Such as?"

"You think I'd tell on myself after that bread and water threat?" she asked incredulously. "What do you think I am—nuts or something?"

"I guess I'd better be on my toes from now on."

Looking smug and far from ill, Tess danced out of his office ahead of him. They found Megan standing next to her car, her cell phone dangling in one hand, an unreadable expression on her face.

"Trouble?" he asked.

"Not exactly. I just broke the news to Todd that I wanted him to come out here."

"And?"

She shrugged. "Let's just say he's resisting the idea for the time being."

"Can't you just order him to take the next flight?"

"It'll be better if I let guilt work him over. He'll come to the right decision all on his own."

As Tess ran off toward the ice cream parlor down the block, Jake glanced at Megan. "I hear you've had quite a morning."

"Let's just say that parenting isn't a walk in the park. I'd rather throw together an impromptu gala dinner for four hundred anytime."

He gestured toward the eight-year-old, who was waiting impatiently for them to reach her. "Are you sure this is the right message you're sending?"

Megan sighed. "Jake, if I thought I knew how to do this, I'd probably have kids of my own by now. I'm winging it."

"You're teaching her it's okay to manipulate you," he pointed out.

"No. I'm teaching her that I'll be there when she needs me. She knows this won't work again."

"It doesn't mean there won't be a next time," he warned. "She'll just be more clever about it. She's already told me she's pulling fast ones on me that I haven't even recognized."

Megan grinned suddenly. "Guess that means I'm better at this than you are," she said with an air of triumph. "At least I knew what she was up to before we ever left the nurse's office."

With that she sashayed on ahead of him, giving him the full effect of swaying hips and kick-ass attitude. If he'd dared, he would have yanked her straight back into his arms and kissed that smirk right off her face. Just thinking about it was enough to turn him on. Acting on it would tie him in knots for the rest of the day and leave him hot and aching and lonely all night.

Better to let her have her moment of victory, he concluded with genuine regret. The day would come—in the not too distant future—when he would have his moment of triumph, and the setting would be a whole lot more intimate than the main street of downtown Whispering Wind.

Dean Whicker didn't mince words. "I'm not wild about this latest batch of tapes you sent in," he told Megan, Todd, Micah and the director during their postponed late-afternoon conference call. "You rushed, and it shows. Now, I understand there are extraordinary circumstances here, but if this keeps up, I may have to look into ways of ending our syndication deal. Whicker Television has always stood for quality programming. I won't send out other slipshod episodes like these."

"You can't cancel our deal," Megan protested weakly, fully aware that he could if he wanted to badly enough. If he'd wanted to pick the one threat that could thoroughly rattle her, he'd done it.

"We have a binding, three-year contract," Todd pointed out.

"Any good lawyer can find a million and one ways to end a contract," Whicker said. "I'm sure you know that, Megan. Look, I'm not saying this is what

I'm going to do. I'm just putting you all on notice that I don't like what I saw when I ran those tapes. You're all professionals. You know what it'll take to fix the problems. Do it.''

He hung up before any of them could respond. Megan was heartsick. She knew she owed all of the others an apology, but she wasn't sure she could get the words past the huge lump in her throat. Finally, swallowing hard, she said, ''Look, I'm sorry. I know this is my fault, but we're going to work this out, guys. I swear to you.''

''How?'' Micah asked bluntly. ''If we're going to be taping at weird hours, I'll have trouble booking guests. Besides that, it's already clear that we can't cram so many shows into a single day. It's tough on you and it's tough on the crew.''

''I have to second that,'' Kenny said. ''There's no time to rehearse, no time to work on blocking. The cameras aren't following you the way they should, because the men don't know what you're doing next and, frankly, I don't think you do, either. They've pulled long hours before, but it's obvious you haven't, Megan. You're on camera and the burden for carrying the show falls on you. We can't disguise the toll it's taking.''

''We'll just have to work harder on preproduction,'' Todd said. ''Megan can do the actual tapings with her eyes closed, as long as she's been fully prepped going in. With these last shows we didn't have time to get all the material to her in advance. We were all flying by the seat of our pants.''

''That should help some,'' Micah said. ''Megan, will you be back in New York next week? Can you budget at least an extra half day for the tapings? That should help, right, Kenny?''

"It'll help," he agreed. "The studio time and the crew will cost us, though."

Megan felt the pressure begin to build. Her head was throbbing. "Todd will see to it when he firms up my schedule," she said tightly. "Okay?"

"Got it," Todd agreed.

After Micah and Kenny got off the line, she told Todd, "Schedule a meeting with Peter, while you're at it."

"Lunch? Dinner?"

She hesitated, then said, "In my office. Tell him to bring figures for every aspect of the company—profit, loss, et cetera. I'll need the material if I'm going to look at long-range options."

"Done."

Todd was beginning to sound more confident. Megan wished she felt half so sure of herself. It was evident, though, that things couldn't go on as they had been. Her years of hard work were going to go straight down the tubes unless she got on top of things fast. She could no longer ignore the fact that something was going to have to change if she intended to keep her media empire thriving.

"Todd, schedule me to fly to New York on Saturday. I want a full day's rest there before we get to work on Monday. Have every last segment for the tapings mapped out and sent over to the apartment so I can go over them on Sunday. We'll do two shows Monday, three on Tuesday, three on Wednesday and two on Thursday. Book the studio and the crews for all four days. Can we make it happen?"

"Absolutely," Todd assured her. "All it'll take is money."

"Right now, that's the least of my concerns," she assured him.

"What about the magazine? It's been pretty much running on autopilot so far, but that can't go on forever. People will start getting nervous. And what about that meeting with your book publisher? Aren't the photos and copy for your next book due soon?"

"Schedule any meetings required for Friday. I'll fly back to Wyoming late Friday night."

"Megan…"

"What?"

"About that discussion we had earlier," he began with obvious reluctance.

"Yes."

"If it will help, I'll fly back to Wyoming with you."

She was too exhausted to gloat. "Thanks. Book yourself onto the same flight."

"Just tell me one thing."

"What's that?"

"You aren't going to relocate everything to Wyoming permanently, are you?"

She sighed heavily. "I honestly don't know, Todd. I just don't know."

Now it was his turn to sigh. "I'll see you this weekend. I'll bring over everything you need first thing Sunday morning."

"With bagels and cappuccino?" she asked.

"Of course."

"Thank you." Maybe her life wasn't spinning as wildly out of control as it seemed. Bagels and cappuccino on Sunday morning sounded so familiar, so ordinary. For one day, at least, maybe she could pretend that nothing had changed, that her life was exactly as it had been before Tex had died.

Unfortunately, it was impossible to ignore the fact that thanks to Tex, the time was also fast approaching when she was going to have to make some very tough decisions.

Armed with photos that he had taken of Janie Morgan's house, Jake wandered casually into Josh Wilson's office on Friday morning. The Realtor's expression brightened at the sight of him. He rushed over to vigorously pump Jake's hand.

"Good to see you, son. You looking to buy something else?"

"Could be," Jake said, wondering if Josh would be half so congenial a few minutes from now. "But that's not what brings me by this morning."

Josh gestured toward a chair. "Sit. Can I get you a cup of coffee?"

"No, thanks."

"So, if you haven't spotted another piece of property, what can I do for you?"

Jake handed him the photos. "Take a look at these. I believe you're familiar with the property."

Josh paled as he examined the picture on top, the one of three overflowing buckets standing in the foyer of Janie Morgan's house as drips cascaded from the ceiling.

"Where'd you get these?" he demanded indignantly.

"Took 'em myself, just last night during that cloudburst," Jake responded. "Check out the rest."

Perspiration beaded on Josh's forehead as he examined the photos one by one. "The place could use a little work," he conceded. "Of course, I've been giving Janie a break on the rent, so it's hard to do repairs with the little I've been taking in on the place."

He was playing for sympathy with the wrong man. Jake had no intention of cutting him any slack. He was finally getting to say and do what he'd wanted to years ago when Josh had played games with his mother.

"Is that so?" he said wryly.

"You know how it is, Jake. Some tenants expect a palace, but they don't want to pay for it."

"How about a place that's been kept up? Is that asking too much?"

"Like I said, the rent's low. It's understood, then, that the tenant takes care of repairs."

Jake pulled a sheet out of his pocket. "Funny, I've been over this lease you signed. It doesn't say anything about that in here. In fact, it says just the opposite—that the landlord is responsible for maintaining the property and appliances in good condition."

It was apparent Josh still intended to try to brazen it out. There wasn't the least little sign of remorse in his expression. "If things were so bad, why didn't Janie complain to me?"

"She did," Jake said, pulling out copies of a half-dozen letters she had written asking that the repairs be done. "On more than one occasion, it seems."

Josh ignored the copies and went to his files.

"Must not have gotten them," he muttered as he pulled a file folder from a drawer. He opened it. There wasn't so much as a rent receipt inside. "See? Nothing."

"How convenient. The postal service in Whispering Wind must not be what it used to be."

Josh's gaze narrowed. "What's your interest in this, son? Why isn't Janie here herself?"

"She got tired of getting nowhere," Jake said quietly, then leveled a gaze straight into the Realtor's eyes. "So she hired me."

Josh bristled. "Hired you? Hired you to do what?"

"Sue you, if need be." He regarded Josh blandly. "I'm sure it won't come to that, right, Josh?"

"You can't sue me," Josh protested.

"Watch me," Jake said with deadly calm. "Unless, of course, you agree to see that these repairs are started no later than this time tomorrow. Otherwise, by the time I'm done with you, Janie Morgan will own that house and have a healthy chunk of upkeep money to go right along with it."

Josh Wilson looked stunned. "You can't be serious."

Jake smiled, pleased with his morning's work. "Oh, but I am."

"Where's Janie going to get money to pay a lawyer?"

"She doesn't need any. This case is on the house."

"Why's that? The two of you got something going? She's—"

Before Josh could finish the thought, Jake had him pinned against the wall. "Don't even go there, you lousy, no-good creep. I know the games you tried to pull with my mother to get her to work off any repairs she asked for. If you even hint that there's anything inappropriate going on between Janie Morgan and me, I will have you in court on slander charges so fast it'll make your head swim. You'll have so many legal bills, it'll make these repairs seem like pocket change."

He released Josh and watched in satisfaction as the low-down weasel sank into the chair behind his desk, clearly shaken.

"Are we clear?" Jake asked.

"Very clear," Josh said, the vein in his temple pulsing wildly.

"Shall we expect a contractor over there tomorrow?"

"I might not be able to get one there that fast," Josh hedged. "Besides, it's Saturday."

"Do your best," Jake suggested. "You know every contractor and repairman around here. I'm sure you can manage it, if you want to badly enough."

Outside, Jake drew in a deep breath of fresh air. He needed to clear his lungs of the stench inside that office, a mix of fear and flat-out meanness.

As he walked down the street to his own office, Janie stepped outside her beauty salon and watched him approach.

"Well?" she asked. "Did you see him?"

Jake nodded. "I'm pretty sure you can expect somebody to come by tomorrow to get started on the repairs. If nobody's there by nine, let me know."

Relief spread over her face. "How will I ever thank you, Jake?"

"Don't thank me. That was more fun than just about anything I've done since I got my law degree."

In fact, it had been so much fun he felt like celebrating. Rather than going inside to shuffle around a few meaningless papers to appear busy, he hopped in his car and headed straight for the ranch. Maybe he could persuade Meggie to play hooky from all her faxes and e-mails and go riding with him.

But when he reached the ranch, he discovered that Megan had already gone riding.

"She left not more than a half hour ago," Mrs. Gomez told him. "She said she needed to clear her head. She took along a lunch. If you wait, I will fix something for you, as well. It is a lovely day for a picnic, *sí*?"

As Jake waited impatiently, she made him a thick ham sandwich, added a small bag of chips, a can of soda and a large package of brownies.

"Megan would not take dessert," she explained as she handed him the bag. "She is too thin. Perhaps you can get her to eat a little something sweet."

"She turned down your brownies? They were always her favorite."

"Still warm from the oven," she grumbled, as if she couldn't believe it, either.

He pressed a kiss to the housekeeper's weathered cheek. "She'll have two. I'll see to it."

"She needs someone to look after her," Mrs. Gomez said, her expression sly.

"Have you told her that?" he asked. He could just imagine how Megan would react to such a suggestion.

"More than once."

"And?"

"She tells me she can take care of herself, that I am being a foolish old lady, but I see what I see."

Jake had seen it, too, this driving need Megan had to prove she could cope with everything. That had always been her way, fostered, of course, by Tex. She would collapse if she didn't slow down.

He squeezed Mrs. Gomez's hand. "Don't worry. She'll be fine."

"She is leaving for New York tomorrow for another week. Did you know that? That assistant of hers made the arrangements today. I took the message. Tess will be brokenhearted when she hears. Her parent night at school is next week and there will be no one to go with her."

"Does Megan know?"

"I do not believe the child has told her. I think she is afraid of asking, afraid of being turned down. She says only that it is dumb, that she does not care if Megan attends, but I can see the hurt and disappointment in Tess's eyes."

"If Megan can't change her plans, I'll go with Tess," he promised. "She won't be alone."

"Why would she be alone at parents night?" an unfamiliar voice inquired from the doorway.

Staring past him, Mrs. Gomez turned pale. Jake pivoted slowly to face a woman with Tess's huge eyes, a thick mane of strawberry blond hair and jeans so tight it was a wonder she could breathe.

"Don't mind me," she said. "The door was open, so I just came on in." She gestured toward the suitcase at her feet. "I figured I'd be welcome in my own baby girl's home."

Jake stepped forward. "So you're Tess's mother."

"Flo Olson in the flesh," she said. "And if anyone's going with my girl to that parent thing at school, it'll be me. It'll be just the right thing to show that her mama is back."

"I don't think so," Jake said softly. "Nor will you be staying here. Not in this house and, if you're wise, not in this town."

"Now why would that be?" she asked, clearly undaunted.

"Mrs. Gomez, do you have those papers I left here?" Jake asked.

The housekeeper nodded and reached into a drawer. She handed them to Jake, who passed them on to Tess's mother.

She took them reluctantly. "What're these?" she asked, without bothering to open them.

"Copies of a restraining order forbidding you to get anywhere near Tess," Jake said. "As soon as I call the sheriff and let him know where he can find you, you'll be formally served with them."

The woman stared at him incredulously. "You can't do this. I'm her mama. You can't keep me from spending time with my own flesh and blood."

"You gave up all rights to that title when you signed her over to Tex."

"I was under—what do you call it?—duress. I wasn't in my right mind, what with Tex pressuring me and all."

"Sorry," Jake said. "There are witnesses who will say that you brought Tess here out of the blue, that you knew exactly what you were doing when you signed those papers, and that you did it not just willingly, but eagerly."

"Who will say that? Her?" she demanded, gesturing toward Mrs. Gomez. "Of course, she'd say whatever Tex wanted. He was paying her."

"Not just Mrs. Gomez," Jake corrected mildly. "Tess. The judge will listen to her."

"She's a kid. It was a very traumatic time for her."

"I'm astonished that you recognize that, since you walked away without a backward glance," he said. "Not so much as a postcard in all these months, as I understand it. Not until you'd heard about Tex's death, of course, and figured there might be something in it for you."

He picked up her suitcase, tucked his other hand under her elbow and steered her toward the door. She stumbled a little in her high heels, but Jake never slowed. "It's time for you to go. I don't want you anywhere near here when Tess gets home from school."

She scowled up at him, but she backed down. "I'll go now, but I'll be back. You can count on that. And I will see my daughter. You can take that to the bank, too. A girl belongs with her mama."

"You should have thought of that before you abandoned her," Jake said.

Outside, Jake noted the car waiting for her with the motor running and a man lounging behind the wheel. If Tess had been here, would they have grabbed her and tried to hold her for ransom? It was a sure bet they weren't here because of any sudden onset of motherly concern. Jake wouldn't have been surprised by any stunt the woman pulled. That meant someone was going to have to keep close tabs on Tess without her being aware of it. He didn't want her scared to death.

As soon as the car had driven off, he went back into the kitchen where Mrs. Gomez waited, looking mad enough to tear the woman apart with her bare hands.

"You do not need to say it," she said. "I will go into town and pick Tess up after school. She should not be alone on the bus."

"And I'll call the school and make sure they know that Tess is not to be allowed to leave with anyone other than you, me or Megan. I'll touch base with Bryce, too, and let him know the tag number on that car. Then I'll ride out and find Megan. She's going to have to cancel that trip to New York."

Mrs. Gomez looked worried. "But her work," she protested. "How can she?"

"Right now, Tess has to be our number one priority," he said firmly. He just prayed that Megan would see it that way, too.

16

"Tess is okay, isn't she?" Megan demanded when Jake found her and broke the news about their visitor. Alarmed by the thought of Flo Olson being anywhere near Tess, she jumped to her feet and started toward her horse. "We've got to go. We should pick her up at school right now."

"Mrs. Gomez has gone," Jake reassured her, taking her hand firmly in his. "And I've spoken to the principal and her teacher. Tess won't be allowed to leave with anyone except one of us. We can eat our lunch before we go back."

Megan sighed, her panic easing. "I was hoping that woman had changed her mind. It's been a couple of weeks since she called. I thought she'd gotten the message after you talked to her. Maybe she gets it now that you've told her about the restraining order."

"I'd been hoping that she'd never show up in the first place, but obviously she was just taking her time getting here from wherever she's been the last few months. I doubt that a mere restraining order will intimidate her, not with all those dollar signs gleaming in her eyes."

"Does Bryce know?"

"I called him before I saddled up and rode out looking for you. Everything's covered for now."

"Good. What do we do next?"

"We keep a close eye on Tess." He kept his gaze fixed intently on Megan.

"Of course."

"That means it would be best if you didn't go to New York next week," he explained quietly.

The suggestion stunned her, though it shouldn't have. Megan sank down on a sun-drenched boulder beside the creek. She knew Jake was right, that she had no business being away from the ranch while there was any danger to Tess. Tex's lectures on duty and obligation resounded in her head.

But what about the tapings, Dean's threats to cancel the syndication agreement? What about her career?

She sighed heavily. It should have been no choice at all—parental responsibilities versus a mere job— but she was so new to being a parent, so unprepared for it. Even so, she knew she couldn't leave Tess. That terrible sensation of being overwhelmed—also new to her—came back with a vengeance.

"I know the timing's lousy," Jake said, sitting down beside her. "If it would help, I could move out to the ranch so you could go."

She whirled on him. "Oh, you'd just love that, wouldn't you? It would give you a foot in the door. Next thing I know you'd be claiming the house and Tess."

He regarded her with silent censure.

Megan closed her eyes. "I'm sorry. I know that wasn't fair. You were just trying to help." Hating her unfamiliar sense of vulnerability, she regarded Jake beseechingly. "What am I supposed to do? It's all closing in on me."

"I've offered one solution, but you didn't like it."

"Moving everything here," she said wearily, staring at the creek. This had always been her special place. It had brought her solace, but there was none for her here today, not even with Jake by her side offering his strength.

"Setting up your headquarters in Whispering Wind would be an option," Jake said. "It could be a temporary move, just until things settle down a bit. Once the facilities are fixed up, they'd become a moneymaker. There are a lot of film companies coming into Wyoming to shoot movies these days. This could become another adjunct to your media empire."

He made it sound so reasonable. Finally, resigned, she lifted her gaze to meet his. "As soon as Tess is home, will you take me out to see those warehouses again?"

He nodded. "Of course."

"Don't gloat," she warned.

"I wouldn't dream of it."

"Sure you would. Just don't do it so I can see it."

He sketched a cross on his chest, then reached for the package of brownies and waved one under her nose. "Eat," he instructed. "There's nothing that can improve a lousy day like chocolate."

She'd resisted the brownies earlier, hadn't even touched her lunch, but she grabbed one now. Jake was right. Chocolate could make up for a lot. Of course, considering the way things were going, she wouldn't be able to fit into a single thing in her closet if she ate enough to keep her spirits up every day.

When she and Jake got back to the house, Megan discovered that Tess and Mrs. Gomez had arrived only moments before. Tess had gone straight upstairs and locked herself in her room.

"She is thinking that is the only way to keep her mother out," Mrs. Gomez explained. "I could not reason with her. She would not even come into the kitchen for her usual snack. I have never seen her like this. It worries me."

Jake offered to talk to her, but Megan shook her head. "I'll go."

For the second time in a few brief weeks, she was knocking on Tess's door, pleading to be let in, wondering what she should say once she was admitted.

Was Tess as conflicted as Megan would have been years ago if Sarah O'Rourke had come back into her life? She had dreamed of that happening, wanted it fiercely for months, but eventually anger and then resignation had taken the place of the yearning. All the good times she'd had with her mother—baking cookies; raking fall leaves, then jumping into the piles; hot chocolate on Christmas Eve while they listened to carols—all of those memories faded and were replaced by emptiness.

Surely Tess had good memories, too, memories that were still fresh after only a few months of separation.

"Sweetie, please, talk to me."

"Go away," Tess said, her voice raspy from crying. "You can't protect me. You won't even be here.

I know you're going back to New York. You have those tapings again."

"I will be here," Megan corrected. "And we need to talk about this, about what you really want to do."

"You're staying?" Tess queried, her tone less defiant. "What about your show?"

"I'm going to call New York as soon as you and I talk. I'll make other arrangements to do the tapings."

"Call now," Tess ordered, clearly not trusting the promise.

"Why now?"

"So I'll know it's a done deal."

Oh, Tess, Megan thought. *What have we all done to you?* Even Tex, who'd welcomed her into his home, made her a part of his life, had abandoned her in the end. She didn't trust the word of any grown-up. Megan honestly couldn't blame her.

"Are you gonna call or not?" Tess demanded. "If you're not, just say so and I'll go back to watching TV."

Megan smiled at the imperial tone. "I'll call. Want me to do it on my cell phone right outside your door so you can eavesdrop?"

The door opened a crack. Tess stared out at her with red-rimmed eyes. "You would do that?"

"If it would make you feel better, yes. I want you to know that when I give you my word, I'll keep it." She was determined to make up for too many broken promises—in both their lives.

Tess seemed to be considering the idea. "Okay. Do it," she said finally.

Megan gently touched Tess's tear-stained cheek. "I'll be right back."

When she returned a few minutes later with the cell phone, the door was still open a crack and Tess was sitting on the floor just inside, her knees drawn up to her chest. Megan settled into a similar position in the hallway. She drew in a deep breath and dialed her office.

"Megan O'Rourke's office," Todd announced.

"Hi," she said.

"Megan? Is that you?"

"Yes."

"You sound funny. What's wrong?"

"Something's come up."

He groaned. "Don't tell me. You can't get here Saturday. Okay, no problem. I'll change the flight to Sunday. I can fax everything to you out there on Saturday. You'll still be up to speed when you get here."

"Todd, stop."

"What?"

"It's not that simple."

"Megan, I hate to tell you, but that's not simple. Anything else is disaster."

"Then that's what we're dealing with."

"Just tell me."

She gave him a brief summary of what was going on, trying not to sound too dire for Tess's sake. "Bottom line, I can't leave here right now."

"What am I supposed to tell Dean?" He sounded more plaintive than furious, which he had every right to be after all the hoops he'd jumped through to put this schedule together.

"Nothing."

"Megan, it's not like he won't figure out something's up. I'll have to ask him to put some reruns into the schedule. He's going to hate it."

"No reruns," she said decisively. That would mean the end of the syndication deal for sure.

"What then?"

"I want you to get on the phone and start ordering cameras and whatever else we need. Have it delivered out here by Monday. I'll get the address for you. Put together a crew and fly them out." She thought of Peggy's picture-perfect kitchen. Maybe they could borrow it for a week until she could get a new studio up and running. "We'll do a location shoot."

"You can't put together a location shoot in a few days," Todd protested, clearly horrified. "It takes weeks of planning. Micah will lose it if you drop this on her out of the blue."

"We have days," Megan said simply. "Micah will have to run with it. She's a pro. I expect her to rise to the occasion. This is important, Todd. Make it happen."

"You will owe me big time if I pull this off," he warned.

"A vacation anywhere in the world you want to go," she promised. "All expenses paid."

"Two weeks," he countered.

"Done." She chuckled. "Of course, it could be next year before you get to take it."

"In that case, make it three weeks," he related. "After Micah gets through with me, I may need a week of that time in a hospital."

"We'll negotiate. I'll see you this weekend, then."

"Yes, God help me. And I'll get back to you before the end of the day about everything else."

"Thanks."

"Megan, wait," Todd said as she was about to hang up. "Are you telling Micah or am I?"

Megan knew she ought to be the one to do it, but she dreaded it. "I'll do it. Maybe I'll even enjoy telling her to pack her bags and head west."

The call to Micah was as horrible as she'd anticipated. Even so, when Megan hung up, she felt slightly better, slightly more in control. The location shoot concept had been a stroke of brilliance. Even Micah had liked the idea, if not the timing. Megan just had to convince Peggy to go along with it. Hopefully, since her kitchen was almost a replica of the one Megan used on the show, she would be thrilled with the idea of having her home on TV.

The door to Tess's room inched open. The next thing Megan knew Tess had crawled into her lap. Her arms crept around Megan's neck.

"It's going to be okay, sweetie," Megan murmured, rocking her. "You'll see."

"If you're going to be here, will you go to parents night with me?" Tess asked in a small voice.

"When?"

"Next week."

"Why didn't you say something before?"

"I figured you'd say no, or you'd be gone or something." She shrugged. "It's not a big deal if you can't go."

Megan looked into her eyes and saw that it was a very big deal, indeed. "I'll put it on my calendar," she promised, and wondered why she felt like crying.

Could it be that she was actually beginning to feel just a little bit like a mom? Or was she thinking of all the parents' nights her own mother had missed?

"Hey, you guys," Jake called from the foot of the stairs. "Everything okay up there?"

"Everything's fine," Megan called back.

"How about a hot game of Scrabble before supper?"

Tess scrambled up. "You know too many words and you cheat. Let's play Monopoly instead."

"Okay by me," he agreed. "Are you in, Meggie?"

"Are you kidding? There's nothing I like better than buying property and putting big ol' hotels on it."

She followed Tess down the stairs. At the bottom, Jake held her back as Tess ran on into the living room to set up the game board.

"Is everything really okay?" he asked quietly.

"It will be," she said.

"Do you still want to see those warehouses this afternoon?"

"Tomorrow morning will be soon enough. Right now, let's just concentrate on Tess."

Jake tucked a finger under her chin and tilted her face up. "You've done the right thing, darlin'. I'm proud of you." He pressed a quick kiss against her lips.

It wasn't quite the same as having Tex here to grant his approval, Megan concluded. In some ways, it was even better.

"You want to do your show right here in my kitchen?" Peggy asked, staring at Megan incredulously.

"I'm in a real bind," Megan told her. She explained about Tess. "There was no way I could go to New York, not this next week, anyway. But if I don't get those shows done on schedule, there's a good chance I can kiss my syndication deal goodbye. I'm going to look at some possible space for a studio later this morning, but there's no way to get a facility equipped overnight. Then I remembered what you've done with your kitchen. It's almost exactly like the set in New York." She watched Peggy worriedly. "So, what do you think? Could we do the tapings here?"

"All day for three days?"

"I'm afraid so. How would Johnny feel about it? We'd put everything back exactly the way we found it at the end of each day. Of course, I couldn't promise that we'd be out in time for you to fix supper. We'd pay for all of you to go out to dinner those nights."

Peggy looked hesitant. "I don't know. If it were just up to me, I'd say yes in a heartbeat. You know I would. But Johnny, he's used to a certain routine."

"You could be on the show," Megan suggested, ignoring her hesitation and trying to sweeten the deal so it would be irresistible. "You could help with one of the segments. Just imagine how proud he'd be."

Peggy was clearly tempted. "Me? I don't know anything about TV."

"But you know about cooking and all sorts of other things. It would be fun. We could talk about the things we did way back when. You could share all my dirty little secrets," she said, knowing that there were none that would be too embarrassing. She'd been a model kid, partly out of fear that Tex would abandon her if she weren't. Loving Jake had been her only rebellion.

"You mean like the way you were head over heels in love with Jake Landers?" Peggy said, as if she'd picked up on Megan's thoughts.

Megan's cheeks burned. "Maybe not that one."

"Too close to real life today, right?"

"Don't be silly. Jake and I are nothing more than old friends."

"It didn't look that way to me the other night when you came to dinner."

"I am not discussing Jake with you. I'm here to talk about borrowing your kitchen for a few days. Can I do it?"

"Oh, what the hell, why not?"

"Do you need to talk it over with Johnny?"

"He'll live with it," Peggy said with an odd touch of defiance. "Or he'll take off in a snit." She shrugged. "If he does, it can't be helped. It won't be the first time. Besides, this is an emergency."

Megan studied Peggy intently, belatedly aware that she might be adding to the already simmering tension in the Barkley household. "Are you sure? If this is going to be a problem, I'll invade Mrs. Gomez's kitchen at the ranch. I thought of yours because it's more up-to-date and I thought you might get a kick out of it."

"No, you'll do it here and that's that." Peggy got an impish gleam in her eyes. "Maybe we should make taffy."

"Oh, no," Megan said with a laugh, remembering the last time all too well. "You aren't getting me to do that ever again. We had to cut off half my hair when that inedible goo we made got tangled up in it.''

"I'm sure we could get it right this time," Peggy said, looking innocent. "When I make it with the kids, it turns out perfect."

"It must have been me, then." Megan shook her head. "No way. I'm not taking any chances. This haircut of mine cost a fortune. I don't want to have to take my own scissors to it."

They were still laughing at old memories a few minutes later when Johnny came into the kitchen. He regarded Megan with what seemed like suspicion.

"Didn't expect to find you here," he said as he snagged a soft drink out of the refrigerator, popped it open and leaned back against the counter. "I figured it would be another ten or twenty years before we saw you again."

"Johnny, stop. Megan came by to see if she could tape some shows in our kitchen next week," Peggy said cheerily. "Isn't that exciting?"

Johnny looked anything but excited. He regarded his wife with disapproval. "And you said yes, I suppose? Just like you always did when she got one of her big ideas."

Peggy stared right back at him, her gaze unflinching. "Well, of course I did. She's in a bind. I knew you'd feel the same way I did, that we had to help her out."

Johnny shook his head. "I don't know. Sounds like a lot of commotion to me."

"It's a few days," Peggy insisted. "We'll survive

it. The kids cause a ruckus around here all the time. This won't be much worse."

"Can't say I like the idea of a lot of strangers tromping around our place."

"Well, I've already said yes, and that's that," Peggy said, regarding him defiantly.

Increasingly uncomfortable with the argument swirling around her, Megan rose. "Look, I'll leave you two to talk it over. Peggy, I'll give you a call later to see what you've decided, okay?"

By the time she reached her car, she could hear voices escalating inside, and regretted ever making the suggestion. She should have been more sensitive to the undercurrents she'd sensed at dinner, and avoided suggesting anything that might give them yet another reason to fight.

Unfortunately, it was too late to withdraw the idea. Peggy was clearly excited about it. All Megan could do would be to call her later this afternoon and give her a chance to change her mind.

Maybe it wouldn't be impossible to turn one of the warehouses into a studio overnight. After all, there were plenty of women across the country who thought she specialized in miracles. What was one more?

17

Megan stood in the center of the cavernous warehouse and listened to the sound of her own voice echoing around the building. The floor was concrete, the walls bare metal. If it had ever been used for anything, there was no sign of what. It had an abandoned, cold, dank air about it.

"Well, what do you think?" Jake asked, as if he were showing off the Taj Mahal.

"It's certainly big enough," she said, then sighed. "I don't know. I'm not a technical person. I have no idea what it would take to make this into a working studio. I do know it couldn't be done by next week. For one thing it's freezing in here. It would have to be heated. Even with all the lights, it would be frigid."

"I didn't think you needed it up and running by next week. I thought you were going by Peggy's this morning to get her on board for those tapings. Didn't she agree?"

"Peggy's for it. Johnny's not so hot on the idea. They were battling it out when I left." She regarded him guiltily. "I'm afraid I caused another rift between them."

"Seems to me it doesn't take much," Jake said.

Megan's gaze narrowed. This wasn't the first little hint he'd dropped about the state of Peggy's marriage. Megan was getting tired of his evasiveness when she asked about it. This time she wasn't going to let him off the hook.

"Meaning?" she asked.

"Just that people who are looking for a fight can usually find one."

"I think you meant something more. Spill it, Jake. What do you know?"

"I've told you before I'm not going to spread gossip—"

"What gossip?" she asked, seizing on the fact that there was some.

He regarded her evenly. "Let's move on to another topic, okay? Otherwise, we're the ones likely to be fighting."

She gauged his mood and decided to give up. "Okay, let's discuss you and Josh Wilson. I heard about what you did for Janie."

He seemed surprised. "How'd you hear about that?"

"I stopped by Henrietta's for a cup of coffee before I met you. It was the talk of the diner. Janie says there are workmen swarming all over that house this morning."

Jake grinned. "I counted a half dozen when I went by."

He looked like a kid who'd just bested the schoolyard bully. "Proud of yourself, aren't you?" she asked.

"I'm just glad Janie and Tommy will have a decent place to live."

"That is a bonus," Megan teased. "You're really glad you had a chance to put the screws to Josh."

"Okay, that, too. I hope it'll only be the first time of many," he said fiercely. "Can you blame me, after the way he treated my mother and me, because she was in no position to stand up to him?"

"Of course not. Any other causes you intend to take on?"

"Hard to tell. Right now, I have this TV host who's in desperate need of studio and office space. I'm devoting all my time to her."

His gaze locked with hers. Megan suspected finding a studio facility for her was the least of his intentions. She had too much on her mind to cope with old, unresolved emotions. She forced her attention back to the problem at hand.

"Let me see what the crew thinks when they get here," she said. "If they think it's workable, we'll do it."

"And in the meantime?"

"In the meantime, I'll just keep my fingers crossed that Peggy wins that argument with Johnny. If she doesn't, Mrs. Gomez is going to have to make room for a camera crew at the ranch."

And Megan was going to have to find some way to keep her attention from drifting all too often to the man who'd been a steadfast presence in her life ever since her return to Whispering Wind.

A half-dozen people from Megan's staff descended on Whispering Wind on Saturday, led by Todd. Megan had booked every room at the town's only motel. She'd put Todd in the guest quarters at the ranch, a decision that raised Micah's ire. She stormed off in another huff.

By Saturday evening they were all crammed into Tex's office going over production schedules. Even Micah had put aside her resentment to pitch in.

Jake, bless him, had taken Tess out for dinner to keep her from being underfoot.

"When can we see this location kitchen?" Kenny asked. "I've got to get the crew in there to start blocking shots."

Megan hesitated. Peggy had confirmed that they could use the kitchen, but not until Monday. The news wasn't going to sit well.

"Sorry, guys. Not until first thing Monday."

Kenny stared at her, clearly dismayed. "You've got to be kidding. How are we supposed to tape on Monday if we haven't even seen the setup?"

"That's the deal and there's nothing I can do about it," Megan said. "You can do the advance work on Monday and we'll wait till Tuesday to tape. We can go through Friday, if need be." She prayed Peggy would go along with that. She glanced at Micah. "Are all the segments ready to go?"

"Right here," Micah said, handing her a sheaf of papers. "The materials are boxed up by episode and ready to go, too. They arrived on the same plane we did. I've checked to make sure none are missing. I'm storing everything in one of those warehouses in town, just like you said. We'll bring 'em out to the location as we need 'em."

There were a thousand more details to be hammered out, and after the initial grumbling, everyone tackled the project as professionally as Megan had hoped they would. By midnight, she was satisfied that the productions wouldn't be total disasters. Even Micah seemed more upbeat. Meeting the challenge of doing an impromptu location shoot seemed to inspire her.

"I can't thank you all enough for pitching in like this," Megan said.

"Hey, our jobs are on the line, too," Kenny said.

"Can I get you anything before you head back into town?"

"Nope, I'm going to that bar down the street from the hotel for one stiff drink and then I'm heading to bed," the director said wearily. "Tomorrow the sound and lighting techs and I are going over that warehouse to see what it would take to turn it into a studio."

"Bring me a budget projection as soon as you have one."

"Since this is temporary, do you want bare-bones improvements or state-of-the-art?"

She considered the question carefully. As desperately as she wanted to believe this was only a stopgap measure, she knew there was a possibility it could turn into something permanent. And there was also Jake's notion of renting the facilities out to other productions.

"State-of-the-art," she said finally.

The response drew groans, then assurances that she would get a complete report the next day.

After the others had gone, Todd regarded her wearily. "This is it, then? You're staying indefinitely?"

"I'm taking one day at a time."

"Megan, there's not even a department store close

by, much less a Bloomingdale's or a Barney's. Are you sure this town is living in the twentieth century?''

She grinned at his dismayed tone. ''There's not a lot of call for designer clothes out here. A good pair of jeans will cover just about any occasion,'' she teased.

''I was afraid of that.''

''Give it a chance, Todd. Please. I can't do this without you.''

''Executive assistants are a dime a dozen.''

''They're not you.''

''I'm a New Yorker, Megan.''

''Aren't New Yorkers known for being able to cope with any challenge?''

He regarded her with suspicion. ''Yes. So?''

''Think of this as another challenge.''

''Riding the subway is a challenge. Walking through Central Park without getting mugged is a challenge. Finding an apartment without roaches is a challenge. This is…'' Words clearly failed him.

''A favor to a friend,'' she suggested softly.

He scowled at her. ''You don't play fair.''

''Not when it's this important,'' she agreed. ''When it's this important, I play to win.''

''Okay, I'll stay for the time being,'' he agreed. ''But I will not wear boots and jeans, and that's that.''

''Deal.''

''By the way, how do I get a taxi out here?''

Megan grinned. ''You don't.''

He stared at her. ''Then how am I supposed to get around?''

''You drive.''

''Not me.''

Surely he wasn't saying what she thought he was saying. "You mean you can't?"

He regarded her defensively. "It's not a crime, Megan. Who needs to drive a car in New York?"

"I'll teach you," she assured him, then chuckled. "Right after I teach you to ride a horse."

"Very amusing," he shot back. "But I'm getting the last laugh. I neglected to mention that when I called Peter to cancel your meeting, he decided to fly out here himself."

"Oh, no," she said weakly.

"Oh, yes."

"When?"

"He'll be here tomorrow. He thinks he's coming in to save the day. I'm pretty sure he watched at least a dozen Westerns on video just to be sure he got it right. He's probably bought a white Stetson, so you'll recognize him as the hero."

Not even the incongruous image of her balding, cherubic-faced accountant in a Stetson could make her smile. Peter in Wyoming was as unthinkable as serving onion dip and chips at a society soiree.

"You couldn't stop him?" she asked.

"Now, why would I do that?" he inquired innocently. "You told me yourself that your social life is none of my concern."

"Peter is my accountant."

"You know that, and I almost believe that, but he doesn't have a clue. I'm not about to be the one to tell him."

"Thank you very much."

"It could have been worse," Todd suggested.

"I can't see how."

"I could have let him surprise you the way he wanted to."

"Yes," she conceded. "It could definitely have been worse."

Jake had had every intention of going to the warehouse with Megan's crew the next morning, but just as they were about to leave his office, Henrietta came flying across the street, apron flapping. She paused at the sight of all the strangers.

"Sorry. I didn't know I'd be interrupting."

"It's okay, Henrietta. These gentlemen work for Megan," Jake said, introducing them. He regarded her worriedly. "Is something wrong?"

"Could I see you outside?"

"I was about to take them out to the warehouse."

"This is more important," Henrietta insisted. "I wouldn't be here if it weren't."

Jake turned to Ken Hawkins and handed him the keys. "You can't miss the place. It's about five miles outside of town. These keys will get you into any of the buildings. They're all available, so just decide which one will suit your needs. I'll get out there as soon as I can."

"No problem," Kenny said. He nodded at Henrietta, then led the others out of Jake's office.

"Nice bunch," Henrietta said. "They had breakfast at the diner. They were real polite. Big tippers, too. I figured they had something to do with Megan. Sounded like New Yorkers."

"You didn't come over here to talk about how well they tipped. What's up?"

"It's Barbara Sue. She showed up for work about

a half hour ago. Lyle's been at her again. I've put her to work in the kitchen, so she doesn't have to show her bruised-up face, but something's got to be done about that man. She says he hasn't gone after the kids yet, but if you ask me, it's only a matter of time before one of them steps in his path.''

''Does she want to talk to me?''

''I didn't give her a choice—I just came to get you.''

''Henrietta, I can't help her if she doesn't want to be helped.''

''You can lay out her options. I don't believe she thinks she has any. Now, are you coming or aren't you? I've got customers to see to.''

A bulldozer was more subtle than Henrietta when her mind was made up. ''I'm coming,'' Jake said.

He found Barbara Sue Perkins in the kitchen washing dishes. She didn't look up when he came in. Even so, he could see the swelling on her face and the growing black-and-blue mark on her jaw. He pulled up a stool and sat behind her at the food-preparation island. It was littered with the remnants of chopped vegetables being readied for lunchtime salads.

''Hey, Barbara Sue.''

''Hi, Jake,'' she said without turning. The scanty part of her face that wasn't bruised flushed red with embarrassment. ''What are you doing here?''

''Henrietta thought you might need legal advice.''

''Henrietta's meddling.''

''Maybe so, but my guess is that she's right about this. Unless you've bounced off a couple of doors in the past twenty-four hours, it looks as if you could use some help.''

She whirled on him. Jake was shocked by the full extent of her injuries. There were more cuts and bumps than he could count. He forced himself not to visibly react, tried only to remember the pretty blond woman with the sweet smile who had once sat next to him in history class and shared her notes and wry comments.

"Okay, you've had a good look now," she said angrily. "Go on back to your office."

"Not without explaining a few facts," he said quietly.

"What facts?" she asked sarcastically. "That if I dare to leave Lyle, I won't live to tell about it? That if I file so much as a complaint with the sheriff, this beating will seem like a gentle nudge? Believe me, nobody knows the facts of my life better than I do. Like my mama used to say, I made my bed, now I've got to lie in it."

"Your mama was wrong. Nobody expects you to stay with a man who abuses you."

"Where would I go? I've got no money, no job skills, nothing more than a high school diploma. I've got two kids depending on me."

"They're depending on you for more than food," Jake pointed out. "They're depending on you to protect yourself and them from harm. They're depending on you to say it's not all right for their father to beat you." He gazed steadily into her eyes. "They're depending on you to stay alive."

Tears welled up and rolled silently down her swollen cheeks. Jake let his message sink in before going on.

"There are places you could go to be safe. You

could file assault and battery charges against Lyle and send him to prison. Even his mama won't be able to save him from that charge. All it would take is a photo of the way you look right now. At the very least you could get a restraining order to keep him away from you and the kids. Folks around here would help you out with the kids and with money till you get on your feet.''

"I can't ask for help like that," she whispered, covering her face with her hands.

"Why not?"

"I'm too ashamed. I'm ashamed that my husband beats me."

"You've done nothing wrong," Jake said heatedly. "Lyle is the one who ought to be ashamed."

"Maybe…"

"Maybe what?"

"Maybe I deserved it. That's what his mother says."

Jake slammed his fist onto the butcher block counter. "No, dammit! Barbara Sue, you did not deserve it. Nobody deserves to be mistreated by a husband, a man who vowed to love, honor and protect you. If Mrs. Perkins says otherwise, she's just blinded by the fact that he's her boy. She would have done him a greater service if she'd laid down a few rules for him way back when they could have done some good. Instead, she's always let him have his own way, encouraged him to think he's never in the wrong."

Jake reached over and covered Barbara Sue's hand. "Tell me something. Has he ever hurt the kids or threatened to?"

She shook her head.

"He will. Believe me, one of these days, he will."

She lifted her gaze to clash with Jake's. "I'll kill him first."

Jake shuddered. Of all the things she had said, none carried more conviction. She had to get out of that house now, before there was a real tragedy.

"Please, let me look into that restraining order. Get him out of the house."

"It was his family's house. His mother gave it to us when we got married," Barbara Sue pointed out. "He'll say I'm the one with no right to stay there."

"The court won't see it that way."

"Jake, I've heard everything you've said and I know you're trying to help, but I have to do this my own way. You don't know Lyle the way I do. He's changed since school. He's bitter about so many things. He can't hold a job except at his mama's store. Even she's losing patience with him. He drinks too much."

"I've known other men like him," Jake assured her. "He won't change, so you have to be the one to take care of yourself."

"You're probably right, but this is the way it's going to be," she said, literally turning her back to him to face the sinkful of dishes.

Jake sighed. Saying any more now would be wasting his breath. "Come to see me if you change your mind."

"I won't," she said emphatically.

Jake walked back into the front of the diner and slid onto a stool. Henrietta put a cup of coffee in front of him, but kept waiting on the packed booths. Only after things had slowed down did she slip onto the stool beside him.

"Well?"

"She won't hear of me doing anything."

"I was afraid of that. She's terrified, Jake. She's convinced he'll kill her if she does anything except go home and take more of the same."

He regarded Henrietta bleakly. "Could be she's right."

"So, what do we do?" she demanded indignantly. "Just leave her there?"

"If that's her choice, there's nothing we can do."

"Well, I don't believe that. If she won't leave, then she at least ought to look out for those kids."

"I tried to tell her that, too."

"Can I file something with the court to get them out of there?"

Jake regarded her incredulously. "You would do that?"

"If it'll protect them from that monster of a father, yes," she said fiercely. "They can come to live with me. When she wakes up and smells the coffee, Barbara Sue can come, too."

"I have to tell you that interfering could put you right smack in the middle of this. Lyle will likely go on the warpath. In addition, you'll be breaking Barbara Sue's heart."

Henrietta sighed. "I know that. Maybe it's not my place to interfere, but thinking of those kids caught up in that breaks *my* heart."

"Give Barbara Sue a couple of days. Maybe when she's thought it through, she'll come around."

"Things like this don't get better by waiting," the older woman said.

"I know."

"Two days," she finally agreed with obvious reluctance. "Then we're going to the court to file for protective custody for those children. Will you help me?"

"You know I will."

She patted his hand. "You're a good man, Jake Landers. I knew I could count on you."

Jake just prayed they weren't asking for more trouble than either of them had bargained for.

18

"Have you seen Tess this morning?" Mrs. Gomez asked when Megan finally came into the kitchen after ten on Sunday.

Still exhausted from her late-night meeting, Megan yawned. "Isn't she still asleep?"

"At this hour? Heavens, no. She is an early riser like your grandfather. She is up with the chickens."

A vague sense of unease stirred in Megan. "Have you looked in the barn?"

"She is not with the kittens," Mrs. Gomez replied. "That was the first place I checked. And before you ask, Tex's horse is still in his stall. I believe she learned her lesson about trying to ride him."

Megan studied the housekeeper worriedly. "You don't suppose...?"

"That her mother came?" Mrs. Gomez suggested, immediately picking up on her unspoken thought. "Tess would not go with her, not without stirring up a fuss. After her reaction the other day when we learned of her mother's return, I am sure of that."

"Then she's probably just gone for a walk," Megan said, trying to convince herself and Mrs. Gomez that there was no reason to be concerned. "As soon as I have some breakfast, I'll go look for her." She reached for a cranberry-filled muffin still warm from the oven and bit into it, even as she poured herself a cup of coffee. "Have you seen Todd?"

"I believe he is in Tex's office. He ate three of my muffins and then said he had work to do," she said, her disapproval plain. "I told him it was a day of rest."

"And what did he say?"

"That he worked for a woman who didn't know the meaning of the word."

Megan pressed a kiss to the housekeeper's cheek. "It's an emergency," she assured her. "Moving the show out here really screwed up our production plans. I swear to you that by next week, things will settle down."

"This I will believe when I see it," Mrs. Gomez retorted. "You are not in a line of work that ever settles down. Now sit. Eat. I will go and look for Tess. You have too many things on your mind as it is."

Megan stayed at the kitchen table and savored her second cup of coffee, enjoying the brief respite before the guaranteed storm of activity that the rest of the day and the upcoming week would bring. She was still there when the housekeeper returned after a more thorough search for Tess.

"She is nowhere, none of her usual hiding places," Mrs. Gomez reported, frowning. "I do not like this. It is not like Tess to vanish without leaving word."

"She did it before," Megan pointed out. "Just the other night."

"This is different. I can feel it."

To be honest, Megan didn't like the feel of it, either. Maybe she was just picking up on Mrs. Gomez's concern, but a little knot of dread was forming in her stomach. If only Jake were here, he would know what to do, where to look. As much as she hated to admit it, he seemed to understand Tess far better than she did.

"If she doesn't turn up in the next half hour, I'll call Jake," Megan said with reluctance.

"That would be best," Mrs. Gomez agreed. "He and Tess are two of a kind. I think your grandfather knew that when he put Jake in charge of his estate."

Megan's gaze narrowed. "What are you saying?"

"Just that Tex knew they would be good for each other."

"But he made me Tess's guardian," Megan reminded her, not sure why she was hurt by what the housekeeper was suggesting.

"You are family. He trusted you to do right by Tess." Mrs. Gomez looked distraught. "I am not saying this well."

"Oh, I think you're saying it fine. I think you believe that Tex didn't trust me at all, that Jake was his backup in case I failed."

"I would never say such a thing," Mrs. Gomez protested. "I helped to raise you. No one knows your strengths better than I."

"And my failings," Megan pointed out. "No, you are too kind to say that I'm likely to screw up, but you believe it just the same."

And the terrible thing was, Megan thought as she left the kitchen, even she believed the housekeeper might be right. For every step forward she took in building a relationship with Tess, there were a half-dozen back.

Because she didn't know where else to go or what else to do, she headed for Tex's office to check in with Todd before launching her own search for Tess. At the doorway, she screeched to a halt. Inside, heads bent over the huge architectural rendering of Peggy's kitchen that Megan had borrowed, were Todd and Tess.

"What does this mean?" Tess was asking, pointing to a note attached to one side.

"It means that the segment on drying cranberries will take ten minutes, that it will use the kitchen set and that it will be followed by the recipe for those muffins Mrs. Gomez made this morning," Todd explained patiently.

"Megan's going to make those?" Tess asked, her expression incredulous. "On television?"

"Yep."

Tess continued to look skeptical. "Have you ever eaten one of Megan's muffins?"

Todd grinned. "It's not important that she be a great chef, just that she can entertain the audience, communicate the recipe and make it sound easy."

"In other words, you have," Tess said. "Her cooking sucks."

Todd glanced up and caught sight of Megan. "I wouldn't say that," he replied diplomatically.

"Oh, go ahead and say it," Megan said. "We all know that I have a tendency to get distracted and burn things."

Todd grinned. "That's why we prebake the finished product, so it's picture perfect. You add ingredients, you stir, someone else bakes."

"You mean it's like a giant fib that she's really

cooking all that stuff?'' Tess demanded. She scowled at Megan. "Did Tex know?"

"It's not really a fib," Megan said defensively. "There's not enough time to bake on the air. Every show precooks the final product so it can be dished up and served at the end of the episode."

"What about those fancy flower arrangements?" Tess demanded, her expression indignant. "Is some florist hiding backstage to do those, too? And what about when you do that quilting stuff?"

Megan felt as if she'd been caught cheating on her high school math test. "I do most of the work," she insisted, "but naturally I have consultants. I have a whole staff of people doing the planning and preparation. Otherwise, I'd never get the magazine out each month or get the show on the air every day."

"But everybody thinks you're like this Suzy Homemaker or something," Tess protested. "What a rip-off. You probably don't even like to do that stuff."

"Of course I do," Megan said. "Okay, some of it's a little tedious, but most of it is challenging and fun."

Tess still looked as if she'd been betrayed. "I'll bet you can't even grow a decent tomato, not the way Tex could."

Actually, Megan was pretty sure she could grow a tomato if she had to. How hard could it be to stick a seed in the ground, water it and watch it grow? Unfortunately, as a practical matter, there hadn't been a lot of places to grow a tomato in her New York apartment. The gardening segments were done at a borrowed house on Long Island...by a landscaping professional and a farmer.

"I could grow one," she insisted to Tess.

"Bet you couldn't," Tess countered.

"Well, it's not the right time of year to try," Megan said, thankful for small favors.

"Ever heard of a greenhouse?" Tess demanded. "Tex has one. He put it in back of the barn so he could get a jump start on the growing season."

Just then Jake joined them. "What's in back of the barn?"

"A greenhouse," Megan said, unable to keep a despondent note out of her voice.

"And that is important because...?" he asked, clearly confused.

"Because she and Tess are having a pissing contest over tomato growing," Todd said with evident amusement. "I suspect we're about to be treated to dueling tomato plants, winner takes all."

Tess looked a little too intrigued by the idea for Megan's comfort. If she weren't careful, there would be a tell-all in some tabloid about how she'd been bested in the garden by a pip-squeak. Her sterling reputation would be left in tatters.

"Forget it," she said emphatically. "I am not going to challenge you to a tomato-growing contest."

"It would be a great segment for the show," Todd taunted. "We could do little weekly updates, measure the height, count the blossoms. Putting you and Tess together on the air would make you seem even more human. The audience would love it."

"The audience will not love it, because they will

not see it,'' Megan insisted. ''This isn't some game where I have to prove myself to an eight-year-old.''

Jake regarded her knowingly. ''Maybe you do have something to prove,'' he suggested. ''Not to Tess. To yourself.''

''I do not have anything to prove,'' she retorted. ''Now, can we get to work?''

''You're the boss,'' Todd said readily.

Jake bent down and brushed a kiss across her lips. ''Think about it,'' he murmured in a voice too low to be overheard. He stood and held out his hand. ''Come on, Tess. Let's go riding.''

Megan's gaze shot to his. ''You're taking her riding?''

''She needs another lesson and you need us out of your hair, right?''

''Right,'' she agreed.

As they left, heading out to enjoy a picture-perfect fall day, maybe one of the last before winter's onset, Megan sighed. She was surprised by the wave of disappointment that washed over her. For the first time in years, she actually regretted that she always made work her first priority.

''Some guy's coming this afternoon,'' Tess announced as she and Jake rode toward the creek.

''What guy?'' Jake asked, not at all pleased by the jealousy that streaked through him.

''Todd says he's some numbers guy who's got the hots for Megan.'' She regarded Jake with evident curiosity. ''What's a numbers guy?''

''An accountant, I imagine,'' Jake responded, taking note of the fact that Tess apparently didn't require an explanation for the rest of Todd's remark. Either she'd dismissed it as unimportant or she knew entirely too much for a kid.

"I don't think you need to worry, though," Tess went on slyly.

"Why would I worry?"

"In case Megan likes him back, silly. But she doesn't."

"And how would you know that?"

"Todd said."

Jake shook his head in disbelief. "You actually asked Todd?"

"Well, of course I did," she said matter-of-factly. "How else are you supposed to find out stuff?"

"Some things are personal," Jake pointed out.

"Todd said, not me. I figured it was okay to ask. Besides, Megan wasn't there to get mad."

"You were still prying into her private life."

"I guess that means you don't want to know what else Todd said," she suggested.

"About this numbers guy?"

"Uh-huh."

Curiosity won out over his desire to set a good example. "What did he say?"

"He said the guy thinks he's some kinda big hero."

Jake tensed. If there was going to be a hero in Megan's life, it wasn't going to be some CPA from New York. "Todd told you that?"

"No," Tess said impatiently. "He said that to Megan before I talked to him."

"And you just happened to overhear it?"

Tess regarded him with pity. "When you're a kid,

you gotta listen. Grown-ups are always deciding stuff about you. It's best to know what's going on.''

Jake admired her logic, if not her strategy. ''Eavesdropping is not a good thing, short stuff.''

''Megan said that, too. What are you guys, the etiquette police?''

Jake coughed to hide a chuckle. ''And what do you know about etiquette?''

''Not much, according to Miss Herter at school. She's always saying I got no manners.''

''And very little grasp of proper English,'' Jake added. Oh, well, one thing at a time. He'd leave the grammar to the teachers, but it wouldn't hurt to reinforce a few lessons on manners.

He gave Tess a stern look. ''Okay, here's the deal. No more listening at keyholes, hiding behind chairs—''

''I never—''

''Oh, yes, you did,'' he said firmly. ''Tex warned me about that little habit of yours and it won't happen again. Private conversations are meant to be just that, private.''

''I still say I got a right to know stuff.''

''If you have questions, ask.''

''How do I know what questions to ask if I don't know what's going on?''

''Maybe you should just stop assuming that something is going on that involves you.''

''Easy for you to say,'' she said grumpily. ''Every time I turn around something's happening, and I'm usually right smack in the middle of it.''

She had a point. ''Okay, I'll make you a promise.

If anything comes up that involves you, I will tell you about it right up front."

She regarded him skeptically. "Cross your heart?"

Jake sketched a cross over his chest. "Promise."

Tess nodded solemnly. "Okay, then. Maybe you'd better start by telling me where my mom's hiding out."

"I haven't seen your mother since she visited the ranch the other day," he said honestly.

"But she's gonna come back, right?"

"She said she would."

"Is Megan just gonna let me go with her?"

"No, absolutely not," Jake insisted. "You know that, Tess. That's why she stayed here this week."

"Maybe I should just go with my mom now and get it over with," she said wearily. "It would make it easier."

"Easier for whom?"

"Megan. You."

"Do you want to be with your mom?" Jake asked cautiously.

"No way. I mean, it's not like she wanted me till she found out about Tex being dead and me maybe having some money, right?"

"Then you can stop worrying about it. Megan and I will see to it that you stay right here at the ranch. Tex wanted you to stay here. He set it up so that you could."

"But he made Megan come home when she didn't want to. That's my fault."

"It's not your fault. It's just the way things had to be. Megan will adjust." He leaned down. "I'll tell you a secret."

"What?"

"I think she's a whole lot happier about being home than she's been letting on."

"Boy," Tess said, "she must be really good at faking it, 'cause, if you ask me, she doesn't like it at all."

"Remember when you first came to the ranch?" Jake suggested.

Tess nodded.

"After a few days, you started to like it, didn't you?"

"I guess."

"But you didn't let Tex or anybody else know that for a long time, did you?"

"No."

"Why not?"

Tess shrugged. "I dunno."

"Maybe it was partly because you wanted to punish everybody for making you come in the first place," Jake suggested.

Her expression was puzzled. "So, Megan is kinda getting even with all of us?"

"I doubt she realizes it, but yes, I think that is exactly what's happening." At least, he prayed it was. More than anything, he wanted Megan to wake up one of these days and realize that she was truly glad to be back in Wyoming.

Glad to have him back in her life again…even if she was too stubborn to admit it to him.

19

Peter had actually bought a Stetson—a white one, yet—just as Todd had predicted. Megan couldn't seem to take her eyes off of him as he stood in the doorway of the ranch house, all dressed up as some sort of western hero right down to the tips of his fancy new snakeskin boots. Barely five-ten, a little flabby around his middle, he looked thoroughly uncomfortable and totally out of his fancy Upper East Side element. A suit could cover a lot of sins that an unforgiving pair of jeans could not.

"Well, howdy," she said, sensing that she'd better slip into a western role herself to keep him from feeling utterly foolish.

Apparently she didn't succeed in reassuring him. His expression fell. "It's too much, isn't it?"

She nodded her agreement. "A little over the top."

"Does that mean I can get out of these damned boots? They're killing my feet."

"Gucci loafers in your luggage?" she inquired.

"Right on top."

"Next to the Armani suit, no doubt." She led him to a guest room. "When you've changed, come back downstairs. Todd and I are in the office working on preproduction notes. We'll take a break when you get

there, and you and I can work on some budget issues.''

That faint flicker of disappointment returned to his
eyes. Megan guessed that he'd hoped for a more personal welcome, something warmer than the peck on
the cheek she'd given him.

It was funny. After all these years, Peter Davis was
still an enigma to her. He'd been recommended to her
by friends the year she'd arrived in New York. His
client list was a roster of Manhattan's wealthiest in-
dividuals and fast-rising boutique corporations. He
traveled in society circles, lending prestige to dinner
parties and his name to charity balls.

Yet there was a shy vulnerability about him, a hint
that no one was more surprised by his success than
he was. Megan had been touched and flattered by his
attention at first, but when it became increasingly evident that his infatuation was turning into sentiments
she couldn't return, she had tried to cool the personal
side of their relationship. Peter had continued to pursue her with dogged devotion, inviting her to dinner
parties, theater openings and regular business lunches.

What he needed in his life was a warm, generous
woman who could make a real home for him, not one
who only pretended to have those skills on TV and
in the pages of a magazine.

An image of Peggy came to mind, only to be hurriedly banished. Peggy was married to Johnny
Barkley, for better or worse. She was definitely an
unsuitable choice for a matchmaking scheme, which
just went to prove that Megan was no better at that
than she was at baking. How she had ended up in her
chosen career was yet another enigma. Maybe she

was trying to prove that anyone could overcome a dysfunctional background to achieve domestic bliss...at least on some superficial level. Heaven knew, her mother had rarely stepped into a kitchen, except when she'd been trying to make up for neglecting Megan. Then she'd baked cookies with a frenzy.

"So, the hero's come to save the day," Todd said when Megan joined him after showing Peter to his room.

"Don't you dare make fun of him," she snapped. "He just wanted to fit in, which is more than I can say for you."

Todd held up his hands in a gesture of surrender. "Okay, I give up. Peter's a saint and I'm a jerk."

She waved off the apology. "I'm sorry. I was just feeling guilty."

"Guilty?" Jake echoed, coming into the room looking tanned and healthy and vigorously masculine.

"Don't get excited. I'm not confessing to my sins," Megan told him, unable to ignore the stark contrast between this man and the one she'd just left upstairs. Measured against Jake, who was all solid muscle, Peter made a lackluster showing. She couldn't help wondering if she'd been subconsciously comparing them for years.

"Too bad," Jake said. "Listening to you recite your sins could have been fascinating."

"Where's Tess?" she asked, deliberately changing the subject.

"In the kitchen eating chocolate chip cookies."

"I'm surprised you're not in there with her."

He grinned. "I've had mine." He held up a foil-covered plate. "Mrs. Gomez dispatched me to bring a batch to you guys."

Todd reached eagerly for the plate, then breathed in deeply. "Still warm from the oven. I've died and gone to heaven."

"You work for a culinary celebrity," Jake pointed out. "Doesn't she ever feed you leftovers?"

"Sure," Todd said, biting into a cookie. "Take-out Chinese is my personal favorite."

"I meant from her own private kitchen."

Megan scowled at the pair of them. "I don't cook at home."

Jake chuckled knowingly. "Still lousy, huh? I thought maybe being the host of *Megan's World* might have taught you something. You make it look so easy."

"Don't you start on me, too," she said. "I've already had this conversation with Tess." She glanced up and spotted Peter in the doorway. He looked more like himself in his tailored slacks, silk-blend shirt and polished loafers. "Come on in. You know Todd, of course. And this is Jake Landers. Jake, Peter Davis."

With Todd looking on in amusement, the two men squared off as if readying for a sparring match. Even dusty and windblown, Jake had the clear advantage. Peter exuded money and polish. Jake exuded pure male sensuality. Megan truly wished it weren't so. Peter was a whole lot easier to cope with. Safer.

"Peter and I have business to discuss," she said, hoping to dismiss Jake.

Instead, he settled into her grandfather's favorite leather chair. "Don't mind me, darlin'. I'll be quiet as a mouse. You won't even know I'm here."

Unfortunately, ignoring Jake's presence was as impossible as pretending that she was still happily ensconced in her New York life-style. "Whatever," she mumbled.

"Megan, these really are private business matters," Peter said stiffly. "Do you think a stranger should be present?"

"Oh, I'm no stranger," Jake said before Megan could reply. "Meggie and I go way back. For a time there, we were practically joined at the hip."

Todd choked on his cookie. Megan glared at him, then at Jake. "If you're staying, keep quiet."

"Not another word," he vowed solemnly.

Of course, the fact that he remained stoically silent while she and Peter discussed her company's financial situation made her even more aware of his presence. A discreet cough every now and then hinted of his disapproval of various plans offered up by Peter.

Jake scowled when Peter shook his head over her plan to create a production facility in Whispering Wind.

"What kind of rent will you be paying for this studio space?" Peter asked. "What are the cost projections for renovations? The kind of equipment you'll need won't be cheap. What about offices? Where will the crews come from? It seems to me to be sheer folly to even consider this, when everything you need is already available in New York."

"I can't be in New York right now," Megan said. "This is temporary."

"Then it truly is a waste of money," Peter countered. "I'd have to strongly advise you against it."

"Maybe so," she said, accepting his judgment. "But can I do it?"

"There's money in the bank, if that's what you're asking," he said tightly. "I thought you were asking my advice."

"I think she's made it clear that she's not, hot-shot," Jake piped up, then gave her a rueful smile. "Sorry. I lost my head."

"Yeah, right," she muttered. "Okay, we're not getting anywhere like this. Why don't we have an-other meeting tonight, when Kenny has given me the cost projections?"

Peter scowled in Jake's direction. "Will he be here?"

"More than likely," Megan said with a sigh of resignation, after glancing at Jake's intractable ex-pression. She reached for Peter's hand. "Come on. I'll show you around."

"Better watch those shoes, Pete. There's a lot of cow dung on a ranch," Jake called after them.

As soon as they'd walked outside, Peter regarded her with a miffed expression. "Who is that man?"

"An old friend," she said wearily. "And my grandfather's attorney."

Peter stared at her incredulously. "*He* has a law degree?"

"Oh, yes. He used to practice in Chicago, till he decided to come back here, more than likely for the sole purpose of making my life a living hell."

Jake stuck his head out the door. "I heard that, darlin'," he said, before disappearing inside again.

"He is a very annoying person," Peter proclaimed.

"Tell me about it," Megan said. The only trouble

was she was beginning to count on that very annoying person. Moreover, he was beginning to make her palms sweat and her knees go weak just the way he had all those years ago. It was a very bad sign.

Satisfied that Peter wasn't outside making moves on Megan, Jake returned to Tex's office and settled in to cross-examine Todd.

"What's the scoop on those two?" he asked point-blank. Jake was fully aware that he was now doing exactly what he'd warned Tess against doing—prying into Megan's private life.

"Megan and Peter?" Todd responded, his expression innocent as a lamb. "He's her CPA, but, of course, she told you that."

"Anything more to it? The guy hovers like he has a right to."

"Why don't you ask her?"

"Because you're here and I'm asking you."

"Then you're flat out of luck, because Megan pays me very well to keep my mouth shut about her private business."

Jake wanted to remind him that he hadn't been half so discreet with Tess, but stopped himself. He considered pressing the point, but concluded that Todd's loyalty was too admirable a trait to mess with. "Does she know how lucky she is to have you working for her?" he asked instead.

Todd grinned. "I remind her every chance I get."

"How do you like Wyoming?"

"Hate it," Todd said succinctly.

"What happens if she decides to stay?"

"I'm praying that won't happen."

Jake gave him a warning look. "I'm praying just as hard that it will."

Todd shrugged. "I guess we'll see whose prayers have more pull."

"I'm not relying entirely on outside forces. I aim to do a little persuading of my own."

"By sleeping with her?" Todd asked, regarding Jake with disconcerting directness.

Jake considered his own response carefully. Discretion be damned. "No," he said finally. "That will be all about pleasure."

"Then you'll use Tess," Todd concluded with evident scorn. "You really are a low-down louse, aren't you?"

"No. I'm a man who cares what happens to an eight-year-old kid who's just lost the only person who ever really loved her. I'm also a man who knows Meggie well enough to understand that she'll never get past the guilt if she doesn't do what her grand-daddy counted on her doing."

"Why here? Why can't she do that in New York?"

"Because this is Tess's home." Jake shrugged. "And Megan's, though I don't think she's realized how important that is to her yet." He wondered if, in the end, that wasn't what had drawn him back to Whispering Wind, despite all the bad memories.

"It's a house, land, a bunch of cows," Todd said disparagingly.

"It's her heritage."

"What makes you think her heritage matters to her? She ran away from it once."

"And I'm betting that she's regretted it ever since," Jake told him, as sure of that as he was of his own growing feelings for her. Meggie needed a home more than most. So did he.

"Not so you'd notice. I keep her schedule. Her life in New York is full, jam-packed with friends."

"And empty of the one thing that counts," Jake said.

Todd looked perplexed.

"Family," Jake said quietly, thinking of how desperately he'd always wanted one of his own. All those years of living on the edge with a mother who'd drifted in and out of an alcoholic haze had made him long for a real home, the kind Tex had made first for Meggie and then for Tess. Jake wanted children and family feasts on holidays and a zillion presents tucked under a towering Christmas tree that sparkled with lights. Maybe it was an idyllic illusion. Maybe it didn't exist in real life, but he wanted to find out for himself.

He wanted all of that with Meggie, a woman who'd tossed everything aside for a single life and an all-consuming career. Maybe Todd was right. Maybe Jake was nothing but a damned fool thinking he could have all of that with Meggie. Just because they'd once shared that dream didn't mean it still meant anything to her.

Supper was a very tense affair. Megan didn't have the energy or the will to referee the nonstop sparring between Jake and Peter. With Tess chiming in on Jake's side and Todd smirking, Megan's stomach was in knots by the end of the meal.

Maybe that was why the unexpected appearance of Flo Olson set her off. When Tess's mother burst into the dining room like an avenging angel come to claim her own, Megan rose from her chair and met the woman before she could get anywhere near Tess.

"I want you out of here," she said with quiet force, waving off Jake, who'd also risen. "You're in violation of a court order."

"I don't give a damn about court orders," Flo said. "Tess is my baby."

Peter regarded her with shock. "Who is this woman?"

Flo barely spared him a glance, before focusing on Tess again. She held out her arms. "Come here, baby. Give mama a hug."

Wide-eyed and clearly frightened, Tess slipped out of her chair. But instead of going to her mother, she crept close to Jake, who circled an arm protectively around her shoulders.

"Go away, Mama," Tess said in a small, but surprisingly firm voice. "I don't want you here and I don't want to go with you. You don't love me. You just want Tex's money."

Flo's face crumpled, and for the first time, Megan felt a vague stirring of pity for the woman. Maybe her presence wasn't entirely about Tex's money, after all. Maybe she really did regret abandoning Tess.

Or did Megan just want to believe that because she needed to think that Sarah had lived with regrets? Her mother had shown no evidence of remorse. Sarah hadn't crawled back and begged forgiveness the way Flo was doing. Megan realized that on some level she was actually a little jealous of Tess. Even after all these years, Megan still thought a dysfunctional mother was better than no mother at all. How pitiful was that?

"Tess, sweetie, I've missed you," Flo said, holding out a hand beseechingly.

Tess took Jake's hand instead. "I don't believe you. You never even wrote me a postcard."

"Baby, I was busy, but I'm here now. I've come to get you. We'll be together again."

"I think Tess has already made her wishes clear," Jake said coldly. "Now, will you leave or will I be forced to call the sheriff?"

Flo looked from him to Megan. "You're a woman. Surely you understand what a mother feels."

"Sorry," Megan said, hardening her heart against the woman's obvious, if belated, distress. "I'm afraid I don't. Mine was just like you."

"I made a mistake," Flo whispered. "I never should have left her here."

"But you did," Jake said. "She's an O'Rourke now. It's all nice and legal. Tex saw to that. You have no claim to her."

"She's my blood," Flo protested.

"And Tex's," Megan reminded her. "Like Jake said, she's an O'Rourke."

Flo seemed about to protest again, but Jake nudged Tess toward Megan, then took hold of Flo's arm and steered her from the room. She was still arguing when they finally moved out of earshot.

Tears were streaking down Tess's face as she stared off in the direction her mother had gone. Megan knelt down in front of her.

"Peter, let's get back to work," Todd said diplomatically, tossing his napkin on the table and leaving the rest of his dinner untouched.

"But—"

Peter's protest was cut off as Todd ushered him from the room as expertly as he guided unwanted visitors from Megan's office in New York.

"What's going to happen to her now?" Tess asked Megan in a quavery voice.

"That's up to her," Megan said. "If she keeps trying to see you, she could be sent to jail." She studied Tess intently. "Unless you'd rather we make arrangements for her to visit you here. It would be okay, if that's what you want. She is your mom. I've told you before it's perfectly natural to still have feelings for her."

Tess bit her lower lip. "She sounded sort of like she really missed me, didn't she?"

"I thought so, too," Megan said honestly, praying she wasn't misjudging the other woman's intentions. If she hurt Tess again, Megan would personally wring her neck.

Tess's expression turned hopeful. "Maybe it's not all about me being rich now."

"Maybe not."

"Would it be okay to maybe ask her to dinner or something?"

"If that's what you want, I won't forbid it."

"What about Jake? Will he freak out?"

Megan grinned. "Probably, but this is your call, Tess. Jake and I will work it out however you want." She tucked a finger under Tess's chin. "Just remember what Jake and I said—you're an O'Rourke now.

That means you've got me to depend on. I may mess up from time to time, but we're family.''

Tess nodded solemnly. ''I guess I'll think about it some more.''

''Take your time. You don't have to decide tonight or even tomorrow.''

''What if she leaves town before I make up my mind?'' Tess asked plaintively.

Megan figured that would tell them all they needed to know about Flo, but she didn't say that. ''We'll find her,'' she promised. She doubted it would be that difficult. Though she prayed it was otherwise, she still didn't entirely believe that Flo would go far from Tess's newfound wealth.

Megan brushed the tears from Tess's cheeks. ''Okay, now?''

Tess nodded, then gave her a shaky smile. ''I'll be better after I've had ice cream.''

Megan glanced at the table. ''You haven't finished your vegetables,'' she observed sternly, then grinned. ''Oh, what the heck. Neither have I. Two hot fudge sundaes coming up.''

''Three,'' Tess said. ''Jake's going to want one, too.''

''Yes, I imagine he will,'' Megan agreed, leading the way into the kitchen.

With Mrs. Gomez gone for the evening, they were left to their own devices. Fortunately, dishing up ice cream was a skill Megan had acquired early on. She loaded the dishes with hot fudge, then let Tess squirt whipped cream on top. Jake returned just as they'd finished.

He took one look at the gooey desserts and pulled

up a chair. "I assume this one is for me," he said, grabbing the biggest sundae.

"It could have been for Peter," Megan grumbled.

"Never. He's probably into poached pears with a carmelized sauce."

He was, but Megan wouldn't have admitted it if her life depended on it.

"Everything okay?" she asked instead.

He nodded. "How about in here?"

"Me and Megan made a pact," Tess said.

"Oh, really? What kind of pact?"

"She's gonna stick by me no matter what." Tess regarded Jake solemnly. "She said you would, too."

Jake reached over and ruffled her hair. "That's a guarantee, sweet pea." His gaze locked with Megan's. "You couldn't shake me if you tried."

There was no question the message was meant for both of them.

20

Total disaster reigned in Peggy's kitchen on Tuesday morning. Megan watched as her old friend stood in a corner and observed the scene with an obvious mix of fascination and horror. Her furniture and appliances were being rearranged, lights were being set up and cameras placed. To anyone outside the business, it must seem chaotic. To Megan it was an orchestrated beehive of activity that had become second nature.

Worried that Peggy might panic over the upheaval and back out, Megan joined her and gave her hand a quick, reassuring squeeze. "You okay?"

"It's so exciting, isn't it?" Peggy asked, surprising Megan with the sparkle in her eyes. A moment later, Peggy's eyes dimmed and worry creased her brow. "Are you sure they can put everything back when we're finished?"

"Absolutely."

"Otherwise, Johnny's going to blow a gasket. He still thinks I've lost my mind to let a bunch of strangers tear our house apart. I asked him what kind of friends we'd be if we didn't help you out when you're in a jam. He asked me just how often I'd heard from you over the years, and then stomped out." She grimaced. "Sorry. I probably shouldn't have told you that."

"It's okay. I haven't been the very best friend," Megan conceded. "But I want to make up for that, Peggy. I really do."

"There's no need," Peggy insisted, her expression bleak. "Nobody understands better than I do that sometimes you just get caught up in living, in making it from one day to the next. There's not much time for anything or anyone else."

There was a troubling note of despair in her voice that tugged at Megan's heart. "Hey," she said, putting her hands on her old friend's shoulders and waiting until Peggy met her gaze. "Is everything really okay with you? Can I help?"

"Not unless you can get Johnny to stop sleeping with every female he takes a fancy to," Peggy blurted in an unexpected burst of bitterness, then covered her face with her hands. "Oh, God, I never meant to say that. I wanted you to think my life was just perfect. That's what I want everybody to believe. Not that they do around town. Half the women have slept with Johnny and the rest know about it. Sometimes it's all I can do to show my face in church on Sunday."

Megan was shocked by the confession and by the humiliation Peggy had endured. "Why haven't you thrown him out?" she asked, genuinely perplexed.

"I honestly don't know. I hate his guts," Peggy said harshly, then sighed. "At least some of the time."

"But you still haven't stopped loving him?" Megan guessed.

"No," Peggy admitted. "How stupid does that make me?"

"Foolish maybe, not stupid," Megan said. "The heart can't always be ruled by the head."

"Even if I really did hate his guts, he's all I have," Peggy said. "The kids adore him. What would I do if he left? I can't run this ranch alone. And I can't hire somebody. We barely make ends meet as it is. The money from this shoot will be a godsend. I didn't tell Johnny you were paying to use our kitchen. I'm hiding every penny in a savings account he knows nothing about. Otherwise, he'll just spend it on his women, the same way he does every other spare penny I manage to save."

Megan sighed. This explained the tension she'd felt between the two, and all of Jake's innuendoes that it was old news and a familiar habit.

"I'm so sorry. I wish there were something I could do."

"Don't be sorry. It's not your doing. I was sixteen when I fell for Johnny, and nothing would do but that I have him the very second we graduated from high school. He was a flirt then, but I thought once we were married, he'd settle down. Far from it. It's as if he's determined to sow the wild oats now that he couldn't because we married so young."

Megan wanted to shake her friend for putting up with it, but Peggy's reasons for staying were her own. Once more Megan thought of Peter and what a good match Peter and Peggy would be if the circumstances were different. Peter truly was the sort of solid, dependable man that Peggy had once described Johnny as being. Even now, despite his avowed disapproval, he was back at her ranch working on a business plan that would permit her to run her operation from Whispering Wind. Peggy deserved someone who understood that kind of loyalty.

Still, Megan cautioned herself to stay out of Peggy's marital situation. It was far too volatile.

"If you ever want to talk about it, I'll be there," she promised, and left it at that.

Peggy regarded her doubtfully. "Even after you've gone back to your exciting life in New York?"

"Even then," Megan insisted, though at the moment there seemed to be no prospect of leaving Whispering Wind in the near future. "Now let's forget about Johnny Barkley and whip up some gourmet holiday treats, so everyone in the country will know what a fabulous cook you are."

Peggy's hands trembled so badly at the mention of the upcoming taping that she had to clench them together. "Are you sure?" she asked nervously. "Maybe you should do the segment by yourself. I'll just make a mess of it."

"No way. They're your recipes and you're a far better cook than I ever dreamed of being." Sensing that she'd better get the taping started before Peggy panicked and backed out, Megan glanced around until she spotted the director. "Hey, Kenny, are we set?"

"In five," he responded. "If you and Peggy will take your places, we can do a sound and lighting check and we'll be good to go."

Ten minutes later the cameras were rolling. Any visible signs of Peggy's nerves settled down the minute Megan started asking her questions about the ingredients they were using in the delicate holiday pastries that had been made by Peggy's family for generations.

As naturally as if she'd done it a hundred times before, Peggy wove in details of her family history. She added cultural traditions from Sweden, where her great-grandmother had been born before moving to the United States with her husband at the turn of the century. Her hands flew confidently as she chopped nuts and dried fruit and mixed in sugar and cinnamon before rolling it in a thin, flaky pastry dough. Megan watched with awe and amusement as her friend literally stole the show.

"That's a wrap," Ken called as Peggy held up a plate of freshly baked pastries for the last shot.

Peggy slowly put the plate on the counter and turned to Megan, an expression of wonder on her face. Her cheeks were flushed from the heat of the oven and the lights. "That's it? That's all there is to it?"

Megan thought of the preproduction work, the scheduling, the thousand other details, then grinned. "Pretty much."

"Oh, wow, that was wonderful," Peggy said. "What a rush! People are actually going to watch me cook on TV."

"A million-plus," Megan confirmed.

As the number sank in, Peggy looked like she might faint. "That many?" she asked weakly.

"Did you think we were doing this just for family and friends?"

"I don't know what I thought, but it wasn't a million, I guarantee that. Thank heaven you didn't tell me that before or I'd have fainted dead away."

"You would have been fine," Megan contradicted.

"In fact, you were terrific," Kenny said, coming over to congratulate her. "A real natural."

Micah joined them. "Nice job, Peggy," she said, though with less enthusiasm than Kenny. "Megan, I'm heading back to town. I've got things to do. Now that we know this will work, I'm thinking of flying back to New York first thing in the morning to take care of some business there."

Megan regarded her with surprise. "You're going back? Now?"

"For a few days at least. Kenny and Todd can handle anything that comes up here," she said with an all-too-familiar edge of resentment. "Do you have a problem with that?"

"No, I'm just surprised."

"I'll check in with you when I get to New York, find out how things are going."

Megan nodded. She had a feeling there was more behind Micah's sudden decision to abandon ship, but she couldn't honestly say she regretted her going. Her attitude was generally adding to the tension, rather than relieving it.

"I'll talk to you tomorrow, then," Megan said, and watched as Micah walked away. She turned to Kenny. "Any idea what that's all about?"

"She hates her room. She hates it here. She hates that Todd has more access to you than she does. She's a very bitter woman," Kenny said. "If you ask me, not that you did, I say let her go for good. She's not adding anything."

Megan was surprised by his outburst. "I thought you two got along."

"I like Micah well enough. I used to respect her." He shrugged. "Something's going on with her, though. I can't put my finger on it. I just think you'd be wise to get rid of her." He turned to Peggy, clearly ending the discussion. "What are you whipping up tomorrow?"

"Venison stew, I think," Peggy said with a questioning look at Megan. "Right?"

Megan accepted the deliberate change of subject. "Yes, that's it."

Kenny responded with enthusiasm. "Wait till I tell the guys. Right now they're gobbling up these cookies so fast they're burning their tongues."

"Maybe they should have waited till they cooled," Megan said dryly.

"No way. They were too afraid they'd be gone."

After he'd walked away, Megan turned to her friend. "You're already a hit with the people who count," she told her. "These guys are the best in the business and they don't hand out praise lightly."

"They're just some cookies from old family recipes," Peggy said demurely.

"This isn't just about the cookies. It's about the way you handled yourself in front of the camera. You were fantastic," she enthused, then paused thoughtfully. "And that gives me an idea."

"What?" Peggy asked.

"Let me think about it and we'll talk tomorrow," Megan promised, giving Peggy a hug. "Go put your feet up and rest. The guys will clean up this mess and put everything back where it belongs."

"It seems such a waste, when they'll need to move it all around again tomorrow," Peggy said.

"Don't worry. They're used to it. It's part of the job on a location shoot like this. Besides, I don't want to give Johnny any reason to get annoyed at you for letting us do this."

"Thanks," Peggy said, clearly relieved. "I think I'll go take a long bath. Johnny won't be home with the kids for at least another hour. After my bath, I'll actually have time to curl up with a book and enjoy the peace and quiet."

Megan was almost out the door when Todd caught up with her. "Are you thinking what I'm thinking?" he asked.

"That she could do the cooking segments on this show with one hand tied behind her back?" Megan asked.

"Pretty much."

She regarded him intently. "You really saw it, too?"

"Would I have said it otherwise?"

"It could make such a difference for her," Megan stated, thinking of the freedom Peggy would have to start over without that louse of a husband. An income from doing the cooking segments would nicely supplement whatever she could make running the ranch. Of course, all of that assumed that Megan would be staying on in Whispering Wind and producing the shows from here.

"You make a great team, too," Todd said. "There's an obvious affection that comes across on the air."

"Would the audience respond okay to me not doing every little thing? Would it hurt my image not to be the sole proprietor of *Megan's World?*" She realized as she asked that she trusted his judgment on this far more than she did Micah's. Maybe Todd should be producing the show. Maybe that would be the lure she could use to keep him happy about being in Wyoming. He'd wanted to be in television. Here was his chance.

"If you dragged in a total stranger, they might hate it," he said, his expression thoughtful. "But the friendship and history you and Peggy share works on the air. I think they'd love it. Just imagine the mileage you could get out of chatting about families and kids and relationships. Those would be a natural extension of who you are, instead of phony talk show advice from some paid expert. I think it brings a whole new warmth and dimension to the program. If you want my advice, go for it."

"If she'll do it," Megan said, wondering if Peggy would dare defy her husband and strike out on her own. It could very well mean the end of her marriage. Once Peggy was financially independent, Johnny would have no hold over her any longer. Was Peggy really ready to take that next step to breaking free?

As they neared her car, Megan spotted Jake waiting in the shadows. That old familiar tingling began low in her belly. If things had been different, at another time in her life, she might have walked straight into his arms. Now she stood awkwardly and waited.

"How'd it go?" he asked, moving toward her.

"Perfect," Todd chimed in. "Not that you were asking me. Now if you'll excuse me, I think I'll catch a ride back to the ranch with Kenny."

"Isn't Kenny heading into town?" Megan murmured, never taking her gaze off of Jake's face.

"He'll detour. No big deal," Todd assured her. "Unless you two want a third wheel along." He glanced at Jake's forbidding expression. "Didn't think so. Good night."

"Smart man, your assistant," Jake observed as Todd walked away.

"Why are you here?"

He shrugged. "It's not so complicated. I wanted to see you. I wanted to hear how it went."

"It went smoothly enough," she said breathlessly as he moved inevitably closer.

"Did I hear you discussing whether to make Peggy an offer to join the show as a regular? Kenny was out here earlier and said she'd done a great job."

Megan nodded, unable to speak as his thumb traced her bottom lip.

"A generous offer," he prompted.

"She's good. Better than good, in fact."

"You're not jealous that she came in and knocked everybody's socks off?"

"Absolutely not."

Jake nodded solemnly. "I'm proud of you."

Her gaze narrowed. "Why? Did you think I was that insecure or that selfish?"

"Sometimes I don't know what to make of you," he said candidly, even as his fingers combed through her hair. "But I do know I want you."

She swallowed hard and backed up a step. "Jake," she protested, "don't say things like that."

"It's true. My saying it doesn't change anything."

"Yes, it does."

"Just making my intentions clear, darlin'. That's all."

"If you were making your intentions clear about buying a tractor, maybe it wouldn't be a big deal. Since it's me you claim to be after, it matters."

He grinned. "Maybe I should start with a tractor and move up. Do you have one you'd like to get rid of?"

"What would you do with it if I did?"

"Plow a field, I imagine," he said distractedly, his gaze locked with hers.

"At this time of year?"

"In the spring," he murmured. "Whenever." He rubbed the tip of his finger across her lips. "Sorry. I can't wait to work up to this."

He bent his head and claimed her mouth before she could protest. The touch was as light and gentle as the flutter of butterfly wings, but her response was lightning quick and hot enough to melt metal. She told herself this wasn't the time or the place, that she was treading on dangerous turf, but that rock-solid advice didn't seem to stop her from swaying into his embrace.

For little more than a heartbeat, she was crushed against him, aware of every solid inch of muscle, of the hard evidence of his arousal. She was stunned when he put his hands on her shoulders to steady her and backed away a step.

"Bad idea," he murmured, looking as dazed as she felt.

"You started it," she reminded him.

"And I'd finish it, too, but not here and not now. In case you've forgotten, we have an audience."

Slowly the sounds around them began to filter through her sensual haze. Trucks were starting as the crew prepared to head back to town. There were a few catcalls as they passed by.

"I'm firing every one of them first thing in the morning," she muttered.

"That would leave you in a bit of a bind, wouldn't it? Besides, there's probably some union rule forbidding you from firing an employee just because he caught you kissing."

"Now you sound like a lawyer."

"I am a lawyer."

"More's the pity. I thought you always wanted to be a rancher. That's what you used to say. Isn't that why you want Tex's ranch?"

"That and you," he said casually, then grinned. "Actually, I got sidetracked years ago."

"I thought you were too bullheaded to get sidetracked."

"The promise of money and power proved to be a terrific incentive. Then there was the beautiful woman."

Megan's gaze narrowed. "What beautiful woman?"

"My wife."

She stared. "Excuse me?"

"I guess no one's bothered to mention that I was married for a few years."

"No, I guess not," she agreed, trying not to sound disgruntled. "What happened?"

"She got a better deal. One of my law partners was on a faster track."

"Ouch. That must have hurt."

"It just winged me. No lasting damage. I should

thank her. It provided the motivation I needed to get out of Chicago and come back here.''

"To claim a ranch?"

"And an even more beautiful woman," he reminded her.

"Don't say that," Megan protested. "You didn't come back to Whispering Wind because of me. I wasn't even here."

"But the memories of you were," he said simply. "There were a lot of things I missed about this place. You were at the top of the list."

She regarded him slyly. "And Tex? After what he did to you, did you miss him, too?"

"I had made my peace with your grandfather." He shrugged. "Or at least I thought I had until I actually saw him. Then I wanted to throttle him for what he'd done to me—to us—all those years ago. When I realized how sick he was, it hit me that he was probably the single most important influence in my life and I was going to lose him. Somehow the rest didn't matter so much anymore."

"You forgave him, then?"

He nodded. "I think I finally understood that he was only trying to protect you, to give you a chance to see just how far you could go. Time proved him right, didn't it?"

"Much to his chagrin, I suspect. He never stopped wanting me back here, wanting me to take over the ranch. In the end, I guess he's had his way. Same as always."

"You're resigned to staying, then?"

"For the time being," she conceded. "Until Tess feels more settled, until she trusts me."

"And your career? Will it suffer?"

She grinned ruefully. "Much as I hate to admit it, Tex was probably right. There's a lot I can handle from right here. We'll take it day by day and see what comes up that can't be managed from the middle of nowhere."

He tapped her chest. "What about in here? Will you be okay with staying?"

She met his gaze evenly, saw the wistfulness in his eyes. "I'd rather be in New York, Jake. I can't pretend otherwise, not even for you."

He sighed. "I see."

"Do you? Do you really understand what it meant to me to go there, to make it on my own, to make a life—a name—for myself?"

"Obviously you felt you had something to prove," he said tightly. "What I can't figure out is who you needed to prove it to."

"Myself mostly. Tex, of course." Because he still looked skeptical, Megan went on. "Try to remember something, Jake. I was the kid whose own mother didn't want her. I was the kid who was thrust on a grandfather I barely knew and then abandoned by the mother I loved. Maybe my mom wasn't the best, maybe she was selfish, maybe she made a lot of mistakes. But she was all I knew and I loved her, the same way Tess still loves Flo, the same way you loved your mother."

"You got the best of it. You were left with a man who not only loved you, but did everything in his power to let you know it," Jake countered. "Wasn't that enough?"

"To make up for being abandoned by a mother?"

she asked. "I'm not sure anything can make up for that. I'll probably spend all of my life craving approval, trying to figure out why she didn't love me."

He regarded her knowingly. "And now that you have approval and love from millions who read your books and magazines or watch your TV show, is it enough?"

It was her turn to sigh. "No," she admitted in a voice barely above a whisper. "It's never enough."

He traced the line of her jaw, his expression filled with compassion. "Then isn't it time you learned to look inside? That's where you'll find the only approval that really counts, Meggie."

He was right, of course. But for reasons she'd never fully understood, every time she examined her life she came up wanting. It was a great motivator. It kept her striving to be not just better, but to be the best. As Jake had just suggested, though, she had to wonder if she'd be satisfied even if she succeeded beyond her wildest expectations.

21

All the way back to the ranch, Megan was aware of Jake's headlights in her rearview mirror. He'd announced that he was going to stop by for a visit with Tess, had gotten into his car and waited for her to start up and head away from Peggy's. Megan had been too exhausted to argue with him.

In truth, she was glad he would be there as a buffer between her and Peter. Jake had a daunting effect on the accountant's amorous intentions. She might as well take advantage of that. Maybe Peter would get the message and go home the second they finished making a few last business decisions. That would also get Peter out of the path of her misguided matchmaking designs in case she lost her head and was tempted to follow through with them.

Five minutes after they walked in, Mrs. Gomez had their very late dinner on the table, with places set for Megan, Tess, Todd, Peter and Jake. Apparently the housekeeper had seen the handwriting on the wall. As long as Peter was around, Jake would be, too. Megan wasn't entirely sure how she felt about Jake feeling so blatantly territorial about her.

"How did the taping go?" Peter asked.

"It was fantastic," Todd answered, to Peter's obvious disappointment. "Couldn't have gone more smoothly."

"Did Peggy do okay?" Tess asked. "Alissa said at school that her mom was a nervous wreck."

"Her mom was spectacular," Megan said, then glanced at Peter. "In fact, I want to hire her to do segments on a regular basis. How much can we budget for it?"

"She'll have to get union scale," Peter said. "With what you're spending on this new studio, transportation and housing for the crew, you'll be lucky to break even this year. Add in another salary and you'll be in the red."

Megan winced. "Overall or just for the show?"

"For the show, but—"

"Good. Then we can manage it. Todd, have a contract drawn up. Jake, will you go over it with him?"

Jake lifted his glass of tea in a toast. "We live to serve, isn't that right, Peter?"

Peter scowled at him. "I beg your pardon?"

"You and I, we're just the flunkies around here."

"Call yourself what you will, I am Megan's financial adviser." He turned to her. "And I can't tell you how seriously I object to this plan of yours."

Megan nodded. "Duly noted. Todd?"

"Consider it done." He grinned at Jake. "You want to draw it up or shall I?"

"You sketch out the terms," Jake said, "since you know what you have in mind. I'll put in the legal language."

"Can you have it ready for me to take along in the morning?" Megan asked.

Jake gave her an amused look. "Maybe, if I stay over."

Peter looked downright horrified by the suggestion. Megan's pulse, however, skipped several beats, before she bothered to shoot Jake down. "Sorry. All the beds are tied up."

"I'm willing to share," he said, his gaze never once leaving her now-flaming face.

"Oh, I'll just bet you are," she muttered.

"He could stay in my room," Tess volunteered. "I can sleep downstairs in Mrs. Gomez's room."

"No," Megan said hurriedly. "Mrs. Gomez is staying tonight, so she'll be here to get breakfast at the crack of dawn tomorrow."

"Then I could sleep in with you," Tess argued. "Let Jake stay, please."

Jake awaited her decision with blatant amusement. "Oh, for heaven's sake, stay if it will make you happy," Megan said finally. "I'm going to bed. Tess, are you coming? It's past your bedtime as it is."

"I want to show Jake the kittens first. They're getting really big. I want him to help me choose which one to bring in the house."

"Okay," Megan agreed. "Make a quick trip to the barn, then let Jake and Todd get to work."

"I believe I'll walk you to your room," Peter said, standing.

Megan barely managed to contain a groan. What enabled her to do it was the expression on Jake's face. He looked as if he'd just been trumped in a high-stakes game.

At the top of the stairs, Peter reached for her hand. "Megan, I have to tell you that I think you're making a terrible mistake letting that child have her way all the time. Children that age need routine and discipline.''

His interference irritated her. ''Her mother abandoned her,'' she pointed out sharply. ''Her father— my grandfather—just died. I doubt that it will hurt to indulge a few of her whims.''

Apparently he opted to let that pass. ''I don't like Jake,'' he continued instead. ''He may be a lawyer, but he's a little rough around the edges, if you ask me. I think he's shady, perhaps even dangerous.''

Megan couldn't argue with that. In fact, that hint of danger was precisely what made Jake so blasted attractive, why she'd never fully gotten him out of her system. Every woman on earth seemed to fall for the rebels, at least until she came to her senses.

''It's part of his appeal,'' she told Peter, sure that he would be appalled by her admission. Judging by his sour expression, he was.

''You can't be saying what I think you are,'' he protested. ''Do you find him attractive?''

''Sorry to say, but yes. Always have. Probably always will,'' she said with an air of resignation.

Peter met her gaze, studied her, then sighed heavily. ''I was afraid of that.''

She touched his hand sympathetically, even though she couldn't help being relieved that he was finally backing off. ''I'm sorry, Peter.''

''No need. I guess I've known for some time that we weren't suited, but I didn't want to admit it. You're the only woman I've ever met who fit all of the qualifications on my list.''

Megan's mouth gaped. "You have a list of qualifications?"

He didn't seem the least bit disturbed by her astonishment. "Well, of course. A man in my position has to choose wisely."

"Oh, Peter," she said, shaking her head. "I really, truly hope I'm around when you finally find true love."

He seemed taken aback by that. "Why?"

"Because you're going to discover that love is quite often messy and unpredictable and nothing at all like what you envisioned."

Once again an image of Peggy came to mind. What could it hurt to just introduce the two of them? Megan thought rashly. The attention of a sophisticated man like Peter would do Peggy's battered ego good, even if nothing else ever came of it.

"Will you come to the taping tomorrow?" she asked, giving in to impulse.

He regarded her with evident confusion. "But why? I have things to finish up here. Frankly, the sooner I can be on my way, the better."

"Just come," she begged. "I want you to see why I was so insistent about hiring Peggy."

"I'm no judge of talent."

"Perhaps not, but I think you'll see what the rest of us saw." In fact, she strongly suspected that he would see exactly the kind of woman he'd never expected to fall in love with.

Sweet heaven, it must be in the genes, Megan thought with dismay. If she kept this up, she was going to wind up being as much of a meddler as Tex.

* * *

Jake spent a very restless night in Tess's bed, as Megan had obviously wanted him to. The thought of Meggie being just out of reach down the hall was maddening. And with Tess tucked away in there next to her, there wasn't a damned thing he could do about it.

One of these days, though, before too very long, he was going to get even. He was going to make love to Megan the way he'd always dreamed of doing. After that, he expected all the pieces of his life to finally fall neatly into place. He would have the running of a ranch to challenge him, a few legal cases that really meant something and the family he'd always wanted.

Satisfied with his plan, he slipped out of the house before dawn to head back into town. It was a calculated move, designed to throw Megan off stride. She would expect him to be at the breakfast table, dancing attendance. Maybe she would even admit—to herself, anyway—that she missed him.

As brilliant as he thought his strategy was, he was still grumpy when he slid onto a stool at the diner and accepted a cup of coffee from Henrietta.

"You certainly look like something the cat dragged in," she noted, leaning across the counter to study him. "Bloodshot eyes, stubble on your cheeks. Were you out on a bender, Jake Landers?"

"Who are you—Perry Mason?"

"Just a friend with sharp eyes."

"And a sharp tongue. Go pester some other customer."

"You're the only one here. The doors just opened."

"Then go pester the help. Where's Barbara Sue?"

"Not here yet."

His head snapped up. "Again?"

"She called in, though. She's on her way. She's just seeing to it that those two kids of hers have breakfast and get their things together for school."

"Are you sure?"

"Have to take her word on it, don't I?" Henrietta retorted. "If I question everything that comes out of her mouth, she'll up and quit. Then who'll keep an eye on her?"

He noticed Henrietta's concern was more for Barbara Sue than it was for her own staffing problems. The woman had a heart of gold. "Okay. You're probably right," he conceded. "But you'll let me know if there's any sign of more abuse?"

"And what will you do? She's made it plain to both of us she won't press charges. I'd like to shake some sense into her, but of course that would just be counterproductive."

"I can mention the problem to Bryce. Let him keep an eye out."

"You're forgetting something. Lyle is Bryce's cousin. It's going to take a lot more than a bug in his ear from you to get him to drag Lyle into custody. His aunt Emma would tan Bryce's hide if he tried to put her precious boy into jail without twice the evidence he'd need against any other man."

"Then I'll deal with Lyle myself," Jake said. "I wouldn't mind getting in a few licks to show him what it's like to be on the receiving end."

"Tell me when and where and I'll help," Henrietta said fervently.

Jake grinned. "You would, too, wouldn't you?"

"In a heartbeat. I never did care much for bullies."

Barbara Sue strolled in then, the collar on her winter coat turned up. She caught their surreptitious survey and asked warily, "Okay, what's wrong?"

"Not a thing," Henrietta assured her. "You working front or back today?"

Barbara Sue's pale complexion flushed at the question. She was obviously aware of exactly what Henrietta was really asking: whether there were more bruises she needed to hide.

Shrugging out of her coat, she said briskly, "I'll help out here. It's time I pulled my weight around this place."

Henrietta gave her a sharp look. "You do your job. Doesn't matter whether it's here or in the kitchen. I have no complaints."

"Thank you," Barbara Sue murmured, and went off to get an apron.

"She looks almost upbeat today," Henrietta noted. "That's always a bad sign."

"Meaning?" Jake asked.

"Right when she convinces herself that things are getting better, Lyle usually sees a need to drag her back down a peg or two."

"He's that predictable?"

"Men like Lyle are always predictable," Henrietta said with disgust. "It's more fun to be mean when the victim's least expecting it."

"Damn," Jake muttered, keeping his eye on the kitchen door in anticipation of Barbara Sue's return. "There ought to be something…"

Henrietta sighed. "I know there ought to be, but

until she's ready to leave him, there's nothing any of us can do except keep an eye out for those kids. He goes near one of them and he's got me to deal with.''

Jake had a feeling Henrietta was single-handedly capable of putting the fear of God into Lyle Perkins. He just prayed it wouldn't come to that.

"Venison stew?'' Peter's face blanched. "Isn't that...?''

"Deer,'' Megan confirmed.

"You're going to cut Bambi up into little pieces?'' he asked, clearly horrified.

"Oh, for heaven's sake,'' Megan snapped. "Eating venison is no different than eating steak or chicken. I know for a fact that you are not a vegetarian. I've been on those expense account lunches with you, remember?''

"It still sounds obscene to me.''

"Well, out here, venison stew is a good meal, and nobody makes it better than Peggy.''

"If you say so.''

Just then Peggy came into the kitchen. She was dressed once again in jeans and a western shirt with a bandanna knotted jauntily at her throat. Her hair was an untamable riot of curls. The extra weight she'd put on over the years had added tantalizing curves. She was every man's fantasy of a sexy cowgirl. Peter stared at her, mouth gaping. Clearly this was not the happy homemaker he'd been expecting, Megan concluded with delight.

"Peter Davis, I'd like you to meet Peggy Barkley,'' she said, drawing them both close. "Peter's visiting from New York. He's a whiz with numbers. I'd be lost without him.''

"Maybe I should let him have a crack at my check-book," Peggy joked half-seriously. "I'm off by sixty-one cents and I can't find it for the life of me."

"Peter prefers to search for thousand-dollar mistakes," Megan said. "I'm sure he could solve your problem in no time, though, couldn't you, Peter?"

"Of course," he said, his expression bemused.

At that moment all three of Peggy's kids came racing in for a goodbye kiss.

"See you, Mom," Alissa said. "Break a leg. I heard that's what they say to all the stars before they go on stage. I think it's so awesome that you're doing this. My mom, the TV star!"

Peggy blushed. "I am not a star."

"You will be," Megan promised.

"Hey, Mom, how come I've got peanut butter and jelly again?" the youngest demanded, bringing Peggy back down to earth.

"Because that's all I had time to fix," she retorted. "You want something different, you know where the refrigerator is."

He gave her a smacking kiss. "Peanut butter's great. Can't wait."

"I thought you'd adapt," she said dryly. "Now get going before you miss the bus."

After they blasted out the door, she turned back to Peter. "Sorry. I would have introduced you, but they had about two minutes till the school bus hits the end of the lane. The driver doesn't like to wait, and obviously I can't take them in this morning."

"Another time," Peter said, looking dazed.

Megan gave a little nod of satisfaction at the way things were going and wandered off in search of Todd. She found him outside on the porch, even though the early morning air was still chilly.

"Hiding out?" she asked, sitting in the rocker next to his.

"Going over this contract one last time," he said without looking up.

"So you and Jake *did* finish it. I'd wondered."

"We wrapped it up about two this morning."

"Did he leave then?"

Todd glanced up finally and shrugged. "I don't think so. He was headed up to Tess's room last time I saw him."

"He wasn't at breakfast and his car was gone this morning."

Todd regarded her with blatant amusement. "Keeping pretty close tabs on him, aren't you?"

"I am not."

"Why not admit it? The man makes your toes curl."

She scowled. "You are so wrong."

"Didn't look that way when we drove past you yesterday. He had you in a clinch that would have made a great cover for one of those romance novels. The temperature couldn't have been much above freezing, but it made me sweat just to look at you."

"Have I mentioned that you are a very irritating man?"

"On more than one occasion, in fact. But you put up with me because I'm smart and efficient and I save your butt from time to time."

Megan sighed. "True enough." She glanced at the papers in his hand. "Is that contract ready?"

"You should probably read through it first, but it looks okay to me. Are you going to talk to Peggy this morning?"

She leaned over to peek in the window. Peggy and Peter were still engaged in conversation. Peter was actually laughing. "Not just yet," she said.

Todd followed the direction of her gaze, then looked back at her, clearly aware of what she was up to. "You are a very sneaky individual. Isn't that asking for trouble?"

"All I did was introduce two friends."

"Both of whom are vulnerable," he pointed out.

Put that way, it did make her actions seem particularly underhanded. "They're adults," she countered.

"Vulnerable," Todd repeated.

"Okay, so it was a low-down, sneaky trick. I didn't know for sure if they'd click. They could have hated each other on sight. Look at her. Peggy is not exactly Peter's usual type. She's June Cleaver in denim."

"I doubt Peter even knows who June Cleaver was. He doesn't strike me as a big fan of *Leave It to Beaver* reruns."

Megan grinned. "My point exactly. If nothing else, Peggy will broaden his horizons."

"What happens if he breaks her heart in return?"

Megan held up a hand. "Whoa! Let's not get ahead of ourselves. Peggy is still married. I figure a little attention and flirting with an intelligent, sophisticated male will be good for her. I'm not suggesting she fall madly in love with the guy or vice versa."

"That's the point," Todd said. "You've set them

up, but now it's entirely out of your hands. I see disaster.''

"You see disaster around every bend. That's your nature."

"My nature is to head disasters off. Yours seems to be to embrace them." He glanced toward the lane. "Speaking of disaster, there's your man now."

Jake's car was speeding up the driveway, kicking up dust. He skidded to a stop behind the trailer being used by the sound techs, cut the engine, then strolled toward them, a determined glint in his eyes. Megan's stomach knotted in anticipation.

He halted on the bottom step, gave her one of those heated looks, then grinned at Todd. "Contract okay?"

"Looks good to me." Todd's own grin broadened. "Sleep well last night?"

"Damn bed was too short," Jake grumbled.

"That must be why you took off so early," Megan said. "I could have warned you about that, but you were awfully determined to stay last night."

"I had another bed in mind."

Todd jumped up. "Okay, that's my cue. I'll be inside if anyone needs me."

"We won't," Jake said, his gaze settling on Megan's. "Will we?"

She swallowed hard. "No, I don't suppose we will."

As soon as Todd had gone, Jake settled into the chair Todd had vacated. "Come on over here, darlin'."

"I don't think so."

"Afraid?"

"Afraid you'll mess up my makeup. We're due to start shooting in a couple of minutes."

"Then we'll have to work fast, so there'll be time left for that makeup gal you're paying to touch up your lipstick."

Despite the yearning humming through her, Megan didn't budge. "You want me, cowboy, you'll have to come and get me."

A smile tugged at his lips. "Is that a dare?"

She regarded him innocently. "Could be. You up to it?"

"Meggie, when it comes to you, I am up for anything," he whispered in a low, husky voice.

Jake moved so quickly, she didn't have time to react. Before she knew it, he'd scooped her up, settled into her chair and snuggled her in his lap.

"Now that's better," he said with satisfaction.

"Jake?" she murmured.

"Hmm?"

"If you're going to kiss me, you'd better do it fast."

"Why is that, darlin'? You getting anxious?"

"No, but Kenny is. Another five seconds and he'll be out here after me. I can already hear him bellowing for me."

"Five seconds doesn't give me much time," he lamented, lowering his mouth to meet hers.

No, she concluded when he released her, five seconds wasn't nearly enough time. But another fifty or sixty years might do the trick.

22

When Megan and Jake arrived at the ranch for dinner, there was an extra place set at the table. Mrs. Gomez wore a disapproving scowl on her face.

"What?" Megan asked as the housekeeper stood silently, arms folded across her chest. "You look as if you've just bitten into a lemon."

"That woman is coming to dinner, that's what."

"What woman?"

"Tess's mother."

Just as Megan was about to explode, Jake stepped in and touched her arm to silence her. "How did that happen?" he asked quietly.

"You'll have to ask Tess about that," Mrs. Gomez responded. "I was in the kitchen cooking when the two of them walked in."

Megan's gaze narrowed. "They were together when Tess came home from school?"

"It is my impression that Señora Olson brought her home."

"Well, I'll put an end to that right now," Megan said, shaking off Jake's hand and heading to the door. "Where are they?"

"In the living room, I imagine. That's where I took a snack to them, at Tess's request. That woman wanted caviar, if you ask me. She got a few cookies and some milk. I'd count the silver before she leaves, if I were you.''

Oh, brother, Megan thought. ''I'll take care of it.''

''With my help,'' Jake chimed in.

She whirled on him. ''I don't need you rushing to my rescue every time there's trouble. I can handle the likes of Flo Olson. You might try finding out why the hell the school let Tess leave with her.''

''Fine. I'll call the school and then I'll just stand around and watch you handle things. Maybe I'll pick up a few tips.''

''Don't be sarcastic,'' she snapped. ''It doesn't suit you.''

As predicted, they found Tess and her mother in the living room. Tess was sitting on the sofa, clearly content with her milk and cookies. She was chattering a mile a minute to a woman who was paying about as much attention as a first grader would at the end of a long day. A sharp sense of déjà vu swept over Megan. How many times had she prattled on to her own mother, only to discover that Sarah was off in some world of her own? Too many to count.

As for Flo, she seemed far more captivated by a rare and delicate piece of porcelain on the mantel than she was by her daughter. She'd just lifted it up to inspect the marking on the bottom when Megan cleared her throat. The bowl tumbled to the carpet and shattered.

''Oh, my, look what you made me do,'' Flo said, scowling at Megan. ''That's all your fault. You shouldn't be sneaking up on people.''

Megan was impressed by her audacity. ''Since

you're obviously so interested, you might as well know that that bowl was worth about three thousand. I believe the appraisal is in Tex's safe. If you don't have the cash, you can pay us back in installments.''

"Now who's being sarcastic?" Jake muttered so only she could hear.

Megan scowled at him.

"Pay you back?" Flo all but shouted. "I wouldn't have dropped it if you hadn't come creeping up behind me."

"Last time I checked, this was my house and you were the one checking out the china."

"I'll pay for it," Tess chimed in timidly. "I asked her to come." She gave Megan and Jake a defiant look. "You said I could ask her to dinner whenever I wanted."

Megan counted to ten before replying. "Yes, I did, but next time, ask for permission first to see if it's a convenient time. You know what a busy week this is."

"She's here now," Tess said, clearly not about to be put off. "Can she stay?"

Megan saw little point in asking the woman to leave. Tess would only view it as going back on her word. "This time, yes. Now please take your dishes into the kitchen and get the vacuum to clean up this mess, okay?"

"Why should I? I know you just want to yell at her while I'm gone," Tess countered.

"Come on, short stuff. I'll help with the vacuum," Jake said.

Tess seemed ready to argue, but she finally relented with a put-upon sigh.

After they'd gone, Megan regarded Flo intently. "How did it happen that Tess invited you to dinner tonight?"

"We were talking—"

Megan cut her off. "Where?"

"At school."

"Do I need to remind you that there is a restraining order against you? The next time you turn up at Tess's school, or anywhere else she is, I'll call the sheriff so fast it will make your head spin."

"You have no right."

"I have every right," Megan said, forcing herself to rein in her temper. "Look, sit down a minute, okay? I don't want to fight with you."

"You could have fooled me," Flo retorted.

"Okay, let's be honest. The truth is, I don't trust you or your motives. If it were up to me, you would never get within a thousand yards of Tess again, but it's not my decision entirely. She still cares about you. If she wants to see you, I'll allow it, but there are some rules that have to be followed. If you can go along with that, we'll work this out. Otherwise, you won't see her at all. It's up to you."

Flo looked taken aback by the straight talk. "You're tougher than you look, you know that?"

"I'll take that as a compliment. Now, do we have a deal or not?"

"How am I supposed to get way out here to see her? There are no jobs in Whispering Wind and I quit my job in Laramie after I dropped Tess off here. I'll probably have to move on to find work." She gave Megan a wily look. "Unless you can maybe give me a little cash to get set up."

Megan ignored the veiled threat to take off and called her bluff. "I'm fresh out of cash. Do you have any skills?"

"I was a waitress before."

Megan couldn't think of a single way she could use a waitress in her company. Nor was she inclined to find a place for her on the ranch. Mrs. Gomez could probably use some help cooking for the men, but she'd quit in a rage before she'd let Tess's mother share her kitchen.

"Can you type?" she asked, thinking of Jake's empty secretarial desk. A devious scheme began to take shape, one that would allow her to get even with one very contrary male in her life.

Flo looked appalled. "I took a class in high school, but I'm pretty rusty."

Megan doubted there would be all that much typing to be done, unless Jake started taking on clients. "How are your phone manners?"

Flo frowned. "I like to chat, if that's what you mean."

"Actually, I was wondering if you could take thorough messages, be polite even when people are being rude, that sort of thing."

"I suppose I could do that. It can't be any worse than putting up with the rowdy customers at the restaurant where I worked."

"Good. You're hired."

Flo stared. "You want me to work for you?"

"Not exactly."

"Then I don't get it."

"You will." Megan grinned as Jake walked back into the room pushing a vacuum. "Hey, Jake."

His gaze narrowed warily as he glanced from her to Flo and back again, clearly trying to gauge their moods. "What?"

"Meet your new receptionist."

"No way!" Flo protested, just as Jake muttered a particularly vile curse.

Megan beamed at their reactions. "Good. This is going to be perfect."

Tess stared around the room. "Mom is going to work for Jake?"

"So it seems," Jake murmured, his displeasure evident, though he was clearly not willing to put up a fuss over the fix Megan had deliberately put him in.

"No funny stuff," Flo said, glaring at him. "Just because you're a lawyer doesn't mean I can't file a harassment suit against you."

"Believe me, there will be no funny stuff," Jake said. He smiled at Megan, but without real sincerity. "Darlin', could I see you for just a minute?"

"Sure," she said, pausing to give Tess a wink as she passed.

In the foyer, Jake pinned her against the wall. Under other circumstances, his closeness could have been very provocative. As it was, Megan had to resist the urge to scoot under his outstretched arm and scamper away.

"What the hell were you thinking?" he asked in a light conversational tone, as if he were no more than idly curious about her reply.

"I was thinking that Flo needs work and we need a way to keep an eye on her."

"So you elected me to be her guardian. Why not you?"

"You heard Peter. My budget's past its limits. Besides, I have Todd."

"Very convenient. What am I supposed to do with her?"

"She'll answer your phones."

"They don't ring all that often."

"She can type letters. I don't think she's fast, so that could take most of the day."

He frowned. "You're enjoying this, aren't you?"

Megan grinned and held two fingers about a half inch apart. "Just a little," she admitted.

"You will pay," he promised.

"No money. Sorry."

"There are other ways," he said, lowering his mouth to hers.

The kiss was a thorough and pricey one. It cost her her composure. She was still rattled when Mrs. Gomez marched in and announced dinner in a voice loud enough to wake the dead, then turned around and marched out. Obviously she kept on going, because the back door slammed a few seconds later.

"She doesn't seem to like tonight's turn of events," Megan noted.

"Who can blame her?" Jake replied. "By the way, where are Peter and Todd?"

"Peter's having dinner at Peggy's. They're dining on venison stew."

"You're kidding me. He's actually eating it?"

"I doubt he'll notice what it is. He seems to have taken a shine to Miss Peggy," Megan announced smugly.

"Exactly where are Johnny and the kids? Are they part of this happy dinner party?"

"I believe they've gone to Laramie to a movie. Johnny refuses to set foot in the house except to sleep as long as we're using it for the show. It's his own little form of rebellion."

"So you left Peter there to share a quiet little dinner with your best friend? Doesn't that worry you?"

"Nope. I think Peter is going to turn out to be very good for her. When I left, he was working on her checkbook. He was also advising her on how to invest the money we're paying her to use the house this week. Peter's very good at predicting the stock market."

Jake groaned. "And Todd? What have you done with him? Signed him up for a rodeo event so he'll get the hang of being a cowboy?"

"No. He went into town to have dinner with the guys. Kenny will drive him out later." She grinned wickedly. "Actually, Kenny intends to put him behind the wheel and make *him* drive. We'll be lucky if the front gate's standing in the morning."

"The prospect seems to please you."

"What pleases me is knowing there's one thing that Todd can't do perfectly. His skills in every other area are scary."

Jake shook his head in obvious bemusement. "The way your mind works terrifies me."

"It should. I'm still working on what to do about you."

"Isn't saddling me with an incompetent secretary enough?"

Megan tilted her head and studied him. "Nope. I don't think so. After all, thanks to you and Tex, I'm holding my career together with duct tape, winging it as a rancher and playing parent to an eight-year-old who's not enthralled with having me as a parent. I think it will be a long, long time before we're even.''

Having Flo on the job wasn't exactly a disaster, but then it was only nine-fifteen on her first day, Jake noted as he tried one more time to explain how the fax machine worked.

"How do I know if a fax is coming in?" Flo asked, regarding the machine with suspicion.

"The machine will pick it up automatically. It's on a separate phone line."

"And I send one by putting the papers in here," she said, repeating his instructions with apparent skepticism.

"Facedown," Jake confirmed.

"Then I dial the number."

"Right."

"And they wind up in somebody else's machine just like that?"

"Pretty much."

"How?"

Jake regarded her candidly. "I have no idea."

She gave a little nod. "Good. I thought maybe I was an idiot for not getting it."

"Nope. Just take it on faith."

She regarded him with a wry expression. "Faith's not something I'm real experienced with."

"Me, either, if it comes to that. Let's just say it works and let it go."

She moved on to the answering machine. Before she could ask Jake a million and one questions about that, Henrietta came running in.

"Oh, Lord, Jake, you've got to come right away."

"What is it?" he asked, already following her out the door. He called over his shoulder to Flo, "Hold down the fort, I'll call you soon."

"It's Barbara Sue," Henrietta said as they crossed the street. "Bryce is about to arrest her."

Jake's heart thudded dully. He'd been worried about something like this. "What's the charge?"

"Attempted murder. She shot Lyle this morning."

The news was every bit as bad as he'd feared. "Is he going to make it?"

"Don't know," Henrietta said. "Personally, I hope the son of a bitch dies, but it won't be good for Barbara Sue if he does."

"No, it won't, so start saying a few prayers for the miserable excuse for a man. Where's Barbara Sue now?"

"At the jail."

"And the kids?"

"I've got 'em at the diner. Bryce had the decency to drop them off. Janie's over there with them. I'll go on back, unless you need me."

"No, you take care of the kids. Do you know what happened?"

"Lyle was about to take a strap to her oldest and I guess she just saw red. Sissy's been weeping and wailing that it's all her fault. Nothing I say has been able to calm her down."

"You do what you can. I'll be in touch as soon as I know what's going on with Barbara Sue."

At the jail he found her sitting across from Bryce, her hands folded tightly in her lap, the beginnings of a bruise on her cheek and a stoic expression on her face.

Jake nodded to the sheriff. "What's going on?" he asked, as if he hadn't already heard the whole story.

"She shot her husband in cold blood," Bryce said. "Won't say another word."

Jake gave her hand a quick squeeze. "Good for you." He glanced at the sheriff. "Did you happen to mention that she had a right to have a lawyer present?"

"Yes, Mr. Big-city Lawyer. I read her her rights. It was as close to a conversation as we've had."

"Then I'd like some time alone with her."

Bryce shrugged. "Fine by me. I'll take a run over to the hospital to see how Lyle's doing in surgery. Don't either of you budge till I get back."

"Wouldn't dream of it," Jake said. As soon as the sheriff had gone, he settled onto the corner of Bryce's desk. "You okay?"

Barbara Sue nodded, but huge tears welled up in her eyes and spilled down her cheeks. Jake handed her a handkerchief.

"Oh, sweet Jesus, what have I done?" she murmured. "What will happen to my babies if I'm in jail?"

"We're going to concentrate on keeping you out of jail," Jake said quietly. "Now, start slowly and tell me exactly what happened."

She drew in a deep breath. "Lyle had a fight with his mama yesterday. She was fed up with the way he's been shirking his work at the store. He was out most of the night drinking," she began.

"When he came in, he was looking for a fight. He

woke me up. I tried to get away from him, tried to agree with everything he said just to keep peace, but he wasn't having any of that. He hit me anyway. I fell against a table and knocked a lamp on the floor. I guess Sissy heard us, because she came running in and told her daddy to stop. She was crying and waving her little fists at him. Punched him right in the stomach, she did.''

"And, of course, that made him even madder," Jake guessed.

Barbara Sue nodded. "He started to unbuckle his belt and I knew what was coming. He never stopped looking at Sissy, so I ran for his shotgun. By the time he realized what I was doing, it was too late. I didn't even aim. I just pulled the trigger. Maybe I wanted to scare him. Maybe I wanted him to die. I don't know anymore what I was feeling, except sick—sick that he was going to beat my baby." She stared bleakly at Jake, her eyes dry now. "I couldn't let him do it, don't you see?"

Jake gave her hand another squeeze. "Yes, I do see. We're going to work it out, Barbara Sue. Even if I can't get the charges dropped, there's not a jury around that would convict you for protecting your daughter."

Her gaze fell. "I want him to die," she murmured, so softly Jake almost didn't hear her. She lifted her head. "Isn't that awful? I loved him so. I had two children with him. And now I'm praying that he'll die. What kind of a woman does that make me?"

"One who's been through too much," Jake said, wishing things hadn't ever had to go so far.

"Are the kids okay?" she asked.

"They're with Henrietta and Janie. They'll be fine," he assured her.

"I suppose my sister would come and take them, if I asked her. She's never liked Lyle much, so we've kind of lost touch. I hate to bother her."

"It's up to you, but I know Henrietta will be glad to have them for as long as necessary. With any luck, it won't be all that long before you're back with them again."

She nodded. "If she's willing, that would be best. Henrietta has been an angel, to me and the kids. I don't know what I would have done without her these past few months. The kids adore her as much as if she were their very own grandmother. She's not a thing in the world like Lyle's mother."

The door to Bryce's office opened. To Jake's surprise, it was Megan.

"Is everything okay?" she asked. "I heard what happened. I wanted to help."

"Come on in. You can keep Barbara Sue company." He turned to the woman. "Mind if Megan stays with you for a bit, while I go see what's going on at the hospital and check in with the prosecutor?"

Barbara Sue shrugged. "Whatever."

Jake paused beside Megan. "If Bryce comes back, don't let her talk to him," he instructed. "She's liable to blurt out that she's glad she shot Lyle. It might be true, but it won't help her case."

Megan nodded. He touched a palm to her cheek. "I'm surprised you came. Why did you?"

She regarded him with an uncertain expression. "I don't honestly know. It just felt like the right thing to do."

Jake grinned. "Don't look now, darlin', but you're actually getting involved in the real world, instead of sitting on the sidelines preaching about the good life."

Her gaze narrowed. "Are you suggesting that what I do for a living is frivolous?"

"Of course not. I'm just suggesting that once in a while it's good to take a hard look at the world that exists outside the pages of a magazine."

She glanced back at Barbara Sue, who was watching the two of them with a bleak, soul-weary expression. When Megan's gaze returned to Jake, she looked shaken.

"This conversation isn't over," she muttered as she brushed past him to pull up a chair beside Barbara Sue. She took Barbara Sue's hand in hers and murmured something Jake couldn't hear.

Watching the two women—one dressed in fancy designer clothes, the other in a frayed housecoat—Jake felt something shift inside him. He'd loved Meggie his whole life, it seemed. He'd wanted her just about as long. But perhaps for the first time ever, he could honestly say he respected her. Some of what he'd said to her about living in the real world applied to him, too. She was growing up, and maybe, just maybe, so was he.

23

The news at the hospital was good—at least it seemed unlikely Barbara Sue would face a murder charge. Lyle was in intensive care in guarded condition. Bryce told Jake the doctors were all but certain he would make a full recovery.

"How hard are you going to pursue this case?" Jake asked.

"I have an obligation—" Bryce began.

"What about your obligation to protect Barbara Sue?" Jake asked, cutting him off angrily. "You knew Lyle was beating her. You had to. Everyone else in town did."

Bryce flushed. "She never pressed charges," he retorted defensively.

"Then you could have made it unofficial. You could have taken your cousin out and beaten the crap out of him. Maybe that would have put an end to it, and it wouldn't have come to this."

Bryce sighed. "Look, I know Lyle's not perfect."

"Now there's an understatement."

"That doesn't give her the right to shoot him in cold blood."

"Not even when he was about to start beating their daughter, the same way he'd been beating on her?"

Bryce's complexion paled. "He was going to hit Sissy?"

"Had his belt off and was going for her when Barbara Sue got the gun."

"Damn."

"All things considered, I think you could do a lot to convince the prosecutor to reduce the charges, go for probation. Having their mama in jail won't do those kids a bit of good."

His expression grave, the sheriff nodded. "I'll see what I can do."

Jake started away, then turned back. "One more thing, Bryce. Keep your cousin the hell away from them when he gets out of here."

"Unfortunately, that may be easier said than done. Once his daddy died, his mama doted on him. Lyle's pretty much gotten his own way his whole life. I doubt anyone can step in now and change that. He's real possessive about Barbara Sue and those kids."

"Make it happen," Jake insisted. "Or the next time might not turn out so well. We could have a real tragedy on our hands."

Bryce sighed. "I'll do what I can."

Back at the diner, Jake found Henrietta at her wit's end. She'd run her fingers through her short hair so often it was standing up in spikes. She was trying her best to keep Barbara Sue's kids out from underfoot so they wouldn't hear the avid gossip about their mama. They'd seen what she'd done. They didn't need to hear everybody else's take on it.

"I can't keep 'em locked up in the kitchen forever," she told Jake. "But there's a lot of ugly talk no child should have to hear about his parents."

"I'll take them with me," Jake offered. "We'll go out to the ranch for the rest of the day. That should distract them."

Henrietta looked startled. "How's Megan going to feel about having more kids underfoot? Seems to me she's barely gotten used to having Tess around."

"It won't be a problem," he said. "She's with Barbara Sue right now. Then, I imagine, she'll be heading back to Peggy's to do another taping. She won't even know about this until she gets home tonight. As for Mrs. Gomez, she'll take these children under her wing just like she did me years ago."

Henrietta nodded. "But you'll bring 'em back into town to stay with me tonight?"

"Absolutely. That's what Barbara Sue told me she wanted, if you don't mind. And with any luck, they'll be able to go home with their mother tomorrow. I think Bryce is going to do his best to get the prosecutor to plea bargain the case out. We should have a deal by morning. Maybe even by the end of the day, if they can hammer it out and get it to a judge."

"Thank the Lord for that. How's Lyle?"

"Still alive."

"More's the pity."

"Be grateful," Jake countered. "Otherwise, it would be a whole lot trickier to get Barbara Sue reunited with her kids."

"He'll come after her the second he's out of the hospital," Henrietta predicted, echoing Jake's own fear.

"Not if Bryce has anything to say about it," he said reassuringly. "I think he's finally seen the light regarding his cousin's potential for violence."

Henrietta didn't seem impressed. "If you ask me, you're trusting the law, when the truth is its hands are tied. Bryce's heart might be in the right place, but if Lyle wants to get Barbara Sue, there's not a soul on God's earth who'll be able to prevent it."

"Then we'll just have to leave it to God," Jake said. "Maybe this brush with death will make Lyle reevaluate his life and start off in a new direction."

Henrietta looked skeptical. "Wish I could believe that, but I don't. I'm telling you, he'll be gunning for her. And we both know a restraining order is a waste of the paper it's written on."

Flo Olson's contact with Tess was proof enough of that, Jake thought wearily. But what more could they do?

"They'll just have to come live with me," Henrietta said decisively. "I'd like to see that man try to get past me."

"That's very kind of you, but you could be putting yourself in danger."

"If Lyle Perkins sets foot on my property, he's a dead man," she countered.

"Now, Henrietta…"

"No, Jake. I mean it. That's a promise you can take to the bank. Not a judge or jury in this county would convict me for it."

"They might not want to, but the law's the law."

"Don't you worry about me, Jake. I know what I'm doing. Now take those kids on out of here," she said, waving him toward the door. "Let 'em run off some of their energy out at the ranch, and I'll see the lot of you at my house later. Bring Megan and Tess along. I'll make fried chicken and mashed potatoes. That always makes folks feel better.''

He headed toward the kitchen to get the kids, then paused to press a kiss on her cheek. ''You're a wonder, you know that, don't you?''

''Oh, get on out of here,'' she said, but her cheeks had turned bright pink and there was a pleased sparkle in her eyes.

Megan walked in after seven to find her entire household in chaos. There were almost as many people running around as there had been on the set for the taping, but half of these were under the age of ten. The noise level was earsplitting. Henrietta and Flo were in the midst of it, deep in conversation. How they could hear each other was beyond Megan.

Jake spotted her standing motionless in the doorway and came over. ''Welcome home.''

''Are you sure this is my house?'' she asked, just as one of Barbara Sue's kids darted past her with a whoop, two more children in hot pursuit. ''What on earth is going on?''

''I needed to get Barbara Sue's kids out of Henrietta's hair for a while earlier today. Tess got home from school and pleaded to have them stay for dinner. Henrietta agreed and said she'd drive on out to pick them up. Then Flo turned up at the diner and asked her if she could hitch a ride out here, too.'' He shrugged. ''I guess it got a little out of control. Do you mind?''

Megan had a raging headache and her first instinct was to say yes, she did mind. But after the rough day they'd all had, the sight of the smiles and the sound of unrestrained laughter reverberating through the house made her pause.

"No," she said eventually. "I don't mind at all."

"Right answer," he said with a wink. "Mrs. Gomez has your dinner waiting for you in the kitchen. Want some company while you eat? Or would you rather I try to guarantee peace and quiet?"

"Company would be nice." She kicked off her shoes and padded toward the kitchen.

Mrs. Gomez took one look at her and began clucking. "Sit. Sit. Your dinner is ready. I made chicken and dumplings again. It is comfort food. I decided everyone needed that tonight."

"Even Tess?" Megan asked, recalling the girl's avowed dislike of the meal.

"Tess likes it well enough. She ate three helpings. Had you been here, she would have turned her nose up just on principle," Mrs. Gomez said. "I remember another little girl who did the same when I made Tex's favorite pot roast."

Megan grinned at the memory. "I wouldn't touch it as long as he was at the table."

"Which was why I always insisted you stay at your place until you'd finished," Mrs. Gomez said. "Once Tex was gone, you ate every bite."

"Perverse little thing, weren't you?" Jake asked.

"Still am," she reminded him.

"I've noticed."

Mrs. Gomez set Megan's dinner in front of her and offered Jake another helping of apple pie. Once she was satisfied that they were both taken care of, the housekeeper announced she was leaving.

"Unless you need me to stay the night," she said to Megan.

"No, go home and get some rest. It's been another long day for you. In fact, I think you should sleep in in the morning. I'll get up early and make breakfast for the men and for Tess."

Jake chuckled.

Megan scowled at him. "It'll be edible enough."

"Were you thinking of serving kiwi and perhaps a cheese and spinach soufflé?" he inquired.

"Very amusing. I can do scrambled eggs, bacon and toast as well as the next person."

"If you say so. Maybe I'll slip on out to the bunkhouse and warn the men to run into town tonight for a couple of boxes of cold cereal and some milk just in case."

"Maybe I should stay," Mrs. Gomez said, frowning.

"No," Megan insisted. "Go. Don't listen to him. No one will starve if you come in late for once. You've been pulling extra duty for too many weeks now. It's time I pitched in."

After she'd gone, Megan ate in silence for a while, then glanced up at Jake. "What will happen to Barbara Sue?" she asked. "I've been thinking about her all day."

"I'm pretty sure we'll have a deal by morning. I talked to Bryce about an hour ago. I'm meeting with the prosecutor first thing and we'll go before a judge."

"What about Lyle?"

"I'd like to think he'll be smart enough to take off

the minute he's released from the hospital, but everyone tells me that's wishful thinking.''

Megan nodded. "It probably is. If memory serves, Lyle wasn't the smartest kid on the block. Maybe Barbara Sue should be the smart one and leave town and take the kids with her. I suggested that to her this morning.''

"What did she say?''

"That this is her home. That she wouldn't know how to survive anywhere else.''

"That's probably true, you know.''

"But it's too dangerous for her to stay here. I offered her the use of my apartment in New York until she gets on her feet. I could make some contacts for her, help her find a job.''

Jake was shaking his head before the words were out of her mouth. "She'd be miserable in New York.''

"But she'd be safe," Megan countered fiercely. "Isn't that what's important?''

Jake stood behind her and massaged the tension from her shoulders. "I love it that you care so much.''

"Why wouldn't I care? I've known Barbara Sue my whole life. We weren't the best of friends in school, not the way Peggy and I were, but I certainly wouldn't stand by and let her go through this all alone.''

"A lot of other people have known about Lyle and have turned their back on her," Jake said.

"Probably because they didn't know what to do. Neither do I, not really. But at least I can offer her a safe place to stay.''

"But to accept your offer, she has to disrupt her life and move hundreds of miles away."

"So you think I'm wrong?"

"Not wrong. I just think you can't make Barbara Sue do something she's not comfortable with, any more than I could make her take legal action against Lyle before this happened."

Megan heard the genuine regret in his voice. "You saw it coming, didn't you? That must have been frustrating."

"Infuriating," Jake agreed. His touch gentled, became more of a caress. "Almost as infuriating as wanting you right this second and knowing that the odds of having you are slim to none."

Her breath caught in her throat. "Maybe not as much of a long shot as you think," she murmured, then turned to gaze up at him.

"You seem to be forgetting all the company in the other room."

"You seem to be forgetting this house has a back staircase."

Surprise registered on his face, along with smoldering desire.

"Right over there," she said, indicating the doorway to the pantry. "Hidden away for quick escapes, I suspect."

"Well, I'll be," Jake murmured, then sighed. "But I think we'll have to test it out another time. Those kids of Barbara Sue's are sneaky little devils. If they think we've disappeared, they're liable to come searching for us."

"The threat of discovery could add to the excitement, don't you think?"

He grinned. "You're deliberately taunting me, aren't you?"

"Why would I do that?"

"Because you figure it's safe enough and you enjoy driving me crazy."

"Well—"

Before she could complete the admission, Jake scooped her out of her chair and headed for the hidden staircase. Megan's whoop of astonishment gave way to laughter, then protests as he headed straight up the stairs and unerringly toward her room.

"Jake, wait. We can't do this. You know we can't."

"Hey, darlin', it was your idea. I heard you plain as day all but begging me to bring you up here so I could ravish you," he said. He nudged the door open and carried her inside, pausing only to kick the door closed behind him.

She got the distinct impression that the game had gotten out of hand. "But I was..." The protest died on her lips.

He gazed down into her eyes. "You were what? Teasing? Testing me?"

"Something like that."

He dropped her unceremoniously on her bed, then knelt over her. His eyes darkened with desire. "Bad idea," he murmured huskily before his lips met hers.

Megan arched into the kiss, then moaned as Jake's hand skimmed lightly from hip to waist to breast, where it lingered. Her skin burned, her nipples peaked into sensitive buds. There was nothing even remotely amusing about the speed with which her body responded to his touch. Within seconds she'd forgotten all about teasing him, all about the noisy gathering downstairs. Heck, she'd pretty much forgotten her name.

And then he was standing beside the bed, a complacent smirk firmly in place.

"In the future, don't start something you can't possibly win," he warned lightly. "Now let's get back downstairs before we're missed."

The sensual stupor she'd been in evaporated in a heartbeat, replaced by a flash fire of temper. Even though her legs were unsteady, she was on her feet before he could take a single step. She blocked his path, then gave him a shove that took him by surprise. He stumbled back. Another push had him landing on the bed. She scrambled on top of him and pinned him down. She had little doubt he could have flipped her over with practically no effort, but he didn't even try. A momentary flicker of astonishment in his eyes had given way to amused acceptance.

"Now what?" he inquired. "Planning to turn the tables and have your way with me?"

She stared at him. "Have my way with you? Where do you get these ideas?"

"Well, you must have had something in mind when you got me back into your bed."

"Teaching you a lesson, for starters."

"And the lesson would be?"

"That I can finish any game I start."

"Oh, really?"

"Yes," she said emphatically, then considered the houseful of people. "Just not here and not now."

He grinned. "That means I get a rain check?"

She stood up and smoothed out her clothes. "If

you're lucky," she retorted, and headed for the door. "On the other hand, you might have blown it by not taking advantage of your one and only chance to get into bed with me."

He reached for her and spun her around just as she got to the door. His mouth claimed hers with a kiss that was totally, thoroughly devastating.

"We'll see," he said mildly, then trotted down the stairs ahead of her.

Megan touched her tender, swollen lips and shuddered. Maybe she was in way over her head.

Maybe, when it came to Jake, she always had been.

24

"Where have you guys been?" Tess demanded when Jake walked into the living room, with Megan trailing distantly behind him after their fascinating little tussle upstairs.

"Megan was just relaxing a little," he said, noting the flush on Megan's cheeks as she came in and overheard him. "She's had a long day."

Tess studied Megan. "Are you sick? Your face is all pink."

"Just overheated," Megan said, giving Jake a sour look.

"But it's freezing out," Tess said. "How could—"

"Never mind," Flo said, giving both of them a knowing look as she steered Tess away. "You ask way too many questions."

"But how am I going to learn anything if I don't ask?" Tess argued, using a familiar refrain.

"Never mind," Flo said. "There are some things you don't need to know."

Megan stared after them worriedly. "You don't think Flo will try to use what just happened here to try to get Tess back, do you?"

"Nothing happened," Jake pointed out. "You came into a room with some color in your cheeks.

Big deal. Flo can't make too much of that. For all she knows we could have been arguing about the price of livestock on the futures market.''

"I suppose you're right."

"It was your idea to let Flo hang around and be a part of Tess's life," he reminded her. "Are you going to be looking over your shoulder every second? Are you going to panic every time she makes a remark about something you do?"

"No, of course not. It's just that—"

"It's just that you're feeling guilty," he said, then grinned. "And maybe a little grumpy because you're sexually deprived."

"Oh, go suck an egg," she retorted as Henrietta joined them.

"Am I interrupting?" she said, her face alight with curiosity.

"No, of course not," Megan said.

"I think I'd better be getting those kids back into town. I want them to go off to school in the morning. They need to get things back to normal." She regarded Jake worriedly. "You don't think you're going to have to bring Sissy in to testify about what happened, do you?"

"I hope not. I'll do my damnedest to avoid it."

"I'll come to court, if you need me," she offered. "I can testify about all the times Barbara Sue came to work battered and bruised. I'd like to hear Lyle come up with an explanation for that."

"I'd appreciate that," Jake said. "If things go the way I'm hoping they will, the judge will agree to the plea bargain without calling any witnesses, but it'll be good to have you there, just in case."

"Right," Henrietta said briskly. "I'll see you in the morning, then. You let me know what time. Good night, Megan. Your granddaddy would have been proud of the way you've pitched in with everything that's been going on around town. He'd be especially proud of the way you're handling Tess."

"I hope so," she said wistfully.

Megan and Jake stood on the front porch and watched as Henrietta, Flo and Barbara Sue's kids left for town. The taillights of Henrietta's car were still flickering in the distance when Jake spotted headlights turning in off the highway.

"Who do you suppose this could be?" he asked.

"Probably Todd coming back from town, or maybe Peter," Megan suggested.

"Peter's still hanging around?" Jake asked irritably. "I assumed he'd gone back to New York today."

"I believe that was his plan, until he met Peggy and had dinner with her last night."

Just then Peggy's car pulled to a stop in front of the house. Not only did Peter get out, but so did Peggy and her kids. She stood hesitantly beside the car.

"Megan, could I speak to you a minute?" she asked, twisting her hands nervously.

"Oh, boy," Jake murmured under his breath. Something told him Peggy hadn't dropped by to compare notes on the recipes for tomorrow's taping.

"Hush," Megan retorted as she left to join her friend.

"What's up?" Jake asked Peter, who hadn't taken his gaze off Peggy since they got out of the car.

"She's leaving her husband. I believe she's hoping to spend the night here."

"This place is turning into a blasted hotel," Jake grumbled. As annoying as the crowds were, he had to admit—to himself, anyway—that Megan's renewed involvement with old friends in Whispering Wind was reassuring. Maybe she was finally realizing that she really did fit in here, that there was a place for her in this community that was every bit as important and rewarding as being in New York. He'd been discovering the same thing himself for months now.

He glanced at Peter. "Just how much did you have to do with Peggy's decision? You didn't make any promises you don't intend to keep, did you?"

"My relationship with Peggy is none of your concern," Peter said in that stiff, uptight way that grated on Jake's nerves. "Not any more than yours with Megan is mine."

"It is if you intend to break up her marriage and then dump her," Jake countered. "She's a friend, and out here, friends look out for friends. We make their troubles our business."

"She's a grown woman who's been living in an untenable situation for far too long," Peter retorted. "I just made her realize that she has options."

"Nothing personal?"

Even in the silvery glow of moonlight, Jake could see Peter flush.

"She's a lovely woman," the accountant conceded. "But...?"

"She lives in Wyoming, for God's sake. I would find that...impossible."

"Did you mention that to her? Or did you allow her to believe that you intended to sweep her away from all her problems?"

"I really don't see—"

Jake moved until he was in the other man's face. "I'd like an answer."

Peter sighed. "Okay, she might have gotten the idea that I'm interested in pursuing a relationship with her."

"But you're not," Jake said curtly.

"I didn't say that." Mr. Polish and Perfection actually looked flustered. "I don't know what will happen. It's...confusing."

Jake almost felt sorry for the man. He really did look a bit as if he'd been run over by a bus. And Jake doubted he'd ever come so close to stuttering before. As Peggy and Megan approached, Peter's gaze sought Peggy's and held it as if he were a drowning man and she were his lifeline. Fascinating, Jake concluded. Maybe Megan had been on to something, instead of dangerously ill advised, when she introduced them.

Peggy brushed past Jake without meeting his eyes, then hurried the kids inside. Peter followed. When they were out of earshot, Jake turned to Megan.

"Well?"

"She's left Johnny."

"I got that much. Now what?"

"Now we'd better get the studio up and running in a hurry, because she refuses to set foot in her own kitchen ever again." She gave Jake a worried look. "Did I set something in motion I shouldn't have? You talked to Peter. What's he thinking?"

"It's a little late to be having second thoughts,"

Jake said. "Your friend Peter is a mite confused at the moment. Every instinct is telling him to hightail it back to New York and his nice, tidy life-style."

"But?"

Jake regarded her with amusement. "You sense a *but* in there?"

"There'd better be one," she said grimly.

"Okay, here it is. He seems to have hit a snag. Whether he's recognized it or not, the man is falling in love. With a woman in Wyoming, yet." Jake grinned. "I love it. You come back to town and the whole place goes topsy-turvy."

"You're not blaming everything that's happened on me, are you?" she demanded indignantly. "Blame Tex. If it hadn't been for him and that cockamamie will he had you draw up, I wouldn't have been back here."

"Sure, lay it all on a poor dead man who can't defend himself," he teased. "Face it, Megan. Wherever you go, things happen."

"Don't you mean disaster strikes?"

"Is that how you see the breakup of Peggy's marriage? I thought you wanted her to dump Johnny."

"I wanted her to want to dump Johnny," she corrected.

"Isn't that the same thing?"

"I suppose," she said. "My version just leaves me out of the middle."

"Well, now, with or without your influence, she has."

"And now she's here," Megan pointed out. "What am I supposed to do with her?"

"Go right on being her friend," Jake suggested.

"Especially since the road ahead with Peter could be a bumpy one till he realizes how he feels. I suppose I can't really blame him for being confused. After all, he flew out here thinking he was in love with you."

"He was never in love with me," Megan protested, dismissing the possibility. "He'd ticked off my qualifications on some list and figured I'd do."

Jake stared. "You're kidding me."

"Oh, no. Peter is very methodical."

"And Peggy is very impulsive," Jake said thoughtfully. He met Megan's uneasy gaze. "You are a very diabolical woman."

"Probably," she agreed unhappily.

"Fortunately for you, I am a man who really gets off on diabolical schemes. That's why I forgave Tex for keeping us apart. He was so damned clever about it. Just tucked those cattle up on the side of a mountain until the dust settled and you were safely gone."

"I don't understand you," she murmured as he pulled her into his arms.

"Then isn't it lucky that we're going to have a lifetime for you to figure me out."

Her gaze shot up and clashed with his. "What?"

He pressed her cheek back against his shoulder. "Don't worry about it now."

"But you said—"

"Just a little offhand remark. Nothing for you to get excited about."

One of these days he'd repeat what he'd said. He'd do it right, with a diamond and flowers and nobody within a hundred miles to slow down what would come after.

"Soon," he murmured, mostly to himself.

"What?"

"Nothing, darlin'. Let's settle down in that swing the way we used to and count the stars."

When she didn't object that it was too late or too cold, he led the way across the porch and settled down with his arms tucked tightly around her. He kept the swing in motion with a gentle push every now and again. Megan sighed, her breath fanning across his cheek.

"How many?" he asked eventually.

"How many what?"

"Stars?"

"Way too many to count," she said, just as she had so many times in the past, and would again in the years to come, if he had his way.

"Did you pick one to wish on?"

He caught the slow curve of her lips in the moonlight.

"The brightest one," she said. "But I won't tell you what I wished for."

"No need, darlin'. I think I already know."

"You don't know everything, Jake."

"Maybe not everything," he agreed. "But when it comes to what's in your heart, sometimes I think I know it better than you do."

At least he prayed that he did, because he was counting on her making the right choices when the time came.

Megan awoke to the sound of pounding on the front door and a stream of high-pitched Spanish from Mrs. Gomez, who'd apparently turned up right on schedule to protect the stomachs of her charges from

Megan's cooking. Since only a crisis of monumental proportions could make the housekeeper revert to her native tongue, Megan was anticipating the worst when she ran downstairs. She found a drunken Johnny Barkley weaving around in the foyer.

"Go. Shoo," Mrs. Gomez shouted, as if he were a stray cat that had wandered in.

"I'll handle this," Megan said.

"Are you sure, *niña?* The man does not listen to reason."

"The man has had too much to drink," Megan corrected, assessing whether Johnny could actually stand up, much less inflict any harm. She concluded the odds were in her favor. In his present condition, a gentle nudge would have him on the floor.

"All the more reason for me to call for help," Mrs. Gomez said, clearly having reached a different conclusion.

"No, it's okay. We'll be fine," Megan assured her. "You might bring in a pot of black coffee as soon as you have some made."

Megan latched on to Johnny's arm and steered him into the living room. He didn't seem to be inclined to resist, even when she gave him a gentle shove that left him sprawling on the sofa. He gazed up at her with bleary eyes. Somewhere in there was a glimmer of the sweet, shy boy he had once been.

"It's your fault, you know," he accused.

"What is my fault?"

"You came in here with all your highfalutin talk and your fancy TV show and your big-shot friends and got my sweet Peggy all mixed up."

"Your sweet Peggy is not mixed up. She is seeing

you clearly for the first time in a very long time,'' Megan said. "Apparently she doesn't like what she sees."

Johnny stared at her sullenly. "You got no right. We were happy till you came."

"I didn't make her walk out on you, if that's what you're thinking. You did that all by your lonesome."

"I want her back home where she belongs."

"She belongs with someone who'll love her and respect her."

Johnny actually managed to look shocked at the suggestion that she got anything less than that from him. "I love her," he insisted. "Married her, didn't I? We've got a nice house, good kids. I give her just about anything she asks for. Doesn't that prove I love her?"

"You'd have to ask her if that's what really matters to her," Megan said, belatedly concluding that this conversation ought to be between Peggy and her husband. "I'll go see if she wants to talk to you."

Johnny covered his face with his hands and mumbled something Megan couldn't quite hear.

"What?" she asked.

"I said she won't want to talk. When she gets ticked off at me, she won't talk. That's how I know I'm in real trouble. It takes a whole lot to get Peggy to keep quiet."

Megan could imagine. "Well, she'll talk to you now. I'll see to it."

She didn't have to go far to find Peggy. She was sitting on the bottom step, dressed in her nightgown and robe, her knees drawn up to her chest. She gave Megan a weary smile.

"You're going to insist I go in there, aren't you?" she asked.

Megan nodded. "This is between you and Johnny."

"But he's always been able to talk me into anything," Peggy whispered, casting a worried look toward the living room. "I want this time to be different."

"Then say no," Megan said. "If that's what you really want, tell him you won't come back, not now, not ever again."

Peggy gave her a rueful smile. "It sounds so easy when you say it."

"Because he's not my husband and I was never in love with him. You two have a long history. It's hard to walk away from that, especially when the future seems so uncertain."

Peggy stood up with obvious reluctance and started toward the living room. When she was close enough, Megan gave her hand a squeeze. "Just remember what it feels like every time you find out he's been with another woman."

The reminder was enough to put fire in Peggy's eyes. She squared her shoulders and marched into the living room without another backward glance. Megan stood where she was long enough to hear Peggy's opening volley, a quiet, very firm declaration that it was over.

"This is Megan's fault," Johnny shouted.

"Hush up, Johnny. Megan has nothing to do with it," Peggy retorted, then lowered her voice.

Megan concluded that Peggy was going to do just fine. She wandered off to waylay Mrs. Gomez and the coffee. She was going to need a whole lot of caffeine to get through the day on the little bit of sleep she'd gotten between Jake's late departure and Johnny's early arrival.

"Peggy is with her husband?" Mrs. Gomez asked. She seemed to be taking the fact that Peggy was here in the first place in stride.

"Yes."

"Will she go back with him?"

"I don't know," Megan said honestly as she accepted a cup of coffee from the housekeeper. She'd barely taken her first sip when Peter wandered into the kitchen, his expression shaken.

"How much did you hear?" she asked him.

"Enough to gather he is trying to win her back, though how he expects to do it with drunken promises is beyond me."

Megan studied him intently. "Would it bother you if she decided to go home?"

"Of course it would. The man has treated her abominably."

"That's not what I was asking, Peter."

He took a long time stirring cream and sugar into his coffee, proof that he was more rattled than he wanted to let on. He took his coffee black.

"Now that you've killed a little time, how about answering me?" Megan prodded.

Peter took a sip of coffee instead, made a face at the taste, then took it to the sink and dumped it out. When he had fresh coffee in his cup, he finally met her gaze.

"I think it might bother me quite a lot," he conceded. "I'm not sure I understand what's going on here. I don't react impulsively. I study things."

"You analyze them to death," Megan countered. "Not a bad trait when dealing with corporate books or the stock market, but a wasted effort when it comes to emotions. Some things you just have to accept at face value."

"I've never even given a thought to being a father," Peter said plaintively. "Peggy has three children. I feel as if I've been plunked into the middle of a bunch of alien creatures. What do I do with them?"

"Take them to the movies. Play ball with them. Do you think it's been easy for me to adjust to being Tess's parent? I was no more prepared than you are. If I can handle it, you can."

He regarded her curiously. "Are you? Handling it, that is?"

"Some days better than others," she admitted. "Sometimes I know exactly what is going on in her head and it breaks my heart, because once upon a time I was exactly where she is. Other times, I don't have a clue."

Megan patted his cheek. "I'll tell you one thing, though, I'm determined to get the hang of it."

"Because you have to."

"No, because every now and then I see a bright and shining glimmer of what it could be like to be really good at it. Tess deserves that. So do Peggy's kids."

Peter's expression turned glum again. "But they already have a dad, a real paragon to hear them tell it. He plays football and baseball with them. He's teaching them all about ranching. Hell, I couldn't throw a pass if my life depended on it. As for ranching, the more distance there is between me and the sort of meat I eat for supper, the better I like it.''

"But Johnny's never taken them to the top of the Empire State Building or to see the Statue of Liberty. He's never taken them to a Broadway play or the opera. It's a trade-off, Peter. He'll bring certain things into their lives. You'll bring others. They'll be better off for having both of you.''

"You're assuming Peggy would pack up and leave here to come to New York.''

"Well, she does have a regular spot on my show now. If you're not enough, she has a career incentive.''

Peter gave her a wry look. "There's just one problem with that little scenario.''

"Which is?''

"As near as I can tell, you're not coming to New York anytime soon.'' He regarded her quizzically. "Or am I wrong about that?''

"I can't,'' she said automatically. "Not right now.''

"When?''

"I don't know,'' she said with a sigh. "I honestly don't know.''

25

Jake spent the morning in court. The judge, known for his preference to exceed sentencing guidelines and come down hard on perpetrators, was not feeling especially charitable toward Barbara Sue. He didn't like attempted murder, whatever the so-called justification for it.

"It was self-defense, your honor," Jake explained, clinging to his patience by a thread. "Mrs. Perkins had reason to believe her daughter's well-being was in danger. The law is very clear on this."

Judge Harry Corrigan gave him a sour look and cut him off. "A spanking would hardly put the child in mortal danger, Mr. Landers."

"We aren't talking about a spanking," Jake began, choosing his words carefully.

At that point Henrietta, who'd been sitting quietly in the first row, jumped to her feet. Obviously, she'd lost patience, too.

"Now see here, Harry," she snapped acerbically, ignoring the hammering of the gavel. "If you'd get off that bench and your high horse and try living in the real world, you'd know what Jake is trying to tell you. The so-called victim in this case is a vicious brute. He's battered his wife for years and everyone in town knows it. He was about to start on their daughter. Anyone with half an ounce of sense—''

"Stop that. Stop it at once," Judge Corrigan bellowed. "I will not have my courtroom disrupted in this way, not even by a woman I respect as much as you, Henrietta."

"Oh, settle down, you old fool," Henrietta shouted back without flinching.

Jake had a feeling the old fool was reaching the end of his tether. A contempt-of-court ruling was on the horizon. He tried to hush Henrietta.

"Don't worry about me, Jake. Let him put me behind bars. I deserve to be there just about as much as this poor child he's got before him. I want you to think long and hard, Harry, before you make your ruling about either one of us. Since when do the courts or you think it's okay for a man to beat his wife? How would you feel if Barbara Sue were your daughter? If Sissy were your granddaughter? I'll tell you how. You'd use the damned shotgun yourself.''

The gavel smashed down so hard it was a wonder it didn't split the solid oak bench in two. Jake waited for an explosion of temper. The prosecutor seemed dazed by Henrietta's outburst. Judge Corrigan's face was a dangerously angry shade of red. It took several minutes for him to speak.

"Okay, Henrietta, you've had your say. Now I'll have mine. If you have any sense in that foolish old head of yours, you'll sit down and keep quiet until I'm through."

With a huff of displeasure, Henrietta sat. The judge scowled at Jake. "You might as well sit, too. This could take awhile and I want you to be comfortable so you'll listen closely to every word.''

Jake sat.

''I cannot and will not condone the method that Mrs. Perkins used to stop her husband,'' the judge said as his color slowly returned to a more normal shade. ''She should have called the sheriff.''

''And been dead by the time he got there,'' Henrietta muttered.

''Silence!'' Judge Corrigan bellowed, his complexion turning red again.

Henrietta glared at him without so much as a hint of contrition.

''Now, then, I do recognize that there were extenuating circumstances. Albeit inappropriately, Henrietta has made an eloquent and strong case. You should thank her, Mr. Landers. I will grant the prosecution's petition for a plea bargain.'' He scowled at Barbara Sue. ''You will be on probation for one year, Mrs. Perkins. I do not want to have any reason to regret my decision here today.''

''And the restraining order against Mr. Perkins?'' Jake asked.

''Granted.'' He slammed his gavel down again, rose and left the courtroom.

Barbara Sue covered her face with her hands and wept. Jake gathered Henrietta into his arms and swung her around.

''You were magnificent,'' he said. ''Though for a minute there I thought I was going to have to bail you out of jail.''

''That old man doesn't scare me. He's the same bully now he was when we were in grade school together. Tried to get me to marry him once using the same approach. I turned him down flat.'' She glanced past Jake. ''I think somebody else is here who'd like to congratulate you.''

Jake turned and spotted Megan standing uncertainly in the aisle.

''I had no idea you were here.''

''You were fantastic,'' she said.

''I barely got out ten words. It was Henrietta who saved the day.''

''The point is that Barbara Sue is free to go back home with her kids. You must feel incredible.''

He shrugged. ''I'm glad I could help. Now all we have to do is make sure Lyle stays the heck away from her. Something tells me that will be easier said than done, even with Bryce staying on his case.''

''When is he due out of the hospital?'' Megan asked.

''Sometime next week would be my guess. He'll probably stay with his mother till he's back on his feet again.''

''Yes, that is exactly where he will stay,'' Mrs. Perkins said, cutting into the conversation. ''And you will all regret the day that you tried to destroy my son's reputation without a fair hearing.'' She glanced at Barbara Sue. ''You are not worthy to clean my boy's shoes.''

Henrietta started to respond, but Jake touched her arm in silent warning. Instead, they just stood and watched as Emma Perkins whirled around and swept out of the courtroom in wave of indignation.

''She's the reason he turned out the way he did,'' Henrietta said. ''She's every bit as much of a bully as Lyle ever thought of being. She spoiled him rotten on top of setting a bad example. It's little wonder he shows no respect for anyone and thinks women were put on this earth to do his bidding.''

"You made an enemy of her today," Barbara Sue said to Henrietta. "She'll probably charge you an arm and a leg for any supplies you need for the diner from now on. I'm so sorry you were drawn into this. You've been trying so hard to help me and all I've done is make trouble for you.''

"I'm not worried about Emma Perkins," Henrietta said dismissively. "I've been going to that new discount store out on the highway for months now. She's the one who's going to lose business when the story gets around about how she defended the way her son's been treating you.''

"Please," Barbara Sue begged. "We can't let that get out. I don't want the kids to hear that kind of gossip about their daddy or their grandmother.''

"It's time you stopped protecting them," Henrietta said sternly. "They're getting big enough to understand what's been going on in that house. Unless they know the whole truth, they're liable to start blaming you when their daddy doesn't come back home.''

"Henrietta's right," Megan said, surprising Jake. "It's always better to know the truth. Kids sense most of it, anyway. I know I did. And for all these years, all they've seen is Lyle's bad example as a husband. They need to know that what he's been doing to you isn't acceptable.''

Barbara Sue nodded. "I know you're right, but right now, I just want to see my babies and hold them.''

"They'll be back at the diner the minute school's out," Henrietta promised. "Janie will bring them by. And then all of you are moving in with me. No arguments. When things are more settled, you can decide what you want to do, but until then, you'll be at my house. It's been way too quiet and empty with my kids grown and gone. I'll be glad of the company."

As the rest of them left the courthouse, Jake lingered. Megan waited for him.

"You did a good thing here today," she told him.

He shrugged off the praise. "It reminded me of why I went into law. I'd lost track of that when I was in Chicago. I got disillusioned with protecting the bad guys, using technicalities to maneuver justice."

"Do you like practicing law better than being a rancher?"

He grinned. "Still trying to talk me out of stealing Tex's ranch from you?"

"No, just asking an honest question. Which do you prefer, Jake?"

"I like them both." He gazed into her eyes, then decided it was time to put his future on the line. "I want it all, Meggie, including you."

Megan was still unnerved by Jake's declaration when she went back to work in the afternoon. They were finishing up their last taping, so they could get out of the Barkley home. As the commotion swirled around her, all she could think about were Jake's words: *I want it all, Meggie, including you.*

So, there it was. She could no longer ignore what she'd been sensing for weeks now. He'd made his intentions crystal clear and this time they included her. He wasn't going to be satisfied with proving something to the town. Taking Tex's ranch wouldn't do it, either. He wanted her. The only question was whether he viewed claiming her as just another triumph or whether he was in love with her. The word certainly hadn't crossed his lips.

And if it had? she asked herself as the afternoon wore on. How did she feel about Jake? The last few weeks had been revealing. Her old feelings for him hadn't died at all. If anything, they had grown stronger, now that she knew the man he'd become. His actions, his values, his caring had earned her respect and, yes, even her love.

But there was still the matter of going back to New York eventually. There wasn't a doubt in her mind that her career—her real future—was back there. The stopgap measures she had taken these last few weeks weren't the answer. She sighed heavily.

"Hey, where'd you go?" Peggy asked, regarding her worriedly. "Everything okay?"

"Just thinking."

"About?"

"The future."

"In other words, Jake," Peggy corrected, grinning.

"I didn't say—"

"You didn't have to. With you, it's always been about Jake, the same way it was always about Johnny for me."

"You've moved on," Megan pointed out.

"I've moved out. I'm not so sure about moving on," Peggy confessed in a voice that barely rose above a whisper.

Megan stared at her in shock. "What are you saying? I thought that was over and done with. I thought you were tired of him humiliating you. I thought you were at least a little bit interested in Peter."

Peggy waved off the suggestion. "Peter's terrific. I owe him the world for making me feel like a woman again. He rode in here like a knight in shining armor, but the truth is, he's a dyed-in-the-wool city slicker and I'm definitely a country girl. It would never work."

"If the show goes back to New York, you'd be a city slicker, too."

"No. My heart's here," she said firmly. "If you take the show back to New York, I won't be going with it."

Megan stared at her in shock. "Has something happened that I missed?"

Peggy nodded, her cheeks turning pink. "Johnny came by again this morning."

"Uh-oh. Did he bring roses? You always were a sucker for a bouquet of flowers."

"He brought daisies, actually, but that wasn't what did it."

"What did?"

"He told me he was sorry. He told me he missed me and the kids. And he said if I'd come home again, things would be different."

"And you believed him? Peggy, how many times has he said this in the past?"

"Never," she admitted. "Because I never walked out before, never even threatened to. Peter gave me the gumption to do it and I guess it scared the heck out of Johnny. He realized he really could lose me.

More important, he realized that it would really matter to him if he did.''

Megan was more skeptical. ''Do you honestly think he'll stick to it once he's won and you're back home again?''

''I was a little uneasy about that myself at first.'' Peggy grinned. ''Which is why I told him I'd be staying on at your house for a while, if you'll have me. If he wants me back, he has to court me, starting with a candlelight dinner in Laramie tonight.''

Megan couldn't help smiling back at her. ''How long are you going to make him jump through hoops?''

''Now, you see, that's where the good part comes in. I can drag this out for a very long time, unless of course you decide to kick me out of your place.''

''No, indeed. You're welcome to stay just as long as you want to. I've discovered I like having roomies.''

''Then I'd say it could take Johnny months—and a whole lot of posies—to get me back.''

Impulsively Megan gave her a hug. ''I am so happy for you. I hope it works out this time.''

''It will,'' Peggy said with confidence. ''I think maybe we're both growing up, learning to communicate. Given the fact that we've both hit thirty this year, I think it's about time, don't you?''

Megan thought of her accountant and wondered if he was inside nursing a broken heart. ''Does Peter know what you've decided?''

''Yes. He was the first one I told. I think he was relieved, to tell you the truth. I believe he's already called the airlines and made arrangements to go back to New York tonight.''

"You've probably broken his heart.''

"I seriously doubt that. He's a nice man. I think I was a novelty for him and I happened along just when you'd dumped him. I'm pretty sure that deep down he was terrified he might have to buy a whole new wardrobe of jeans.''

"Since we're finished for the day, I'd better go and find him,'' Megan said. "I'd hate to lose a good accountant and financial adviser over this.''

"I doubt there's a chance of that. He seems pretty confident you'd be heading straight for financial ruin without him.''

Megan laughed. "Yes, now that you mention it, Peter does have a fairly strong ego. He'll survive.''

Back at her ranch, she found him inside with his bags packed and his cell phone in his hand. He certainly didn't look especially distraught. She sat down opposite him and waited. When he'd hung up, she said, "Business as usual, I see.''

"The market doesn't wait for every little blip out here in the hinterlands,'' he said briskly.

"You okay?''

"Of course. Why wouldn't I be?''

"Because, despite what you may have told Peggy, I think you actually cared for her. Jake thought so, too.''

"Let's not give Jake too much credit for being insightful,'' he grumbled. "He had his own reasons for wanting me to be otherwise occupied, romantically speaking.''

"Peter, seriously, are you okay?''

"Let's just say between the cows and getting dumped twice in less than a week, this hasn't been the vacation of my dreams." He chuckled. "Then again, I will have a story to tell my grandchildren."

"If you're counting on grandchildren, you can't be too distraught."

"Distraught, no. The men in the Davis family always muster up the courage to move on in spite of adversity. This was nothing more than a minor setback."

Megan wasn't quite sure how she ought to feel about being dismissed so easily. "Why do I get the feeling that someone's waiting in the wings back in New York?"

"Because, despite that tough facade, you're a romantic at heart and you're looking for happy endings?" he suggested.

"Maybe, but it's that glint in your eye that really does it. You look as if you're heading out on a mission. Who have you been keeping on hold for too long now?"

"What makes you think I've been keeping anyone on hold?" he asked stiffly.

"For one thing, you're actually blushing. Peter Davis, I think you've been keeping secrets."

"Maybe I have. Maybe I haven't." He winked as he picked up his bags and headed for the door. "Maybe I'm just discovering the value of being a man of mystery."

At the door he paused. "I'll be in touch about the budget. If you let Kenny have his way with that studio, you'll go broke. And tell Todd he's to rein in expenses. The crew needs to fly coach, not first-class."

"And you?" she asked, regarding him with amusement.

"First-class, of course. Not to worry, though, this trip was on me." He gave her a wink. "Personal business."

He was either a master of the quick recovery or of sheer bravado. Megan couldn't really tell which. "I'll see you soon."

"In New York," he said firmly.

"Right. In New York."

Why, Megan wondered as he drove away, didn't the thought of going back fill her with as much excitement as it once had? She spotted the churning dust at the end of the drive long after Peter's car had disappeared and guessed that it was Jake. Could that be it? Was Jake the reason why, after all these years, Whispering Wind was finally beginning to feel like home?

A couple of minutes later, when he stepped onto the porch, her heart did its predictable lurch, and she knew. For better or worse, she was going to be stuck with these feelings she had for him. Time, distance, Tex's maneuverings—nothing had killed the love she'd felt for Jake most of her life.

"Everything okay?" he asked, studying her curiously.

"I suppose that depends."

"On?"

She wasn't ready to discuss her feelings with him, much less a still very uncertain future. "How you feel about potluck for dinner? Mrs. Gomez has gone home. Johnny has taken Peggy out for dinner in Laramie and all the kids are on a sleep-over with a friend from school.''

''Peter?''

''On his way back to New York.''

''Very promising. Todd?''

''At the new studio with Kenny and the techs. They'll be there most of the night.''

''Fascinating.'' His expression brightened. ''It's just you and me then?''

''And whatever leftovers I can whip into a meal.''

''I'm not worried. After all, you are reputed to be a whiz with leftovers.''

Megan laughed. ''You are about to discover that I've been duping the world. You'll be lucky if you don't get food poisoning.''

''I'll take my chances.'' He beckoned to her. ''First, come here.''

''Why?''

''If I'm going to die, I at least deserve a kiss before I go.''

Megan stepped into his waiting arms. Jake's mouth claimed hers with an urgency that scrambled her thoughts. The man surely did have a wicked way with a kiss.

''Jake?'' she whispered, when she could finally summon breath to speak.

''Hmm?'' he murmured, scattering kisses down her neck.

''Since dinner's not likely to be much to write home about, how about we put it off?''

He pulled back and gazed into hers. ''And do what instead?''

"If you can't figure that out, you deserve my cooking."

His expression sobered. "Meggie, are you sure?"

She nodded.

"Because once I've had you, I won't let you go, not ever again."

"I know," she whispered solemnly. Caught up in the moment, she pushed aside the consequences of making such a rash statement and added, "I don't want you to."

He scooped her into his arms and carried her up the stairs, as he had on another night recently. This time, though, there was no teasing undercurrent, just pure anticipation. Her body was humming with it.

As they reached her bedroom, night was already falling outside, filling the room with shadows. In the remaining light, she stood silently before him, then slowly, deliberately began to remove her clothes. The brightness in his eyes was enough to guide her. He swallowed hard when she stood naked before him.

"Do you have any idea how long I've dreamed of this?" he asked. "How many times I've wondered if it would ever happen or if we'd simply missed our chance?"

"I wondered that, too," she confessed.

She reached for the buttons on his shirt, then took her time undoing them, pausing to rake her fingernails along his chest with each new exposure of skin. Touching Jake made her brazen. Nothing in her past—no man she had made love with—had prepared her for the utterly feminine, totally sensual way she felt as she caressed him, watched the flare of fire in his eyes that matched the rush of heat building inside her.

When Jake bent his head and took the tip of her breast in his mouth, shock waves rippled through her. Every touch stirred unmatched excitement. They fell onto the bed in a tangle of arms and legs and throbbing need.

His gaze locked with hers. "I swear to you that next time will be slow and lovely, but right now I want you too desperately to wait."

"Me, too," she whispered back, thrusting her hips up to complete the joining. Only when he was deep inside her did she sigh at the sheer joy of it, the sense of rightness and completion she'd craved. "Make love to me, Jake. No man has ever done that before."

He stared at her, obviously startled. "No man?"

She smiled. "I've had sex. I've never made love. I don't think I knew that before."

"Then let me show you," he said, starting a slow tide of sensations that rolled over her as gently as waves at first, then rocked her with the passion of a stormy sea. When the last glorious waves crashed over her—through her—she almost wept with the wonder of it.

And even then there was more. Jake carried her back to the edge, sent her over it with a flick of his tongue against her most sensitive, intimate nub of desire. Then, when she was still trembling, he entered her again, and this time when they reached the top they took the frantic, joyous leap into sensual oblivion together.

Afterward, slick with perspiration and the musky scent of sex, they curled against each other and slept.

Megan woke first, bemused by the tender ache between her legs and the weight of Jake's arm across her middle. Her breasts were as sensitive as they had been when Jake's teeth had raked the peaks. She skimmed her hand over one and felt the nipple harden, felt yet another sharp tug of desire stirring low in her belly.

When she glanced at Jake, she saw his gaze fixed on her hand. "Let me," he whispered, his voice raw.

His touch on her breasts alone was enough to send her reeling again.

"Sweet heaven, if we keep this up, I think I'll die from it," she said.

Jake's hand found its way between her legs. "Let's see," he taunted.

She was still shuddering from his touch when she rose to her knees, straddled him, then took him inside. "If I'm going, you're going with me," she said, drawing him into the passionate madness.

Only later, after they had slept again, did the thought of dinner intrude.

"I'm starving," Jake announced.

"Then you'd better cook. My skills are better suited to hors d'oeuvres than rack of lamb."

"I'll settle for scrambled eggs and bacon. I'll even make toast."

"All this and you can cook, too," she said in wonder.

"Given your international reputation, that should have been my line."

"I've allowed you to know my darkest secret," Megan told him. "Will you ruin me?"

Jake gave her an impudent grin as he pulled on his

jeans. "As long as you keep up the sex, your secret is safe with me."

"Deal," she said, holding out her hand.

He took it and pulled her to her feet. When she was toe-to-toe with him, he looked into her eyes. "Megan, this is for keeps. You know that, don't you?"

"So you've said."

"I won't lose you a second time."

"Tex isn't here to keep us apart," she reminded him.

"Tex couldn't have kept us apart back then if you hadn't been so ready to believe the worst of me." Jake regarded her with grim determination. "This time there's even more at stake. I'll fight harder to keep you."

Megan could have told him that it wouldn't be much of a struggle, but it would have been a lie. Her career was between them now, and it was as much a worthy adversary as Tex had ever been.

26

Todd's expression was pure doom and gloom as he handed the phone to Megan when she walked into Tex's office the next morning. "Dean Whicker," he announced, then mouthed, "he sounds weird."

Megan's heart thudded dully. "Dean, how are you?" she said brightly.

"I've been better."

She recognized that tone. No wonder Todd had picked up on it. It usually spelled trouble. "Okay, what is it? You've seen the tapes and you hate them, right?"

"No, the tapes are fine. I actually think that little friend of yours—what's her name? Peggy?—I think she'll go over big with the audience."

"Then I don't see the problem."

"Okay, I'm going to lay it out straight. I think you're terrific. I think you have incredible potential." He used the word as if it weren't quite enough.

"I thought you invested in potential," she said quietly.

"I do, but I also know when to cut my losses."

Megan gripped the phone tighter. "Excuse me? When did *Megan's World* become a losing proposition?"

"It's not," he agreed. "Yet. But I'm in a business that necessitates quick calls, and I don't see your show going anywhere, not with your attention divided the way it has been."

"You know the circumstances," she protested, feeling as if she were suddenly in an uphill battle for her life. "It's been a few rough weeks. We'll get past it. The new studio out here will be ready in another week or so."

"Not soon enough. A few weeks can turn the tide in television. Audiences drift away and then it's all but impossible to get them back."

"Are the ratings down?" she asked, even though she'd seen them herself not an hour earlier and they'd been as strong as ever.

"No," he admitted.

"Then there's something else going on here and I want to know what it is. I think I have a right to know if you intend to pull the plug on me."

"I just don't see it working out," he said again. "I'm sorry. I like you, Megan. It's nothing personal."

"That really means a lot," she said with a biting edge of sarcasm. "No doubt you'll be hearing from my lawyer."

She hung up before she could say things she'd never be able to take back. Todd was staring at her sympathetically.

"Don't you dare say it," she warned.

"Say what?"

"That you told me so. Or that you're sorry. Or anything else, for that matter."

"How about I tell you what's really going on, then?"

She stared at him blankly for a full minute. "You know?"

"Oh, yeah. I heard the buzz from a friend in New York this morning, about an hour before Dean called to break the news."

"Tell me."

"It seems that a few of your staffers in New York got tired of being out of the loop while you've been here. They've staged a little coup. They told your buddy Dean that they were the real brains behind *Megan's World* and they proved it with a week's worth of sample tapes that reportedly knocked his socks off."

Megan stared at him in shock. "They did this on my time?"

"Actually, they did it at night, since you weren't minding the store. Used your studio, too, since it was paid for."

Megan saw red. "Who's behind it? I'll sue them and Dean Whicker. They'll be tied up in legal red tape for so long they'll never get a show on the air. And who the hell is hosting this new show?"

Todd's expression faltered.

"Who, dammit?"

"Micah."

Micah, the woman she'd trusted almost as much as she'd trusted Todd. Micah, who'd bailed out on them a few days earlier. Micah, whom Todd had fallen for the minute she'd come to work for them. It appeared they'd both been betrayed. Megan could see from his shattered look that it had hit him just as hard as it had hit her.

"I'm sorry."

"Don't say it," he said grimly. "Whatever I thought of her once doesn't matter. She's slime. I say we go back to New York and rip her into tiny little bits."

"I'm delighted to see you haven't been affected by this news," she said wryly.

"Who was it that said don't get mad, get even? One of the Kennedys, I think."

"Revenge does hold a certain appeal," Megan agreed. "Any ideas?"

"There are other syndicators," Todd pointed out. "Or you could force Dean's hand. I went over the contract earlier. It's airtight. I'd get Jake to take a preliminary look at it, then call the entertainment guy who drew it up. We haven't defaulted on a single term, even as rough as the last few weeks have been. Dean has no legal grounds for pulling the plug. He can't even use the age-old creative differences, since he doesn't have the documentation for a single creative dispute, unless Micah's been busy helping him trump up some paperwork."

Megan nodded. "Perfect. Get Jake out here. I think he's got really good instincts about going for the jugular."

Todd hesitated. "He also has really good reasons for wanting you to stay right here. How hard can we count on him to fight, if it means you'll end up back in New York?"

Megan wasn't sure. Maybe this was going to put him—and their love—to the ultimate test even sooner than she'd anticipated.

"Call him," she said again. "I guess we're about to find out just where he stands."

* * *

Jake listened to Megan's recital of the morning's events with mounting indignation on her behalf. He glanced at Todd.

"How sure are you of your facts, that this so-called coup is behind Dean Whicker's decision to cancel Megan's show?"

"A hundred percent."

"Then I say we nail the sucker," he said grimly.

Megan met his gaze evenly. "Jake, it could mean I'd have to go back to New York, at least for a while, to prove I'm on top of things."

"We'll talk about that later," he said, giving her hand a reassuring squeeze. "If it happens, we'll figure something out. In the meantime, nobody messes with you without taking on me, too. Remember what I told you yesterday. Chicago trained me for fighting down and dirty."

"Damned if he isn't straight out of a Western," Todd said, grinning at them. "The good guys always win, right? Heck, I might even buy me a big ol' white Stetson."

"Doggone straight we do," Jake said. "Now get me the contract."

"Done," Todd said, and handed it to him.

"Latest ratings," Jake suggested. They were in front of him before he'd finished the request. He glanced at Todd. "Does she pay you enough?"

"Not nearly," Todd said. "But life around her is fascinating, which is its own reward."

Megan chuckled. "I'll remember that when you want to negotiate a raise."

Jake glanced over the papers, then looked at the

two of them. "We're going to need proof that Micah used your studio time to make her demo tapes."

"Done," Todd said. "I'll have the studio sign-in sheets faxed out here. And there will be the bills for the crews. I doubt she footed those herself. She probably used people we bring in as backup and figured she could slide the invoices past Peter, since he was out here with you."

"Oh, I hope she did," Megan said fervently. "Suing her personally for fraud and misuse of corporate funds or whatever else we can get her for will be the icing on the cake. I should have known she was up to something when she left after the first day of taping."

"Get the documentation first," Jake warned. "And do it before anyone back there gets wind that we're onto them."

For the next hour, he watched with a certain amount of awe as Todd worked the phone with the skill of a military tactician or a political strategist. Faxes spewed in, each one more damning than the next. He even got ahold of long distance phone records logging calls between Micah's line and Dean Whicker's office. She could have been making those calls on Megan's behalf, but under the circumstances it was doubtful any jury would see it that way.

Jake sat back with a sigh of satisfaction after studying the material. "This is a great start. Think we can get anyone to appear as a friendly witness to testify to what's been going on? Or has everyone in New York gone over to the other side?"

Megan glanced at Todd. "Why don't you go back

to New York? Take stock of things firsthand. See exactly who's acting guilty and who's still on our side.''

Todd nodded. "I'll book the flight now."

"Charter one if the connections are terrible," Megan said. "We can't afford to waste time. Once the news of the cancellation hits the trade papers and the mainstream media, it'll be all over. We have to try to force Dean's hand before that."

Jake could see that it was killing her to let Todd go back and do the sleuthing and battling she was itching to do herself. "Meggie, why don't you go with him? I'll stay out here with Tess. Peggy and the kids are here, too."

Her hesitation cut straight through him.

"Still don't trust me not to use it against you, do you?" he said quietly.

Todd glanced up from the notes he was taking on his travel arrangements. He grabbed the notebook, switched to the portable phone and left the room without a word.

"I'm sorry," Megan said. "That's not it. Really."

"What then?"

"I just don't feel right about going. Tess is just beginning to feel secure. Peggy's marriage is on uncertain ground. And there's Barbara Sue."

"She's doing fine with Henrietta," Jake assured her.

"But Lyle could get out of the hospital any day now. Who knows what he'll try."

Jake barely resisted the urge to smile. "What are you planning to do to stop him?"

She frowned at him. "Okay, maybe there's nothing I can do, but I should be here."

He moved closer and took her hands in his. "Look, nobody wants you to stick close to Whispering Wind more than I do, but this is a critical time for your career. If you don't jump in and do everything you can to save it, you'll never forgive yourself or me."

"I suppose you're right."

"Darlin', I am always right. Now go. Tell Todd to book another seat. Pack."

In the doorway, she hesitated again, her expression thoughtful. After a moment, she came back to lean against the side of the desk beside him. "Maybe you should come, too," she said. "When we act, we'll have to act quickly. It'll be faster if you're there."

He considered the suggestion. He could certainly see its advantages. And a few days alone with Megan in New York might cement their relationship. He shook off the idea. This was no time to be contemplating a romantic getaway. There was business to take care of.

"No," he said at last. "I'll do you more good if I'm right here drawing up legal briefs. Todd can fax me whatever I need." He pulled her down in his lap. "Besides, you'd be too big a distraction. We're both going to need to stay focused."

He gave her a long, mind-numbing kiss. "Too many of those and we'll never get any work done."

She grinned. "I see your point."

"By the way, you're going to need to contact your New York lawyer and get him involved. He knows the ins and outs of this deal better than I do. He'll probably need to be the attorney of record, too, since I'm not a member of the New York Bar. How's he going to feel about me being in the middle of things?''

"He'll be fine with it," Megan assured him. "Evan Porter's a great man and he knows the entertainment business inside out, but he's a gentleman. Given the way Dean's going about this, I think he'll be glad to have someone who can play down and dirty."

Jake wasn't entirely sure he shouldn't be insulted. "Thanks, I think."

"You know what I mean."

"Do I?"

She touched his cheek. "Don't look like that. I trust you, okay? That's what counts."

Yes, Jake thought when she'd left the room, trust counted for quite a lot. Love would have counted for more.

Megan waited until ten o'clock to walk into her New York office. She wanted Todd to have time to do his own sleuthing before her unanticipated arrival.

"Good morning, Ms. O'Rourke."

"Hey, Ms. O'Rourke."

"Hi, ya, sweetheart. Long time no see," the newspaper vendor called out to her as she crossed the lobby. "You need a copy of the competition?"

"Not today," she told him. "I grabbed one at the airport."

"How was your trip? I'll bet you picked up a lot of new ideas while you were out West."

"A few," she agreed. "See you later."

He handed her a candy bar. "Here, it's on the house. Knowing you, you won't get out for lunch, first day back and all."

"Thanks. You're probably right. I've got a lot of catching up to do." If he only knew how much, she thought as she moved on.

As she rode the elevator upstairs, she realized that her day was starting just as hundreds of others had. The greetings were as friendly as ever, but for some reason she no longer felt quite as at home as she had a few short months ago. The excitement had dimmed, too.

Maybe that was because she was dreading the scene that was bound to ensue once she stepped off the elevator. She prayed she could keep herself from going for Micah's pretty little throat. Jake and Evan Porter had warned her again and again not to let on how much she knew.

She drew in a deep breath and braced herself for the show she was about to put on. She stepped out of the elevator with a smile firmly in place. Striding briskly through the offices, she spoke to every single person whose path she crossed.

Were the *welcome backs* a little subdued? Were the expressions a little guilty? Or was her imagination working overtime? Maybe some of each, she concluded as she finally stepped into her suite of offices and met Todd's worried gaze. He forced a smile, but it was clearly for the benefit of Micah, who was standing right beside his desk looking as innocent and complacent as a lamb.

"Megan," she said brightly. "No one knew you were coming back today."

"I had a few things here that needed my attention," Megan said. "Everything okay around here?"

"Terrific," the traitor said cheerfully. "Well, I'll be in my office if you need me."

"I'm sure I'll want to talk to you later," Megan said. "You can catch me up on everything that's been happening."

Micah left at a leisurely pace. The instant she was gone, Todd shut the outer door and the door to Megan's private office. "Want to bet she's on the phone to Dean Whicker right this second?" he said.

"More than likely," Megan agreed, dropping her purse and coat onto a chair. When she spotted the Howdy Doody puppet on her desk, she grinned despite the seriousness of the situation she was facing. It was a bittersweet reminder of the kid within, the one she'd rediscovered despite herself back in Wyoming. Somehow she was stronger than ever for having found her.

"So, what have you learned?" she asked Todd, braced for the worst.

"Not a lot," he admitted with obvious disappointment. "A few of the magazine people have made it a point to stop in this morning and bring me up-to-date on production for the next issue. Either they don't know about the rest or they're covering their butts. I can't tell."

"And Micah's cohorts in crime?"

He hesitated, then said, "To be honest, I think it's everyone on that side of the operation. They're all looking guilty as sin, except for Micah, of course. I'm just realizing what a terrific little actress she is. She's the one who should have been on a soap. She'd have made a fine villainess."

Megan sighed. "Todd, I didn't ask you this before

and I should have. You don't have to give me a name, but was it an insider who warned you about what was happening here?''

''No. The tip came from outside.''

''And you're absolutely certain it's accurate?''

He regarded her quizzically. ''Why the doubts now?''

''I guess I'm just hoping that you got bad information. I know this is a cutthroat business, but I thought I was working with friends.''

''Megan, I didn't manufacture that call from Dean Whicker.''

''No, I suppose not,'' she said wearily. ''Wishful thinking, I guess.''

''So, what do we do next? Confront Micah directly?'' he asked eagerly. ''I can't wait to see her face when she finds out we know.''

''No. I was thinking about this on the plane. I think I should have meetings with everyone on staff. Private meetings,'' she stressed. ''Don't let anyone know who's being called in next. After all, it would be perfectly normal for me to want to catch up on what's been happening in my absence. I want everyone to think these sessions are just routine.''

''Starting high or low on the totem pole?''

''Low,'' she said. ''Save Micah for the end, but I want everyone in here before lunchtime so she doesn't have time to run out and get advice.''

''Are you going to let on what you know?''

''Not directly, but I think I will ask some fairly straight questions about the outside studio use. You know, something along the lines of whether our time was cancelled, whether accounting was notified not to pay any bills for the dates we were out of town, that sort of thing. Maybe someone will crack.''

"Do you want only people from the production side or the magazine staff, too?''

"Both," she said. "This has to look as if it's business as usual, not as if I'm on a fishing expedition.''

"Got it. I'll have the first person in here in ten minutes.''

Megan kept the ensuing meetings brief and friendly. For two solid hours she took endless, tedious notes on details that were of no real consequence to the issue at hand. When she finally met with the head of accounting, she asked first about the magazine's budget.

"Everything on track? Advertising and circulation revenues keeping pace with expenses?''

"Better than ever on both counts," Frank told her.

"How about the production side? I know we're overbudget because of the new studio, but I've okayed all of that and gone over it with the outside CPA. Peter's on top of it. Any other unusual expenses?''

Frank regarded her uneasily. "I don't know if you'd call it unusual exactly, but I did wonder about something.''

Megan's heart skipped a beat. "Oh?''

"I was a little surprised when some of the production and studio bills here came in as usual, even though you were out of town. Shouldn't somebody have cancelled the studio time and the crew?''

"Maybe it was a slipup," she said.

"Probably. That's what Micah said, too. She took the bills and said she'd look into it.''

"When did she do that?"

"This morning."

Bingo, Megan thought triumphantly. She would have bet anything that those bills were about to be passed along to Dean Whicker, who would no doubt pay them expeditiously. The extra cost would mean nothing if the show was as profitable as he anticipated it being, especially without the high cost of having Megan's name attached to it.

"Thanks, Frank. I'm sure everything's being handled. Any problems I should know about?"

"Not a thing."

"Good. Let me know if anything comes up."

"Will you be around more now?"

Megan didn't know how to respond to that. "That's still up in the air," she said finally. "Any particular reason you're asking?"

He shrugged. "Things just seem to run more smoothly when you're here. This company is your baby, after all."

His choice of words left her with an odd feeling in the pit of her stomach. *This* was her baby, but Tess was just as much her responsibility. Megan knew from her own experience how critical it was for Tess to feel secure and loved. How could she measure that against a business? Obviously it was a dilemma that men had been facing for years, with children sadly coming out the losers all too often.

She was still thinking about it when Todd announced that Micah was waiting to see her.

"Send her in," she said. "Let's get this over with."

Far from wearing the downcast look of an about-to-be-discovered traitor, Micah sailed into the room with the confidence of a woman who knew she had a future.

"Tell me what's been going on around here," Megan suggested casually, as if she were interested in no more than the latest office gossip.

"We've been busy," Micah said. "Everyone's been trying to take up the slack with you and Todd out of town."

Very noble, Megan thought but refrained from saying. "I'm glad I could count on you. Next to Todd, you're the one person I can trust to stay on top of things."

Micah had the good grace to blush at that. "I try."

"By the way, tell me about those bills Frank passed along to you this morning. He says there was a mix-up on the studio cancellation."

"Not a problem," Micah said, her expression suddenly tense. "I don't know why he bothered you. I told him I'd take care of it."

"Did someone forget to cancel the studio time?"

Micah nodded. "Yes. I'm sure that's exactly what happened."

Megan regarded her solemnly. "That's not like you to let something like that slip through the cracks."

"I know, but I was in Wyoming, remember? I guess we just got so busy with everyone pulling extra duty around here. I'm sorry. I'll talk to the studio and see if we can't get a credit or something."

Megan tapped her pen on the desk in a nervous rhythm that normally would have driven her nuts. She was hoping it would have the same effect on Micah. "It's odd, though."

The woman's head snapped up. "What's odd?"

"That the bills weren't just for studio time we didn't use. There were bills for the crew, too. Surely they didn't go in there and sit around doing nothing."

"Of course not," Micah said. "That bill was probably just another slipup. I'm sure I cancelled the crew for that day. Don't worry. I'll take care of it."

Megan nodded. "Okay. Let me know if there are any problems."

"Absolutely," she said, looking relieved to have the discussion ended. "Anything else?"

"I can't think of a thing, unless there's something you'd like to get into."

"Nope. Not a thing," Micah said, all but racing for the door. "Glad you're back."

Megan stared after her. "Oh, I'll bet you are," she said softly as the door closed behind her.

Megan experienced the same odd sensation of being out of place when she went back to her apartment that night. She was surrounded by all of the things she had chosen with such care—beautiful art, exquisite porcelain, a one-of-a-kind sculpture, priceless antiques. There wasn't so much as a hint of her western roots in the decor. That had been incredibly important to her when she'd made her choices. Now none of it seemed to matter. Apparently she'd adapted to being surrounded by oak and leather again.

She wandered over to the wide expanse of windows that overlooked Central Park and the spectacular view beyond. Usually she found such peace and satisfaction in knowing that she'd earned the right to look on such grandeur every single day. Tonight she would have given almost anything for a view of a snowy expanse of nothingness and a star-filled sky.

Had she changed so much in a few brief weeks? Had her priorities shifted so dramatically? Apparently so, because the truth was she missed Tess and Jake and even Whispering Wind and the friends who'd come back into her life.

Without realizing it, she'd begun anticipating Christmas, looking forward to filling the house with the fresh scent of pine, the sparkle of lights, mounds of presents and a host of friends. She couldn't wait to see Tess's eyes widen with wonder when she found everything she wished for under the tree.

Maybe it was foolish, but Megan hoped that by giving Tess her heart's desires, it would make up for the things Megan's mother and Tex had never given Megan herself. Even as she had the thought, she realized that those weren't what mattered. She and Tess had both had Tex's love, and that counted more than all the rest.

And then there was Jake and the steadfast way he'd made a place for himself in their lives. Beyond the extravagant gifts, she realized she could hardly wait until she and Jake were alone together with only the lights from the tree to illuminate the room and the sound of carols as background for quiet talk and the sort of kisses to which she'd become appallingly addicted.

She sighed heavily when the phone rang, but when she heard Jake's voice, her spirits brightened.

"You okay?" he asked at once. "You sound down."

"Just thinking about home," she admitted.

Silence fell for what seemed like an eternity before he asked, "Does that mean what I think it does?"

"That I miss you and Tess and the ranch? Yes, I'm afraid it does."

"You don't sound happy about it."

"I'm..." She searched for the right word, settled for saying, "Confused, I guess. I didn't expect to feel like this. I thought I'd want to jump into the fray, take this fight with Dean Whicker to the bitter end, strangle Micah."

"And instead?"

She chuckled. "Well, I still want to strangle Micah," she said. "But I don't much care about the rest. There are other syndicators who'll pick up the show. I suppose I want to sue Dean on principle, but I can't work up a lot of enthusiasm for the battle itself."

"Then allow me to have enthusiasm enough for both of us," Jake offered. "Nobody messes with Megan O'Rourke while I'm around. I talked to Evan Porter today. He's every bit as outraged as I am. He'll file the papers tomorrow. We're going to take them all to the cleaners."

"You sound downright eager."

"There's nothing I like better than a good fight, a worthy opponent and a just cause."

"It's only business," Megan said.

Jake seemed to be stunned into silence. Finally he said, "Excuse me? Did I hear you say this was *only* business?"

"I know. I'm as astonished as you are. I must be losing my touch. What's happening back there? Is Tess okay?"

"Tess is safely tucked into bed. She got through the school day without getting sent to the principal's office even once. Flo came for dinner, then spent the evening helping me finish up the legal papers to fax to your guy in New York. She's got a quick mind, even if her typing leaves a lot to be desired."

"Don't tell me she's actually working out," Megan said, startled by the tone of approval in his voice.

"As a matter of fact, she is. I owe you."

"Does that mean that someday she'll be ready to be a full-time mother to Tess again?" Megan asked with an odd little quiver of trepidation in her stomach.

"I think she'll be ready to be a part of Tess's life, but it'll be a long time before she's eager to take on the responsibility of raising a daughter. This arrangement is working out well for all concerned, especially Tess. She's beginning to thrive, Meggie. She's beginning to have faith that she's surrounded by love. Flo is a part of that, but so are you."

Megan found she was surprisingly gratified by his assessment. "And Peggy?" she asked, realizing that she felt strangely left out after only a day away. "How are things going with Johnny?"

"She's making him jump through hoops. She called him an hour ago—past his very early bedtime, as I understand it—and hinted that she felt a wild craving for mint chocolate chip ice cream. Johnny was here within thirty minutes. They've gone into town. If you ask me, she was just testing to see if he was at home when she called."

"No doubt it was the first of many such tests," Megan said. "Is Barbara Sue okay?"

Jake hesitated. "For the moment," he said finally.

It didn't take much to figure out why he sounded so worried. "Lyle's out of the hospital, isn't he?"

"Oh, yeah. He's at home with Mama and mean as a snake. I'm not at all sure Bryce can handle him. He's got a deputy posted to keep an eye on Barbara Sue, but there's not enough manpower to do that for long."

"Lyle's been served with the restraining order?"

"Yes, but we both know how much good that will

do if he decides to ignore it and the deputy turns his back for a split second."

"And Barbara Sue won't even consider taking a vacation, leaving town for a while?"

"Not a chance. Henrietta's backing her up, more's the pity. She thinks it's important for her to finally take a stand. She says it will be a big boost to Barbara Sue's self-esteem that she stood up to him."

Megan glanced down at the sheet of upcoming topics for her magazine. There were articles on refinishing junkyard furniture finds, making silk flowers, restoring vintage clothes, designing quilt patterns to fit a child's interests. Did anybody really need to know that stuff? she wondered. What mattered were the things going on in Whispering Wind. That was real life. She sighed heavily.

"What's wrong?" Jake asked.

"Nothing. I just have some thinking to do. I'll talk to you in the morning."

"Okay," he said, sounding puzzled. "Love you, darlin'."

"Oh, Jake," she whispered. "I love you, too."

For the first time ever, she finally realized that that alone was more than enough to make her truly happy. The rest was all window dressing.

Jake perched on a stool at the diner in the morning, sipping a cup of coffee and pondering the odd mood Megan had been in the night before. All the while he kept a careful eye on Barbara Sue, who was waiting tables and laughing with the customers.

"She looks happy, doesn't she?" Henrietta asked as she refilled his cup.

Jake nodded.

Henrietta sighed deeply. "I have to wonder how long that will last."

"As long as Lyle steers clear of her, I imagine," Jake said, then caught Henrietta's expression. The color had drained out of her face and she was reaching for the phone.

"What is it?" Jake said.

"Bryce, get over here right now," Henrietta barked into the phone, then jerked her head toward the window for Jake's benefit. Lyle was making his way toward the diner, limping and in obvious pain, but with a grimly determined expression on his face. Barbara Sue caught sight of him just then. Her order pad slipped from her fingers. Her whole body trembled.

"I'll stop him," Jake said, heading for the door. "You get Barbara Sue out of sight. Keep her in the kitchen. Take her out the back door. Just don't let her come out where Lyle can see her."

Henrietta moved quickly. Jake didn't wait to see if Barbara Sue moved. He headed outside and met Lyle on the sidewalk.

"It's a public place. You can't stop me from going in there," the man told him, trying to push his way past. He was too weak to shove a toddler, much less a very determined man like Jake.

"That is exactly what I'm going to do," Jake replied. "Go on home, Lyle. You know you're not supposed to go anywhere near Barbara Sue. Henrietta's already called Bryce."

Lyle stared at him with bloodshot eyes. Apparently he'd spent the night mixing booze with his painkillers. Or maybe he'd skipped the painkillers altogether.

Before Jake could guess what he intended, Lyle had reached in his pocket and pulled out a gun.

"Either you get out of my way or I'll take you down with her," Lyle said with blood-chilling calm. "It makes no difference to me. I have nothing to lose."

"You have your freedom to lose. Any hope of a future," Jake said, not flinching. He kept his gaze trained on Lyle's face, avoiding so much as a glance toward that wavering gun. He had to stall him until Bryce could get here. Where the hell was the sheriff, anyway?

"My future's over and done with," Lyle said. "She's ruined my reputation. Do you know Mama fired me from my job over this? She said the customers would stop coming in if I was there. Barbara Sue shoots me and I lose my job in my own family store. Now where's the justice in that, I ask you? You're the big-shot lawyer. You going to represent me, help me get my job back?"

"Either that or help you find another one," Jake offered. "In another town where you can make a fresh start."

"Right. I know you're on her side," he said bitterly. "You'll say whatever it takes to keep me away from her."

Out of the corner of his eye, Jake saw Bryce easing down the street, gun drawn. If he could just keep Lyle's attention, keep him talking, maybe this would end without bloodshed.

"Hey, you said it, Lyle. I'm a lawyer. It's my job to help anyone who needs it. Representing Barbara

Sue wouldn't keep me from helping you get your job back.''

"Nice try," Lyle said sorrowfully. "But I'm not buying it."

He lowered the gun, and for an instant, Jake thought he'd gotten through to him. Then, before Jake could even guess his intentions, Lyle aimed for Jake's leg and pulled the trigger. Even as he fell to the ground and the pain exploded through his leg, Jake heard Barbara Sue's scream of protest.

"Stay inside," he yelled, as another shot rang out and then another. Lyle seemed to fall in slow motion, landing just inches away. He was clutching a gaping wound in his chest.

Then chaos erupted around Jake. The last thing he remembered was the sight of Henrietta peering down into his face and all but commanding him to stay alive. "Don't you dare die," she said. "If anything happens to you, Megan will never forgive either one of us."

Megan hung up the phone after an illuminating conversation with Dean. He'd been eating crow and backpedaling so fast on his threat to cancel her show it was a wonder he hadn't choked on the words.

"Well?" Todd demanded. "What did he say?"

"He seems to have had second thoughts."

"Did you tell him he could take his second thoughts and shove them?"

"You were standing right there. Did you hear me say such a thing?"

"I was hoping maybe you were so subtle it eluded me. So, what have you decided?"

"I told him I'd get back to him, that I'd been hearing from other syndicators all morning and I wanted time to consider their offers." She grinned happily. "He's squirming, Todd. I love it."

Just then the phone rang. Todd reached across her desk to pick it up. "Megan O'Rourke's office." He paused. "What? Slow down. Who is this?" A moment later, he handed the phone to Megan.

"Henrietta. She refuses to talk to anyone but you."

Acid began to churn in Megan's stomach. "Henrietta? What is it?"

The older woman sucked in a deep breath, then blurted, "It's Jake, honey."

"Jake? What's wrong with Jake?"

"He's been shot."

Megan's knees gave way. She sank down into her chair. After swallowing hard, she managed to ask, "Is he...?" That was as far as she could get.

"He's alive. It's his leg. I'm at the hospital now. They're taking him into surgery in a few minutes."

People didn't die from being shot in the leg, did they? Oh, sweet heaven, could there be more? "Henrietta, there's nothing else, is there? He's not going to die, is he?"

"Not if I have anything to say about it," the woman said grimly. "You just get on back here as soon as you can."

"Wait," she said when Henrietta was about to hang up. "What happened? Who shot him?"

"That son of a bitch Lyle Perkins did it." She hesitated. "He..." Her voice choked up. "He got Barbara Sue, too."

"She's...?"

"Dead," she said, her tone flat. "Barbara Sue is dead."

The phone dropped from Megan's fingers. Watching her anxiously, Todd reached over and picked it up. As if from a great distance, she could hear him talking to Henrietta, asking questions, murmuring replies. Then he hunkered down in front of her.

"You okay?"

She nodded.

"I'll charter a plane. You can go straight to the airport from here. I'll pack up whatever you need from your place and bring it out later."

Megan nodded again.

"At this rate, we probably ought to buy a plane," he said, his gaze fixed closely on her as he dialed the charter company.

"Do it," she murmured. If she was going to be jetting back and forth across the country at the drop of a hat, she'd better have a plane and a pilot at her disposal.

Todd took one of her icy hands and held it as he made the flight arrangements. By the time he'd hung up, she could feel the warmth returning.

"You sure you're okay?" he asked. "Want me to ride out to the airport with you?"

"No, just stay on top of things here and fly out later."

"He's going to be just fine," Todd reassured her. "Henrietta said—"

"Henrietta's not a doctor," Megan retorted, then stared at him, feeling utterly bewildered. "Barbara Sue is dead."

"Lyle, too," he added. "The sheriff got him."

Tears spilled down her cheeks. "What about those children? What will they do now?"

Todd returned her look, his own expression just as helpless as she knew hers must be. "Go, Megan. You'll do what you can for them when you get there."

She was still numb as she left the office. She caught a cab in front of the building, then went through the motions as she made her way through the airport terminal to the waiting charter jet. The trip west seemed to take an eternity, though it was only late afternoon local time when she arrived. A driver was waiting for her at the airport.

"I'm sorry. I don't need a driver. I'll just rent a car," she told him.

He smiled. "The boss said you'd say that and I was to give you this." He handed her a note.

Megan, I know you think you don't need a car
and driver on your own home turf, but I think
you do. Just this once listen to me. Todd.

She gave the driver a rueful look. "Lead on."

"This way, ma'am."

He pulled up in front of the hospital in Laramie a few minutes later. "I'll be right here, whenever you're ready to leave."

"You're in a no parking zone and I could be here for hours," she pointed out.

"I'll be right here," he repeated.

"Thank you."

"I hope you find that your friend is doing fine," he said.

"Me, too," she whispered as she went inside to find Jake.

She found him sitting up in bed and yelling at the nurse to get the blasted needle away from him.

"Well, that answers one question," Megan said briskly as she walked into the room. "You're going to live."

"I will if they stop pumping me full of drugs," he grumbled.

"It's for the pain," the nurse said.

"The only pain around here—"

"Enough, Jake," Megan said, crossing the room to silence him more effectively with a long, lingering, life-affirming kiss. "Do you have any idea how glad I am to see you?"

A discreet cough interrupted Jake's reply. Megan turned to find Henrietta sitting in the corner. She stood up.

"I'll be going now that the big guns have arrived," she said with a wink at Megan. "Keep him in line, girl, before they decide to toss him out on his rear end. Trust me, if he has his way, he'll hobble out of here despite doctor's orders."

Megan followed her to the door. "Thank you for calling me."

"What else would I do? I'm just sorry it came to this. It's all my fault for dragging Jake into Barbara Sue's troubles in the first place. Me and my meddling."

"You didn't meddle," Megan said adamantly. "You cared. How are the kids?"

"Janie has them at her place. I'll go by there and get them."

"What will happen to them?"

"I don't know. Barbara Sue didn't get along all that well with her sister and that's the only family she had left. I'll shoot somebody myself before I let them wind up with Lyle's mama."

Megan squeezed her hand. "We'll think of something. Just give them a huge hug from me for now."

After she'd gone, Megan walked back into the room. She took a good long look at the bandages on Jake's leg and the cast that went from ankle to thigh.

"You're a pretty picture," she observed.

"And you're a sight for sore eyes. You didn't have to rush home. I was in good hands."

"Oh, yes," she corrected. "I did have to rush home. I had to see for myself that you weren't at death's door. Do you know how many times on that long flight I panicked? I was terrified that Henrietta had lied."

"Henrietta? Not a chance. That woman wouldn't know how to sugarcoat the truth."

"She was scared, though. I could hear it in her voice. And she's blaming herself that Barbara Sue is dead."

"Why on earth would she think a thing like that?" Jake demanded. "This was Lyle's doing, every sorry, sordid bit of it."

Megan shuddered to think of how much worse it could have been. Lyle could have taken Jake down with them. She sat gingerly on the side of Jake's bed opposite his injured leg. Only when she had his hand firmly tucked between hers did she begin to relax just a little.

"I've been thinking," she said slowly.

"Heaven help us."

"Hush. I'm serious. Do you think Henrietta would be willing to take the kids? They're at home with her and I can see she loves them."

"I think that's what Barbara Sue would want," Jake agreed. "We talked about that very thing when she was in jail, though neither of us could have predicted that these would be the circumstances."

"It's a lot to take on at Henrietta's age."

Jake grinned. "Don't say that to Henrietta. She may be sixty, but she thinks she's thirty. She has the stamina to raise two kids."

"Mrs. Perkins will fight her for them," Megan said. "She'll claim they're all she has left of her precious boy."

"I think the rose-colored glasses are off in the legal system where her son is concerned. I'll help Henrietta if she decides she wants those two children to stay with her."

"Then she can't lose, can she?"

"You know, darlin', I'm delighted that you have so much faith in my abilities as a lawyer, but I was kind of hoping that your interest in me was more personal."

"Personal?" she echoed, being deliberately vague.

"You know, a daddy for Tess, a husband for you. Something permanent that no one can rip apart."

"An interesting idea," Megan said, surprised to find that the prospect of marriage didn't terrify her half as much as it once would have. "Are you sure you're up to it? Tess and I, we're a lot to take on."

"Maybe I'm not up to it right this second," he

conceded. "Give me a couple of days, though, and I'll be waiting at the church."

He would, too. And he would be waiting at the airport when she needed him to. He would be there for her forever. She was just beginning to realize how vitally important that was.

Megan slid down until she could lie next to him with her cheek resting on his chest. Satisfied by the reassuring beat of his heart and the warmth of his arms around her, she uttered a soft sigh of contentment. The future was taking on a shape far different from the one she'd had in mind even a few short weeks ago, but it was every bit as exciting. She could have it all, if that's what she decided she wanted.

"Maybe Tex knew what he was doing, after all," Megan whispered.

Jake laughed. "Oh, darlin', there was never a doubt in my mind—or his—about that."

Let **DEBBIE MACOMBER** take you into the **HEART OF TEXAS.**

Let her take you back to...

PROMISE, TEXAS

Dear Reader,

In Promise, Texas, people know that family, home, community are the things that really count. They know that love gives meaning to every single day of their lives.

Some of the people in Promise are from old ranching families—like the Westons and the Pattersons, who first came to the hill country more than a century ago. And there are newcomers like Annie Applegate, who agrees to marry a widowed veterinarian for the sake of his children...and discovers that this marriage can lead to a great deal more.

MDM502A

In Promise, everyone's life is a story! The people here, like people everywhere, experience tragedies as well as triumphs, sorrow as well as joy. But— whether times are good or bad—you're never alone in a place like Promise. And that makes all the difference, doesn't it? Join me there!

Debbie Macomber

PROMISE, TEXAS

"I've never met a Macomber book I didn't love." —Linda Lael Miller

On sale mid-September 1999 wherever paperbacks are sold!

Look us up on-line at: http://www.mirabooks.com

MIRA

MDM502B

From *New York Times* bestselling phenomenon

BARBARA DELINSKY

DREAMS

For five generations Crosslyn Rise has been the very heart of one of Massachusetts's finest families. But time and neglect have diminished the glory of the once-majestic estate. Now three couples share a dream...a dream of restoring this home.

For Jessica Crosslyn and Carter Mallory, Gideon Lowe and Christine Gillette, and Nina Stone and John Sawyer, Crosslyn Rise has become their mutual passion. And as they work to restore the house, that passion turns personal, making their own dreams come true....

Join these three couples as they build their dreams for the future in Barbara Delinsky's unforgettable Crosslyn trilogy.

On sale mid-September 1999 wherever paperbacks are sold!

MIRA

Look us up on-line at: http://www.mirabooks.com   MBD627

www.mirabooks.com

MIRA Books has what you're looking for—the brightest stars in fiction.

...romantic suspense...political intrigue...espionage...
historical romance...mystery...domestic fiction...
adventure...heartwarming romance...thriller...
women's relationship novels...

At **www.mirabooks.com** you can

- see covers of upcoming books—before they're released
- read excerpts and sample chapters—unavailable from any other source
- check out author background information, photos and bios
- take advantage of web-only promotions and special offers
- locate our books on a variety of bestseller lists
- join in discussion forums with like-minded readers
- order current and selected backlist titles from a number of authors
- link to author web pages
- chat with a new author each month
- get our Editorial Guidelines for writers

AND SO MUCH MORE!

Whatever your reading needs,
you'll meet them with
MIRA Books.

www.mirabooks.com

MWEB

New York Times Bestselling Author

ELIZABETH LOWELL
CHAIN LIGHTNING

**They were strangers, stranded in a breathtaking
land where nature wields a power of her own.**

For Damon Sutter, the trip to Australia's Great
Barrier Reef is a chance to escape civilization…
alone. And Mandy Blythe, a beautiful woman
haunted by her past, is the last person he wants to
share the beautiful island retreat with. Though
Mandy's been tricked into the trip, she's not fooled
by Sutter. The arrogant womanizer is the last man
she'd ever fall in love with. But the tropics are a
different world, where emotions run as deep as
the ocean and paradise is only a heartbeat away.

"For smoldering sensuality and exceptional
storytelling, Elizabeth Lowell is incomparable."
—*Romantic Times*

On sale mid-September 1999 wherever paperbacks are sold!

MIRA®

Look us up on-line at: http://www.mirabooks.com   MEL538

From *New York Times* Bestselling Author

SANDRA BROWN

THE STORY OF A MAN AND A WOMAN LOST IN PARADISE…TOGETHER.

Caren Blakemore was on vacation. Away from her high-stress job and her painful divorce, all she wanted was sun, sand and relaxation.

Derek Allen was fleeing a scandal-hungry press eager for stories of the notorious Tiger Prince. He found the perfect hideaway…and the woman of his dreams.

But as quickly as it began, their passionate affair was over and Caren learned the price she would pay for love. Because every move the Tiger Prince made was a headline, and Caren had just created international havoc….

Tiger Prince

"The formidable Sandra Brown heats up our blood to a fevered pitch."
—*Rave Reviews*

On sale mid-August 1999 wherever paperbacks are sold!

MIRA

Look us up on-line at http://www.mirabooks.com   MSB531

From one of America's best-loved authors...a story about what life, joy and Christmas are all about!

DEBBIE MACOMBER

Shirley, Goodness and Mercy

Greg Bennett knows he's made mistakes, hurt people, failed in all the ways that matter. Now he has no one to spend Christmas with, no one who cares.

Greg finds himself in a church—and whispers a simple heartfelt prayer. A prayer that wends its way to the Archangel Gabriel, who assigns his favorite angels—Shirley, Goodness and Mercy—to Greg Bennett's case. Because Gabriel knows full well that Greg's going to need the assistance of all three!

Shirley, Goodness and Mercy shall follow him...because it's Christmas.

On sale October 22, 1999, wherever hardcovers are sold!

Look us up on-line at: http://www.mirabooks.com   MDM529